A COLLECTIVE
BARGAIN

To Pam—
Best Wishes +
Many Thanks for your
help over the years

John Schierer

JOHN SCHIERER

authorHOUSE®

AuthorHouse™
1663 Liberty Drive
Bloomington, IN 47403
www.authorhouse.com
Phone: 1 (800) 839-8640

Published by AuthorHouse 04/08/2019

ISBN: 978-1-7283-0184-6 (sc)
ISBN: 978-1-7283-0182-2 (hc)
ISBN: 978-1-7283-0183-9 (e)

Library of Congress Control Number: 2019902285

Print information available on the last page.

DEDICATION

Dedicated to the American factory
workers everywhere.

CHAPTER 1

---•◆•◆•◆•---

THE LONG RUN

The dim, green numbers gently punctured the darkness. 4:59. As the numbered tiles inside the clock silently tumbled over to 5:00 a.m., the radio on the bedstand began to play until a practiced hand swooped through the darkness with all the accuracy of a night hawk, first alighting on the snooze, then flicking off the alarm entirely. If playing "Name that tune" you would have needed only three notes, a remarkable feat of dexterity given Trey was sound asleep just seconds before. The accuracy was the product of routine and the routine was to arise and run three miles before work without waking his wife in bed next to him.

Her part of the routine was acquired immunity to the three notes that played on the radio. It may have gently roused her, but the noise had become a comforting signal that she had another 90 minutes of sleep to go. Necessity is the mother of adaptation.

Trey Bensen was officially past 30 years old. He noticed a thickening midsection that was not going away, so, reluctantly, he shoehorned this run into his daily schedule. The miles deflated his spare tire and his attitude shifted from a steely reserve to endure the run, to actually craving it, indeed missing it when his routine was interrupted. Part of the success in sustaining the habit was the efficiency and ease in moving from bed to kitchen to curb. His running clothes were in the hallway bathroom along with his toothbrush. A quick swish to banish morning breath, followed by slipping on socks and shorts and sneakers before heading downstairs 12 steps to the kitchen for a small glass of white cranberry juice to wash down a handful of vitamins. He slipped a house key on a coiled elastic over his wrist and crept out, quietly closing the door and carefully locking the storm screen so the deadbolt gently met the doorframe rather than bang against it. It was a routine that was honed and taut, even if his body was not. Some would find this a numbing monotony. Trey found challenge in whittling the steps and eliminating every noise possible.

As he stepped past the front lawn of his townhome and onto the curb in the cul-de-sac, he measured the late April day. This was a month for the seasons to do battle and indeed there had been snow flurries in the first week of the month. But clearly, summer was winning the day today. The muggy humidity was the telltale sign this was to be a brutal day where the air settles around you like a damp blanket. Ever the optimist, Trey saw it as good fortune that he would complete his run before the day turned to a complete blast furnace. So he started out, slowly at first to test his energy level and as a warmup, but quickened his pace in the first few minutes.

He loved this time of day and the rhythms of the town waking up. It was still officially before dawn but the light was plentiful and rising, revealing the neighborhood before him. His first turns in the development were past manicured common lawns, well-kept, watered and fertilized by the townhome association. Like most of New Jersey, the town of Seawell was a mishmash of urban planning. The town was not so much an archeological dig of modernity lain upon antiquity, but a blanket weave. The warp and woof of the town rose and fell, exposing various plans and theories of how to create a community. Trey's own townhome was the newest plan to bring in middle income families to what was once a forlorn industrial moonscape of abandoned properties. After an old chemical outfit went bankrupt, the site was pockmarked by the detritus of buildings hastily razed. Flat expanses of poured concrete slab took off in each direction and gave hint to once large industries now withered and blown away. Stubborn outcroppings of concrete rose at odd angles, survivors of the wrecking ball, while the hardiest weeds poked through the tiniest seams in the slabs. The concrete chunks neatly concealed decades of chemical pollution that saturated the soil. Faced with a bill it could not pay, the chemical company went bankrupt and left the debt to an unknown future. Twenty years of fighting over the pollution on the site and five more years of cleanup led to an auction of the property that partially defrayed the ecological remediation. The site was now zoned residential in the master plan so the bidding was among developers who constructed a vast bandage of townhomes, tennis courts, a pool and walking trails over the ecological wound.

But the townhomes were just part of his Trey's three-mile jog. Over the course, he would pass the history of urban planning. A quick right turn out of the development led to an older neighborhood of single-family homes with larger, overgrown shrubbery and shade, many with weatherworn— even rusted—chain-link fences that neatly delineated property lines. These homes were built just after WWII and represented the American dream to returning soldiers looking for a yard for their kids and a job in the nearby factory. The biggest difference between the old and the new neighborhoods was the shade the older developments provided. The new developments had immature trees and cheap surface-rooting Lombardy poplars that would take years to provide canopies. The new townhomes sat and baked in the sun and were whipped in the winter by wind and ice. The older neighborhoods sat in shade and repose under a generation of carefully tended foliage.

Trey jogged past the old homes and quickly into the industrial section of town. The proximity to the labor pool was no accident but the area was bound by a large stone quarry. When Trey would run during the day he could not see but rather hear the equipment wrenching boulders that would later be pulverized into ornamental stone. Now the gaping hole in the ground created odd thermal anomalies that sent updrafts of hot and cold air to the running path that skirted the quarry. Today the air ran cool and felt good to Trey, giving him respite from the humid air closing in around him, squeezing any comfort from the atmosphere. The rest of the outbound run cut through rows of small factories renting space in pre-fabricated square boxes subdivided quickly by drywall to fit the expanding and contracting needs of the businesses inside. Some of the factories already were in full thrum, indicating good times of three-shift operations driven by hungry customers while others were dark and shabby. As Trey ran past the buildings, the sun played peek-a-boo on every street, but there seemed to be no happy medium today. The shadows were too cold and lasted too long while the bursts of sun blinded him between each block and introduced what was sure to be the heat and humidity to dog the rest of the day. His comically elongated early morning shadow was swallowed every few feet by the factories.

At last Trey emerged from the industrial section to the apogee of his run and what was the functional center of the town consisting of a small square, grammar school, library and fire station. Geographically, it stood on the northernmost edge of the town and reflected every era. A Depression-era schoolhouse sat next to a modern community center alongside a strip mall hosting nail salons, dry cleaners and a bagel shop.

The run each morning gave Trey a physical workout and a time to reflect. As he made the turn at the halfway point he saw sweat had already soaked his grey athletic T-shirt through and it clung to him uncomfortably. The form fit assured him the results of the morning runs were worthwhile. Some sweat dripped past his threadbare baseball cap and wore a path into his eyes, which stung him into a new level of alertness. He mopped his brow to redirect the sweat rivulet past the corner of his eye and reflected on the workday before him. He realized while he had a lot of issues to be addressed today and this week, there were few long-term plans in place. The unrest of the realization quickened his pace, even though he did not cognitively perceive it. He was restless and a little unhappy. He could see as far as the next building but had no vision beyond it. His day would be full, to be sure, but somehow he had to carve out the future in greater detail. It all seemed a little overwhelming so he turned his thoughts to home. He felt a sense of unease there too, an unease that was unfamiliar and hard to place a finger on.

Trey's wife, Carole, lay home in bed asleep, but she, too, saw an inflection point in their lives. They were now married six years and her job as an elementary school math teacher had its own proscribed rhythm without much variation. She was talking more affirmatively about a family. The distant noise was the ticking of her biological clock, and for her it was like awakening in the night to hear your own breathing. Carole knew it was always there but now she was keenly aware of the ticking and it was not going away. Conversations with Trey were not yet testy, but recently had a harder edge. There were decisions to be made, conversations to be had. There was so much uncertainty about the future and a baby was not going to add any certainty at all. Trey wanted more time, but he knew a delayed decision was a decision made. The push of time made its way like a tectonic plate—perhaps imperceptibly, but certainly. Adulthood was getting more complicated every minute.

As Trey headed for the home stretch in his run, he picked up his pace and the sweat poured off him. All thoughts got pushed to the edge of his consciousness as he accelerated and his lungs burned with effort. He paid greater attention to the road and traffic so he did not twist an ankle or get hit by a car driven by someone late to work or school. It was hard to see fools in shorts gadding about in the flat light of dawn. Worse yet, as he retraced his steps on the return through the older neighborhood, the tree roots pushed the sidewalk up at odd angles, creating another hazard. He cut the corner and found his way into the beautifully flat, new pavement of his pristine development so he could concentrate on the effort rather than the obstacles. He could feel the difference between the old neighborhood and his new subdivision. The overhanging trees and vegetation, grown over several generations in the old neighborhood, gave way to a clear-cut where the developers razed all vegetation and replaced it with seedlings and immature trees that gave the townhomes a clean, defined, yet sanitary, look and feel. He leaned into the final curve and pulled up 100 yards short of his home, walking, catching his breath and mopping his sweat-drenched face with the bottom of his shirt. It seemed of no use—the shirt was as wet as his face so it was merely smoothing it away from his eyes. He stood on his lawn, held in common with his neighbor, and bent over, tugging at the bottom of his shorts in recovery mode.

Quietly, Trey slipped in the front door, carefully sliding the deadbolt behind him. He glanced at the clock—still before 6 a.m. Although he knew he was on time, a glance at the clock comforted him. He grabbed a towel he left in the kitchen and mopped his brow and neck. Their cat, Belvedere, crunched at some morsels in a plastic bowl on the floor. Belvedere looked up briefly, then turned his back to resume his snack. Belvedere was both furry and fat and bright orange. His head seemed to disappear when he lowered it to eat. The snap and crackle of dry kibble resonated in the pristine morning silence. Belvedere seemed to revel in the noise like a teenager defiantly popping gum. A round fur ball with no head making crackling noises. The sight and sound made Trey smile.

Trey crept up the stairs on the left side because the right side creaked. Once he reached the top, he glanced in the bedroom at Carole, still in a light slumber. He showered, shaved and dressed, his clothing pre-arranged at the back of the closet. He combed his hair. Because it was short cropped, he needed no blow dryer, just a brush and some time. He went back down the stairs in socks, making no sound as he wheeled back around to the kitchen. Just then, the silence was shattered by the phone ringing. It was no louder than midday, but in the quiet it rang out like a Klaxon. Although it seemed to ring interminably, the phone was close enough that Trey actually stopped it in mid-ring. He did not even get to say hello before the caller started in.

"Where the fuck are you and do you plan on getting here anytime soon?" the caller demanded.

It was a cigarette-smoker's tone Trey knew very well. He answered in a low voice and turned to the corner to absorb the sound.

"What is so goddamn urgent and what time do I fucking get there every day?" Trey responded.

Trey was not the most profane person but when called upon to communicate with the earthiest sailors on their terms, he could—and did—when he felt it helped him in context.

The growl on the end of the phone continued.

"Well, he's in there again and it would not be the worst fucking thing if you happened to see this for yourself. But I guess the longer he is in there now the better off it'll be. How long before you get here?"

"I'm at least a half hour away—haven't even had my coffee yet. By the way, did I mention my wife is trying to sleep?" Trey shot back.

"Best part of the day is gone already. About time she got her ass up and made you that coffee, Ghee," the caller said with a small, ironic laugh and a raspy cough.

"I'll ask about who makes your breakfast in bed when I get there, and I can't get there if I'm talking to you—so how about hanging the fuck up?" Trey answered.

The caller needed the last word: "Get here now, Ghee"—and then hung up before Trey could respond.

Slightly exasperated, but not unnerved, Trey picked up the pace only slightly, pouring coffee into a worn travel mug with the fading emblem "Garden State Bank" on the side, then adding cream. He put the coffee on the end table by the front door and bounded up the stairs two and three steps at a time. He hopped over Belvedere who by now situated himself in harm's way, one lope past the top landing. Trey bounded over Belvedere and made his way to Carole's side of the bed. The alarm clock blinked 6:23.

"G'bye sweetie, gotta go, have a good day," he said, kissing her forehead. Carole rolled back in a slight daze.

"Did the phone just ring? Were you talking to someone?" she asked.

Trey thought about it for a millisecond. He decided there was one answer that would get him out of the house quickly.

He shot out: "It must've been a wrong number. They hung up when I grabbed it. Sorry if it woke you. See you later tonight. I'm stopping by to see my parents right after work, maybe take Mom grocery shopping if she needs it, remember?"

"Yeah, I would've remembered eventually, like when you weren't here. Why can't people dial more carefully early in the morning?" Carole sank back in the pillow but mumbled from the side of her mouth, "Drive careful, huh? Love you."

Trey went back downstairs, slipped on a pair of black loafers and was out the door. As he started his car, he thought about his early morning call and what he had to do for the raspy-voiced caller intruding on his home life.

CHAPTER 2

A NEIGHBORHOOD GUY

Those who live in New Jersey understand town names are irrelevant. What really counts are exit numbers. Trey made his way onto the Garden State Parkway at 117 and drove north to 142B onto Route 22, which dropped him into Newark. Twenty-five miles translates to 45 minutes, even before 7 a.m. But even as the time matures dawn into day, the miles transform the terrain from suburban to urban. The Garden State earns its nickname in April as the roads and median shake off the ugly gray carcass of black-tinged frost and snow to grow a luxuriant coat of green grass and trees. Somewhere north of Union Township the gray becomes a multi-seasonal thicket of dreary industrial buildings and pavement overtaking the green. The grass and plants gasp up through the smallest cracks in driveways and asphalt roads. Unlike most vegetation showing off curves and symmetry worthy of a beauty pageant winner, the vegetation here is a mutation, growing in fits and starts, gnarled and angry, punching through with defiance.

None of this bothered Trey in the least. He grew up in East Newark and now, ironically, worked there. In grammar school and high school, Trey saw himself going to college out of state and gaining the reputation in the neighborhood of the guy who moved away. But instead, he saved money by getting in-state tuition to Rutgers-Newark, taking the bus to school. Now somehow, he ended up working in a factory less than a mile from where he grew up. After getting a business degree, he took a job as a headhunter in a placement firm. There he worked in a telephone boiler room making cold calls to prospective clients and working on commission.

The job was brutal and he felt like a pimp, peddling bodies to earn a decent wage. But he was tenacious and learned the recruiting job well, even as he grew to hate it until one day one of his clients, impressed by his ability to spot talent, asked him to interview for a job at his factory in Human Resources as a recruiter. Even though he worked for the client for three years, the address did not strike a chord until he arrived on site for the interview. Grean Machining existed in East Newark for over 60 years, turning out precision machine parts.

Trey took the interview as a lark, practice for when he would get a lead on the BIG job he wanted. When he traveled into the bowels of the neighborhood, the factory sat like an oasis in a wasteland. It was an old brick building surrounded by high fences and barbed wire. It had the vague appearance of a Stalag. It was a red brick building encrusted with a half century of smog and chemical residue. It evoked the image of a natural redhead who dyed herself a brunette. The red brick peeked out at the edges while the center of each brick was smeared with grit. The city sidewalks were unkempt and uneven. The street surface was a series of covered potholes knitted together in a weltered history of macadam patchwork. The alternating brutality of cold winters and hot summers bent and eventually broke the streets, showing the lines and character of an 80-year-old face. It was wear matched with experience. But once you passed the guard shack at Grean, the lawns were thick and well kept, the edging perfect, the American flag snapped in the breeze. Once inside for his interview, Trey was impressed by the light yet professional atmosphere. It was like passing through the door of some exclusive nightclub and into an unknown world pulsing with energy.

In his final interview, Trey met with the plant manager, Isaac "Ike" McKnight. McKnight was a tall, awkward-looking man whose hands shook nervously as he spoke. His fingers were long in relation to his hands. The first time Trey saw Ike punctuate a comment with the wave of a hand, he thought Ike would have made one hell of a piano player. Ike was known for his tenacity at work, but the tenacity did not reflect in his appearance. His wardrobe was straight out of the early 1960s. He wore thick, black horn-rimmed glasses, polyester pants and short-sleeve cotton shirts that revealed a tattoo of an anchor on his forearm. His hair was a study in tenacity; remnants of his hairline now clung to his skull in what could only be described as a comb over of denial.

But that tenacity—OK, stubbornness—made Ike a success in other ways. Ike grew up poor on a farm in Okarche, Oklahoma. The town's name was an amalgamation of the tribes of Oklahoma, Arapaho and Cheyenne. The town was largely the product of the U.S. government resettlement of defeated Native American tribes over time. As a child, Ike was befriended by a fascinating old Cheyenne tribesman who passed himself off as a seer and a medicine man. Ike spent many dusty afternoons listening to the old shaman tell fortunes for a quarter.

One hot August day, Ike invested a quarter he earned collecting scrap newspapers at 10 cents per 100 pounds. The old Indian sat in front of a smoldering fire pot of burning leaves until Ike's eyes watered from the smoke. Emerging from his trance the shaman told Ike that all he could see for him was water in many directions, some of it smooth, some of it rough, but all of it teeming with life. While dissatisfied with what a quarter bought him in terms of understanding his future, Ike was clear there were few ways out of town or even less of a chance to pay for his education. Perhaps with a nod to the vision of his Cheyenne seer about water, Ike joined the Navy as soon as he graduated high school. His natural nervousness and impending sense of doom was not a good match for life on a battleship, so he left after one tour of duty.

As Ike left the Navy, he was discharged out of the Brooklyn, New York depot. Told by his mother there was no work in his hometown, he boarded a bus for Newark, New Jersey, asked to be let off in the industrial area and walked door to door looking for a job. The year was 1964 and the neighborhood did not yet require a fence or barbed wire. Grean had just won a big contract to machine parts for the Ford plant just south in Edison Township. It was Ike's lucky day. Ike diligently cleaned equipment onboard ship and was immediately hired to do roughly the same job at Grean. He was the classic success story and company man as he rose through a combination of effort and years of night school on the GI Bill to get his BA and then his MBA. He was steadily promoted from the depths of the entry-level job of sump sucker to plant manager. A sump sucker was the very lowest job there was in the factory. The machines cut metal and the cutting blades depended on a steady stream of coolant to extend their life and sharpness. The coolant circulated in the machines and was lard based. Combining the heat of the plant with the bacteria present in the metals meant the oil would go bad, creating a rancid smell that lingered in the nostrils. The sump sucker arrives at each machine as the oil goes bad and empties the oil pans that contain the coolant at the base of the machine, replacing it with fresh oil. During the summer, when the oils went bad with great frequency, the smell clung to Ike like grim death. Ike hid the fact that he took daily bubble baths just to combat the stink of his job. The good part of the job was that Ike traveled the entire plant and understood how the pieces fit together. He realized where the bottlenecks in production were and how different departments depended on one another. He used this knowledge to his advantage and set his keen eye on positions of greater authority.

Ike understood Trey was both a neighborhood product and a recruiter who had identified several talented engineers currently working at Grean. He offered Trey the job as a recruiter on the spot. Somewhat like Ike, Trey rose through the HR ranks through several assignments. He grew out of the narrow job of recruiter and was now the Human Resources Manager-Industrial Relations. Trey was essentially the liaison between Grean and its union: Local 412 of the Brotherhood of Metalworkers. For the past three years, Trey reported to Ike.

Today, Trey zigzagged through the city streets toward the plant, anticipating and avoiding traffic lights where he could. The inner cities were both the worst and most interesting examples of planning and zoning. The Grean factory sat squarely inside a residential neighborhood and that neighborhood was dotted with an odd assortment of outposts and businesses. A VFW hall sat next to three homes, followed by a bar, two more homes, a six-family duplex, and a funeral home. The driveway past the funeral home opened into a large parking lot behind this whole lineup to the point where a symbiotic relationship evolved. The bar's back door led out to the funeral home's secluded parking lot. So as to enable mourners to properly toast the dearly departed, the bar received permission to install a small swinging gate on the outgoing side of the parking lot with "RILEYS TAVERN—A NEIGHBORHOOD TRADITION OPEN TO 2AM NIGHTLY" and on the other side of the gate a more sedate but ominous greeting to those exiting the bar, "Arrive Home Safely- Runge Mortuary."

Trey eased past this quilt of life to the corner where he parked his car illegally in front of Page Family Luncheonette. Trey knew the Page family when they owned the place, but about 10 years ago they sold the business to Korean immigrants, the Kim family. the Kims, wishing to avoid neighborhood backlash, left the Page name in place, leading to the neighborhood snicker: the new owners had opened The Yellow Pages. Howard Kim, proprietor and family patriarch, was blissfully unaware of the joke. While purported to be a small restaurant, the business actually sold diverse items such as milk, eggs, Spam, rodent repellant, diapers, cigarettes, lottery tickets and a small assortment of aspirin and cold remedies. The Kim family would stock anything if it sold well, which led to the odd sight of citronella candles sharing shelf space with walnuts. The whole enterprise was supplemented by a Taekwondo school Howard Kim operated in the storage room behind the luncheonette in the evening hours. By all accounts, the Kim family was the prototype of hustling immigrant entrepreneur.

Trey knew he would not be long and that there was no one who would ticket him for the three minutes it took him to pour hot coffee into a paper cup, snag a buttered hard roll from a pile of the delicacies on the counter and pay for it all. Howard Kim depended on speed to clear the scarce parking spots—even the illegal ones—so he was at the ready when Trey appeared.

There was one snag in this plan for speedy service: The Council of Elders. The Council was essentially retired neighborhood guys with nothing better to do at 6:45 in the morning but meet at the luncheonette, pick up the early papers and solve world problems. At one point the Kim family tried to simultaneously dislodge the Council and play to the growing Asian clientele by replacing two tables in the window with 100-pound sacks of rice. This had the effect of a BB gun on a rhino. The Council foiled the whole scheme by hopping on the rice sacks and using them as bean bag chairs. They had an opinion on everything and a name for everyone, just not their given name.

As Trey breezed in, the Council pounced.

"Whoa, the lawyer must have a case today the way he is hauling ass," one said, with a nod to Trey.

The Council based this solely on the fact that Trey wore a tie every day, had dubbed him The Lawyer, irrespective of the fact that there was not a law office within 30 blocks of the luncheonette. The Council numbered four today although that number could grow to as many as six, depending on who had a doctor's appointment or galloping constipation on a given day. They all had coffee and a newspaper and absolutely nowhere to go. Their attire this day- long dress pants and sleeveless undershirts—some might call them wife-beater shirts—indicated they understood the day would grow hot and they intended to be there as the temperatures rose.

"Your Honor, slow down. You're gonna have a heart attack," one called to Trey. "Tell us who you are hanging today. What's the federal case on the docket?"

Trey tried to indulge them pleasantly but on their own terms.

"We are debating whether you can be charged with loitering when you are inside a luncheonette and if the death penalty would be appropriate. You are all criminally pale and not wearing sleeves. This *should* be a crime. What say you, proprietor Kim?" Trey said with a wink and a smile.

"I say they are cheap bums who buy one cup of coffee and chase paying customers out. Jesus, look at them sitting in the window in their UNDERWEAR!" Kim feigned in mock horror. Deep down, Kim wished they would not hang out as long as they did in the shop. But he knew them as good guys and their imprimatur helped ingratiate himself and his business into the fabric of the neighborhood.

"Sorry," Trey answered, "we can have a dress code but there is no taste code. You are stuck with them—case dismissed!" Trey used the buttered roll, wrapped in butcher paper, as his gavel to bring the verdict.

The Council of Elders erupted in indignation.

"You think you can get some fucking models in here?" one shot back. "If it weren't for us, you'd be outta business, you Kung Fu sonuvabitch. Consider us advertising here in the window. The kind of people Americans want to associate with!"

The rage was all bluster and good natured, but the conflict was verbal cover for Trey as he ducked out the door.

Once back in his car, Trey normally proceeded with a quick left to get to Grean, but today he took the long way around, making a right, heading up two blocks and cruising past a neighborhood gin mill known as Karl's Bavarian. In their heyday local taverns would set out beers and shots across the bar at 11:45 a.m. awaiting factory workers on 30-minute lunch hours. Now, alcohol was not the accepted noontime beverage for those operating heavy equipment. Those operators were now an endangered species, victims of automation, layoffs, age and changing social acceptance. Now, the taverns were a haven for those most desperate for a beer. One rusted green van sat in Karl's parking lot. Trey made a mental note and proceeded back toward the factory.

The guard recognized Trey right away, hoisting the wooden arm of the security gate and waving him through. He proceeded to his marked parking spot: T. BENSEN HR. It was the last of the reserved spots indicating Trey was on the top tier of the local management, but just barely. By virtue of the fact that the neighboring spot was unreserved, it could have been anyone parked there, but as usual, he opened his door carefully so as not to ding the shiny dark-blue Trans Am with a vanity license TUHOTBB. The early birds also get the best parking.

The promised heat was beginning to steam the parking lot but the sun was still low enough to cast a long shadow from the factory. Trey could feel the relief of the shade immediately. As he stepped in through the open bay doors in the shipping dock, Trey felt the factory was still cool from the night air, but this would not last long. The hum and beat of the various machines and processes were still faint but growing. It was shortly before 7 a.m. and the only machines running were those on three shift loads. But the factory had its heartbeat stirring in the whines and thumps of metal hitting metal.

Walking through the back of the factory floor, Trey felt the vibration of his pager already. He looked down and saw 911215. He knew this meant his counterpart in the plant in Bellmawr, Pennsylvania, outside Philadelphia, Ed Wendlocher wanted to talk to him desperately. This 911215 was their code—911 (emergency), 215 area code of Bellmawr. But Trey knew Ed had a flair for the dramatic, so he dismissed the page with a flick of his thumb and made a mental note to call Ed as soon as he could.

Trey could see the machine operators beginning to congregate near the lathes, presses and milling machines on the floor. They were girding for the battle of the hot day and had already soaked rags in cold water and tied them around their necks in a pre-emptive move. Now, their dark blue work shirts were darkened with the cool water. Somewhere in the day the dark blue would switch in significance from water to sweat stains.

Each operator would wave or nod at Trey and he would greet each by name. Many had been there 20 or 25 years. Trey had only been there eight, long enough to make the plant fraternity. Choosing to walk through the factory to the front office rather than taking the sidewalk around the building like the accountants earned him the nods and waves as he moved.

Trey opened the door to the offices and stepped into a cool, light space cut into many neat smaller spaces. His HR office was closest to the factory floor and afforded him a windowless but large office complete with a table and four chairs in addition to his desk. Next to his office was a much smaller one belonging to his assistant, Barbara Brixner, also known as BeBe. She was the BB who owned the Trans Am with the plate TUHOTBB. She was a single mother of a teenage daughter. TUHOT was an homage to her days as a bartender at a local strip club of the same name. Her body was killer but, in truth, her face kept her from the main stage for better or worse. This disparity in body and face brought out the cruelest designation among the union rank and file who decoded her vanity plate as The Ugliest Head On The Best Body. While attractive, she recognized her looks and glory years as a bartender were fading fast so she picked up administrative skills at community college and got a job at Grean. Her title was HR assistant, and her primary duty was helping employees unravel medical claims. Her looks certainly helped draw in those who needed help, but it was her kind ways and persistence on behalf of "her boys in the factory" that kept them coming back. She was smart, worldly and self-assured. She liked the rough edges she encountered in her job and could see through the tough factory guys and find a lot of soft hearts and sad stories. Her time slinging drinks at the strip club prepared her well for this job. It was an odd transference of skills. She seemed to thrive in operating in such a masculine world and handled the ham-handed attention of the old factory war-horses with great grace and a light but firm touch. If an oaf came in to make a crude comment, she knew that one day that same oaf might depend on her to ensure that the insurance paid every penny of his kid's cancer treatment. Her tenacity in getting payment might mean the difference in making the rent. She inherently understood the long game and her value.

CHAPTER 3

---◆·◆·◆---

WARSAW'S GRIEVANCE

The 7 a.m. meeting was a ritual in the factory day. Ike would arrive about 6:30 and scan the production reports in 10 minutes and almost tell from the output on the page what was going right or wrong. Trey marveled at this ability. It was like the people who can look at an unlabeled phonograph record and tell you what song is recorded on it. Savant-like stuff but with an industrial twist.

The meeting had all the key players—Finance, Production, Purchasing, Engineering, Quality, HR, Facilities—anyone who could fix an aberration. Ike called it at 7 a.m. to ensure everyone arrived bright and fresh. He admonished the team constantly with sayings like, "The day goes as the day starts" and "How do we make our people successful today?" It was generally a friendly meeting, as would be expected as the East Newark plant was in the top 10% of the four dozen plants owned by Grean in terms of overall performance. That did not stop the meeting from getting heated occasionally and Ike liked it when passions rose. After one such session got into a bit of fist pounding over a materials issue, Ike pulled Trey aside and whispered, "It shows they care when you see the veins in the neck." Trey made a mental note and scheduled a time to raise his voice every three or four months for his boss.

This morning was pretty perfunctory. Machine malfunctions were rescheduled through Production Planning and a discussion about capacity planning and vacation requests were in full swing when BeBe appeared at the door, pointed to Trey and silently mouthed the word: "union." The rest of the meeting-goers were just happy they got a glimpse of BeBe.

Trey knew he was needed and anything to do with labor was his free pass out of Ike's production meeting. As he rose to leave the meeting, his pager went off again: "911215."

"Goddamn Wendlocher can't keep his pants on and BeBe can't keep him calm," Trey thought to himself. It would have to wait; Trey was not going to antagonize the union by making them cool their heels because of Ed Wendlocher's twitchiness. It was likely nonsense anyway, the latest dirty joke Wendlocher heard.

Trey decided to go directly to the Blue Room, but as he passed near his office, two union officials stood in the hall and cocked their heads, indicating they wanted to see him in his office first.

The two were dressed in gray factory uniforms and worked the floor like everyone else. They did get more time off the floor because of meetings like this and got a stipend from the Union International for their status as local officers. Bound in union brotherhood, they could not have been more different.

Muhammad Morris was short and black with fringes of gray hair on his bald head. His given name was Mike, but Mike Morris was too common. He was a Baptist through and through, not a Muslim. But in the 1970s the local Civil Rights leaders needed to be noticed and a little feared by the white establishment, so he took on the name of Muhammad as much as a tactic as a choice. He was the product of Newark Tech and learned to be a lathe operator. He had been with Grean almost 30 years.

Tommy Pherrell was tall and lean. His scraggly beard barely disguised the fact he had no chin. As a younger man he had a thick head of red hair and a pale complexion. His hair had faded to some kind of undistinguished brown shock, but the paleness seemed to intensify. He sometimes was asked by the plant ball-busters if he had a side job as a casket model. Pherrell started at the plant "only" 15 years ago, coming to Grean from a smaller shop that had closed and left him one paycheck short of bankruptcy. It was a story he liked to tell when he ran for union office to illustrate his suffering.

Together, Morris and Pherrell had led the local union for three straight two-year terms. They were a good team and decent guys who liked each other and their position of power within the structure. They understood the contract and were not going to be bullied or tricked. Their ire was reserved for anyone who tried to play them for a fool. Trey worked with them long enough to respect them, but knew how to push their buttons.

"What's up so early?" asked Morris.

"Let's see if you guys are in a bullshitting mode," said Trey. "If we are here this early, what—or should I say who—is the topic?"

"How should we know, you called us," said Pherrell.

"The last couple of times we met this early, who was the topic of our little breakfast club?" asked Trey, probing to see if they would acknowledge the issue at hand or play games.

Morris wanted to get to the point a little quicker. "So you want to congratulate Warsaw for his improvement? Just give me the check and I'll present it to him," he said.

Now Trey was getting his buttons pushed.

"Very close, Mo," Trey said, continuing the dance. "You are in the neighborhood of the real issue with our friend Mr. Grohowski. But in the neighborhood was where I saw him this morning and not at his workstation when I walked in. Any chance he could try to be here on time since we gave him his final written warning last week? I would say he has not gone three months without being tardy like his warning defined as success—or should I say the first step toward success. As a matter of fact, I don't think he has gone three days without missing time. I am thinking the check you will present him might be his last check."

"Naaaah," Morris dismissed. "You got that all wrong. He was here. He was in the men's room with the shits. I saw him." Morris' tone was not particularly persuasive.

Mo is quick this morning, Trey thought.

"If he *did* have the shits, I would say that he had them at his little Nazi bar down the block as I saw his piece of shit van parked at Karl's and him not here in the plant wiping his ass when I walked in," Trey asserted.

Morris was not shaken by Trey's words. He spoke with cool authority and an upturned chin. "You would see his van there and he leaves it there and walks over so he does not have to move it when he leaves work," said Morris. "He knows it is a piece of shit, too. Maybe if you paid him a little more he could afford a good car he doesn't have to worry about not starting again!"

Trey knew he made a mistake now, revealing too much. He thought he was just going to ambush them with the revelation about the van, but they clearly had been figuring ways to protect their brother-on-the-edge.

Stan "Warsaw" Growhowski was a material handler with a drinking problem. Now in his late 40s and single after his second wife left him, it appeared his drinking was out of hand. His lateness was disruptive because he delivered materials to operators who could not work without his efforts. Worse yet, he drove forklifts and narrowly missed running over two coworkers. The employees were conflicted. They did not want to (and by union rules could not) rat out their brother, but they also valued their life. Trey was pulled to the side by several employees who engaged him in quiet conversations, begging Trey to intervene and stop the madness before someone was seriously hurt.

Trey needed to draw this to a head, but it would not be easy.

"Since he is here, why don't we just page him and talk to him a bit," Trey said, raising his voice so BeBe could hear.

"BeBe—page Warsaw for me to come to the Blue Room, "Trey directed at BeBe.

Pherrell tugged nervously at a pack of cigarettes in his breast pocket, looking very uncomfortable. Mo was quick to countermand the page, but with sweetness.

"Put a pin in that, dear," said Mo. "We'll go get him and bring him here."

Trey knew that, assuming Warsaw was in the building, if the union got to him first they could concoct some story their union brother's pickled brain could hold and thus evade the issue.

"BeBe—page him, please," Trey said firmly. Morris, Tommy and Trey had such a practiced relationship that they knew why Trey wanted Warsaw paged without a word passed between them. They did not protest.

Mo turned around and gently guided Pherrell out the door and into the plant, saying, "We'll see if we can hurry this along and find him. He can't hear the page in some of the corners of Receiving, where he works all the time."

This was pure bullshit and Trey knew it. But this was not the hill to die on in this confrontation.

"Very helpful, Mo, very helpful," Trey said. "If he is not here in five minutes I'll assume he is...somewhere else?"

20

"He's here, you'll see," Mo responded.

Trey watched the two head into the plant. He picked up the phone and called the supervisor of the materials department. He wanted to be sure Warsaw was indeed in the plant and asked for his timecard be pulled from the rack and safeguarded. In cases like this he liked to invoke the President Reagan doctrine: trust but verify. Trey was assured the timecard had been punched in but Warsaw had not been physically seen.

Trey grabbed the cold remnants of his luncheonette coffee and added some fresh brew to the paper cup from the departmental pot BeBe kept fresh. He sprinkled a generous portion of creamer powder and put the plastic lid back on the cup, swishing it to stir the ingredients like a lab experiment. He grabbed a yellow legal pad and a pile of resumes he was vetting and headed into the Blue Room to wait for Warsaw and the union guys. If this turned into a protracted wait, he could pass some time productively by looking at the resumes.

The Blue Room was actually pale green. Lore had it that the room had been blue once, but the name stuck. Further, the language heard inside was often blue, so the name still seemed appropriate. It was a windowless room with a long meeting table. The walls were bare except for a small framed map that showed the path of an emergency exit. There was one door in and out and Trey liked to sit far away from the door as a sign of trust. He wanted to show no fear when the union was in the room in a contentious situation. Trey's predecessor, a big, nervous man named Cam Stockton, sat nearest the door and warned Trey that he always wanted to have an exit strategy in case the discussion turned physical. Trey sensed in his earliest meetings the union reps felt weakness when sitting by the door and attempted to use Cam's nerves against him. When Trey initially changed his seat and sat at the far end, the union protested. But he just continued to get there first and stake his claim to the seat he wanted, occasionally ceding it on a first-come, first-served basis, not as a safety measure. The tiniest signals were not important alone, but strung together they set a tone. Trey watched for what worked and what gave him any advantage in conversations.

The rules of the Blue Room were pretty simple between management and the union officials although they were not spelled out in any document. You could say anything, in any tone or language desired—no holds barred.

What was said stayed in the Blue Room unless agreed to mutually, and grudges were not allowed. It was like a safety valve and the whole idea of the room worked. Either side blew off steam and no pressure built insidiously over time.

Trey hardly finished five resumes when the union walked in with one Stanley "Warsaw" Grohowski. BeBe trailed in at the end of the group and placed Warsaw's timecard face down in front of Trey. Mo and Tommy sat on either side of Warsaw, who they seated at the far end head of the table facing Trey. It occurred to Trey that the union sat Warsaw at the farthest point because he smelled like booze. Trey filed away the mental note in case he needed it.

Warsaw looked like shit. His head was bowed and even at that he looked like he had just tumbled from a moving car. He had a bristly beard with a day or two of growth. His fingers seemed like sausages and the folded fingers seemed to pile up rather than fold together. The awkward silence in the room was initially broken by the pager on Trey's belt illuminating again. It repeated "911215" but this time added the letters SEF. Trey was getting more annoyed by the minute. He uncapped his coffee, letting fresh steam waft, but the creamer powder made the brew look vile and gray.

Mo broke the silence.

"Your meeting," Mo started, "What's up?"

"Mr. Grohowski," Trey said. "Nice to see you this morning. How are you feeling today?"

"OK I guess—a little tired," said Warsaw, hoping the small talk might derail the discussion. "This heat is gonna be a bitch today."

"Do you remember last week and your final written warning about coming to work every day and on time?" Trey asked.

"Yeah, I was here," Warsaw said.

"If I turn over this card, will it show me that you punched in on time?" Trey asked.

"It should. I was here. Maybe your clocks are screwed up sometimes," said Warsaw.

Mo chimed in. "Get to the fucking point, Perry Mason, was he late or not?" he said.

Trey turned the card over and looked. He read it aloud.

"7:02 a.m.—two minutes late."

Warsaw was battered, his head still swimming in alcohol, but he knew his lines.

"See—I'm OK—contract says we round to the nearest five," Warsaw said.

"But you were late," Trey countered.

"Not by contract—I'm OK—I'm trying and your clocks are not that…" warsaw said before he was interrupted.

Trey had had enough.

"You know, Stanley," Trey started in, switching to his given name deliberately, "I am not as concerned as much by exactly when you did or did not come in this morning or how long it took you to drag yourself to the floor to do your job as I am by the fact that as I drove to the plant this morning and I saw your van in the parking lot of Karl's at 6:30 in the morning."

Mo was not happy at the turn of the conversation.

"Is *this* what you want this morning? What he does on his own time is his own business and I don't give a shit if you drive around the block a million times and see me picking my ass. He has a job. He is here on time. His warning was not violated. He is trying hard. This is bullshit."

Mo was winding up into a dull roar.

Trey was equal to the challenge

"What he does on his own time?" Trey began. "You know what he might be doing on his own time? He might be getting a toot, which I don't care about. But then he comes in here and gets on a big piece of equipment, he gets his union brothers the wrong material so they look bad and can't make their numbers, he drives over some union brother and hurts them…"

Every time Trey used the words "union brother" he added a touch of derisive emphasis.

Pherrell tried to break the momentum by raising a hand of objection, letting his long fingers punctuate in midair. "Now just hold on here a second, "he said. But Trey was reaching his crescendo and would not be denied the floor. He basically ignored Tommy, which was a heck of a lot easier than trying this with Mo so Trey plowed ahead with gusto.

"I don't call that a brother, I call that a *selfish buddyfucker*. There I said it," Trey yelled. "If you fuck your buddy you are a buddyfucker. If you do things that make it possible to hurt your coworkers I have to step in to stop the buddyfucking. I saw the van there; I don't care if he was here on time on a technicality. I think he is under the influence and I have probable cause. I am going into my office and ordering up a drug and alcohol test and you know the rest. He has one hour to get there."

Trey was almost winded by the time he concluded his rant.

Trey picked up the remnants of his coffee swill and tossed it in the garbage then headed out past the three, out of the Blue Room and toward his office. As he passed, Mo was calm as a counterpoint to Trey's outburst.

"You know we will win this," Mo said in an almost soothing tone. "We will grieve it and arbitrate it, so don't even try this shit nonsense."

Trey countered as he left. "He has one hour—I'll be back with the paperwork."

As he walked back into his office, Trey asked BeBe to type up an authorization for a drug and alcohol screen.

"I figured," she said, "I have it here already and I'll call it over when you tell me."

Trey wanted to give the situation a few minutes to marinate so he sat and opened the resume file and picked through more candidates. He thought about calling Wendlocher to stop his pager fusillade of 911 notes, but decided to let him wait a bit more. In moments like this, Trey hated his pager.

He had only gone through three resumes when BeBe appeared and slipped the lab authorization for Warsaw's drug and alcohol onto the corner of his desk. As she did, Mo appeared in the doorway behind her and spoke in a quiet baritone.

"C'mon in here again, we have some talking to do," Mo growled.

Trey left the resumes in piles on his desk, grabbed his notes and picked up the lab screen authorization. He trailed after Mo, who left the door open to the Blue Room as he went in. Warsaw was still at the head of the table closest to the door, which meant his back was to Trey as he entered, but Warsaw looked headless. He was stooped over even further than before, his head now in his hands. He was perfectly still, almost catatonic.

As usual, Mo took the lead. He spoke quietly and calmly, barely above a whisper.

"First, I have to say that the Brotherhood does not agree with your position or your accusations of Mr. Grohowski here," Mo started. "What you said and what you did is not right. If you continue to proceed on this path of forcing our brother to an unjust test, we will bring to bear all the resources of the union. We will go to arbitration should the actions turn out in any negative way to Mr. Grohowski."

Pherrell was tugging at that cigarette pack and pleaded with his eyes for Mo to get to the point. Tommy needed a cigarette in the worst way. Pherrell and Mo both shot a glance at Warsaw, who was still motionless.

Mo continued, "However, we are going to offer you another path to resolve this, justly. Mr. Grohowski, as is his right under the contract, is asking for help under the rehab section 22 of the contract, which says he can receive treatment if he has a problem. He is not sure if he has a problem but he thinks he wants to see if he does. Let this man pursue his health issues."

Then Mo raised his voice. "We are *not* agreeing that he did anything wrong or should be subject to discipline or violated his warning status. Do you hear that?"

Mo's eyes popped a little wider to underline the point and he jabbed his finger on the table for emphasis. Having been dislocated a few times in various street brawls as a kid, his bony finger landed on the table at an odd, almost 90-degree angle.

Trey let the words hang in the air and wiped the corner of his mouth in contemplation before answering.

"This is kind of convenient to play this card now," Trey said. "I could make the argument we had him dead to rights before he asked for the help. I am very concerned about all the rest of your brothers' and sisters' safety."

Pherrell, perhaps under nicotine stress, leaned forward and started in. "Are you saying you won't help?"

Trey waved him off to continue his thought before Pherrell complicated the matter.

"The only thing I really want to hear is Stanley say something," Trey said. "He has not said a word and I want to be 100% sure and on the record that this is what he wants—not just some kooked-up stunt you guys came up with to save his skin."

Pherrell was still cranky.

"Now he has to holler uncle, too?" said Pherrell, indignation rising in his tone. But this time Mo interceded. He leaned over and spoke to Warsaw gently. "Tell the man what you want, Stanley," said Mo.

Warsaw's hands were cupped over his brow, obscuring tired, red eyes, and his thumbs were on his cheeks. As his thumbs rode up his face the scratching sound from the bristle on his face was audible. He picked up his head and looked right at Trey.

"I don't know how I got to this point, but I need to figure this out," Warsaw said in a mutter. "I want some help. I gotta go in."

He looked pathetic, beaten and utterly sincere.

Trey met his tone of voice with a similar calm.

"Stanley," he responded, "I am happy for you. I am proud of you. This is not easy for anyone to ask for help but sometimes we need it. We can do this. I just wanted to hear it from you."

Mo sat back in his chair and with his right hand waved in disgust at Trey for his show of sympathy. Part of him wanted to point out that this compassion was a big act, a management ploy to use any means to control union members. But he let it go in light of the tone of the meeting.

Trey started to describe the process to get Stanley into a rehab center. Mo and Pherrell noted they were aware of the process and made sure the union took steps to escort him there. Trey needed a few minutes to be sure the center could take him as a patient, and the union needed time to discuss all the steps and outcomes with Warsaw. This was not the first time this had happened, but the first time in the context of a potential grievance. Trey took the lab drug and alcohol screen authorization, wadded it up and tossed it into the waste basket. It was a visual signal to Mo and Pherrell and they acknowledged it.

"Come see me when you are ready. I'll need about 15 minutes, but come see me sooner if you need to," Trey said as he stood to leave the room.

As he passed Stanley, he touched his shoulder. It was damp from sweat even in the air-conditioned room. Trey's pager went off again. He glanced down and saw "SEF" light up. What a pain in the ass Wendlocher was today.

Trey got to his office. He asked BeBe to step in.

"Change of plans, Warsaw wants to try rehab," Trey informed her. "Give them a call, please, and let me know what you find. You know the drill."

BeBe stood in front of his desk, palms down.

"Good, I'm glad for him," she said. "He's not a bad guy. He just needs his act together."

Trey realized then that BeBe and Warsaw were classmates at some point. The fact that there were no more than three years between them seemed impossible. BeBe looked 20 years younger. Warsaw did need the help. Badly.

Trey knew it might be a few minutes before he had to go back in the Blue Room so he picked up his phone and started to call Wendlocher, thinking "before he has a shit hemorrhage." He had only dialed two numbers before Mo appeared in his office quietly and shut the door.

"Ghee," Mo started.

The word Ghee was an honorific given to the boss. No one quite knew where it came from, but even as Trey grew up in the neighborhood he knew even the leader on the stickball team got dubbed Ghee. It was not a title used when in conflict so the opener by Mo relieved Trey. Mo continued, "You were outta *line*, that time. Buddyfucker? You actually called him Buddyfucker? No, no, no, no—do not ever call our guys buddyfucker again." Mo punctuated each little "no" with a wag of his misshapen finger.

While the message was delivered in earnest, Mo could not conceal his glee for a new level of creative cursing. He had a half-crooked smile on his face.

"Hard issues require hard words sometimes," said Trey, adding quickly, "and would you *mind* not calling so early in the goddamn morning? What did you plan on doing if you woke my wife and she answered?"

Mo was quick to respond: "Big fucking deal. You are the one who needs the beauty rest by the way, sad looking as you are. What can I say? He was in there in that bar. Who knows when we would get an opportunity like this again? You needed to get your ass here and it should have been sooner. And remember buddyfucker is O-U-T. I cannot let that pass again."

"I thought it was pretty good," Trey said, "but point taken. Is he going to be OK? Do you guys have this covered taking him over there? Do not let him tell you he will get there later. They will be waiting for him and you know guys in this spot are dying to wiggle out. If he does not get there I will..."

"Do I look like the Virgin Mary here?" Mo asserted with a renewed testiness. "We got this. Tommy is the guy I'm more worried about. I gotta go in there and sit with Warsaw so Tommy gets a smoke before he has a stroke. He didn't like buddyfucker either, you know."

"Go. Get out of here, already," Trey said. "Take care of Warsaw. Tell me how he does when you two get back."

Mo left the room and as he opened the door, BeBe was right there with written authorization from the insurance company to admit one Stanley Grohowski to substance abuse evaluation panels and up to 28 days of detox and rehabilitation, if required. Mo turned charming as he took the papers from her.

"Thank you, dear," Mo said, smiling to himself as he sauntered out the door.

CHAPTER 4

————◆◆◆————

TALKING TO PAULEY

Trey felt good about the session. It could have gone a lot of different ways and many of them ugly. Mentally he looked at situations like these as trying to dock a great sailing ship in a shallow, rocky shore. There were obstacles all over and he was somewhat at the mercy of the winds but when he maneuvered the big ship into dock, he felt accomplished.

In this case, the rising outcry from those in the factory about Warsaw's drinking was becoming loud and frustrated. People sympathized with their coworker and union brother and wished him no harm, but it was clear his life was out of control. His life careening was one thing. A careening 2000-lb. forklift with Warsaw at the wheel was another. In cases like this, the union was sometimes helpless unless the brother in question sought help. Nobody had to tell Trey this and it was not hard to document Warsaw's deteriorating orbit. The union knew, too, Warsaw would self-destruct by simply not showing up at work. Had it been a new brother, they may have let that scenario run its course to termination, with all the obligatory protests along the way. The simple fact was that the plant was populated by senior employees who did not like to see their dues spent on protecting these new kids with drug problems. There was a soft spot for those with some time under their belts like Warsaw. Surely the union protected all their members, but it was a delicate dance—and the union would dance longer and harder for a guy like Warsaw.

Trey needed no script. He observed the environment throughout his eight years. He knew what the union needed was a way to get out of this jam. As he exerted pressure regarding attendance woes, Trey signaled

29

consistently he would move to terminate Warsaw, hoping Warsaw would ask for help in the process. When he didn't, Trey merely mentioned to Mo and Tommy that if there was any hope of saving their brother, he needed either a miraculous turnaround in the form of an extended period of sobriety and good behavior or a hammer. That hammer was ultimately creating a situation where the union could tell Warsaw there was no further help they could offer unless he participated in his own rescue. What Trey had not counted on was all of this happening this morning, starting with the call at home. Trey could not know that the rank and file was putting pressure on Mo and Tommy to fix this, but when Trey sensed the pressure, he had to respond quickly. Rearranging priorities on the fly was something he had to do in his job, and he did it well.

The pile of resumes was still strewn on his desk. Trey had to think hard about which the keepers were and which were the rejects. It was getting closer to lunch and Trey gauged where to spend his time. Just then, the pager from hell went off again with the message "SEF." He knew it was Wendlocher. He knew what "SEF" meant but he could not necessarily piece it all together. His morning crisis complete, Trey thought about calling Wendlocher but decided he needed to go walk the plant floor and see what the mood was. Warsaw was a popular and polarizing figure. Most people liked Stan Grohowski the man, but disliked the irresponsible drunkenness of Warsaw. Trey knew there were as many stories as there were interested parties. The confidential nature of what had just happened to Warsaw put Trey at a disadvantage. Out on the floor, it was the kid's game of telephone on steroids. The misinformation could flow exponentially and who knows what the union guys might say. Trey needed to get on the floor and get the pulse. While he could not control the wild thicket of rumor and information, he could prune and shape it a little. Perhaps.

As soon as Trey exited the office area he was reminded of the heat. It was not mid-summer uncomfortable but after six cooler months, this was the first blast of sapping heat. The first hundred yards were more of a thaw as the office was normally too cold. This was due to the fact that the HVAC system was 30 years old and scores of internal moves of walls and renovations mismatched the ducting.

The plant did not have a core area but was distributed in various departments depending upon the task. It followed a rough flow from receiving dock through primary rough cut operations through secondary operations and onto inspection and finally shipping. Grean took on machining work of all kinds, but the work of this plant was generally taking raw bar stock of steel and cast iron and adding various threads or perhaps reaming out rough metal into precise dimensions. They did bending and shaping of aluminum and more pliable metals, too. There were departments with enormous 100- and 200-ton presses stamping out shapes with a thunderous cadence. These presses were so large that their repeated impacts could eventually destroy the structural integrity of the building. Before they were placed, Grean engineers dug holes in the floor and poured a cement base several feet below to absorb the repeated shocks, dissipating them so the building would be spared the blows. Without the concrete pad the building would literally shake itself apart. Such was the raw power at play. The population of the plant was in inverse proportion to the machine size. The larger the press, the fewer people needed in that area. Looking for bodies, Trey headed deeper in the plant to where rows of lathes sat, each attended by an operator. At first glance, the operators all looked alike in gray factory uniforms with an oval "Grean" logo on their chest. Upon closer inspection, the gray-clad operators personalized their appearance. Some covered the Grean logo with "Live Better Work Union" badges. More than a few women had pictures of their kids or grandkids behind their badges and often flipped the badge outward to show off their families. They personalized their clothes reminiscent of how soldiers recalled their families while in the foxholes. Instead of shell blasts, the factory floor boomed out a steady cadence of metal hitting metal. All the employees wore earplugs but this was a relatively recent occurrence. It was the rare 25-year employee who could actually hear the music at his or her retirement party.

When Trey entered the machining area he had a choice of people he could sidle up to and chit-chat with to benignly take the pulse of opinion. As he walked down the main aisle, his eyes passed through the department to the delivery dock in the distance, where he saw a couple of people taking a break. It was cooler and quieter there so after a few nods and waves in Machining, he made his way back to the dock. Strictly speaking, there was no smoking in the plant, but the dock area was a bit of no man's land. The building ended at the cement dock but Grean constructed a wooden overhang so trucks pulling in could be protected in inclement weather, a special favor to those in receiving who had to wrangle long steel rods and plates off flatbed trucks. The overhang also afforded a sheltered spot for smokers. Trey occasionally got complaints but he generally deflected the issue to the union in that its leadership was populated by smokers. He had enough issues to deal with daily without taking on emotional flashpoints like the exact size and boundary of smoking areas.

It was late morning already so some of those congregated on the far dock scattered, perhaps guilty of sneaking an extra break or fearful that they would be perceived as such. Trey didn't care because the one person who did stay was Paolo "Pauley" Firrigno.

Pauley had been with Grean 28 years. He was a little over six feet tall, almost undernourished looking. What little hair he did have was slicked straight back, an unfortunate choice in that it accented Pauley's nose, which was both large and mangled, having been broken several times. It had been broken in Lord-knows-how-many fights. He was born in Western Pennsylvania outside of Pittsburgh to poor Italian immigrants, the second of six children. An early childhood ear infection went untreated, leaving Pauley almost deaf. Hearing aids were expensive and thus out of the question. Pauley fell behind in class and was deemed slow. Kids pick on slow kids who talk a little funny so Pauley fought back.

When he was very young the fights got him thrown out of school and into the state system for troubled children. Having one less mouth to feed seemed to be a blessing for the Firrigno family at that time so they relinquished him to the state of Pennsylvania. He was shipped eastward three times in the system until he landed at a school near Philadelphia that taught him the machinist's trade. Grean was a regular at career fairs for the Pennsylvania state school. Recruiters hoped to pick up young labor trained in the basics and who then could hone their skill set at a factory next to some of the older employees.

While teaching him his trade, the state fitted Pauley with a hearing aid that helped him up the learning curve faster than any time in his young life, but the damage already done bent his potential curve irrevocably. His nose was a mash of fights against odds that were too long. The fights also left him with a string of concussions that likely were the source of the permanent hum that plagued him. The isolation in the state school system caused a lifelong social awkwardness that made him "Most Likely to be Picked on for Life," if the school yearbook awarded such a dubious laurel.

After eyeballing the list of jobs available at Grean, Paulie spotted one that paid a premium of 25 cents an hour. He hopped the bus from Pennsylvania to East Newark. He began as an oiler for the machines and took residence in a nearby men's boarding house where he got a bed, a place to plug in his hot plate and a bathroom he shared with six other men. Rising earlier than any of the other residents to catch the 6 a.m. bus, Pauley always could get in the shower first. The only problem was the hot water might not appear until hours later.

He made the slow climb through the ranks at Grean, eventually rising to his current status as a die setter and press mechanic. The job paid well and Pauley was not afraid of the raw power of the press. He was a bit too fearless as he was missing his pinky. But he wore the wound like a badge of honor and waved it in front of the newest mechanics not as a cautionary tale, but as a symbol of his intimate knowledge of the trade.

Pauley's personal situation was bit of a puzzle. He lived in the boarding house for years after he was able to afford a better place and seemed to be saving for some unknown goal. He eventually met an older Columbian woman named Pilar who inherited guardianship of a grandson, Tomas, from a junkie daughter who died in a car crash. The relationship between Pilar and Pauley was more of convenience than love. Together they bought a small run-down house in nearby Newark and made a life. If there was a deep connection present, it was between Pauley and Tomas. After moving in with Pilar, Pauley's conversations in the plant were dominated by the absolute awe and wonder of the world as seen through Tomas' eyes. Pauley would go on endlessly about the boy's discovery of the birds in a tree on the sidewalk, or a fascination with the on/off switch of the lights. If Pauley was robbed of his own childhood, he seemed to be recapturing it through Tomas, whom he protected with a great ferocity. Trey was amused by the reaction of many in the plant to Pauley's personal situation. One day after Pauley had been rambling on about Tomas' latest adventure chasing a cricket down the sidewalk, a fellow die setter could stand it no more and interrupted the story asking, "With how you are taking care of this kid, are you getting any pussy?" The intellectual curiosity of the workers was boundless. It was the direction that was completely uncertain.

Trey was happy to see Pauley on the dock, taking a long draw on a cigarette. He was slathed in black grease from elbow to wrist. His hands were a fleshy white until the black fingernails that held the cigarette.

"What gives, Pauley? How is little Tomas?" asked Trey.

"Not so little but he's good, he's good," Pauley said, looking off into space.

"Things good in your neighborhood?" asked Trey. "Neighborhood" in this case was the pressroom and Pauley understood.

"We are busy and that's good," said Pauley, who was a noted overtime hound who regularly worked Saturdays and averaged 60 hours a week. "I wish we had more time to do the stuff we need to keep the machines running. That's the bad part of being busy. When you get slow you guys say we can't have the time and money to do the same stuff. I don't care; I'm taking the little guy to the Shore for a week in July, see how he does in the sand and waves."

Pauley turned and flicked his cigarette off the dock and into a small pool of liquid. Given the uncertainty of the contents of the puddle, Trey eyed it to be sure the liquid snuffed the cigarette, not that the cigarette ignited some unseen chemical or oil trail.

Pauley half-knew what Trey was looking for and did not mind sharing. He felt Trey had always been fair to him.

"I heard you guys tried to shitcan Warsaw but he beat you to the punch and checked himself in," Pauley said. "He thinks he outsmarted you, but the poor bastard was going to be dead soon if he didn't shape up so it's good for everyone."

Pauley took the tip of the one grimy pinky he had left and turned his hearing aid down so he could dampen the noise as he went back into his work area.

"Gotta get back," he said and headed back into the plant.

Trey riffled through his mental cards, trying to pick another opinion point. While Trey never knew who complained to the union about Warsaw's deteriorating behavioral orbit, he tried to think of who was just cranky enough to lodge the complaint. Or maybe who took up the complaint for a fellow union member who escaped a careening forklift piloted by Warsaw. That calculus made Trey set his compass for Lee "Choo-Choo" Thomas.

Lee was a story unto herself. She was one of the few female employees who did not work in the assembly area. Lee worked in Deburring. When the parts came off from machining or stamping, they often had sharp and even potentially dangerous burrs that sat up high off the cold rolled steel as it progressed through various forming processes. Before the parts went to assembly, they passed through Lee and her counterparts in Deburring. The assemblers liked to work quickly and a burr on a part could leave them bleeding if they grabbed the sharp part in the wrong spot. Worse yet, if the part somehow made it past assembly with a sharp edge, a customer could suffer the injury. Lee would take each part and remove any burrs by pressing it against a wide belt of industrial-strength sandpaper. The Deburrers wore extra heavy work gloves to protect themselves from the burrs and the fast turning sandpaper. They spun the sharp burrs like jugglers against the belt to wear down the dangerous edges. From there the smoothed parts were safe to pass on to the Assemblers. It was monotonous and slightly dangerous work. Trey noticed one day at lunch that several Deburr employees sat next to each other eating sandwiches. Their hands bore tiny scars. Each scar a reminder of the stitch or two they suffered to close a wound suffered by grabbing at sharp metal hundreds of times a day. Sometimes their luck simply ran out. They wore the scars proudly and recalled a story behind many of the scars the way a prizefighter can explain stitches above their eyes, wounds opened by a worthy opponent. They scoffed at the inexperience of new employees in the department until the newbies sustained a scar or two.

Lee was distinctive in so many ways. For one, she was the only female in the group. Second, she was black. Black employees were not uncommon but the racial mix in the plant better reflected the community demographic of 30 years ago than the present day. Third, Lee always wore a dazzlingly train conductor's cap, adorned with thousands of sequins of various colors. Lee was not clear how this came to be her preferred headwear in the plant, but it became her trademark and led to her nickname "Choo-Choo." The caps came in all colors and varied by season and whim. Even Lee did not know exactly how many she owned but it was difficult to discern a repeat pattern in a month. She bought the conductor's caps from a local thrift store but the sequins were of her own hand and creativity. When Lee ever retired, it would be time to sell any interest in sequin investments.

In the 1950s East Newark was still predominantly a white community, but a rising black middle class began to take an interest in some of the older, more affordable homes in the area. Lee's father moved his family from the ghettos of New York City to the suburbs. She was thrust unwillingly and unknowingly into the forefront of the integration of East Newark. She could not know that the usual adolescent struggles were also stoked at home by parents who resented the influx of blacks into their community. Predatory realtors urged Lee's white neighbors to sell their homes while they still had value. The practice was called blockbusting. All the fear and resentment carried over directly and indirectly to the schoolyard. As a freshman in high school, some of the older white girls picked on Lee until a fight ensued. Lee took a pretty good beating but she gave one of her opponents an even bigger beating. What Lee could not sense was that the girl she beat up was the daughter of a low-level neighborhood mobster. Incensed that his daughter took a beating from "that black bastard," he sent his sons to even the score. The three older boys beat Lee so severely she spent four days unconscious in the hospital and ultimately lost sight in her left eye. The result was she wore an odd set of glasses, both lenses somewhat darkened. The lens covering the left eye was fogged to obscure the hideously deformed eye behind it. Trey often wondered if all the wild conductor's caps were inspired in part by a desire to draw an observer's gaze to a plane above eye level.

Lee never returned to school and drifted for a while hustling untaxed cigarettes. After one arrest, she decided jail was not a place in her future. She applied at Grean several times but was never offered a job, owing in equal parts to both her black skin, odd appearance and her free admission of a conviction for peddling bootleg cigarettes.

Old man Grean was well aware of the savage beating of some young black girl in the neighborhood and that no one was arrested for the crime. He also was aware of the odd-looking young black woman who seemed to apply every two weeks or so. Old Man Grean was no social activist but once he stitched those two facts together, he demanded that she be hired and trained in Assembly. Lee worked almost 10 years in Assembly before applying for the Deburr job. Many were quick to say the job could not be done by a one-eyed (black) woman. The job was too heavy. She risked blindness if a chip flew the wrong way. She might encourage women to leave assembly en masse and threaten productivity. (Everyone then knew women were not as productive. Why else would they get paid less than the men?)

Lee never wavered. She tenaciously adhered to the union rules for bidding on jobs and used her seniority to claim the spot. She then used her effort and skill to outperform most of the other Deburrers. She could have outperformed them all, but Lee was savvy enough to know that to show up her union brothers was unwise. She remained almost exactly in the middle of the department in terms of output for the next 20 years.

Trey had known the story of Lee's beating since he was a child. It was neighborhood lore. Depending on who told the story it was either a shame upon the neighborhood, or the last valiant but unsuccessful stand against a black community that overwhelmed a once-proud neighborhood. When he first discovered that Choo-Choo in Deburr was the same Lee of legend, he expected to find a bitter, angry woman. What Trey found was almost the exact opposite. Lee was gregarious, warm-hearted and sought-after for her opinions. Even though she had deserted Assembly for a "man's job," Lee was still a spokesperson for a lot of the grievances and annoyances in Assembly. On breaks, Lee would be found on a bench on the side of the building, a cigarette (presumably taxed) dangling from her lips as she held court. Since the factory was a non-smoking area, Lee still talked out of the side of her mouth, balancing an imaginary cigarette in much the same way an amputee stretches a missing leg.

Lee bridged so many areas and demographics, thus was a good barometer of opinion and Trey knew it. He made his way over to Lee. Trey had to raise his voice over the dim roar of exhaust fans that pulled tiny particulates away from the sanders and the employees' lungs and deposited them in filters on the roof. The exhaust fans were relatively new, added only five years ago but resisted by the operators as maddening for their hum.

"Lee, how are things with you?" Trey asked. "I like the hat. Brand new or part of the rotation?"

Lee was short, maybe a shade over five feet tall. Between the exhaust fan, her concentration on her job and the constant whine of the belt sanders in the area, she sensed Trey long before she could really hear him. She adjusted her head so she could peer up at Trey with her good right eye above the tinted lens.

"Hey honey, what are you doing out here with the poor folks who just happened to pay your salary?" Lee said. Her voice had a deep phlegmy edge that made Trey fear she might spit up a burr with the next cough. The greeting was pure Lee. Friendly, but with distinct edges.

Trey decided that pretense would make him seem cloying. He knew Lee was plugged into everything so there was no use beating around the bush.

He replied, "I just came out to say I am sorry about your friend, Warsaw. I know you two know each other a long time. We need him healthy and his family needs him."

"Say no more," Lee interrupted. "We all have our hardships and crutches, but when somebody's crutch nearly runs over my broken-up old ass, I am glad when things get straightened out. He'd *better* come back here straightened out or I am going to sharpen one of these things and– uuuUUUUHHH." Lee cackled hoarsely as she made a playful lunge with an imaginary shiv..

She continued: "If anybody around here begrudges that man getting right, then they just don't know what's right in this world so I am not listening to them crazies anyway."

There was no mistaking where Lee stood on any issue.

"Well, I'm glad we all got it right for once," said Trey.

"Don't be so happy with yourself," Lee said. "Even a blind pig can find an acorn once in a while and that was one big frigging acorn—that Warsaw." Lee pulled another piece away from the belt sander and tossed in the shop box with a thunk, unofficially dismissing Trey.

Trey was satisfied that even if Pauley and Lee's opinion and information varied even 25% from the mainstream, the twisted game of telephone regarding the fate and treatment of Warsaw was not going to hurt the mood.

Trey took two steps back toward the plant when the paging system boomed from the rafters: "Trey Bensen, call 200." Extension 200 was Ike's secretary, Ida. If the page was in the switchboard operator's voice, it was one thing. If Ike asked Ida to page that was a minor crisis. Almost on cue, Trey's pager lit up again: 911 SEF. Trey knew he had to call Wendlocher right after seeing Ike, if for no other reason than courtesy at this point.

As he circled through the plant, Trey could discern no other telling signs about mood. The few people he did see nodded or waved as usual, but any impact of the Warsaw issue was unseeable for now.

Trey ducked into the back door of the offices on the far north end of the complex and down a long corridor before he appeared at Ike's door, which was closed. Ida never looked up from her typewriter. "He said for you to go right in," she said flatly.

Trey opened the door and the effect was no different than hitting the wall of heat in the plant. He almost ran directly into all 6 foot 3 inches of Harlowe Mikkelson. Mikkelson also went by the initials SEF, which had jammed his pager all morning. Harlowe was The Squinty-Eyed Fuck.

CHAPTER 5

THE GREAN BROTHERS IN ORLANDO

Orlando, Florida, was swept by a pre-dawn tropical downpour cleaning the streets better than the grimy brushes of the municipal street sweepers ever could. The fantasy created inside the famous theme parks like Disney and Universal Studios ends at the gates. The city of Orlando itself is a mash of cheap souvenir shops and some industry. The fantastic growth of the city population strained the municipal budgets so when it did rain as hard as it had the night before, the Orlando Street Public Works called off the street sweepers and let nature do its work. By the time rush hour began, water receded from the streets in fetid black streams of watery gunk, driven by gravity to the lowest point and running off the crown of the road, exposing a hot, dry pavement. The runoff snaked down to storm sewers. One of those wide-mouth storm drains sat directly in front of a three-story office building on the south side of town. Above the windows of the third floor, blue letters were slanted forward, seeming to hurry to some unknown destination ahead or around the other side of the building and announce the occupant: *Grean Machining.*

Cal Grean Jr. stopped his three-month-old black Mercedes Benz at the curb before the driveway to the building leading to the parking lot around back. The runoff for the storm would trail down to the drains for hours after a hard rain, bringing along with it any amount of municipal detritus. Today, Cal calculated the angle around a sodden corrugated box washed along the urban stream and into his path with unknown content. The box looked somehow rooted in his path as an ugly black torrent swirled around it.

"Shit," Cal mumbled under his breath as he slowly accelerated through the water. He thought, "I just had these wheels detailed." But he made his way into his reserved parking spot without incident or damage to his wheels.

Grean Machining was the legacy of his father, the late Caleb "Cal" Grean Sr. Unlike his son and namesake, Grean *pere* considered himself a very lucky man. He liked to mention that he was the son of a seventh son and that fact portended his charmed life. Born in 1910, Cal Sr. was too young to participate in WWI and too old for WWII. While a great patriot, he knew that good fortune alone meant he had an uninterrupted time to build his business and, in fact, build his business upon the war effort.

The seventh son that was his father Virgil owned a small corner grocer in Patterson, New Jersey. Cal planned to stay in that business, but the Depression killed the grocery by choking the paying customers. In 1932, the stress of the business and the economy also killed Virgil and left Cal— an only child—to take care of the business and his mother. Cal struggled for a few years, eking out a living and extending groceries and credit to a neighborhood burdened with 35% unemployment rates. He was just getting by until one day in 1935, Cal noticed a machine shop in a garage three doors down that had not opened their doors in weeks. Peeking in the window, he saw three lathes and some drill presses, all abandoned. The penniless owner of said machines fled to parts unknown and left the equipment for the bank to seize and sell. Cal, sensing he might make more money in one week scrapping the equipment itself than he could selling a year's worth of bananas, considered breaking in and stealing the equipment. He thought better of such a nefarious plan and contacted the bank instead. The bank wanted the building cleaned up so it could find a decent occupant, or at least an empty building it could raze, so the deal was struck: Cal would remove the equipment, clean the building interior and keep the proceeds for salvage or sale. Three backbreaking weeks later, Cal hauled away the equipment on a flatbed truck, searching for the best price as he traveled from junkyard to junkyard. On his third stop, in East Newark, Cal came across a salvage yard owner uninterested in the equipment at any price, but motivated by putting his unemployed bother-in-law/machinist to work. He proposed to Cal they try to revive the machining business in a tin-roof shack on his junkyard property. The one stipulation was Cal employ his brother-in-law as the machine operator. Cal was dubious, but felt it was worth a try. He could always sell the equipment for scrap if demand rose and scrap prices spiked. This was how Frank Reilly—unemployed brother-in-law deluxe—became employee No. 1 of Grean Machining.

Frank and Cal struggled along for the better part of a year, Frank being paid in groceries now and then. But they got their first break when Maxwell House Coffee in Jersey City gave them a recurring order for machine parts for the coffee-processing equipment. That order alone was more than Frank could handle by himself, so the unemployment rolls dropped by another tool and die maker with the hire of employee No. 2.

Gradually, Cal came to understand the machining business better than the grocery business. He formed a partnership with the bank to clean out abandoned businesses. He mined veins of defunct businesses discovered by the bank and the tin roof shack gave way to a more permanent structure with modern conveniences like walls, plumbing and heating. Soon Cal sold the inventory and fixtures at the grocery store to finance the expansion of Grean Machining.

Over time, Cal bought up small machine shops in New Jersey, New York and Pennsylvania. He especially looked for distressed businesses needing fast cash and willing to sell cheap. His favorite targets were family businesses that did not quite understand the value of the business. Some of the larger machine shops he left in place to house smaller shops he acquired. He filled unused space with the smaller purchases, cutting costs and gaining efficiency.

By December 6, 1941, Grean Machining had eight shops and claimed to be "of the finest mettle where metal meets metal," per their first sales brochure. If Grean was just stirring as a business, Pearl Harbor and WWII jolted the business awake. The war years were a period of frantic growth as the business received almost unlimited orders from the U.S. Department of Defense. The hodgepodge of machinery Cal acquired over the first few years could be configured to make almost anything and everything. It so happened the war effort required anything and everything. It was a match made in heaven.

Cal's personal life was just as prolific and productive. He married Maysie in late 1940 and by the time the Japanese surrendered, the young couple jump-started the baby boom with a son, Caleb Jr., and daughter Georgeanne. Their youngest son, Jack, arrived five years later in 1950.

Like kudzu, Cal Grean, Sr continued to expand throughout the 1950s into neighboring states. In the image of a great army logistician, Cal slowly extended his supply lines, careful not to jump into strange geographies and faraway places. As most of those who survived the Depression, he eschewed debt and avoided risk like the plague.

The strategy served him well. By 1980, Cal thought about retiring and turning the business over to his sons. Grean Machining was debt-free and worth over $100 million. It operated in 11 states and had 32 machine shops. Many were now in shiny state-of-the-art buildings using the finest computerized systems requiring less raw manufacturing talent than software know-how. But no matter how much the business thrived, Cal Grean Sr. ran the business from East Newark. The factory he started with Frank Reilly expanded at least a dozen times and included an office building that served as the nerve center for administrative functions like Accounting and Sales. The site, which started as a junkyard, was acquired by Grean over time and the junkyard disappeared. Rusting automobile carcasses leaking unknown multi-hued fluids gave way ever so slowly to a bright green front lawn protected by a barbed-wire perimeter. Cal had an unimposing, cluttered office in the structure where he would work long hours and often rest his feet on his desk at the end of the day. If this state of repose exposed a toe peering through a threadbare sock, Cal declared victory: "I got my money's worth out of these, for sure!"

Frank Reilly became a venerated part of corporate history. His status as employee No. 1 took on a life of its own. A parking spot simply marked "1" waited for him each day. Frank still roamed the floor as a kind of trouble-shooter-and-engineer-without-portfolio, puttering with the technically tricky issues, searching his mental database for answers acquired over the previous four decades. Frank was part of a dying breed who garnered the title "Engineer" as an earned honorific rather than as the outcome of a college curriculum. Despite generations of hiring degreed engineers, when the going got tough, technically, it was Frank who was the fountainhead of solutions.

The subject of transitioning this business to the next generation seemed straightforward but was not without its intricacies. Cal Jr. was Ivy-League educated and took an early interest in the business. He was the financial wizard the old man needed and helped steer the course since he joined the business in 1970. He worked in various positions in the accounting and finance areas. By 1981 he was named CFO. He merited the job and had been a watchful eye and steady hand.

Georgeanne, on the other hand, never took an interest in the business, which she saw as grimy and coarse. Her tastes tended to the finer things in life. She, too, went to the best schools, but leveraged her time to find a wealthy suitor who took her off to Virginia where she raised horses. She adored the family name and in fact wore it in hyphenated fashion. "Georgeanne Grean-Lewis" was her preferred title long before the practice became accepted.

Jack went to the finest colleges, too. Several of them. His issue was staying enrolled and a step ahead of disciplinary boards with distaste for drunken students with low grade point averages and lower class attendance rates. He understood at an early age that a lot of attention focused on the child who held the suffix "Jr." For his part, Jack created his own attention for better or worse. He staggered through college in seven years, but joined Grean in Sales. When Jack discovered the magic of an expense account and the two-drink lunch, he hit his stride in the business. He was good with a joke and a golf club and his primary role was to soothe ruffled customers. He took the axiom "people do business with people they like" to new heights. People liked Jack and Jack liked making them like Grean. It did not matter to Jack whether they liked Grean for its ability to produce precision-machined parts or Jack's ability to entertain at strip clubs in and around New Jersey. In reality, because Jack understood very little about the technical side of the business, he took particular pride in landing business based upon his ability to lubricate purchasing agents with copious amounts of the finest liquor mixed in equal parts with topless dancers.

By 1982, the old man turned the business over to Cal Jr. and Jack. Under their combined stewardship, they kept Grean Machining a very successful operation, and continued to expand the business under the same model. They kept the family image pristine, providing their father a fine office where he came and went as he pleased as the Chairman of the Board Emeritus. They created a legend around his success story, funding Grean Scholarships for local schools, in particular trade schools that turned out machinists with contemporary skills. It was philanthropy with a purpose, and they understood it well.

In 1988, Cal Green Sr. was diagnosed with cancer and died the following year. After a respectful period of mourning, Cal Jr. and Jack decided East Newark was just too dreary. With Cal researching the best tax rates and Jack the best nightlife, they compromised on Orlando, Florida, as their destination. Their arrival in the Orlando business community was heralded with great anticipation. The truth was they moved only some administrative and headquarter functions to Florida, but for the buzz created by the Green PR firm, it was as if they had moved General Motors to Orlando.

After a few years in Orlando and now pushing 25 years in the business, Cal had a bigger vision: cash out. As a private business, all three siblings could live a life of leisure at any pursuit they chose. Surely, Cal Sr. would not approve of such an idea, but he was gone and the time was right. Quietly, Cal cultivated a series of potential buyers. It was now 1994 and quiet conversations turned into serious due diligence. There were three suitors to buy Green and on this day Cal sat in his large office expecting a phone call to see just how serious an interest had developed.

There was one problem: it was 9:55 a.m., just minutes before the conference call was scheduled to begin and brother Jack was nowhere to be found. This was only a problem in that Jack insisted on being included in the discussions. Cal did not want to appear disinterested or disorganized to the potential buyers, so while he considered the idea of postponing the call, he quickly dismissed that option. There might be hell to pay from Jack later on, but as the stakes got higher, he needed to make command decisions and if Jack was not going to act responsibly then…

Just as Cal had worked himself into a full froth of frustration, Jack bolted through the door of the office.

"Thought I forgot about the call, Junior?" Jack blurted out, delighted in attaching the sobriquet "Junior" to his older brother. It was loving, but carried a distinct, edgy message. It shouted out that they were equals in this venture.

Cal sat at a large, round table in the middle of the office. His notes and files were arranged so he could reference any of them quickly. He wore a dark suit and non-descript blue striped tie. The speakerphone was set precisely mid-table. Cal was ready. Jack was ever-so-slightly hung over.

"No, Jack," Cal answered. "I was not concerned. Like a great prizefighter, you are always ready at the bell. I just thought we needed a little prep time."

Jack was not aware his brother was annoyed. He said, "That reminds me- and preparation is a good word—tell me about this one? Which group is it? What is my role in this call? Anything you want me to say? Am I the good cop or the bad cop?"

"No one is a cop," Cal said in a tone more wearied than one would expect so early in any conversation. He was not so much annoyed by Jack's rapid-fire questions as the fact they had little time to go through all the variables. He was still worried Jack could go off the rails and say something to spook the potential buyers. They did not need flash; they needed substance on this call. These investors would not be impressed by a night on the town, so any impact Jack might have was muted in these circumstances. Even if an oddball comment by Jack knocked the value of the deal by 1% it could mean several million dollars. Cal decided to try and fit in as much as he could in the three minutes they likely had left.

"We are talking to TerVeer Industries today. They make interiors for the mobile home business. They do a ton of machining and metal bending and think they are getting raped by their suppliers who do this for them but TerVeer knows nothing on how to do it themselves. The idea is they buy all of Grean, keep the capabilities they want, maybe run a few more of the profitable businesses and likely sell off a whole bunch. They get lower costs and hope to make a buck when they flip what they don't want. We are here to listen. We should say as little as we need to and volunteer nothing if not asked. If you are not sure, hit the mute button and ask me, but they want this call, not us, so just *listen*."

Cal emphasized the word "listen" in a pleading yet firm way to drive the point deeply for Jack, whose success thus far in life was more broadly based on talking.

Jack knew his brother was half informing, half lecturing.

"I got it. Low key. My role on the call is low key. I know when to lay low," said Jack.

Cal knew he needed to stroke his brother a little.

"You are the best at reading these things. You will do fine. Conference calls are tricky—they take away all the visuals and for you it is like taking away your superpowers," said Cal. He knew he did not need Jack in a mood where he had to prove anything.

Jack got up and looked out the plate glass window at the city below. It was now a beautiful day the tourists would love. The withering heat turned a lot of the morning rain into mystical plumes of steam that would rise just enough to segue into more drenching rain later that afternoon. Jack sat mesmerized for just a moment, distracted by the curls of steam off the pavement and momentarily looked for them to turn into some kind of divine message. An Orlando street genie maybe, granting wishes. Cal, not as antsy, but oh-so-more anal-retentive and neater than Jack, sat arranging his papers again.

The intercom soon buzzed and a disembodied assistant announced the TerVeer call. Cal popped the speaker phone into live mode without acknowledging the introduction.

"Cal Grean here. I have my brother Jack with me. Who are we speaking to?"

There was a pregnant pause, followed by a bit of rustling. It was obvious that the TerVeer callers were just settling in. Their offices were in Chicago and close enough to O'Hare that you would occasionally here the muffled roar of a jet engine in the background.

TerVeer Industries was represented by three people on the call. Two were bankers trying to make the deal attractive so they could collect fees. They could give a damn if the deal made sense for either side. It was their experience that both the buyers and sellers in these situations overestimated their potential gain and both would likely be disappointed. The bankers were there to feed the over optimism on both sides just enough so the deal would be consummated and the fees would begin to flow. The call was led by Duncan Rucks, the Senior VP at TerVeer in charge of Mergers and Acquisitions. Duncan was in his late 40s and a rising star. He needed a high-profile win to keep his corporate star ascending. An acquisition like Grean was a high-risk/high-reward play for him. He needed to get this just right. Duncan had vetted this acquisition with everyone up to his Board of Directors, who gave him some loose parameters on the size of the offer. While the bankers were there to advise him, the potential of buying

Grean was his to close or walk away from. He wanted the Grean team to understand his pain points clearly.

"We continue to be pleased with our financial projections," Duncan began. "We think Grean, if acquired, would fit nicely within our organization and give us a capability we lack today. The numbers you have given us bear this out to some degree. You are a sound organization and you should be congratulated for that. Your father was a very sound businessman and the apples have not fallen far from the tree." He was not above blatant ass kissing at this stage of the game.

He continued: "While we have not settled on a final number, I think it is safe to assume that we are thinking of a number that would be a significant multiple of sales."

Duncan let this sentence hang a bit. On the Grean side, Jack looked like he was ready to speak, so Cal decided to take charge.

"Significant is a hazy word that can lead to misunderstanding. So I can compare this better to other discussions, can you be a little more concrete as to your interpretation of 'significant?'" Cal said politely, while raising a silent hand to Jack, begging his patience.

Duncan pounced with words he hoped would land with great impact.

"As much as $300 million, if our diligence continues to be favorable."

Jack pounded the mute button in Orlando hard enough that Cal was sure it was heard all the way to Chicago. His once-fatigued eyes were agog with excitement.

"Did he just say $300 fucking million?! That is $70 million more than any number we have heard!" Jack looked to be searching for a pen to sign on the dotted line. Cal, for all his cool rationality, ran his freshly manicured fingers through his hair—a telltale he was unnerved. Cal hit the button again carefully to unmute the line, hoping Jack's frantic move to mute the conversation was not heard or understood in Chicago.

It was then Duncan spoke the word the Grean's dreaded hearing: "But..."

There it was. For Jack, it was like reading his lotto ticket and knowing he had the first five numbers, certain the sixth would come a cropper. Duncan continued. He had the Greans attention.

"Our greatest concern is your unionized facilities. As you know you have six. Five of the six are not a great concern. Either they have weaker unions or they belong to units we intend to sell. It is the plant in East Newark that bothers us. It has the nastiest union. You have had three strikes there over the last 20 years. It has all the equipment essential for this to make sense from our side. It is where your father started the business, so we don't think you want to touch it from an emotional standpoint—which is understandable. If that plant is not reliable as a source of production, the valuation comes way down. We cannot have that plant be the wild card in this. There are about a half dozen other items we need, mostly environmental issues and visibility into lease agreements, but we see this plant and the union issue as the big stumbling block. We are non-union and if we had to deal with this, frankly, it is not an area of expertise we currently have nor do we want to add to our costs by buying that expertise."

The Grean brothers processed this information in polar opposite fashion. For Jack, it was a detail. Done. No problem. Cal immediately knew it was the $70 million question. Again, Cal pleaded with Jack not to jump in with the wave of a hand. He did not need to worry. Jack was trying to figure out how long he could stay in Barbados and if Cal and Georgeanne would want him home *every* Christmas.

Cal knew his company history well and was to the point, saying, "So exactly what do you want us to do about this? The East Newark plant is very well run; has not had a strike in almost a decade and the last one was for two days. Factories are more prone to unionization in this line of work. It is a cost of doing business."

"It is not currently *our* cost of doing business," Duncan interrupted. He wanted to be in command of the conversation. "We still think this is a deal worth considering, but I thought you'd like to know our concerns."

Jack had been so good for so long, but with his Barbados fantasy receding into the distance he could be quiet no longer and said, "What would you want us to do—close that plant? Do you know how long and costly that would be? With all those employees who have been there longer than dirt, the severance cost alone would…"

Cal looked at Jack aghast, knowing he had just squeezed every bit of toothpaste out of the tube and there was no putting it back in. Cal quickly determined he would have preferred Jack's wrath if the call had taken place without him versus this verbal blunder. Duncan heard it and knew it too.

"Precisely my point. I think that was Jack who just talked of severance costs? If that plant is a choke point for what we want out of the acquisition and we have to close it or move it or remediate God-knows-what-chemicals are in the soil underneath it—that changes our bid quite a bit. It is not a small risk and if it comes to pass, the costs of the risk can be significant. Further, the key skills we need are embedded in that plant," said Duncan. With each word he envisioned the purchase price being hammered down.

Cal wanted to wrest the momentum of the conversation back. He did not want Duncan and the TerVeer team to bully them.

"Understood. And I am sure you know that each potential buyer views risk and the likelihood of that risk very differently in some cases. I don't want to jump the gun here. I know you have a half dozen concerns and I am sure if you have not done so already, you are willing to reduce them to writing so we can respond to them as fully as we have all your other requests," Cal said. For good measure, Cal concluded his statement with a glare Jack fully understood that called for his silence through the duration of the call.

Duncan was not ruffled in the least, saying, "We will indeed lay out our concerns. The issue in East Newark is perhaps the vaguest. What we are looking for is some sign that you have control of the situation. We are not sure what that looks like exactly. How do we know that the union will not shut us down? Can you get a longer contract? Can you guarantee us labor peace and a productive plant? The answer to that last question is certainly no, but help us feel good that the situation is stable. We can discuss this again in the future after you have had time to think about it some more. It is really a math equation. The smaller the risk, the greater the value."

The call continued for another 20 minutes as the two sides traded additional facts and definitions and finally, some personal small talk about great golf courses. They agreed to exchange information within six weeks.

When Cal ended the call with a flick of his finger, he did not strike a relaxed pose but stayed sitting straight up, contemplating some space in the air about two inches past his nose. Jack was pacing the room.

"He *did* say $300 fucking million, right?" said Jack. Even Jack was capable of this math. Three siblings. $300 million. That is $100 million each.

Cal was unmoved, in front of Jack anyway. This time he ran both hands through his receding hairline.

"It is all Monopoly money until we get a check. He could have said a billion. There is no offer on the table, so wring out your panties. We have a lot of work to do and two other great offers on the table," said Cal.

Jack retorted, "But no others at $300 million."

"No—but only one offer will be real in the end," said Cal.

Jack was back in Barbados again and knew which offer he wanted to be the realest.

"I don't think the East Newark thing is a deal breaker. They love us up there. Half of them knew the old man. They're not a bad bunch of guys and they are getting older. They aren't the ball-busters they were when they were younger," said Jack.

Cal tried to drag Jack from the island fantasy back to Orlando and explain things to his younger brother saying, "That is precisely the fucking point. You know and I know those old farts up there are out of piss and vinegar. They have tuition bills now to pay so they are not going to strike anymore. But TerVeer doesn't know that. If Grean is sold and the name comes off the building, there is no memory of Dad. TerVeer knows that too and they are only making that big offer because they want us to do the dirty work and close it or absorb all the costs on this side. Then, they still don't have to make that big an offer—just a dollar more than anyone else. It is something that would just suck up our time and energy."

"Are you willing to bet $70 million on that?" Jack asked. "I'd spend a lot of time on an issue for that kind of change."

"Strong words for a guy who gets antsy at a three-hour movie," said Cal, only half-teasing.

Cal picked up the phone and punched in three digits for an internal extension.

"Is he in the building? No? When is he back? Next week? Do you know where he is? Even better. Ideal, as a matter of fact. Call him and have him call Ideal, OK?" Cal hung up the phone and smiled perversely at Jack. He began to quiz Jack in mock schoolhouse fashion.

"Now Jack, who is the one person who can handle this better than anyone?"

"Harlowe," answered Jack.

"Correct. Now on to question No. 2. Where is Harlowe this very minute?"

"East Newark?" Jack guessed.

"Bingo."

"Sounds like fate is on our side right now," said Jack, looking out the window at a hazy sun and imagining what that sun looked like over Barbados. "When will he call in?"

CHAPTER 6

HARLOWE

As Trey entered Ike's office, he did not expect Harlowe Mikkelson, aka The Squinty-Eyed Fuck, to be so close to the door. Trey's nose ended up almost in the knot of Harlowe's polyester tie. Harlowe was imposing enough at 6 feet 3 inches tall and thick everywhere. His hair was sparse but slicked back, dyed an unnatural color of black. The hair combed straight back exposed a face that appeared more like a bas relief, his large features jutting from an oversized round head that sat atop an even thicker neck. Somehow, every time Trey saw him, he had an image of how bowling balls are displayed at the local pro shop. Taken in total, Harlowe's head would be the delight of any caricaturist on the boardwalk at the Jersey Shore. His eye sockets sat perfectly round but the eyelids narrowed to slits. His eyes combined with his height gave him the appearance of looking down on those he talked to, adjusting his head to address his audience like a person with trifocals struggling to find his focal point while looking at a menu. This habit of peering down on people, combined with his supercilious and greatly dismissive mien, earned him his nickname The Squinty-Eyed Fuck.

The nickname was coined by the serial-pager Ed Wendlocher ("Will he ever stop paging me?" Trey thought, as his hip vibrated yet again as he stood nose-to-Windsor knot with Harlowe) late one night at a hotel bar in North Carolina. Trey and Ed just concluded two days of a Grean-sponsored Human Resources conference. As the senior and most trusted HR executive, Harlowe was given the honor of concluding the session with a 45-minute stem-winder. His topic had been the judicious use of placebos or "sugar pills," as Harlowe termed them. He suggested each HR director present go out and buy a large jar of the brightly colored pills in a form closely approximating the appearance of prescription medication. If an employee appeared with a malady or symptom and an inclination to go home, leaving precious production behind, Harlowe advocated taking three pills ("two pills seems skimpy," he noted) and giving them to the employee along with a story that these pills had been left by a passing pharmaceutical representative (why the pharmaceutical rep would be plying his or her trade in a factory was a detail left unexplained), who described just these symptoms as the target of this wonder regimen. Harlowe claimed this tactic led to 75% of the employees staying and doing productive work on behalf of Grean. He further reminded each of the HR leaders their bonuses were tied to productivity scores at their individual location.

Many of those in Harlowe's audience seemed too fatigued or too numb to care, but as Trey shot Wendlocher a look across the room, Wendlocher caught the glance and made a tiny motion like he was jerking off his pencil—visible only to Trey's understanding eye. Back at the hotel bar that night after a communal dinner, Wendlocher and Trey recapped the day's events, fueled by an antsiness of two days of lecture and about five beers.

Wendlocher decided to unburden himself, saying, "Does Mikkelsen *really* think our people are that fucking stupid that they are going to buy that cartload of shit about *just* having the drug, handing them some shitty pills out of a candy store and them making some kind of recovery? Are we going to sell snake oil next? Trey, your guys will tell you to shove the pills up your ass, and then they will call the cops and Harlowe will be on the 6 o'clock Eyewitness News press conference expressing shock at your illegal drug trafficking. With my luck, I will hand those fucking sugar pills to some diabetic who goes into a coma. That Squinty Eyed Fuck."

Wth that denouement, Trey laughed until he fell off the barstool. While he started in rage, Wendlocher finally saw the humor and the two of them ended up on their knees in the bar, screaming with laughter. Thus begat The Squinty-Eyed Fuck—or SEF in pager code.

Technically, Harlowe's title was Senior Director of Corporate Health and Safety. Whose health and safety he was safeguarding was open to interpretation—most likely the health and safety of the Grean family fortune. Harlowe came to meet Cal Sr. in early 1970 when the old man was looking to buy several run-down machine shops in Georgia and combine them at one central site nearby. He located two parcels with the right zoning and settled on a price with one of the parcel owners, but the other, smelling weakness, held out for an outrageous price, one that old man Grean could not stomach. Grean the elder was sitting at a local saloon squired by Harlowe, who worked as a shift supervisor at one of the companies due to be acquired in the deal. Harlowe was hoping to curry favor with his new potential boss and assured him he could save the deal. He asked for the address of the property already purchased and $120, fully refundable if the properties were not secured. Over the next week, Harlowe paid a dozen black college students $10 each to inquire as to the availability of the property Grean had already agreed to purchase. Each went there in the middle of the day. For emphasis, Harlowe made sure to be at the coffee shop when the holdout owner stopped in for lunch. Harlowe expressed support and admiration for how the man welcomed people of color (or, as was more likely at the time, "those colored people") to buy the property that Grean had no use for anymore. To be fair, Harlowe was no bigot at heart, but he understood fear and used it as deftly and carefully as any swordsman would use a sabre. Within the week, the holdout landowner dropped his price, Grean Machining closed on both pieces of property and Harlowe rose to legendary status in old man Grean's eyes. Forever after, when there was nasty business to attend to at any of the Grean sites, Harlowe Mikkelsen was dispatched. Without fail, the problem was resolved and few at Grean cared to know the details of exactly how it had been fixed. Jack and Cal Grean Jr. understood the value of Harlowe and kept him on as an advisor of sorts, performing the same tasks as he had for their father. They often lamented how difficult it would be to replace Harlowe if he retired. The ability to act without burden of conscience was apparently in rare supply in the workplace. Harlowe understood this job security and magnified it by wrapping the most mundane jobs in a cloak of mystery. A favorite piece of wordplay between the Greans and Harlowe would begin by them inquiring "Anything we need to know?" Harlowe answered with great emphasis, "There is *nothing* you need to know." This was followed by uproarious laughter.

Since Grean operated in a reasonably dangerous business environment, it was not uncommon to see OSHA inspections and complaints. There was no better diplomat than Harlowe. He kept OSHA at bay and dressed up the safety programs with a host of efforts, some of which included sugar pills. Harlowe was in his official role when he literally ran into Trey this day.

"Well hello, son," said Harlowe, a small wry grin from ear to ear. Trey cringed at hearing himself called "son" by the Squinty Eyed Fuck. Since Harlowe gave no ground, Trey backed up and walked around him to an open area of Ike's office. Ike was behind the desk, reviewing some purchase requisitions. Ike glanced up to be sure it was Trey who entered and returned to the paperwork.

"Harlowe here is in for the day and wanted to see where we are on safety," said Ike, "I assume you can make time for him even on short notice?"

"No problem. We can make time for Mr. Mikkelsen. I can get the union to get the safety committee, too," said Trey. He knew the union hated and distrusted Harlowe as much as he did. They saw him as a spy for the corporate side, one who wanted to make them look bad compared to the other plants. Harlowe did not understand nor care that this plant in East Newark was the genesis for his job. Trey sometimes wondered if at least part of the union mistrust was projecting from his own feelings about The Squinty-Eyed Fuck. While he never said a bad word about Harlowe to anyone in the union, he could not bring himself to be enthusiastic either. This was not healthy and he tried to check it as best he could. But he was sure he could not project sincerity. You can't shine shit.

Harlowe had more on his agenda and decided to get to the point, something he was good at.

"I need to talk to you about our Safety Award too, the Grean Machine?" said Harlowe.

The Grean Machine was literally that—an award with a miniature lathe on top. It was awarded quarterly to the plant with the greatest improvement in safety metrics. The winning plant got to display the trophy and the company picked up a lunch for the whole plant.

Harlowe continued: "I'm sure you saw my secretary put out the standings for the first quarter and it looked like East Newark won."

In truth, Trey had not seen the note. It likely was in his in-box, but he bluffed.

"Yes, I was very pleased and I hope you were too," Trey said. "It shows that we..."

Ike perked up hearing the exchange. "Trey, how come you didn't tell..."

"Hold on now everyone, simmer down now," Harlowe interrupted as his pinky finger dug deeply in his ear. "That is what I am trying to tell you. That list should not have gone out that way. Yes, East Newark did have a great improvement, but do you think that we need to send the union that kind of message? First of all, if they are going to be in a union, we should only give them exactly what they bargain for and second, their record was so bad they had the most room to improve. It's almost like cheating for them."

Trey processed the word "cheating" coming out of Harlowe's mouth with equal parts irony and disgust. He also knew that East Newark had a record that was smack dab in the middle of the overall rankings for safety in most months, adjusted for size.

"So are you saying we weren't the most improved in the first quarter?" Trey asked.

"Your guys certainly did not have the least amount of accidents, if that is what you are asking," Harlowe said, trying to turn the discussion ever so slightly, a tactic Trey had seen many times before.

"That is *not* what I am asking," said Trey. "I am asking if the award is for most improvement and if we, by those criteria, were the most improved over the last three months. If so, give them their lunch. You get a lot more flies with honey, you know."

"These guys love the honey. I only wish there were some more worker bees out there," said Harlowe, again slightly shifting the conversation.

Ike now had a dog in this fight and chimed in. Harlowe was squirming and folds of skin seemed to ripple back through his slicked-back, receding hairline and down where his neck disappeared into his white collared shirt.

"Nothing wrong with our productivity here, Harlowe, but I get your point," said Ike.

Trey saw the entire issue being muddied with the criteria for the award, labor relations philosophy and now productivity questions. He also saw Ike—ever the careful politician—had already given some ground. Ike was never sure of the depth and breadth of Harlowe's powers, but if he was going to test them, this would certainly not be the issue. It was not a hill Trey was going to die on, either. Trey's wheels were already turning and he figured he could make up some reason for an unplanned plant lunch out of his budget in the next few months. Trey also wanted a parting shot.

"You know, when we do stuff like this, whether the union knows it or not, the potential is that they will find out," Trey said. "If we give them the lousy lunch, it costs us maybe a grand. If they even get a whiff they got screwed out of their lunch, or hear a rumor, I cannot tell you what it costs us in a thousand conversations I have to have with them. They won't give an inch on some other pissant issue because we have no trust. They are not stupid. They have contacts at other plants, even the non-union ones."

The last comment about communications with non-union facilities was designed specifically to needle Harlowe, whose other unofficial duty was keeping the non-union plants exactly that way. Harlowe was nonplussed.

"Then that is why we have you," Harlowe said in an overly sweet but not-quite-sarcastic tone. "You understand what we are trying to do as management here and can make sure the facts are presented so we do not have bad feelings."

Trey was done. Harlowe was not going to budge. It was good to know so he could go and rip up the memo on the safety rankings and ensure it was never found. The union guys had honed the skill of reading memos on his desk upside down into an art form. For all his sliminess, Harlowe's audaciousness and lack of a shame-bone helped Trey course adjust and calculate any blowback.

"How long are you here for?" Trey inquired of Harlowe.

"Just the rest of today," said Harlowe, "I have to go over some environmental issues with your pollution folks over at the plating tanks, and then I'll be back home."

Trey thought about inviting Harlowe to stop by before he left, just to be polite, but then realized he really had nothing to share of consequence. Ike told Trey that this was a shortcoming—the inability to engage the corporate folks in small talk, he advised. Just remain visible. Ike always seemed to have a half dozen points to engage corporate types. Trey struggled to find context.

As Trey walked back to his office, BB was in her office and spotted him. She shouted out, pleading: "*Please* call Ed in Philly. I admit it—I failed miserably keeping him calm."

Trey went to his office and punched up Wendlocher's number. It was creeping close to noon and he wondered if he would be out to lunch yet. The phone barely rang once before Wendlocher answered.

"Where the hell have you been, I've been trying to warn you that that Squinty Eyed…"

Trey interrupted. "Got it, Eddie, and appreciate it. Everything's OK. When did he get in?"

"Must've been last night," Wendlocher noted. "He could only get a flight in here to Philly and drove up there to you in Jersey this morning. Barely saw him. He just kind of breezed through. At least he brought good news this time. We won the quarterly Grean Machine. I am trying to get a caterer who can bring in surf and turf. Think anybody'll notice that bill?"

Trey was now truly amused.

"Yeah, Harlowe told me you guys nosed us out. Good for you. See, he isn't always a prick," said Trey.

"Well, he also was out there at 6 a.m. counting cars to see how many people were here. He called it his 'Commitment Index.' Lectured me for 15 minutes on this shitty index no one has heard of outside of his head. So, no, he isn't a prick, he's a Squinty-Eyed Fuck." Wendlocher never gave a centimeter in his estimation of Harlowe. "You didn't mention he was visiting when we talked last so I didn't want you ambushed," he said.

"Nah, everything's OK, Ed. He is actually here on some environmental issue I know nothing about. He is out of here later today, thankfully," said Trey, trying to be a counterpoint to Wendlocher's hysteria. It was no use.

"He's probably trying to tell someone those three headed fish in the river behind the plant are actually a high-yield food experiment to solve world hunger," said Wendlocher in a lather. "I hope his plane fucking crashes."

CHAPTER 7

EARL ALOYSIUS

The rest of Trey's day was a trudge of productivity. He finally did get through those resumes for the accounting job. He went over pension options with a female machine operator who was trying to decide if she had enough money to retire at 63 after 30 years of service. The last part of the day was resolving another union haggle. The claim was that some of the non-union, salaried production planners moved some inventory to the floor—work that belonged by contract to the Metalworkers Union. Such a move by the planners was not unknown, but rare. For their part, if the planners were guilty, they would report it to Trey so he knew how long and hard to fight the case. Practically, it was sometimes worth it to just admit it and just move on, paying some union brother 30 minutes of work that had been done by management. If the materials moved freed up a $10,000 order while cost $10 in wages, it was easy calculus. Still, Trey could not be nonchalant or admit to such a blatant contract violation with some kind of fight, indignation or at least a promise of a thorough management investigation and refresher training for the management miscreants. For their part, it was important for the planners to spread their ignorance around. If one of them was singled out as a habitual offender, they were seen as indifferent to the union and a lightning rod for any kind of controversy going forward.

When Mo Morris and Tommy Pherrel came knocking on Trey's door at 2:45 p.m. they looked wilted from the heat. Trey knew any discussion was going to last until the end of the shift so he paced his argument accordingly, denied any misconduct by the management, and then settled for 30 minutes of pay for what was likely five minutes of unsuccessful covert operations by the feckless planners.

As the meeting wound down, BeBe appeared silently at the door, waved good night and pantomimed—hanging herself in an imaginary noose indicating that she was glad Trey was in there and not her. She would formalize the settlement of the issue in the morning in an official document.

Trey left the plant a little before 5 p.m. The promise of a scorching day had been fulfilled. He got into the car and headed to his parents' home. About a dozen blocks away, it was almost close enough to walk, but on any day the threat of crime made a walk ill-advised and on this day the heat made the choice of a car ride easy.

Trey's given name was actually Earl Aloysius Bensen III. Highfalutin' for East Newark, for sure. Earl Aloysius Jr.—Trey's father—resisted the idea of such a namesake. The elder Bensen remembered the playground taunts of "Earl the Girl" and "Earl the Squirrel," but Earl's mother Margaret loved the idea of an offspring trailed by roman numerals. After Margie (as she was known to friends) became pregnant, nine months of debate ensued about the name for their baby, interrupted by a truce in case it was a girl. The nickname "Trey" (a substitute for "3" in card playing parlance), was a nod to those Roman numerals, was the compromise. Trey did not discuss his given name often and was quietly thankful for his father's humility, but proud to share his name.

The Bensen home for the last 52 years was part of a row of attached homes very close to the Newark border line. The border was so close, in fact, that when Trey played stickball in the street with his friends home plate was in East Newark, while most long hits landed in Newark. Fifty-two years ago, the houses were gleaming palaces, but now they sat decaying at the edges but well kept. Five decades of fallout from the nearby New Jersey Turnpike and the adjacent gas refineries pitted the exteriors and dulled the once-a-decade paint jobs. Occupants owned their unit and it was not uncommon to see the owners pay as much attention to keeping the sidewalk, curb and gutter as well-swept and clean as the 900 square feet inside.

As Trey pulled down the block he searched for street parking (the row homes had no driveways or garages) and settled on a snug spot about a block away and walked back. The sights and smells of the neighborhood were comforting to him, especially on the first warm day. The doors and windows were open, it was suppertime and every smell of every ethnic seasoning filled the air. When Trey was growing up, it was a predominantly white, Italian neighborhood that had gone through several evolutions. Today is was a mixture of Dominican and Cuban families. The Bensens were the lone constant over the five decades.

As Trey walked up the sidewalk and past a creaky, rusted gate on a spring hinge, he was not pleased that the air conditioner in the front window sat covered in a makeshift plastic tarp. Before entering he picked at the corners of the plastic, held in place by duct tape and clear plastic packing tape. Once the first efforts to carefully unwrap the unit tore the plastic, Trey saw the fruitlessness of the effort and clawed at the wrapping, shredding it in all directions. He globbed the plastic together and tossed it in a garbage can concealed in the front corner of the yard under a plastic table and proceeded into the house.

Earl sat in a folding chair on a narrow enclosed porch. His eyes were closed is a light sleep. At his side an oxygen bottle hissed a quiet lullaby of white noise. Earl was diagnosed three years earlier with a lung disease of unknown origin. In the past year, his battle to breathe became more pitched and the oxygen bottle had become his constant companion. Earl was dressed in an undershirt and long dress pants and formal shoes. He had a bowl next to him, filled with what was once cold water and a face cloth. The cold wet top of his father's undershirt told Trey the face cloth had been used already. Trey leaned down and kissed his father on the top of his head, awakening him.

"Pops it's me. Everything OK today?"

Earl stirred and immediately smiled. He gathered his breath and marshaled some energy to say a few words.

"Good day today," Earl said in a raspy voice. "Just a little… hot."

"Well, you picked the coolest spot in the house out here for sure, Pops," said Trey.

Trey turned and went into the house. It was 10 degrees warmer in the house than out on the street and his mother was boiling water for potatoes. This created a sauna-like atmosphere. Before proceeding in, Trey plugged in the now-liberated air conditioner and turned it on full blast. He ran his hand over the vents and was pleased to see it had awakened from its winter's nap able to produce cool air.

"Mom, I'm here to take you food shopping," said Trey, "Why are you cooking when we are going to the store and why are you heating this house up like this? Make a sandwich on a day like this, huh? Pop will die in this steam bath."

Margie stepped back in her narrow kitchen to see her son walking through the dining/living room and into the kitchen.

"Did you turn on the A/C? Shut that off. All the windows are open and we are just throwing money into the street. It's not that bad in here," Margie protested, ignoring all of Trey's questions.

"Not that bad? Dad's in a coma out there. Let the man have his A/C a couple of minutes. It can only push the hot air out for the next few minutes. I took all that wrapping off and it is working just fine."

"You don't have to live here," said mother Bensen, stating the obvious. "Your father will come in here and be cold even on a day like today. I think that oxygen freezes his blood or something."

Trey's parents lived through many summers in this house when they had no air conditioning at all. The wiring in the house was so bad that when they first put in a window unit, they could run only one appliance before the fuses blew. In the most brutal summers Trey read comic books by flashlight on hot evenings when the choice came down to air conditioning or television. It was not a hard choice.

Margie finally responded to Trey.

"You gotta eat in any temperature and your father still needs a hot meal now and then. I don't think we need anything right now. No use in having a lot around that can go bad quicker. Thanks for asking, though, sweetie. I should have called to tell you we wouldn't need to go this week. It's good you came, though. Your father always likes to see you."

Earl stopped driving about two years earlier when he suffered a few fainting spells brought on by his deteriorating lungs. Margie had never learned to drive, preferring the city buses that took her most places she needed to go. She had been a patron of public transit all her life, taking the bus during the day for a variety of chores while Earl took the car to work. Now Trey stopped once or twice a week on his way home to see what errands needed to be done. Grocery shopping, because of the heavy bags, was a burden on his mother. Going out with Trey was an hour out of the house, too. A minor indulgence.

Earl Sr. was a great provider for his family, but was simultaneously snake bit and exceptionally lucky. He was snake bit in the fact he worked at a string of factories and jobs that closed their doors or moved. He was lucky in that he never had a time when he was unemployed. Like some action movie star, he seemed to run across the bridge of his career a step ahead of the collapsing structures behind him. In sequence, he worked at a commercial laundry, a printing shop, a plastics factory, a book warehouse, a TV assembly plant and a food packager. He leapt across the chasm and into retirement with social security and not much else, his career quilt never containing a pension thread.

Earl hoisted himself up and moved into the living room with a shuffling gait, his oxygen bottle trailing behind him on tiny wheels as a child might pull a wagon or favorite toy. He fell back onto the sofa with a small gasp of accomplishment. The house was warm, but the windows provided some relief to supplement the tank that was his constant companion. The doctors could not tell how long he could last; the trajectory of his descent was not linear but seemed jagged. He rallied for periods, but inevitably his bad days were coming to outnumber the good ones. Trey struggled with the equation constantly. His father practically knew no other home, but Trey could see the day when he would need more care than his mother could provide. Trey found himself thinking about the options more and more. More and more he liked none of them.

Trey found his way into the living room with two glasses of ice water and pulled out a dining room chair so he could sit in front of his father. Dinner would not be ready for another 20 minutes, and since grocery shopping was no longer on the agenda, he wanted to talk with his father. Trey felt that his father rallied and got stronger when they talked. Not only did it take his mind off the ever-present green tank, but the talking was like some kind of therapy. Trey once worried talking would fatigue his father, but it seemed to be a form of exercise. Now slapped with his father's mortality, Trey wanted to pull every answer he ever sought from Earl.

"Pops, we really improved our safety at the plant recently. Almost won an award, but not quite. Didn't you tell me some horrible story about what went on where you worked?" Trey liked to hear these industrial war stories.

While he and his father were separated by a generation in the workplace, the stories always had some parallel Trey liked to use, especially if he could illustrate a notion of progress to the union in some debate session.

Earl straightened up a bit and eyed the ceiling, going through his mental catalogue to match with Trey's request with his experiences.

"I think you mean Trunceleto's old print shop. That was pretty early in my career. Before the war. It was a nasty old place. The smells were bad enough. Ink was everywhere. There was no ventilation and the biggest press was in the basement. You'd come home on a Friday and be blowing ink in your handkerchief all weekend. Maybe by Monday you had cleared up, but you could never get that black crap out of your nose."

Trey focused on the two plastic tube nubs occupying that nose and wondered how deeply the ink could be inhaled. Earl continued, his voice getting stronger.

"Yeah, the ink was everywhere. It was a slop house, for sure. This was before they had OSHA or any of that stuff where anyone cared what the hell happened in a shop. People were so desperate for any work, no one cared if the work was dangerous or not. I think it was worse for the young kids. They didn't know from nothing. They didn't know how dangerous the machines were. They used to hire kids like me to wipe down the presses and clean them. I saw one boy get his sleeve caught and dragged his arm into the press. The kid's arm was caught and smashed and he was crying and the owner, Trunceleto, he was yelling at me to get the basket of finished work out of there before it got ruined. They took that kid away and we never saw him again. I have no idea if he lost that arm or kept it or what. It was awful. You never get that kind of thing entirely out of your head."

Earl paused to take a draw from the ice water. It was a sign that he was warming up not winding down. This pleased Trey.

"But the most dangerous and stupid thing in a press house like that are those blades," Earl continued. "They cut the papers to all various sizes and trim off edges and get them ready for binding. You can be careful all you want, but hour after hour, day after day, you lose your sense of how dangerous this stuff is. I'll give Trunceleto credit; he tried to make it so you were more aware. He had rigged up some kind of dead man feature. You had to operate the blade with a foot pedal and in order to do that you had to have your hands on the buttons on top and out of the way of the blade. The problems were that on thick jobs, the blade came down and moved the paper like squeezing toothpaste from the middle of the tube. The pressure on the blade squeezed the paper stack in the middle and made it rise on the edges. You kind of had to have your hand there to steady the paper you were trimming. Second, he put the button for your hand too close to the blade. I'm not sure if he did that on purpose so he could get more work or if it was just a stupid design, but it was set up that way anyway. Well, to top it off, it was a job with an odd horizontal shape we were cutting. The poor guy working the machine had just gotten hollered at for his production, so he's nervous. He has this odd job and the first time the blade comes down it scatters the papers everywhere on the floor. He is a wreck. So he pushes down on the hand safety bar with his elbow and is trying to hold the papers steady so the blade makes a clean cut. He's done this before so he's feeling pretty good about it and getting this oddball job done. Except he forgets that because it's a horizontal job, his hand is closer. Down comes the blade and it takes off the top of his finger. It was awful. He's screaming. He sees the blood and passes out. We wrapped his hand up in the worst rags, nothing was clean down there. They get him out of there to the hospital."

A hot breeze pushed the curtains into the room and near Earl's face. He turned his head to feel the breeze and gather himself at the same time. Earl braced for a cool breeze but the blast of warm air caused him to make a face that expressed his discomfort, sticking his tongue out defiantly. Trey sat back and soaked in the story and the storyteller. Earl felt he was losing Trey's full attention so he brought him back to point with a light rap of his wedding band on the oxygen tank that made a gentle clang.

"I wish that was the end of it but it was not," said Earl. "I'm down there mopping up the blood and trying to figure out which jobs could be saved and which had to be thrown out because of the blood stains and a kid comes running in from the street. He said the hospital sent him and they wanted to know where the finger was to see if they could sew it back on. Nobody ever thought of that. We were only worried about the guy who hurt himself. Since I was the littlest guy they sent me under that contraption. It was full of grease and ink and crap under there and it had a catchbin with what looked like snow in it, which was really little fine trimmings from the paper. The big stuff we would sweep up and take out but this little fine stuff would sift down under there. Sure enough, I feel around and there is the finger. I wrapped it in clean paper and gave it to the kid. I was making 25 cents an hour and they told him they'd give him 50 cents if he found the finger and ran it back. If I'd have known that I would have run it there myself."

Trey's mother came out of the stifling kitchen looking amazingly comfortable. Fifty-two hot summers acclimated her to the heat so well she seemed to be unaffected. The small room served as half living/half dining area and just a few feet away she laid out a small bowl of green beans and potatoes and nodded toward the table. Earl knew his cues so he got to his grand conclusion.

"They never could reattach the finger so a few weeks later the guy comes back. The whole time he was gone, Trunceleto kept looking at the machine. He was proud of his little contraption, but could not figure out how the guy lost his finger. So when the guy comes back, Trunceleto says, 'Show me how you did it.' The guy keeps saying he doesn't remember, he was in shock, it all happened fast and so on. But the boss doesn't let up. He keeps asking him if his memory is coming back and to show him how he thinks he did it. This goes on for weeks. Finally the guy gives in and he brings Trunceleto over there. Don't you know he ends up doing the exact same thing and loses another joint on the same finger?"

Trey shook his head in disbelief and helped his father to the table. The story invigorated Earl, so Trey felt a sense of accomplishment no matter how small. But he also felt guilt. Trey could come in and stoke these little rallies but in the end, his mother was going to deal with the setbacks more often.

Trey looked at the table and thought of all the hot meals his mother served on that table in the swelter of summer. Somehow, it never bothered him then, but the thought of eating hot pot roast in what amounted to a sauna made his stomach turn a little. Where he stood, between the dining room table and the front door, he felt the air conditioner start to make a dent in the dense air. He kissed both parents and headed out to the street. As he walked to his car, he wondered how he became addicted to central air conditioning. He also wondered what effect sugar pills might have on industrial amputations.

CHAPTER 8

DINNER WITH CAROLE

When Trey got home to Carole, it was closer to dusk and the light was flat. She already had the air conditioner humming when Trey entered the front door. It was a relief to feel the cool, dry air. He popped his head in the kitchen, gave Carole a quick kiss and a hello and headed upstairs to change into shorts and a T-shirt.

Carole was home for hours already. She had marked papers for her class, looked over her lesson plan for the next day and prepared a salad for dinner. While she knew what Trey did and who he worked for, she did not always understand the details of his day. What she knew for sure was that she could not work in that awful factory—ever—in any capacity. It started with the not-unpleasant but-distinct chemical smell that clung to Trey. It had become his de facto scent of choice. It was actually a mixture of various vaporized oils and cutting fluids from the factory floor plus the heavy soaps the toolmakers washed their tools in at the end of the day. One morning while driving to Newark Airport to catch a flight, she drove past the corridor of manufacturing plants that surrounded the airport. As she rolled down the window to pay the toll, she made the connection that the whiff of chemicals in the air brought to mind the image of Trey. This involuntary association simultaneously astounded and frightened her. She was associating loved ones with toxic chemicals.

She worried about the crime as Trey entered and exited the factory's neighborhood. She came from a quiet suburban upbringing. Her play took place behind a fenced-in schoolyard or playground, not the street. She understood that Trey felt comfortable in the East Newark environment, but she fretted that the familiarity and ease in which he navigated the side streets of the city made him lax and vulnerable. He was not a non-descript kid. He was a man in a suit and guys in suits in East Newark had some kind of inferred status that made them look like targets. She particularly hated it during the winter months when daylight was short and Trey's long days caused him to both arrive and leave in the dark at the plant. She hinted to Trey that perhaps he should look for a job at a pharmaceutical company somewhere in the neighborhoods where the researchers liked to go to work. He was not all that macho to be feared but she figured he could take a guy in a lab coat. But Trey seemed to like what he did and where he did it. While he initially resisted the idea of working in his neighborhood, he now wore that fact like a badge of honor. He was working with the people where he once went to grade school. Whatever the circumstances, they liked the fact Trey still was among them, even if they eyed his suit and tie with suspicion. They watched to see if he put on airs but found nothing to further their misgivings. Many of them still lived with their parents, working or barely working, taking up space in paneled basements or spare bedrooms.

When Trey entered the kitchen, Carole put the finishing touches on the salad and Trey set the table. The salad was topped with strips of turkey. The cat, Belvedere, patrolled the floor beneath their feet with some kind of gurglepurr indicating he would not mind a few handouts. Trey did not like feeding the cat scraps, fearing he would beg and be a pest. As Trey set the table, Carole silently dropped a small clump of shredded turkey on the floor. Belvedere swallowed the evidence in conspiratorial silence.

The kitchenette table just inside the sliding glass door led to a small back deck of red stained wood. On cooler nights, they would eat outside, but not tonight. The darkness had broken the back of the heat but the sunset glowed red and foreshadowed at least one more day of the unusual heat. Trey thought about the comfort of his meal and wondered what his parents were doing.

"Did anybody pass out in the factory today?' said Carole. "It must have been awful."

"C'mon," Trey pleaded, "it's only April and they have been making parts there for half a century. It is not nice in there but no worse than it ever has been. I predict they will survive." Trey stabbed unproductively at a crouton that flew off his plate and onto the floor before the ever-watchful Belvedere.

"Pretty easy to say from where you sit in there, isn't it?" said Carole. She was not picking a fight, just making an observation. Belvedere was underfoot, pawing the crouton, more as a toy to be swatted and chased than a treat to be eaten.

"It's not like I look at them through some glass window and taunt them by putting a sweater on. I bet it is harder to teach a bunch of kids math," said Trey, clearly trying to deflect the conversation. "I bet they were whining all day and cranky."

"I am trained in whiny and cranky. The kids will survive, but by 3 they were ready to go back to their nice air-conditioned homes for sure," said Carole. "I want to tell them about your parents and their house but I feel like I would be such an old fossil to them. And not even a genuine fossil. I won't be saying: 'You should have seen it in my day!' I'll be talking about how bad my in-laws have it. It will totally get lost. By the way, how are your folks and how bad was it over there?"

Trey picked at his salad and felt Belvedere brush his leg.

"Pops was pretty good tonight. I uncovered their window air conditioner and turned it on for them and…"

Carole interrupted. "You mean they did not have it on when you got there? Why do they do that? Isn't it hard enough for your father to breathe? Were they just waiting for you to…"

"Again," Trey took back the conversation, "everything is just fine. They didn't even have an air conditioner until after I moved out of the house after school. Now they think if they turn it on they'll be in the poor house with the electric bill. I wish there was a way I could just pay their bill or something without them knowing."

The minute the words left his mouth, Trey regretted it. He knew it was a bit of a family sore point with Carole. Her parents helped with the down payment on the townhouse and assisted with purchases like appliances. Trey's family seemed to turn inward with worry while Carole's were not better off financially, they seemed to be more generous with a rosier and more optimistic world view. Trey could not tell if the eye contact with Carole was her tacit statement about finances or he was imagining it all.

Trey knew his parents needed more peace of mind than financial help, but the two were not necessarily distinct.

Each of them looked for the next topic. Something safe. Trey patted Belvedere on the head just because it was somehow comforting. In his mind Trey envisioned a Jeopardy category board and sought frantically to be able to say "I'll take Safe Conversations for $300, Alex."

"How was your work today?" Carole buzzed in first, or at least she thought so. Her intent was pure, but the question poked at Trey. How would he explain not getting the safety award they earned? How would he explain Warsaw and how he ended up in rehab? To the uninitiated, it was madness. To answer truthfully would invite a lot of questions that could not be answered neatly. Even in this now-pregnant pause he was pushing the calculus forward. Truth in this case was not binary. If he did not answer, he would seem angry or disinterested. By answering fully, it would open up an environment formed by decades of industrial history and intrigue for scrutiny and unanswerable questions, a culture that worked well if you looked at the forest. This forest had some very twisted and angry trees. Trey wanted so much to share, yet he was already worn down by the complexity of his work. He wanted simple. He wanted relief. Why did work seem so logical while he was there, and sound so illogical when he rehearsed discussing it in his head? What strange-looking glass did he step through on the way home? There was another option, an option he picked out in a million tiny calculations in between bites of salad.

"It was sad," Trey began. "One of the older guys in the plant had to come in and ask for help with an alcohol problem. The union brought him in and he got a 28-day program going. I don't know how you get yourself to that point, but I'm glad he felt good enough to come in and get help. What's on TV tonight?"

CHAPTER 9

PERFECT LAUNDRY

The next morning came with hazy skies and heaviness in the air to foretell another muggy, uncomfortable day. Trey ripped through his run with an energy that surprised and pleased him. The months of running was starting to have an effect as now he even felt good running in less than ideal conditions.

Trey was driving to work, thinking about his father. He knew there were some stories that had been told and re-told over the years, but suddenly Trey needed them told again. There were details missing he needed to know, wanted to know. While they had been revealed previously by Earl, Trey glossed over them and forgot them when the vista of time stretched out endlessly. Now he saw his father in decline and knew he needed to stop by more often and fill in those precious details. Some of it was family folklore. Trey would like to relate these somehow to his kids, if he ever had any. Trey also saw them as cautionary tales. In some ways the workplace had evolved, perhaps to the same place that just looked different. Getting Earl to fill in the details seemed to help the old man, too. It invigorated his spirit and pushed the edges of his waning endurance outward. Trey could see the sands of the hourglass and the acceleration of the pour made him tense.

Trey drove to work almost on auto pilot, thinking of what he needed to flesh out.

June 1935

Earl Aloysius Bensen worked for Perfect Laundry in Elizabeth, New Jersey, for less than two years. Perfect Laundry was what its name implied—the perfect laundry service for any number of area hospitals and housewives. Their fleet of panel trucks made a weekly stop at homes in the dense urban areas. Housewives who wanted the whitest sheets and linens left a small knotted cloth bag emblazoned with a blue "Perfect Laundry—Every Time" logo at their door. Inside the bag was any bit of laundry—shirts, tablecloths, sheets—that needed cleaning. For most living in apartments, a washing machine did not physically fit in their tiny abodes. Further, any whites needed bleach and bleach was expensive. But while bleach had a financial impact, being seen with soiled, dull whites when company came calling had a social cost. The Perfect Laundry route man filled that need. They would pick up the bag at each home and identify it with a small coiled tag and drop off packages containing glowing white linens carefully wrapped in brown paper.

If the lady of the house was home he would double park his laundry truck in the street, ring the doorbell, collect payment for the dropoff and pick up the next week's load. In the event no one was home, the payment was in a collection pouch sewn inside the laundry bag of dirty items. It was not an issue to leave the money in the laundry bag unattended. It was a system built on trust.

Once the truck was weighed down with bags of dirty laundry, the driver would return to the laundry, back up to the receiving dock. There, workers like Earl would scramble in and unload the truck and inspect for things that were not intended to be white ("Jeez would you get a load of Mrs. Klaus' blue bloomers!") because just one non-white item could cause an entire load to take on an off-white, ugly hue. And an entire load in an industrial washer was a lot of tablecloths. Earl and his coworkers separated them into metal bins, assigned them a name and an address and placed them on a conveyor belt, where they disappeared into a steamy anteroom that resembled the bowels of hell with bleach added for aroma.

The boys worked quickly because they were paid a nickel a bag processed. Each bag had an order slip and a perforated corner. As they loaded and separated them, the "towel monkeys," as they were known informally, greedily took the paper corner and stuffed it in their pocket. At the end of the day they would turn the precious tatters in to be paid. There was nothing happier than finding some housewife who accidentally put two order sheets in one bag and nothing sadder than seeing one of the slips float away on the breeze created by the enormous 9-foot industrial fans that sat on each side of the dock. The fans had the dual purpose of keeping the area at a bearable temperature while dissipating the smell of bleach before it settled in like a toxic fog. Earl paid no attention to the rumors that the fans paid for themselves a nickel at a time as the poor towel monkeys saw their pay chits float away.

The workers in the factory were not the issue for the management of Perfect Laundry; it was the damn prima donnas on the trucks. The drivers traveled the city and like bees gathering pollen they brought it all back to the factory. Some of it was good—like the tales of the unemployed who would love to have jobs like the ones in the laundry—while other tales were far more alarming. Many of the hospitals and restaurants had unionized staff that discussed wages and paid holidays. The drivers brought these stories back to people like the towel monkey, fomenting dissatisfaction.

The tension between the drivers and management ebbed and flowed over time. In most cases, the drivers spoke as loudly as they could on the docks and used the prevailing wage and benefit information they gathered as a lever. They had the best of both worlds—improvement in wages and benefits without union dues. But once in a while, things would get testy and the most dissatisfied drivers would make some inquiries about organizing. Recent days had seen that ebb tide in relations over the fact that one of the drivers, Chet Crovicz, lost pay while attending his young son's funeral. Like any dispute, it gathered momentum based on as many real as perceived slights. In this case, Chet, upon his return, suffered through two weeks of breakdowns of his truck, a fact he attributed to retribution of bosses who wanted to be sure his productivity suffered and assigned him the oldest and worst trucks. The veracity of that fact may have been in question, but it was certain he could not find five minutes of overtime availability as he tried to make up for lost wages.

The situation escalated to the point where a few drivers did seek an informational meeting with the local service workers union that represented workers at the large hotels. The meeting promised free beer and sandwiches to anyone attending. From the union point of view, they wanted to see if the drivers represented a wider unrest and if they could not draw a big crowd with free food and beer, Perfect Laundry was not ripe for unionization.

As word of the union gathering spread to Perfect Laundry management, they were determined not to be outdone. They announced that due to exceptional productivity and outstanding work, they would sponsor a cruise for all employees—the same Saturday as the union session, by chance. The cruise would leave from the Atlantic Highlands dock, feature free food and beer, and in an effort to one-up the union sirens, include a polka band on board as well. There would also be a drawing for a fresh ham at the conclusion of the trip. The cruise and the union buffet/beer blast had the unofficial impact as a straw poll of sorts. Both sides would know where they stood by day's end.

The reliability of headcount as an indicator of true interest in either side was called into question by many variables. For one, the union hall was on the outskirts of Elizabeth in an area that did not have reliable bus service on a Saturday. While the cruise from Atlantic Highlands was not exactly accessible, Perfect Laundry provided free transportation by bus to any employee who showed up at the factory that morning. In addition, the union flyer promised non-descript "sandwiches" while the Perfect Laundry cruise featured "hot grilled bratwurst and roast beef." Point for Perfect Laundry. On such minute details as the quality of meat are labor wars won.

That Saturday morning also favored Perfect Laundry as it was warm and perfect, a great day for a sea cruise. If the early votes were counted, the company was winning by a landslide. They rented one rickety bus but enough employees showed up to fill more than three buses. It was decided to hold up the departure of the cruise until every employee could be loaded on to buses bound for the dock. This would turn out to be a fateful decision, but the greatest fear was any employee left on the curb would head over to the union hall, even if the sandwich choices might be chintzy.

Earl Bensen was one of the employees lined up on the sidewalk. Rumors spread that the boat would be leaving soon and a few of the employees left the line to go home or to the union hall. Managers appeared with soda pop and assurances that the boat would be held up until all employees who wanted to go were on board. A second bus was commissioned and the ride to the dock sputtered along the two-lane highways that led to the Jersey Shore.

Upon arriving at the dock, Earl was astonished that the boat operators had not yet let anyone on. It was also clear to Earl that Perfect Laundry management were not optimists. The size of the crowd in and around the dock seemed to dwarf the size of the boat, even though the boat had several decks. He feared for a riot. After all, employees on both ends of the bus ride had been waiting for some time. Anticipation was now heightened. If they had to turn away anyone, it would be a disaster.

The crowd itself was an odd-looking lot. Many of them had arrived in their work uniforms as if they thought they might be assigned to fold or press the sheets. Almost all wore white sailor hats with "Perfect Laundry" stenciled on the brim, courtesy of the company that wanted the crowd to forever associate the gaiety of the day with their beneficent employer.

With the arrival of the last bus, the excursion operators slid back a wire gate and the crowd, sensing the capacity limitations, surged forward, running up the stairs to stake out the best seats available. The testiness of the crowd was evident as there was some pushing and shoving and the entrance to the craft was narrower than the dock, creating a pinch point for those trying to board. Earl stood back to see how it would play out. He quietly thought being left behind was not such a bad idea. He looked back to where the bus had dropped him off to see if an early round trip back to Elizabeth was possible, but the buses were gone in a flash. The initial surge of people actually tipped the boat slightly to the dock, creating a small drop for those entering the boat. Earl could see heads bobbing downward upon entry, but as the employees dispersed over the larger part of the boat it seemed to level itself to the dock. The boat was getting crowded, but Earl entered as the crowd thinned on the dock. It was still slow going as the forward part of the crowd had less and less space to disperse. Again, Earl thought they might stop boarding and turn away the stragglers. To his right, he could see a frantic and animated conversation going on between plant management he vaguely knew and the boat operators. The captain of the ship grabbed a megaphone and shouted commands in his captain's basso profundo voice, urging all on the lower decks to proceed up a deck, if they could, to make room. His command alone seemed to quiet the crowd and Earl shuffled on board.

He was not more than 4 feet onto the deck when he heard the metallic screech of the boarding gate being closed behind him despite the fact his face was only about 3 inches from the person in front of him. The engine roared to life and the smell of diesel permeated the air where he stood, falling on him in a sickening cloud of exhaust from above. They were late departing, and the captain was a precise man. Earl briefly thought he might be sick but settled himself with an optimistic thought that the crowd would find spaces and this whole disaster would only get better.

As the boat pulled away, the fresh breezes blew the diesel fumes off the deck, creating a momentary respite, but they were fighting the tide and the ship bobbed in an uneven cadence for a bit before it all smoothed out. Earl heard some polka music playing from a deck or two above, but it was clear no one was dancing unless they danced in place.

Little by little, some space appeared on all decks, although the boat was tightly packed. Those who were lucky enough to find seats on benches that ringed the interior stayed put, sure that their seat would be gone the second they abandoned it. The ship hugged the Jersey shoreline. It was a trip to nowhere. The captain's orders were to go as far south as he could until 2 p.m. and then circle back and deposit the happy employees back on the dock by 4 p.m.

Earl found some elbow room and began to squeeze in and around his fellow employees. He noticed that a few of the men had given up trying to find the bathroom and were happily peeing off the side of the boat—downwind—thankfully.

It was a pleasant day to begin with and being out on the ocean was even more pleasant with dazzling sunshine and a refreshing breeze. They were about an hour into the journey when Earl smelled the bratwurst. He looked around and tried to figure out how he might get an angle on the food as it seemed pretty obvious that while they had gotten everyone on the boat, it was highly doubtful they could feed the crowd without some kind of rationing. The thought had not crossed his mind for more than a few seconds when a feeble PA system crackled out a weak, distorted message.

"FOOD WILL BE SERVED ON...DECK IN...PLEASE WAIT UNTIL...YOU WILL..."

The promise of the feast was too much for the crowd. While Earl tried to process the message and what it meant, he could hear the collective sound of hundreds of shoes on the decks. He could not make out which way they were going, but it was certain they were moving with great pace and purpose. While the boat stabilized in the path it cut through the water, there had been swells and some movement. So when Earl felt himself trying to catch his balance, he thought it was just another bob in the water. Quickly he realized that the tilt was not temporary or rhythmic as might be caused in the waves. The rush of people to the stern and port was causing the overcrowded boat to list to one side. The mob in search of bratwurst on the overcrowded boat gasped as they recognized the unnatural, severe tilt of the ship. Earl knew he might fall backward now and threw his left arm back hoping not to fall flat. He feared he might be trampled by the panicked crowd. His arm landed on the deck and initially he held himself up by one arm as he tried to twist his body to *counteract the roll of the ship. This was when he felt a very sharp pain in his left shoulder as it held his arm at an odd angle from his body.*

He collapsed in pain and rolled over to his right side in reaction to the shock of his dislocated arm and slid into the corner of the boat. The PA system sounded out in agony as well, an unintelligible hiss and mumble of half syllables. Those sounds that did come through were loud, but disconnected. Someone was trying to get a message out, but it was failing miserably.

Panic washed over Earl as he slid back in the corner only to see seawater slosh up over the deck, dousing his pants in salty brine. The boat was tilted to the stern by the rushing crowd. There were just too many people on the craft. Earl thought for sure that the boat was ready to capsize, and again he heard the sound of those many feet—this time traveling away from the low side of the boat and toward the front.

He slid forward from the spot he sat as the center of gravity shifted violently again. He tried to protect his useless left arm as he slid but this time he hit a pole and simply passed out from the pain.

The rest of the day was a jumble of sights and sounds for Earl that made little sense. But he knew he was alive when medics helped him to his knees and off the boat several hours later in a town far south from Atlantic Highlands, where the captain made an emergency landing. The Newark Evening News headline summed it up the next day in a screaming headline: "COMPANY CATASTROPHE AT SEA OUTING."

It was reported that 55 employees sustained injuries when an overcrowded boat that hosted the company picnic nearly capsized when panicked employees engaged in an on-board stampede that destabilized the craft. Three of the employees either fell or jumped overboard but were later retrieved. The Coast Guard would launch an investigation into the incident that ultimately would lead to the revocation of the ship's commercial license for failure to obey capacity limitations and safety standards.

Earl Bensen was treated for a separated shoulder that plagued him the rest of his life. He was presented with the bill for medical treatment and paid it off over the next two years on an installment plan. He was unable to return to work and was terminated for absenteeism three weeks later, although he tried several times to return to his duties as a towel monkey.

Fourteen months later, the Service Workers Union won an election to represent the workers at Perfect Laundry, Inc. They served roast beef sandwiches at the victory party, which was held at the Elks Lodge in Elizabeth.

Trey arrived at Page's Luncheonette to get his morning coffee but he could not remember the drive. He was jolted back reality by the Council of Elders, already holding court inside.

"The lawyer will know," one of the elders asked. "Does the governor commute a sentence or pardon it?"

CHAPTER 10

THE TURK

As Trey pulled into his spot at the Grean factory, he noticed that the reserved spot marked #1 set aside for Frank Reilly was taken. Although Reilly was now in his 80s and rarely arrived, when he did, he gloried in having this spot of honor as the first employee. Further, being so close to the back door, the spot allowed Frank to enter the plant with a minimum draw on his finite energy. The fact that someone other than Frank took the spot annoyed Trey and he made a mental note to have the security guards track down the person and get the car removed.

Trey grabbed two Styrofoam cups of coffee from his car and ducked into the plant through the receiving dock so he could walk through the plant on the way to his office. Trey preferred the walk through the plant to gauge the tempo and mood. He circled through the press area and saw Pauley trying to bring the press to life. While the leviathan press was silent for at least eight hours, Pauley had a routine to resurrect it to thundering glory. This routine had a number of steps. For openers, he would jog the press through one stroke at a time. It was a 16-stage press, which meant it created parts through a series of 16 impacts on the metal forced through the various stations. Like a series of cels creating a cartoon, the press gently and gradually reshaped flat, cold-rolled steel into an intricate geometry. Pauley dutifully jogged the press one station at a time, and then peered into the press at various odd angles to see that all was well. The worst possibility was a press explosion when some piece of the monster machine might come loose, fall into the area where metal hit metal and caused a chain reaction. That could create all kinds of random havoc and send what amounted to shrapnel all over the room. Even though the press was guarded with Plexiglas shields, the sheer forces and random nature of the arc of flying metal were frightening. It did not happen often, but when it did, this was the most likely time of day—when the machines were awakened from their slumber after a night of inactivity.

Trey saw Pauley was preoccupied but left one of the coffee cups on top of his toolbox. There was no doubt Trey had a soft spot in his heart for Pauley, who he saw as a sweet guy with a very hard shell.

"What's that for?" Pauley asked.

"So you stay awake and I don't have to fire your ass," Trey shouted back. The din of the plant coming to life already caused the need to shout, even at this early hour.

"What am I, a fucking charity case? Keep your coffee and just give me the money!" Pauley was speaking in mock anger, his eyes wide open but his face betrayed a big grin.

As usual, BeBe was already in the middle of something when Trey arrived.

"Mornin' BeBe. Can you check who is in Frank Reilly's spot and have Security..."

BeBe had already gotten up and trailed Trey and stood in his doorway interrupting him.

"I would bet that the car is Mr. Mikkelsen's," BeBe said. "He was already here looking for you. When he was here he asked if we see Frank much anymore so I am putting two and two together."

Trey was not happy with Harlowe's choice of parking spots, but he was even more annoyed that he was still here. Wasn't he supposed to leave?

"Did he say what he needed or where he'd be?"

"No," BeBe answered. "I would guess he is over with Ike, but I can see where he wants to meet."

Trey was thinking through the order of his day when the phone rang. It was Mikkelsen. He could just envision the too-wide polyester striped tie through the phone.

"Morning there, son," Harlowe began. "I guess I am here another day. I got a call from the Grean boys in Orlando and they asked me to do a few more things while I am here. Can you get me the International Rep for the union, Larry, right? Can you get me Larry but I need this on the

QT, OK? We need to have a private conversation without the folks here in East Newark."

Trey's irritation level went off the charts with every syllable Harlowe slurped out.

"What's the issue? I think he'll want to know. By that way, I'd like to know too. Maybe I can help you?" said Trey. He knew this would be an exercise in dragging every single detail out of Harlowe. Harlowe liked to play it close to the vest and see if others would just be disinterested enough to do his bidding without question.

"I'll tell you more when we all get together. I just thought I should get here early and see what you can do to get him. Let's meet at the country club at noon if we can, OK?" asked Harlowe.

Trey intuitively tried to lower expectations a bit.

"You know, Harlowe, I have no idea if he's even been in town. We've had no issues in a long time, so I don't know if he can meet us today at all."

"All I ask is that you try. I know you have the kind of relationship with the union that if they can they will make it happen. You have a way of making things happen," said Harlowe. This was exactly the kind of wordplay that infuriated Trey. Harlowe would often challenge those around them to accomplish what he needed as if it was a routine heroic act only *they* were good at. It was manipulative, but it was impactful. Trey knew he was in a situation that would change the course of his day but he had to make this meeting happen. He was sure Harlowe was sitting within earshot of Ike when he asked for the meeting. He felt Harlowe was patting him on the head in the most condescending way.

"I'll do my best and get back to you as soon as I can. Larry is not exactly an early riser and the first thing I don't want to do is piss him off by waking him up," said Trey.

"I know you'll get your man," said Harlowe.

Trey was wary of the whole thing and aggravated. He had the local relationship with the union, but when Harlowe had some kind of secret mission he had to pull it together without understanding what the issue was or how it would play out. Trey's strength was in understanding the issues, the end game and altering his approach to maximize the potential outcome. When Harlowe made him drive blind, the margin for error with the union became huge. For his part, Harlowe thrived on withholding information that made him more powerful. Trey knew that to question Harlowe further at this point would have been futile, and Harlowe had already cut him off at the first question of the motive.

The person Trey sought was the Metalworkers International Representative, Larry Turkel, also known as The Turk. Mo and Tommy were the local union leaders, the guys on site at the plant who actually worked the floor and the machines and were elected by their brothers at the Grean plant. They in turn paid dues to the International Brotherhood of Metal Workers. There, a hierarchy of leaders set larger bargaining objectives, supplied legal counsel to the locals and training in a host of issues like contract administration, grievance handling, investigations and bargaining technique. The International Reps were a cut above the locals, often handling the toughest issues or broader policy interpretation. If the locals were seen as too cooperative or pliable, the international ensured the union showed a harder edge. This is why the meeting request troubled Trey. Whatever Harlowe and the Greans wanted, they felt it was beyond Trey's pay grade to handle with the local leadership.

Larry Turkel was an interesting and tough character for a lot of reasons. For openers, he was a dwarf.

Larry was born in a suburban New Jersey community. His parents never allowed the fact that he was a dwarf to interfere with their expectations or how the community would come to treat him. When the school district suggested Larry might be better served in some kind of alternate educational arrangement, his parents politely and firmly insisted their child get no special treatment or placement. They wanted him to be with all the other children of his age.

In time, Larry actually used his disadvantage to his advantage. While not a spectacular student, he got access to the advanced placement classes and hung on for dear life, barely passing, benefitting from whatever sympathy he chose to arouse and rubbing elbows with greater intellects. He also was not averse to taking a quick peek at the exam of the smartest students at nearby desks. He felt confident no one would accuse a dwarf of cheating.

To say Larry was gregarious was an understatement. Over time, he became a symbol of how accepting the school could be. His classmates were lavished with praise as a community that nurtured and accepted their disadvantaged classmate. This, in turn, set into motion a positive cycle of good feeling and good behavior toward Larry. While many in his position might have been the target of bullying and ridicule, Larry enjoyed life as a minor community celebrity. In high school, he was elected class president all four years with no opposition. He graduated, if not with academic honors, as an honored member of the community.

Once outside the loving bosom of his community, Larry's arc flattened. He went to college but struggled with the coursework. He transferred to community college and got an associate's degree, but could not stand the thought of two more years of school. He turned to business and bought a small convenience store in his hometown. He ripped out half the aisles and installed a small soda counter so he could converse with the locals on a specially constructed riser that sat behind the counter. It allowed him to converse eye-to-eye with the patrons. Thus Turk's Corner was born.

The business was popular but not exactly financially successful as more people came by to talk to Larry than buy a soda or milk from the refrigerated cases. To make best use of his square footage, Larry decided to add a bookie operation to the menu and run it out of the back room. This distinctly changed the clientele, but helped Larry's finances.

Whether Larry was just careless or had an insatiable need for more financial success is open to question. What is certain is Larry decided to keep more of his bookie profits than had been agreed upon, and Turk's Corner suffered a devastating gas explosion. This ruined the business and convinced Larry to sell it at a modest profit to interested buyers. The Mob did not think Larry was cute at all.

Casting about for a new way to make a living, Larry answered an ad from the Metalworkers Union. They needed people to assist them with organizing campaigns at non-union businesses. After being rejected initially, Larry showed up at the union day after day until they gave him a bunch of leaflets outlining the benefits of unions and told him to get them on the windshield of every car in a metal tube extrusion plant employee parking lot in Patterson. The union had been unsuccessful several times because plant security cameras caught the organizers placing the leaflets on the cars and escorted them off the lot. Moving below the camera line and placing the leaflets in every car handle, Larry blanketed the parking lot with great success. While they initially rejected Larry because they feared the patina of a circus instead of a union, they soon came to treasure the advantages Larry brought. Larry, for his part, had no shame exploiting any angle that gave him an advantage.

In time, organizing came to fit Larry like no other interest before. His outgoing nature made him an instant success. His size made him a sympathetic figure. When on private property, the sight of Larry being carried away by armed security guards, legs dangling, made him and the union instant martyrs. Larry once again turned his handicap to an advantage and sought to exploit every inch of that edge (or lack thereof). Union organizing, in retreat for decades, saw a local string of victories throughout Northern New Jersey and Larry made sure he was at the scene of every triumph. He surged up the ranks of International Union leadership, running with a slogan "The Turk Stands For The Little Man" with absolutely no shame.

His success did not make him pleasant to deal with if you were in management. Perhaps no matter how kindly he had been treated by some in his life because of or in spite of his size, Larry knew well the power of getting the upper hand by belittling another person. Trey knew he was the object of Larry's dismissive tactics, particularly in a public setting. Larry often dismissed Trey's every word. If Trey asked a question or made a point, Larry would answer Ike as if Trey was not there. Trey understood the posturing and accepted it, but he did not like it and sought to change it somehow. At the local level, Tommy and Mo knew they worked well with Trey, but delighted in every time Larry dismissed Trey. It was a disadvantage that Trey understood, but did not brood over. Just part of the calculus of the situation.

Trey picked up the phone with an unknown mission. He readied himself for Larry's abuse, but knew he would make the meeting with The Turk happen—somehow.

CHAPTER 11

THE COUNTRY CLUB

The Essex Knolls Country Club was an odd oasis in the middle of Newark. All around the club, the city sat ravaged by the lingering effects of the 1967 riots and the systemic political corruption for the decades that followed. Not far away, the Central Ward of Newark looked like Dresden after WWII. Crumbling and abandoned buildings and drug dealers prowled the city blocks in too-nice-for-the-neighborhood cars. Industry fled Newark in the 1960s, but Grean and small manufacturing companies lingered at the fringes in places like East Newark. The smaller suburbs stayed small enough to provide needed city services.

Somehow The Knolls, as it was known by its members, remained viable—a green oasis behind barbed-wire fences. Once through the gates, a long row of trees provided members and their guests an arbor. It acted as a portal of sorts. Under the tunnel of cool, shaded greenery, one felt transformed in time and place before coming out the other end, where a lush green golf course appeared on both sides of the road and golf cart paths warned drivers to slow down. Members felt a palpable sense of the world slowing down at The Knolls. This feeling was accentuated at the large clubhouse, where valets took the cars and members stepped into a large foyer with high ceilings full of light. The Knolls somehow remained not only relevant, but a sought-after status symbol by the primarily white dealmakers who fed on the carcass of Newark. They hid in plain sight, just behind lush shrubbery disguising the barbed-wire fortress.

The Grean family was respected and honored members for decades. Once the elder Grean died and his boys moved to Orlando, they kept their membership and used it as a corporate perk, mostly for those from the East Newark plant. They would host retirement parties and small holiday celebrations at the club, or entertain customers and suppliers, twisting arms and lime rinds over long lunches and too many drinks. It also was a perfect venue for meetings with Larry Turkel and other union brass. They would reserve a private room and have long discussions over some issue. Many times the basic outline of the labor agreement itself might be sketched at such a lunch. Here there was no posturing. Each side could state their objectives plainly and expose where flexibility existed. In many ways, it was where the true bargain was struck, or at least the parameters set. The final agreement might have some flourishes or minor things moved around, but Larry was able to understand how far he could push the issue with Grean and likewise give Grean an idea of the mood at the local level. It was a dirty little secret, but one that advanced the cause of both sides and eliminated misunderstandings.

For Larry, lunches at The Knolls were a bit of a status symbol. It was the ability to be in the same building and dine with some of the wealthiest people in Northern New Jersey. To be escorted to a private dining room just added to the mystique and allure for him. He was needed and the center of attention yet anonymous at the same time—and he loved the feeling.

Trey saw such meetings as a necessary evil. He could never reveal to Mo or Tommy or any of the local union members the fact that such discussions existed. He once wondered if Larry was playing both sides by letting the local know he was truly brokering the deal and claiming to manipulate management. But that seemed too risky, and Larry would be unlikely to share such secrets because he liked operating in the mysterious shadows of the issues. In this way, he was a lot like The Squinty-Eyed Fuck. Like a magician, Larry enjoyed hearing the gasps of the crowd as they observed his misdirection, but he certainly did not like to give away the trick.

This particular lunch troubled Trey. Normally they might talk to Larry six months before the end of the contract, but now it was almost two full years before this contract expired. Harlowe's unwillingness to discuss the agenda ahead of time was troublesome. Trey liked to understand his role and this was too close to improvisation for his liking. He felt ill-prepared and edgy as they were served their salads and drinks. Trey ordered iced tea as he wanted to be on his game, unaffected by alcohol. Harlowe, Larry and even Ike ordered mixed drinks that would be refreshed when they were half-consumed by the attentive Knolls staff lurking at the edges of conversation. Trey was deathly afraid of being asked a question so he decided to make sure his mouth was full of food at all times—better to give him pause if questioned. Trey cut his salad in pieces and took small bites, chewing thoroughly as pleasantries were exchanged. Ike seemed to know something of the topic as his scalp glowed red beneath the combover and he adjusted his black horn-rimmed glasses obsessively.

"Turk," Harlowe began. He liked to call Larry by his nickname to build some kind of familiarity. "We have a tougher one than usual and we need your help." As the salads were cleared away, Trey stuffed his mouth with bread and tried to look as informed as he could.

"It seems that the Grean family needs to move some of the plant to another part of the country," Harlowe continued. "This has nothing to do with you or the local. It merely is a customer demand to be closer to their plant for quick turnaround. We didn't want to spring this on you in front of the local and wanted to talk through the implications. It would entail layoffs but we have severance clauses. In time we could see what we could do to bring some of the work back in here. But we wanted to run this by you." Harlowe added an inappropriate smile to the end of his statement. Nobody at the table except Harlowe knew he was lying through his teeth. The only "customers" were potential buyers of the entire business who wanted to see if the union could be controlled.

Trey was floored. How could Harlowe *not* discuss this with him ahead of the lunch? He stuffed a larger piece of bread in his mouth and cycled through the implications wildly in his head. Trey felt the beat of his heart increase involuntarily.

Larry raised an eyebrow toward Harlowe and settled back in his chair. If he was panicked or angry, he did not betray it. He responded almost too calmly.

"How many? When?", The Turk inquired.

Harlowe fidgeted with his butter knife and replied: "Maybe a quarter, up to a third of the plant? We haven't figured it out exactly. Need to run the numbers. We have some play in there. We'd like to do it in the next month or two."

Larry was still calm, but his tone was getting firmer.

"Cutting it a little close, aren't you? Any later and you would be telling me at the same time as the local. Pretty fucking close to be telling me."

Ike looked like he wanted to run away. His body was still but his knee bobbed nervously now. Trey chewed slowly—there was no way he was going to add a syllable. Harlowe broke an awkward silence.

"Turk, this all came on us pretty…"

Larry quieted Harlowe with a wave of a meaty hand tipped in stubby fingers saying, "Give me a second to think this through." His face was still the picture of composure. His eyes were fixed on some indefinite space. If he wore a turban you would have sworn he was in a trance.

Harlowe would not let the moment linger too long and was desperate to fill the dead space. He turned to Trey and asked: "If we did lay off a third, how far back up the seniority trail would that leave us?"

Trey chewed even more slowly. This was an impossible question to answer without knowing exactly what jobs would be affected. Trey knew that if Larry had any pent up anger, it was about to be directed at him because Larry and Harlowe needed to leave the table with a relationship intact. Trey understood he was the whipping boy at the table, and he did not like it. He chewed in exaggerated fashion to buy some time. Larry broke in, more annoyed this time.

"He won't know," Larry said. "And I just need a moment here to *think*." This was a good moment for Larry. He insulted Trey *and* put Harlowe in his place in one sentence.

Fortuitously, lunch arrived: thinly sliced filet mignon with baby carrots and Lyonnaise potatoes. Larry cut his food while doing some kind of calculus in his head. Ike usually salted everything, and heavily, but refused at this moment to ask for the salt, respecting Larry's call for quiet to the extreme. Larry chewed the first few bites pensively, then placed his knife on the table and kept his fork to jab the air for emphasis. Trey never saw Larry as a mental heavyweight, but the statement Larry was about to make awed Trey for its detail, given the short time to think it over.

Larry started the conversation again, saying, "I'm going to assume you really need this otherwise you wouldn't bring me out here to the palace and kiss my ass like this but we can discuss that again later. Here is how we do it. First, no more than 25% of the heads go. Period. End of sentence. I don't care if you have the rest paint the parking lot with a fucking toothbrush. Next, I want you to come in and say you are closing the plant. Done. Over. No more plant," said Larry.

At this point Harlowe no longer owned the title Squinty-Eyed Fuck as his eyes got unusually large at Larry's suggestion. Harlowe looked like he was about to say something but Larry waved him off with a fork.

"Then," Larry continued, "we caucus. I take the local team back there for quite a while. We come back in. I scream and rant and rave. I call you all lying, backstabbing sons of bitches. I threaten to bring down the hounds of hell on Grean. You caucus, we set another meeting. A few days later, you reconsider and say you want harmonious relations. We give you something like the clothing allowance to cut costs, you give us 75% of the jobs back *and* you add 50% to the severance for those impacted. We saved the plant, you get what you want. Everyone is happy." Larry stabbed his fork into the next slice of beef and jammed it in his mouth and looked at Harlowe for reaction. Trey could see Harlowe was stunned and processing everything that was said. Ike's hands shook as he buttered a piece of bread.

Trey was simultaneously awed and repulsed by how quickly Larry created a fiction. He always knew he was self-serving, but this took the cake. In the space of two forkfuls he turned around a situation where he lost a quarter of the plant and transformed it into a case where it appeared he saved 75% of the jobs. When facing a crisis, create a bigger one and solve most of it. Brilliant. Nefarious. He also managed to slip in a huge sweetener for those who would lose their jobs as well, and Trey wondered if Harlowe or Ike picked that up. He imagined Larry had already figured out what increase he needed in union dues from each remaining member to make up for the loss of jobs. By this two-act play Larry insured the remaining local members would gladly pay it given Larry's marshaling of union might to save the plant for all. Trey realized his mouth was empty and picked up the biggest forkful of carrots he could and stuffed his mouth. He needn't have worried; Larry was staring at Harlowe. The ball was in his court.

"Well, I have to say, Turk, that is a lot to think about," said Harlowe.

"We are thankful that you understand what we have to do and are willing to participate in the discussion."

Larry pounced. "It really is not a discussion. If this is what you want, that is pretty damn close to the way it is going to be. And when will the work come back in?"

Harlowe answered quickly, trying to parry with his friend The Turk, who did not seem so friendly at this point. "We can't say when the jobs might come back. We have not even gotten through this. We also need to cost out all that additional severance. And don't you think things will be a little tense after all these people think the plant was about to close?" said Harlowe.

This was not a fair fight. Larry was several steps ahead in the logic already. Trey could not stuff another morsel in his chipmunk cheeks if he wanted to.

Larry never looked up from his plate, but still answered.

"You had enough severance budgeted for this little move for a third of the plant, now it's 25% so your costs aren't higher," he said, using forcefulness as a substitute for math that was clearly not going to work.

"As for the morale," he continued, "do you think it will be better if you just take a third or if you nearly close the plant and give back the vast majority? Morale is your issue not mine and that is also why you have Boy Wonder Trey over there. He can throw them a little party or something."

Trey was not sure whether to despise Larry for his condescending swipe or be grateful that he made him indispensable for the near future.

Ike bypassed his scotch and soda for the glass of ice water. It trembled in his hand and the ice tinkled like a tiny alarm. Ike felt the need to say something so as he took his sip of water he added a vote of confidence. Larry never took his eyes off of Harlowe but he clearly saw the tremor in Ike's hand.

"Trey can handle the morale," said Ike. "He is a good man and the local knows he did not make the decision."

"The local knows what I tell them," said Larry. He was gaining confidence and poise with every word. He knew he created the advantage and was pressing it hard. He pushed a very clean plate away from his place and turned to Harlowe.

"Are we doing it my way?" Larry asked. "I hope so because that is the only way it fucking gets done."

Harlowe popped the last piece of meat on his plate into his mouth, looked at Larry and said, "The devil is in the details here, but I understand how you want this done. I think we can get there."

Larry was unimpressed.

"Well if you want to 'get there,' tell me soon," Larry said. "No surprises and let's talk before we have any formal meeting down at the plant. Now are we getting dessert or what?"

CHAPTER 12

IN IKE'S OFFICE

After lunch, Trey, Harlowe and Ike retreated to Ike's office and shut the door to recap what just happened. Harlowe seemed rather pleased in the whole.

"Overall I'd say we got what we needed today. He didn't throw up on the idea," said Harlowe with no small amount of admiration for anyone who might out-sly him. "As a matter of fact, he got neck deep pretty quick with the whole idea about closing the plant and saving it. I never thought of that angle."

Ike chuckled a bit and sat back in a chair near the conference table.

"Neck deep is not exactly a long way for him." Ike was not a clever man, but this little joke pleased him to no end and he continued to laugh at his own joke.

Trey was still curious and asked Harlowe about this new customer, where they were and what kind of machining they would need. He was trying to fill in the blanks but Harlowe was evasive, calling the customer and the project "very confidential" and still in the planning stages.

"One thing I will tell you is that we have to help The Turk a little," said Harlowe. "Pretty soon you guys will see a raft of orders come through here. We are going to pull some of the future orders up a bit as a hedge. For one thing, it will make the rank and file happy to get some overtime and see the place humming. Second, if there are any problems here with morale, we will have a little build-ahead. We do not want to see a sag in output. Those who will stay will see a lot of work and fatter paychecks. It may help them ignore the fact some of their coworkers aren't there."

Harlowe was informed by the Grean brothers about the potential sale in enough detail to understand there was a nice reward waiting for him if he maximized the sale price. For their part, the Greans decided to stimulate a little good will by accelerating orders from the future to stuff the plant. A busy plant created good will that might count for something in the eyes of the buyers, particularly a jittery TerVeer Enterprises. Accelerating orders was also risky in that it might dry up the pipeline if the market declined even a little bit. This little production illusion was like a form of heroin. Once you started distorting demand, it was hard to get unhooked from this rush without a lot of pain. Right now the Greans were willing to bet that the detox was going to be someone else's problem.

Ike noted that any build of product capacity would likely have to wait until after the summer as the machines were heavily scheduled and summer vacations did not leave a lot of excess hours.

"Do what you can, Ike, we'll need the cushion because when those machines leave, they will be out of commission for weeks until they get moved, settled and humming along," said Harlowe in his finest command mode.

Harlowe switched his attention back to Larry and the union. He was certainly impressed by the depth and breadth of the plan Larry spun over lunch.

"Is there any way he saw this coming? And does he really hold that kind of sway over these guys?" Harlowe asked to no one in particular. Harlowe was staring at the street from Ike's office window. The light from outside cut across Harlowe in horizontal lines, recalling a zebra as he stood, almost entranced by the view. Harlowe's question hung in the air and was really an idle reflection, but Ike felt the need to answer and be supportive.

"Yes sir, I do think Larry has always been able to deliver on his promises. He knows his guys better than anybody. If he says he can do this, then I firmly believe he can. I bet he comes back for something else, but he will make this happen—and come out looking better after losing some dues-paying members. Amazing," said Ike, betraying admiration for The Turk.

Harlowe stared out the blinds in the office. It was still blistering hot outside as two homeless men in overcoats and scraggly beards pushed a shopping cart full of who knows what down the middle of the street. He swung around to face Trey.

"You have been very quiet on this, but you know these guys," said Harlowe, who stepped a bit more in front of Trey to make eye contact. "What do you make of all of this?"

With not a morsel of food around to jam in his mouth and delay his response, Trey sat up straighter in his chair and cupped his hands behind his head.

"I think Larry is underestimating how hard his group will take this. We don't have a lot of new people. Our average age is 55. The average seniority is 21 years. You take 25% out of this place you are walking 25-year employees out the door. I don't care how many jobs you 'save,'" Trey said, punctuating his word with air quotes to tip his disgust. "We are still walking senior guys out the door very likely. This is not going down easy, I don't think."

Harlowe had his first dissent and it did not take him long to show he did not like it. The message was not one he wanted to hear and he was zeroing in on the messenger. A red tinge of scalp peeked through his thin cover of hair.

"These guys have had it pretty good for years here. Their members may get more than they originally bargained for—literally—if we buy into their extra severance game. People are getting walked out of factories all across America, so if they lose a couple of guys, the rest of them will have pretty fat paychecks—and they will all have the name *Grean* on them," said Harlowe. His squint was in full view as he spat out the words.

Trey wanted to remind Harlowe that in fact they were not "saving" any jobs; that assertion was a fiction created by Larry. In fact, it was a fiction Harlowe already embraced as fact. Still, Harlowe and Trey both knew that strategically and financially—even emotionally—Grean needed East Newark. The land the plant sat on had been a dump and soaked with tons of unknown chemicals. In the earliest days of the operation there was no Environmental Protection Agency and no government oversight. The machines themselves sat on wooden planks. Thousands of gallons of solvents soaked into the earth. Old Man Grean was trying to make a living and no one had yet figured out what about the solvents were toxic, nevermind how to dispose of them. For all Old Man Grean knew it was fertilizer that could help farmers in the next century. Today, if they ever wanted to mothball the operation it would become a money pit to clean and remediate. As it stood, the plant was a concrete slab that sealed all the toxins below. On top of that slab was a money-making operation. Once they stopped production above the slab, it was a bottomless money-sucking pit. What Trey did not know was that East Newark stood between the Grean family and $300 million.

At this moment, Trey quickly weighed how big a fight he wanted with The Squinty-Eyed Fuck. He turned somewhat conciliatory. "Harlowe, you and I get the same paycheck with the same name on it, too. I am not saying this won't get done. I am just saying we'd better not get lulled here either. Let's not assume the best and be prepared when it does not go as well as Larry says."

Harlowe was not content to let this go.

"Let me give you a little finance lesson, son. Every month I sit down there in Orlando at the right hand of God and listen to financials. After they show the value of production—the next line is a deduction—do you know what that is?" he asked Trey

Ike, half to show his knowledge, half to break the tension now building piped up and answered:

"Manufacturing Losses."

"That is right," said Harlowe, shooting a quick squint of annoyance Ike's way before refocusing on Trey. He wanted to be sure who answered the next question.

"And Trey, what are Manufacturing Losses?"

"I do not know," said Trey, sensing correctly not to hazard a mere guess.

"That is right," Harlowe snapped. "No one does. Manufacturing Losses are the unknowns. A thousand pieces go in one end and 997 come out the other. Three pieces are gone. Kicked away. Fallen into a machine. Pocketed and used as a paperweight. Made into a fishing line sinker. Who the fuck knows? It is rounding. It is a plug number to make it all balance and make us feel better that we have this all under control. I know you come here every day and this looks like the center of the world, but I am telling you, we are all just Manufacturing Losses. Rounding. It isn't pretty, but you need to start thinking that way and making sure we get this done and not make this into a big hullabaloo. In the big picture, this is a couple of machines moving to a new zip code."

Ike was very uncomfortable with any conflict, and this conversation made his skin crawl. He did not want any doubt going back to Orlando and the Grean brothers through Harlowe. Trey knew he was done with the argument and nodded understanding.

Ike capped the conversation with reassuring words.

"We have never let you down, Harlowe. When the bell rings, we will be there and make this thing happen. Always have. Always will."

This was alpha-dog Harlowe. He wanted to show who was in charge and be sure he safeguarded the deal to the best of his ability. While never a man who showed his cards, Harlowe knew he was in a high-stakes game and he needed blind obedience. This rant was a preemptive strike at Trey—the most likely person to ask a lot of questions about what was going to rapidly become a set of more implausible actions. Harlowe did not want to give Trey any room to feel comfortable. It was almost predictable Ike would want to smooth any ruffled feathers; at least it indicated he might help check any hesitation from Trey. Harlowe turned and resumed his blank surveillance of the street outside the window. He muttered in a low tone, repeating Ike's words in a guttural, intimidating growl

"No, you won't let me down," Harlowe said, almost menacingly.

CHAPTER 13

EARL AND THE MAYOR

The next morning, Trey crept out the front door of his townhome and onto the sidewalk for his run. The sun had just begun to ignite the skies. As he felt the air, he knew the first assault of summer would be beaten back today. The morning air was cool and dry now. It actually had a nip in it. Trey was thankful for this. It might invigorate him as his sleep last night was fitful and shallow. Each time he awoke, he thought about Larry and Harlowe and the hard days ahead; the faces of disappointment when employees got their layoff notices. Worse, the looks of worry as each person silently calculated how close the waves of cuts would come to their personal shore. Layoffs wear away at every person, whether they are laid off, uncertain about getting laid off or simply miss the person who was just laid off. Looking at an idle spot where a coworker once stood was like a deep ache. It receded slowly. Trey knew the time just before the cuts were the worst. The uncertainty gnawed at everyone. He needed to think it through, and this was the time of day to do his thinking.

As he took off out of the cul-de-sac, Trey found himself preoccupied with images of his job, but somehow thoughts of his father took over his ideas like an incoming tide. Earl's failing health was more evident with each visit. With his father now more mortal than any time, Trey allowed his thoughts to drift to his favorite conversations with his father. They pushed his unrest about Grean to the recesses of his consciousness in the cadence of his run.

May 1924

Earl did not realize they were poor in 1924, but he knew free stuff was good to get. He also knew he could not travel the Newark city trolleys alone at age 6. Not only was he not allowed to, he did not know how to. So when he heard the other kids on the street talk about how the mayor was about to hand out food and drums and rubber balls, he began to pester his older sister, Ingrid, to take him. Since Ingrid brought him everywhere she went anyway, he thought it might interest her to get a bounty of free things from the city. So Earl was greatly perplexed when his sister staunchly refused to buy into his little plan. This trip to city hall looked like an even better day than Christmas had been five months earlier. As far as Earl could tell, there was not even a need to pass Santa's goodness test.

Ingrid's refusal was a real annoyance to Earl. He could not figure out why she refused to take him to see the mayor. His next step involved pestering his sister. Ingrid was not sure her little brother would understand her reticence but after several days of enduring his badgering, her sanity demanded a try.

"We are not going to see the mayor for whatever silly thing you think you can get," Ingrid said flatly, mustering up the maximum amount of authority she could find to put an end to her brother's insistent lunacy. "Besides, where are we going to get the nickel for the fare? What do we say to Momma? We are going to see the mayor? For what?"

"To get all the free stuff they are giving out down there," pleaded Earl, as if he really had to explain this return on investment.

Ingrid looked at him with a crooked set of pursed lips, measuring her next statement carefully. She was on a mission akin to describing the color blue to a blind man.

"Free," she began. "That is the problem word right there. Free. Charity. Like we are not hard working or American and buy these things for ourselves. If Papa saw us standing in line like ragamuffins waiting for the city to give us free food or hoops or whatever your friends think they are giving out, he would be very stern with us. He did not like when Momma got the cheese from the city worker who stopped by to see us. He said they gave that to people in pity and he did not want pity. He wanted to work for what he received. Besides, he said if the city gives you cheese it must be ready to go bad or something."

Ingrid hoped that would be enough to stop the whole conversation in its tracks, but of course it was not. For little Earl, it was just a minor setback. A statement that begged more questions.

"But if they are giving it out and they tell everyone, they must want you to have it," Earl implored.

Ingrid sighed a deep sigh.

"So who told you about these wonderful things?" asked Ingrid, arms akimbo.

"My friend, Euchie," said Earl. "He said the man from the city stopped his car and got out and told them all to come down and that the mayor wanted the good kids in town to get some stuff from him."

Ingrid raised an eyebrow in disbelief.

"Then let Euchie go and bring you back something when he gets it," she said. She turned on her heel, ending the conversation once and for all. Or so she thought

In mentioning Earl's good little pal Euchie, she opened up new, unintended vistas for her little brother. Until the moment she mentioned Euchie bringing treasure back from city hall, Earl had not the imagination to think of his universe beyond the tether of his sister's hand. But Euchie was two years older and traveled via the trolley all the time to bring glass bottles downtown to the soda plant and collect deposits for his family. Usually, Euchie had two dozen bottles at a penny apiece. At 5 cents trolley fare each way, he netted 14 cents and his mother let him keep a nickel for his efforts. Earl would travel with his worldly friend Euchie, see the mayor and maybe split any food he got with him.

While Earl initially fretted about the problem of the nickel trolley fare, Euchie said not to worry. They would get there somehow.

The next morning Earl better understood the somehow was due to the fact Euchie actually made out with 15 cents on the deposit chore because he paid no fare either way on his trek. The plan involved standing on Mulberry Street, where the trolley slowed to take a curve, and hopping on the back of the car at just the right moment and then hopping off at any given point somewhere close to the destination when the trolley slowed because a car stalled on the tracks or a horse crossing or any similar impediment. When Euchie first described the act, it seemed like a reasonable plan. But when the first trolley car came down the tracks, it appeared like a huge, iron, screaming dragon to young Earl. He hesitated at the first passing car, frightened of jumping too soon and falling under the wheels that looked like round razors, or jumping too late and landing in the mossy mess that filled in between the tracks, thus ruining his clothes and exposing his deceitful plan to his mother. So, in that first pass, Earl froze. Euchie somewhat expected this and kept an eye out for Earl. When he saw Earl getting smaller by the curb, Euchie jumped off and ran back to Earl, who was nearly in tears. Two more trolleys went by but were going in the wrong direction. This allowed Euchie to demonstrate the boarding jump to Earl and gave Earl enough time to screw up his courage and test the strength in his legs required for the maneuver. All of the fear was overlaid by the fear of being seen by the paying customers and turned over to the authorities. Earl was beginning to weigh the cost of the free goods he would get from the mayor. This was where Earl learned that "free" was a cost in and of itself. Juvenile hall seemed a certainty by the end of the day and Earl fought back tears imagining himself behind bars.

Finally, like marauding pirates, Euchie and Earl hopped the trolley and clung to a back rail, obscured from view of the passengers by advertising that covered the back rail. They hopped off when the car slowed just short of their intended destination and scurried down a cobblestone embankment and toward city hall.

Once at the seat of power, it seemed pretty obvious where to collect the loot as a long line of children—all seemingly older and bigger than Earl—ran up the steps of city hall before a large platform featuring a larger-than-life photo of the mayor.

The line led up the stairs to a long table with the mayor himself. He did not look nearly as imposing at his 5-foot-8 stature as he did in his 10-foot-high likeness on the canvas. As they slowly approached the table, Earl feared any free goods would be exhausted by the time he and Euchie got there. As the lucky kids at the front of the line passed by those still waiting, it appeared that a brown paper bag contained some variation of fruit, a slingshot, a rubber ball and matches as well as two wads of gum twisted in wax paper.

When Earl and Euchie approached the front of the line, the treasures inside the paper bag were just in their grasp when a taller man standing next to the mayor stepped out and approached them. "You two look lucky today," he said. He grabbed the boys and brought them behind the table and closer to the mayor himself. Earl thought the mayor smelled like an odd mixture of aftershave and stinky cigars. In a moment, Earl and Euchie were lifted by strong hands and seated right in the lap of the mayor. The mayor's wool suit scratched Earl's bare arms, which were exposed from beneath his jacket that had now ridden up. Earl eyed the bags of bounty on the table. From behind the table, he was not sure what the view might be like and he saw the long line of kids still snaking down the stairs awaiting their loot. Just then, fear gripped Earl. Before him was a knot of commotion punctuating a sea of silver and black and a dozen men hollering at the mayor to look their way. He realized they were photographers and above all Earl knew that while he wanted his bag he could not be photographed accepting this charity. He was not poor. He belonged to a family that could pay for anything they chose to have. Now they certainly chose to have fruit, but a slingshot, a rubber ball and gum were certainly not an option. Being photographed with such lucre was even less of an option.

As small as he was, Earl made a sinuous turn under the arm of the mayor and hid his face. Somehow, this made the photographers even more interested in him.

Get him up on your lap, mayor," one of the photographers pleaded. "This is the shot you'll want."

Earl felt the mayor's rough grip get even tighter but he was able to squirt under his arm and then the table. With so many flashes going off, he was not sure if he had been caught in the act or not. Looking at an array of feet beneath the table where he hid, he thought they might still come to get him or try to take his picture under the table. The whole adventure had gone terribly wrong. He had no idea where Euchie was. He had no desire to jump on another moving trolley. He was not going to get his free stuff. He was trapped under a table and just outside photographers wanted to chronicle this whole sad travail. Earl could barely see sunlight peeking under the dark tablecloth on the table where he was hidden when suddenly the light blinded him. He thought it might be a photographer, but it was really just a friendly female face. She smiled and cooed at him in the voice of an angel.

"Are you scared? Would you like to come out and go home? It's alright," she said, extending the most dainty, pale-white hand he had ever seen. He took her hand and emerged from the side of the table. The mayor was preoccupied with the next kid and the photographers seemed to now think of Earl as yesterday's news. Earl was grateful to his lady angel and was surely going to take her up on her offer to get him home. But just as suddenly as angels appear, they drift away and she was gone again and he was on his own. Why did she leave him with a promise half-fulfilled? Panic was setting in as he looked for Euchie on *the mayor's lap, which was now occupied by two curly-haired girls who kissed the mayor's cheek. No Euchie there, for sure.*

As he looked up, Earl realized he was near the top of the steps and had a good view of the city. Some movement in the not-too-distant horizon caught his eye scooting between buildings two blocks away. It was the trolley! He could see it. It was at least some trolley and it was a start to get home. Earl took careful note of a point in the distance where he saw the trolley and resolved not to take his eye off that target so he could at least find the tracks. From that point he could follow the tracks and perhaps even walk on them on the way home. The trick was navigating the 20 to 30 stairs down to street level while still fixing on the point where he saw the trolley. In a determined gait he took his first steps, but he quickly lost his balance. As he fell, he was more concerned about getting turned around and losing sight of the trolley than getting hurt. But he was further confused as he tumbled a few steps and something else fell on him, tangling in his fall. He was not going fast and was able to stop himself, coming to rest on top of the foreign object—a paper bag half filled with fruit and slingshots. As he rolled to look up from his point of origin, he saw the long table where the mayor was seated. But in the foreground he saw Euchie. It was Euchie who had pushed him down the stairs and thrown a paper bag on top of him. His older friend was clearly disgusted.

"Cheeze you are a mess. They thought you was retarded or something so they gave me your bag to hold. Didja think they were killing you? I told them you had fits at night so they gave me your bag. I oughta keep it just because you're stupid. Then you're lookin' around like a zombie. You woulda done better if the trolley did run ya over."

Earl was so happy, he would have given Euchie everything in his bag, but he settled on surrendering the only two things Euchie wanted—the rubber ball and the gum. On the way home Earl and Euchie devoured their fruit and their memory of their day with the mayor. Earl hid the slingshot beneath his bed in a cardboard cigar box. He also now understood why his father hated accepting charity.

Trey eased into the last hundred yards of his run. He had almost no memories of the three-plus miles of his trek. He was amazed and had to think about where he had just been. He had not thought for one minute about the upcoming trouble at work. But he felt good. He felt strong. He could figure the rest out as he went along.

CHAPTER 14

RAMPING UP

As Trey pulled off the Turnpike and into East Newark, he passed by Riley's Tavern. He made a mental note to find out what detox center Warsaw was in and write him a note of encouragement. At times, Trey had been known to craft a note to a sick employee and bring it to Ike to sign. Ike's reputation as a warm, caring manager was largely the manufacture of Trey's efforts. Ike was no writer for sure, and was not particularly in touch with the issues of the employees, but Trey carried a list of home addresses and a supply of blank Green notecards in his briefcase and could whip out a note, often deciding who should sign it much later. It is not certain how many employees noticed or cared that the handwriting and the signature on the card did not match, but the impact was the same. Ike appreciated Trey's efforts and acknowledged it in Trey's performance review one year with the comment, "Much of your most valuable contribution does not show up in the box score for all to see." That comment brought Trey his greatest satisfaction, although he was not sure if it meant anything to anyone except Ike. As Trey mentally composed the note to Warsaw, he decided he needed to sign it as a token of reconciliation—he had, after all, called Warsaw a buddyfucker. Trey hoped Warsaw would not even recall the meeting.

When Trey pulled up and double parked in front of Page's Luncheonette, he was thankful for the cooling temperatures—the Council of Elders were dressed in something warmer than their undershirts. It did not make them any less talkative or more attractive.

"Good morning, Your Honor. What is on the docket today?" a daring council member inquired.

Trey glanced their way. He did not know the names of this crew but had assigned them names in his own mind. The Elder who addressed him this morning he called Bee because he had the oddest shape. He was a slight man with silver hair and a chest shrunken by age and an outsized potbelly. When he stood in profile he looked like a lower case letter "b." Today, Bee sat atop the highest pile of rice bags, his feet dangling a foot off the floor. Trey tried to envision exactly how Bee got hoisted onto his perch but decided he did not like the visual. Trey knew that ignoring the Elders was not an option. They would accept abuse; they simply would not brook being ignored.

"I'm letting them all go today. Everyone gets released," said Trey. "It's not their fault they grew up poor and disadvantaged. They were all framed anyway. They were misunderstood by their mother." If he was trying to raise the collective blood pressure of the Elders, he succeeded.

Bee smacked his forehead in disgust and howled in coffee-fueled agony and indignation.

"Jesucristo, another goddamn liberal," said Bee. "No wonder this neighborhood is falling apart. We get them arrested and you let them out and they come right back here."

Trey went over to the coffee pots and poured two cups. He added cream and lids as well as a cardboard sleeve to protect his fingers from the heat emanating from the cups. He turned to pay but there was no one there to take his money.

"Where is Howard and Sun?" Trey asked the Elders. They were the de facto security detail.

"He's back there teaching some kids some of that kung fu shit in the back room before school. Probably the kids that get the shit beat out of them. He'll teach them a few moves and they'll try it out on a kid who tries to take their lunch money. They'll stand there waving their arms around and the kid will come in and punch them straight in the mouth. That kung fu ain't worth a crap," said Bee. Trey wondered exactly what was in their coffee to fuel that kind of indignation.

Somewhat disgusted by the description, another one of the more attentive Elders growled a more accurate report.

"He's back there teaching old ladies tai chi- not kung fu. I don't know where the hell Sun is. Probably taking a piss."

Somewhat amused by all this, Trey shoved a dollar under the corner of the cash register and took off out the door. No time to linger with the car narrowing the street to one lane.

Once in the plant, Trey breezed past Pauley's area. He was nowhere to be found but his press was already pounding out a healthy pulse and his toolbox was open, hinting at his presence. Trey slipped a coffee behind the toolbox to shield it from the oil vapor aloft and headed into the office.

Once inside, he had not even emptied his briefcase when BeBe came in and rattled off a list of needs.

"Ike called already and he said to make sure you did not miss the meeting this morning. He wants to be sure you are here. The union is looking for you. I need your help in getting the medical carriers to fix a screwed-up medical claim—they aren't being helpful at all and won't budge without you stepping in. And over there," BeBe said, pointing to a 3x5 card tucked in the corner of Trey's desktop blotter, "is the home address of Warsaw and the address of the rehab center in case you want either, or both."

Trey turned around and saw BeBe still had the best body. She was dressed in a tight wraparound dress that showed off every curve, but she was still dressed professionally. Several years earlier, Trey actually sent BeBe home for showing too much skin in a short dress. He spoke to her frankly about dressing appropriately and the impact it had on her being perceived as a professional. BeBe was furious and a chill fell between Trey and BeBe for weeks, but she got the message. She found nice clothes that covered everything that needed to be covered and let her body send its tacit message. Trey could not help but pick up the maroon color of the dress but kept his eyes fixed very firmly on the pupils in BeBe's eyes.

"Thanks, I think. You really know how to schedule a day. I appreciate the Warsaw info. That is a good idea. If there is a Mrs. Grohowski, send a fruit basket there. I'll get a card to him at the center. Tell the union to come by at 10. I'll be sure to go to Ike's meeting. And you look very professional today," Trey said, a lingering nod to his previous fashion run-in with BeBe.

BeBe was pleased to receive the compliment.

"I always do," she said, just the slightest jab at Trey's dress code guidance of the past. It was the kind of sly shorthand only two people who have worked together for a while develop.

Trey was not sure why Ike made it a point to remind him about his attendance at the daily production meeting. For one, Trey was almost always there unless he was traveling or handling a union matter. Second, he knew of nothing special he had to report on, so this invitation made him wonder if he overlooked an issue, but he could think of none.

Once the meeting was underway, Trey understood why he was needed. The wave of orders Harlowe promised hit the production planning system. There was a central production planning system in Orlando that took incoming orders, their due date and matched it against the capabilities and equipment capacity at each plant and then factored in the lead time for raw materials as reported by suppliers. Then current scheduling plans and any additional information like machine breakdowns got added to the mix. All of this got mashed together in an algorithm and, like impulses from the brain that moved an arm or a leg, the production system set in motion the distant locations to build finished product. When the rough-cut production plan reached a location like East Newark, all hell might break loose. It was only 7:30 in the morning but the production planners looked like they had been digging ditches. Their hair was mussed already. Reams of computer paper sat in piles before them with red circles drawing attention to potential choke points and risks in the plan. Fulgencio "Fully" Alcara was the Director of Planning. He was a 25-year veteran of the planning wars. He seemed to relish a crisis and ran his hands continually through his thick black hair. The fact that he added copious amounts of gel to his hair caused an odd series of furrows to form one finger's length apart across his hairline. Fully was in full battle mode today. Sleeves already cuffed above powerful forearms.

"Where the hell did all these orders come from? We just did the plan for the summer and let everybody pick vacations and now all this shit hits the fan? We won't know until Purchasing gets all the info from the vendors on their ability to deliver the raw bar stock, but we do not have it on the shelves here, that is for shit sure," said Fully. His attention was fixed on the computer printouts in front of him. His eyes darted back and forth as if he was deciphering enemy intelligence. A junior member of his planning staff carried a yellow legal pad and was taking notes as Fully talked and picked up more challenges to be met in making the schedule. It was like dropping a rock in a still pond. The ripples went everywhere. Purchasing had to check every vendor and be sure all material was available. Maintenance had to change scheduled downtime for machines that would now need to run two shifts instead of one. Finance had to be sure they had enough cash to pay for the material now needed. Some of the material would need to be expedited, allowing the vendor to charge a premium for the privilege. That variance in price needed to be picked up in the financials. The ripples began from a single point but met points of impact at different times and angles.

Ike sat back, pleased to see his staff in such a controlled frenzy. He said very little but adjusted his thick, black-framed glasses every few seconds. Once in a while he had to mediate small disputes regarding turf and timing. Trey observed this with great respect. Harlowe moved fast to make this happen.

As the meeting wound down after about an hour, Ike held court.

"Remember, these are not problems but challenges," Ike began. "Lots of people would like to be in the position we are in right now with too much work. Remember, if you come to me with a challenge, bring me your solution, too. Let's be thinking about how to make this happen, not focus on all the reasons it might not happen. Let's keep our eye on the prize—and that prize is making the customer happy."

At other times, Trey might have been mildly inspired by Ike's words but today he wondered how many more clichés he could possibly fit in five minutes. As Ike spoke, Trey could sense exactly how false and disingenuous Ike's encouragement was. He now understood why Ike wanted him there. He wanted feedback on this performance.

As soon as the meeting exhausted itself a little short of 90 minutes, Ike asked Trey to stay back a moment for a word. As soon as they were alone, he eagerly asked for feedback.

"Did I fire them up enough? How did I come across? Did I look excited?" he asked.

Trey was always surprised at Ike's need for reinforcement after all these years and briefly pondered the fact that with no superior on site, feedback for Ike was obviously more important than it seemed. Trey pondered the question for a beat. On the best of days Ike could come off stiff and contrived, if competent. The utter truth was his act was good but he always seemed to be acting with forced emotion. But that would not help Ike now.

"You were great. They would follow you through hell in a gasoline suit, you know that? The best signal you got was that their heads were buried in the details. They are not giving this another thought. Just another day inside the blender while it is set to 'puree.' The guys I'd worry about are on the other side of this wall," said Trey, extending a thumb to the unseen factory and the union.

Ike seemed only briefly pleased as he digested Trey's words.

"Do you think they won't see this build as real? They are real orders; customers need this stuff," said Ike. Panic made Ike change direction like a puma chasing a gazelle.

"No, that's not what I'm saying. The union is coming in at 10. I'll gauge them. What I am saying is that these guys in the planning area can plan anything they want. It is the guys out there who execute. If their hearts are not in it, the plan is worth shit. I think we have two things to worry about. One is that somehow Harlowe is so proud of himself that he cannot help but tell somebody and they get a whiff of it out here. The second is that we do not overload them. Not a lot of people are going to love us—overtime or not—if we cancel vacations and get a heat wave that saps them."

Ike pondered Trey's words, which were unusually strong and frank. It betrayed a little of Trey's disgust for the entire affair and Trey heard it in his own voice. He made a mental note to dial it back in the future. Still, he was glad he said it.

"Go get them fired up and thinking about how good this will be for them," said Ike. He was not sure he was happy he asked Trey's opinion.

By 10 a.m. the union appeared at Trey's door. Mo and Tommy looked like they had been on union business most of the morning. They had not changed into their work uniforms but were still in casual street clothes— Mo in khaki pants and a knit shirt, Tommy in jeans, a white short-sleeve undershirt and an unbuttoned long-sleeve cotton shirt. The smell of tobacco clung to Tommy, but it was not unpleasant. Mo quit smoking several years ago after a mild heart attack, but under stress he was known to bum a few cigarettes from Tommy.

Mo slowly closed the door and let it click quietly. He talked at the door, letting his words echo back to Trey at his desk.

"When the fuck were you going to tell us about all this new work, Ghee? Do you like making us look bad?" asked Mo.

Trey realized that by using the term "Ghee"—factory slang for "boss," Mo was not angry but maybe a bit perturbed. The fact that the factory was ramping up was the saving grace. Had this been a slowdown and the union not informed ahead of time, the tone would have been curt, even angry. Tommy was already slumped in a chair in front of Trey watching his reaction as Mo turned to face Trey and continue his thought.

"All these people with all this vacation are coming and asking us about if they can still take their time off. We are sitting out there with our ass hanging out looking like two mo-mos. Is that how you play it now?" Mo asked, peering over his bifocals at Trey. Mo and Tommy were there making a point about neither communication nor production. That was very clear to Trey.

Trey got out of his seat and came across the desk. He did not like the desk to be between them, especially when he was trying to make a point. This was a little trick he had picked up from Ike.

"Why don't you two just unbunch your little panties a bit," said Trey, refusing to give ground. "You think I knew any earlier than this morning when I got in? Is my name Grean? BeBe told me you were coming in at 10 so I thought it might hold, especially since we are still trying to figure it all out."

Mo tapped his finger on the desk to make a point.

"Management gets paid to figure this out. All we do is make the shit and pay your salary. Now what can you tell us?" said Mo. He wanted to get on with it.

"I think I am about to disappoint you. We get the nightly downloads from Orlando. Planning got surprised. Looks like customers pulled in a bunch of orders and wanted them sooner. They throw it in the computer. Bingo, the floor gets busy. Still too early to say how busy for how long. The boys in Planning will need a few days more, but safe to say anybody who does not want to go on vacation with their old lady has an excuse. You can blame the fuck ups in management. See, we keep the family strong. Some of your guys would be divorced by the end of the summer if not for this, spending so much time around the old lady."

This line of thought amused Tommy who covered his mouth to hide an emerging grin, but Mo would not allow himself be amused.

"When will you know and when will you start hiring?" said Mo, mindful of union dues 60 days after an employee started.

Trey knew the tradeoffs and put them out front.

"You guys want more overtime or more union brothers? At least in the beginning, I say we load them up with OT. If they can't absorb it, we get some more people in here."

Tommy piped up.

"They'll want the overtime." This drew a glare from Mo. He wanted to defer any decision to figure out the maximum leverage and Tommy spouting off annoyed him.

"We'll see," Mo cautioned, tempering Tommy. "When will you know something solid?"

"Today is Wednesday—maybe next Friday." Trey knew they would have this buttoned up in a day but he was gauging the union's interest in the answer and setting up a situation to exceed expectations.

Mo was not happy.

"Nonononononononono. Too long. Friday *this* week. All of them have to go home this weekend and make decisions about vacation and weeks they can be here and whatnot. Tell your planners to get their shit together," Mo said.

"I'll see what I can do. I do not hold the keys to that kingdom," said Trey, adding, "By the way. What did you want this meeting for?"

"That was the topic," said Mo, "your lack of cooperation with your union." He only slightly twisted the facts.

"You're fucking kidding? You knew before I arrived? Before I knew? Why even bother me then? Whoever your little tattling bitch-buddy is in Planning, go take the next meeting with him. Whoever he is, he sounds like he knows more about the contract so maybe he can do my job too," said Trey. He was not mad. But he was envisioning choking a planner or two just to send a message. Mo had gotten the last laugh. His eyes twinkled with delight because he knew about the production ramp before Trey.

"Sounds like management needs to get their shit together," he said, opening the door and motioning Tommy out behind him. Tommy was reflexively reaching for a cigarette and headed outdoors where he could light up.

Mo turned toward BeBe with a parting shot.

"Your so-called Boss is always mad at us for what he can't do. How do you work for him?"

BeBe blew a kiss at Mo as he walked away.

By 1:50 that afternoon, Trey headed to the floor for the social event of the week. One of the production workers was about to retire after 32 years on the job. While the workforce was predominantly male, females made up about a quarter of the population. Inspectors, rework operations, packing and assembly were female bastions in the testosterone-laced factory world. It wasn't that females could not be tool and die makers or press operators—automation had eliminated a lot of the physically imposing work there—it was the mere fact that today's factory was generally hired 30 years previous and at that time females were diverted from the Metal Shop to Home Economics in the East Newark school system.

Mary Czvornyek was one of those girls encouraged to learn to sew. It was just that she hated it. In the early 1960s, although she was Polish, she was encouraged to marry a refugee from the 1956 Hungarian uprising who landed here and wanted to stay in the U.S. With no skills, her suitor worked janitorial jobs and thus forced Mary to look for a job. Mary put in applications everywhere in the neighborhood within walking distance, following smokestacks to the personnel offices like a bloodhound on a scent. She was hired at Grean to remove stray metal chips from the inside of machined parts in an operation called Finishing. She expected her job to last three months but it stretched to 32 years, not counting the five years she left to have two daughters. After each pregnancy Grean welcomed her back. Her reference came from the Old Man Cal Grean himself, who noticed Mary slogging to the plant in the aftermath of a snowstorm to staff her finishing station. He promised her she would have a job after any amount of pregnancies. Together, she and her husband put both girls through college and on the path to a better life. Now 60, she wanted to be a nanny for her grandchildren. She would retire at the end of the week.

The retirement parties were a proscribed rite of passage with well-worn traditions. A drab gray break bench in the middle of the production floor was covered with a bright vinyl tablecloth. Balloons were tied to each corner of the bench. Each employee brought food in a covered dish. Wood pallets that normally ferried production throughout the plant were stacked to create an impromptu stage. Grean contributed a sheet cake brought in from the local bakery (the baker's father had been a Grean machine operator, thus was given the sheet cake franchise *ad infinitum*). The 2 p.m. 15-minute break would get stretched a little on both ends.

Mary represented the changing demographics of the neighborhood and the plant. Older workers tended to be Eastern European and Italian. The newer employees were more likely to be Latin American and Asian. Trey looked around for Ike. He reminded Ike about the party and the need for him to be there to say a few words. At the moment, Ike was nowhere to be found. Mary was a short, stout woman with strong forearms, sculpted by three decades of manual labor. Trey waived plant security and safety rules to allow Mary's husband to join the party. He was a janitor in the school system and already retired. He looked at least 10 years older than Mary. He had a shock of gray hair that stood up on top of his head. His body was stooped, and his face bore a craggy smile. He looked happy that Mary would soon join in his days. A crowd of about 75 gathered, eating snacks and drinking punch. Several of her coworkers gave short speeches. Trey looked around for Ike but prepared to fill in for him with a few words if necessary. As Trey composed the speech in his head, Ike suddenly appeared in a rush and broke through the ring of well-wishers to give Mary and her husband a hug.

"If Cal Grean were here—and I know he is here in spirit—he would acknowledge Mary as one of the hardest working, loyal Grean employees. A person who built the success of the company when our success was not assured," said Ike. Invoking Cal Grean always brought a few solemn nods to the older employees. Ike should have ended there but he could not resist extending his time upon the pallet dais.

"For me, I can say Mary never gave me a nickel's worth of trouble," he said. To Trey, it seemed faint praise but no one else betrayed anything but admiration for the speech. Perhaps the mere fact Ike showed up gave him enough of a pass.

After Mary said a few words some of the older female employees formed a circle around Mary, holding hands. Trey noticed how strong their hands were, all of them equal to Mary's. Some bore the scars of surgery to relieve carpal tunnel injuries brought on by the repetitious motions of their assembly jobs. As they locked hands, the scars looked like they met, crossing from one hand to the next—a sinuous barbed wire of toil. Then they began to sing in Polish. They started, but by the second line of the song almost all of the employees, regardless of nationality, joined in. Even if they did not know the exact words, they hummed the tune:

> Sto lat, sto lat,
> Niech żyje, żyje nam.
> Sto lat, sto lat,
> Niech żyje, żyje nam,
> Jeszcze raz, jeszcze raz, niech żyje, żyje nam,
> Niech żyje nam!

Trey did not know the exact translation, but in essence, it wished her a hundred years of good health. The song was part of every plant celebration there was—births, weddings, retirements. The song was the highlight of these gatherings and brought the employees together in one language, one gesture that transcended the company or the union. These employees had spent the majority of their waking hours together. They had seen each other at their worst moments, at points of exhaustion and times of uncertainty. Working together, there was a nakedness of emotion employees could not even share with their family. It came through so vividly at times like these.

Mary covered her face and wept, followed closely by her inner circle of well-wishers.

Trey felt a strong need to go see his father.

Chapter 15

Superior Plastics

When Trey arrived at his parents' house, his mother was outside, sweeping the sidewalk and the gutter in front of their house. It did not matter that any manner of things might wash another load of grit from up the street and back in front of the Bensen abode. Margie Bensen swept the day's dirt from in front of her home daily and stubbornly.

"What are you doing here, dear," Trey's mother said, greeting him and steadying herself on his arm as he drew near.

"Just wanted to see Pops and how he is doing now that it's cooler," Trey answered.

"If *it* would stay cool or hot, he would be best off. It is the changes that seem to get him. It takes him a day or two to adjust to each change. But he's right there," she said, nodding to the porch. Trey could see the silhouette of his father, a frail outline somewhat smaller than he hoped or imagined.

Trey popped up the four stairs in two nimble steps and poked his head in to see Earl. His eyes were closed in a peaceful rest as he sat upright in a vinyl lawn chair. The louvered windows were open all around him, giving him both light and air. His companion oxygen bottle sat at his side and the plastic tubing snaked from the tank and hissed into his nose, affording him relief. Trey's kiss on his forehead brought Earl awake with a smile.

"Hey," Earl rasped, "what brings you here twice in a week?" The constant flow of oxygen and his condition forced him to breathe through his mouth a lot and dried his throat. Earl coughed and cleared his throat to gain the full range of his voice.

"Just wanted to drop in and make sure you didn't melt in the heat.

I wanted to see you better," said Trey adding, "you know I think of you a lot."

"Don't worry about me; I'm better than you think," said Earl. He straightened up in his chair a bit and offered Trey a drink.

"Nah, Pop, I can't stay that long, but I was thinking—tell me that story about the plastics shop again," asked Trey.

"Why are you so interested in ancient history?" said Earl, though clearly pleased to recount the story.

May 1950

Earl was working at a plastic extrusion manufacturer for three years. The factory manufactured tubing for pools and irrigation systems. It was a reasonably simple process: get plastic pellets, heat them until they melted and then force the goo across rollers that extruded tubing of various diameters, colors and thickness. But like all fairly simple ideas, the execution was far more difficult than the concept. The temperature had to be just right. The machines had to run at a constant speed. It could be a mess when things went wrong and plastic began to set up. It could destroy machinery or ruin precision. The rising affluence of America created swells of demand as people wanted to keep their green suburban lawns lush in the driest of summers. That created a demand for plastic tubing and the rise of Superior Plastics. Superior was actually two companies in one. Half of it was devoted to plastic tubing and extrusion. The other half was another growth business—plastic credit cards. The management at Superior invested carefully in the credit card business. It appeared to have little or no growth. Who would want to owe money and run up debt? But somehow the business was growing. By the time Earl joined, there were about 350 employees over three shifts and about a thousand issues. Although owned by a number of private investors, the managing partner was a man named Bob Potz. Potz owned a degree in the emerging field of plastics and a volcanic temper. It was nothing to see him degenerate into a rage and toss wrenches past the heads of unsuspecting workers. As one of the investors, he also liked to keep wages as low as possible. As an engineer, he saw the employees as interchangeable cogs—strictly mindless machine tenders. Seniority and longevity were cost escalators. Social convention, he thought, required raises while the operator added no greater value next year than last year. This attitude reinforced his pattern of abuse toward all employees at any level of the organization. If they could not stomach his tirades, they should do better work or leave and afford him the opportunity to pay lower wages to new employees. It was not so much an intentional strategy but an outcome and rationalization of his rage and incivility.

When Earl arrived, he learned how to tweak the delicate extrusion machine and maintain the temperatures key to the quality of the product. He listened for differences in the churning of the product. He came to understand how as the heat of the day rose, the machines and the mixture of raw materials needed to be altered. Earl liked the factory and the people and became fascinated with the science surrounding plastics. But he also winced every time another coworker quit or broke down in tears in the crosshairs of a Potz tirade.

It was only natural that talk soon turned to how a union might help Superior Plastics employees level the playing field, both emotionally and financially. Over a short period of time, Earl emerged as an articulate spokesperson for the issues at Superior. His gut told him there had to be more dignity in the workplace. While he did not invite the union representatives to the factory property, he listened to them intently when they arrived. It seemed an easy but reasoned choice: Superior Plastics employees would benefit from a union. When asked, Earl was unapologetic and open about his support for the union.

Earl's openness did him no favors. While no one in management approached him directly, his overtime was cut to near zero and he was shuttled to the night shift and then on to the graveyard shift—midnight to 7 a.m. based upon "emergency production needs" he was uniquely qualified to address. If it was a plan to send Earl a message, it only backfired and allowed Earl to make his case across all shifts. The union organizers, for their part, held Earl up as an example of the kind of unfair and unilateral actions management could take. They promised these kinds of actions would stop when a union represented the employees of Superior.

As the momentum for the union grew, management did not sit still. In addition to making life difficult for Earl and others recognized as strong union supporters, they took other actions. Perhaps their most effective was a very public announcement that Bob Potz had been sent to business school to learn more about the finances of the business. This public announcement was followed by a series of leaks from other top managers that "business school" was synonymous with "rehabilitative charm school" for Potz and that he was going to be kicked upstairs to some unnamed finance role.

What management failed to realize was that Potz was just the most visible symbol of widespread problems. Wages were still below that of other factories in the area. This was evident when the company became informally known as Superior University—a de facto training school for other companies that could lure talent away. In addition, Superior lagged in holiday pay, health benefits—heck—even the prices in the company cafeteria were higher than anywhere. Beyond that, an air of favoritism prevailed in the allocation of the best jobs, overtime and promotions.

As the union gained precious momentum, Superior management sat behind closed doors and evaluated the likely outcome of a ratification vote. They sat locked in a room for nearly 20 hours scouring over each employee's name and the likelihood of their vote. Sadly for the company, their most optimistic outcome still showed the union prevailing by almost a two-to-one margin. They were in desperate straits and 30 days from a vote directed by the National Labor Relations Board. Desperate times called for desperate measures and in this case it was Project 51. The 51 in Project 51 symbolized the 51% of the vote required to defeat the union attempt. Managers locked themselves away for another marathon session. They listed all employees they felt would vote for a union and ranked them from most likely to support management to least likely. Forsaking the hard-core union supporters as lost causes, they chipped away at the list, guessing at what it would take to sway the vote. Bathrooms were suddenly cleaned three times a day. A new window was placed in a dark corner of the credit card area adding light and air to a stifling room. Prices fell in the cafeteria. Bob Potz disappeared two weeks before schedule. Overtime became plentiful. Unplanned spot raises to reward outstanding performance flowed from every department. Of course, every raise came with a plea for confidentiality so that the deserving employee (who coincidentally held a swing vote) would not be the subject of petty jealousies of those other less-deserving (read: union supporting) folks who were not getting this generous increase.

Project 51 chipped away at the union's edge. The biggest single breakthrough came with the announcement of a summer jobs program. Dozens of students would be hired for the summer. Most of them were children of employees in the swing vote category. Each job offer came with a note at the bottom in bold print: "All employment is subject to change due to varying economic conditions." Some parents beamed at the sight of their kids working beside them on the factory floor. Some beamed at the notion that every hour spent earning a paycheck was an hour less their kids pursued spending money. How could the union top that?

Earl and others in the "hardcore" regions of the Project 51 list were beyond the reach of this new, targeted largesse. They saw their support chipped away but remained confident of two things: 1) the vote would still support the union and 2) all employees would certainly benefit from the presence of a union.

"If the company has responded this way in fear of the union, imagine what we might gain with an actual union," Earl said to any of the wavering middle.

Three days before the election, Project 51 had made great progress, but it now looked like a narrow union victory instead of a landslide as before. Rosier projections saw it as a dead heat. The final push was on.

Project 51 now relied on an exhibit mapping the home addresses of each employee radiating out in color-coded circles. Each pin was an employee. Green pushpins were company supporters. Red pushpins were immovable union supporters. The yellows were the fence-sitters. An odd pattern appeared. For no discernible reason, the fence-sitters clustered heavily to the north of the plant in a large apartment complex known as Rose Manor. Because the apartments had limited parking, very few of the residents owned cars—it was just too inconvenient. Once you owned a car you moved somewhere else. Because few had cars, the only viable grocery shopping was a block away at AAA Markets. So many of the housewives were seen on foot toting groceries in little wheeled personal shopping carts behind them, the apartments were dubbed "Refugee Manor." Project 51 had its last bullet to fire at the heart of the union campaign. Two days before the election, AAA Markets had bag boys in bright red smocks leaflet right next to the union organizers. The AAA boys had a green sales flyer that read:

"AAA OFFERS A LIMITED TIME SPECIAL TO OUR LOYAL CUSTOMERS AT SUPERIOR PLASTICS.

FOR ONE NIGHT ONLY.

SHOW YOUR BADGE AND GET 50% OFF YOUR FOOD ORDER."

It was a masterstroke. Quietly, word got out that the company had prevailed upon the supermarket to offer this sale to the employees who were captive to the only accessible source of food close to their home. Secretly, the company would write a check to AAA to cover the cost of the promotion. Publicly, it was the work of the marketing department of a supermarket rewarding its loyal customers. It was good to work at Superior. Your pantry was full. Your kid was employed. Overtime was available.

Earl shook his head in disbelief. He was sure his coworkers would remember their tears and anger more clearly than their groceries. He had seen the frustration in their faces. This would not possibly sway them—would it? Although Earl was not aware of the level of organization and purpose proceeding from Project 51, the effort was obvious, if unidentified. The night before the election, the union held a reception and rally at its headquarters. The union hall was packed, but Earl felt a vague uneasiness. He saw many familiar faces. To be sure of a win, they needed to go beyond the familiar. But heck, it was a Tuesday night and no one wanted to come out. What he could not see were the aisles of AAA Market, 20 blocks away. It was the busiest Tuesday night in store history. And it seemed that each shopper had an ID from Superior Plastics.

By Wednesday night at 8 p.m. the votes had been counted. The employees rejected the union by a vote of 267 to 183. The union would petition the NLRB for a recount, but they knew the vote was not close enough in the end for that tactic to matter. They lost the vote. Earl was disappointed but not crushed. Practically, he knew his days at the factory were numbered. The union, having lost the election, would be barred from organizing activities for another year. In that year, Superior would make his job uncomfortable if not downright miserable. If the efforts of Project 51 had been covert and sly, the impunity of a year without the union organizers would make their next steps far more overt.

Even the employees who supported the company throughout admired Earl and how he went about his advocacy—evenhanded and without rancor. They understood that the mere action of unearthing and confronting the workplace issues made life more pleasant and lucrative. Many of those who shifted their allegiance in the last days could not make eye contact. They had their groceries. They had their kids in summer jobs. They were rid of Bob Potz and his temper tantrums. They had no deduction for union dues coming from their check. By refusing to make eye contact with Earl, they avoided seeing the one thing they sacrificed—their advocate.

As Earl left the union hall, he stopped at the corner deli to pick up the evening edition of the newspapers. He needed to search the want ads.

CHAPTER 16

ORLANDO

Cal Grean Jr. sat at his desk while brother Jack sat on a small ledge near the window nursing a soft drink and the lingering effects of a hangover. It was shortly before noon and the insistent sun made the ledge hot and uncomfortable for Jack. It also made him cranky.

"Where the fuck is Harlowe and why are *we* waiting on *him?*" asked Jack, obviously peeved.

Cal shot his brother a glance, thinking about Jack's spotty record of punctuality and considered picking a fight, but Cal thought better of it and decided to explain.

"Harlowe controls a lot of things but the airlines are not one of them. He called from the airport, he is on his way. He should be here any second." Cal was eying a mountain of papers on his desk, trying to decide which one he might approach next. Jack eyed his watch, counting down the minutes to tee time with the sales team.

A few minutes later Harlowe entered, brushing past the normally forbidding administrative assistant seated just outside Cal's door. Harlowe had free rein in the office anytime he wanted. He looked relaxed and tan and wore a linen guayabera shirt and tan pants. Normally he would don a suit and tie but he had not factored in his flight delays and knew this was not a time to be a second later than he had to be. Even allowing that he was late, Harlowe exuded the presence of command.

"Gentlemen, I think we are about in as good a position as we can be at this stage," said Harlowe, not waiting for an invitation to speak. "The little Turk not only bought in but bought in big. He came up with all kinds of

121

extra ideas. This is his idea now. He owns it. This is why it is important we talk to him and keep lines of communication open to him, especially the back channels. We could not have thought of all the angles he came up with."

Harlowe went on to describe in detail Larry's plan to "save" the plant. As Harlowe recounted the conversation, Jack broke out in a grin at the sheer cleverness of it all. When Harlowe concluded Jack commented: "Dad would love this kind of shit."

Cal walked around from his desk to a chair at the table where Harlowe and Jack sat. He looked like he had been sucking on a lemon. While impressed with the thoroughness of the plan, Cal was uncomfortable with all the complexity. Cal noticed that Harlowe usually talked in a slow drawl, but today, Harlowe was rapid-fire, perhaps even a bit anxious.

"What Dad liked was to get things done. All of Larry's little games help him but not us. This extra intrigue costs time and TerVeer wants to see whether or not we have that situation in hand. In the end, if there is a press release of some kind, we just want to talk about the transfer of the work, not any of the details. TerVeer can then make their offer. They also want this to happen soon—any idea when that might be?" asked Cal.

Harlowe had not survived in the good graces of the Grean family by reading the tea leaves incorrectly. He knew Larry wanted a month before they met.

"I'll go back there and call a meeting in two weeks," said Harlowe. "We can pick up the pace."

Harlowe knew the Greans were dressing the company for sale. He signed a non-disclosure form prohibiting him from discussing it. In return for his silence, and in recognition of his long service to Grean, Harlowe would receive a huge severance payout, one so large he would never have to work a day in his life again. For a man who lived to keep and leverage secrets, the payout was icing on the cake. What Harlowe did not know was that the rough offer by TerVeer Enterprises was so far above other potential offers. He could not know that to sell at such a huge premium was the path for Cal and Jack to step out of their father's shadow. The old man had the genius and foresight to build the company. It allowed the boys to make a great living but they heard the doubts: Would they have been successful without standing upon their father's legacy? To sell the company on such terms would cement their place as industry titans. The other offers below TerVeer's would merely be indications the boys had enough talent not to screw up what their father gave them. The difference was desperately important to the brothers in ways Harlowe could not possibly sense.

Cal was all in on this bet but needed to explain to Harlowe the stakes.

"We pulled a bunch of orders forward and flooded East Newark two days ago. They are scurrying around trying to make it happen. We even added some volume based on what customers may order in the future. If we do not make this happen, we have a big hole at the end with no orders. Some of it we can absorb. Some we may need because once we move machines, production will be interrupted anyway," said Cal, before Jack interrupted with, "... and if we are lucky, just as it becomes a problem, it will be somebody else's goddamn problem, not ours."

Cal saw no humor in Jack's remarks despite the fact that he added a wide grin and the raise of his glass in a toast as he concluded his remark.

"We need to plan as if all challenges are our challenges," said Cal, correcting the tone of Jack's remarks, and making eye contact with him that encouraged him to be quiet.

Harlowe saw the tension between the brothers before and was not uncomfortable. He had seen this play out many times before.

"We will make this happen, I assure you," said Harlowe.

"I know you will pull out all the stops on this one," said Cal to Harlowe, who took that as his cue to exit the meeting.

As Harlowe left their sight line, Jack quietly closed the door.

"I'm glad he is on our side. He is one crafty old bastard," said Jack admiringly.

"Harlowe may not be pretty but he always finds a way to get things done," said Cal.

Jack swirled ice in his glass as he looked out on the steamy Orlando landscape. Cal knew his brother had a golf date and was not one to linger.

"What's bothering you?" Cal asked.

Jack paused and continued to ponder a bit, trying to decipher his feelings and describe them properly.

"Odd isn't it?" Jack began. "It is like the gods are testing us."

"I am not following you. What gods? What test?" asked Cal.

"Dad began in East Newark. Somehow TerVeer chooses that particular spot as the litmus test as to how big a bag of money to throw at us. Dad loved that place. It is a grimy mess but he loved that grit and the people there. Yet those are the people we have to fuck with? Dad's office is there in East Newark, locked up like a shrine to some future set of beings. TerVeer will empty it into a dumpster," said Jack.

Cal, ever the logical thinker, seemed almost poised with an alternate theory.

"You are looking through the wrong end of the telescope, maybe," said Cal. "If the Old Man did not make the hard calls, East Newark would have been where he stopped. That is where he grew up. It was his start, but he made lots of hard choices. Maybe it is a coincidence those choices never included East Newark as part of the equation. We will never know. All we know is that he made a lot of good decisions over time. They had to include hard choices. Closing and moving operations. Doing unpopular things. His legacy is not in watching what he built slowly atrophy. Given a choice between making the good choice or leaving his business a museum that cannot be touched? He would want us to make the right call. As long as you believe we are making the call, you can sleep tonight."

Jack turned to Cal to let the words soak in. Cal extended his thought.

"You are right about his office," said Cal. "The day he died we locked it up and have not gone back more than once or twice. We like seeing it as it was. It reminds us of him. But it has no use, no purpose anymore except as a reminder. It is no use to TerVeer, so they will trash it. Standing still, locked in place has no value."

Jack slid his glass across the conference table.

"I've got to make my tee time," he said.

CHAPTER 17

———◆•◆•◆———

FRIDAY BEER NIGHT

By the time Friday rolled around, Trey was mentally exhausted. The planners digested the production surge and changed their minds a dozen times as to the impact. Every time a variable changed, the estimate of hours required changed. In this particular case, the revision was always upward. When suppliers found they could deliver raw materials early, it added the need for more people. When maintenance found a way to repair mothballed machines and place them in service, it meant more people. When some employees could not change their vacations on short notice, it required more people to sop up the hours and calculate the union rules on how the additional overtime would be divvied up. Two employees went out on disability leave; one with a gallbladder attack, the other with injuries suffered in an auto accident. More people were required to meet the surge.

With each change, Trey found himself more concerned about the effect this surge in production would have on the overall plan Larry and Harlowe dreamed up. While the timing was not yet certain, it was sure they needed to have the meeting with the union to announce the pullout within 60 days. After 60 days, any new employees hired to staff the surge would become voting union members. The larger they were in number, the more they would add uncertainty. How would they vote on any issues like additional severance? Would they pose a greater threat of vandalism once they knew their jobs were gone? After all, they had no stake in the long-term health of the plant. There would surely be a rise in Worker's Comp cases as the short-timers would try to wring every available dollar out of the situation. Trey did not blame them; he just needed to add this to his calculus.

Most of all, he wondered if Larry was thinking this all through. Trey would hate to mention these factors to him. Even if Larry was not thinking through the fine details, he would never admit to that fact and would deride Trey as stating the obvious. Like facing a tooth extraction, Trey wanted this over.

The counterbalance to all of this was that in order to increase inventory to sustain the move, the plant needed time to work the production plan. The plant itself was more like a giant liner not a speedboat. It accelerated by degrees, subtly, over time. The difference between the tempo of 63 strokes of the press run by Pauley and 60 was indiscernible to the eye and the ear. Over the course of a month and 100 similar processes, it could amount to 10 million more pieces a month. The key is having the material there, the machines running and enthused, trained people to make it happen. But Trey had to be sure the first two pieces of the puzzle were in place before fulfilling his role of staffing the people to run the place.

Throughout the week, Trey met nonstop with Mo and Tommy to discuss how the work would be done. Certain jobs were considered plum jobs and the union wanted to be sure current employees got a chance to fill those. The least desirable jobs and shifts would be filled by the eager new employees, just hoping to impress their boss long enough to make it past the probationary period and into the union. It was not unheard of for some employees to be 60-day wonders: highly productive and punctual until they made it into the union, only to devolve into an unrecognizable morass of absence and apathy on the 61st day.

It did occur to Trey that another strategy might be to not accept any new employee after 59 days. The company had the sole right to terminate any employee for any or no reason before they became union members with all the protections their initiation fee and dues provided. This had the advantage that none of the new employees would be eligible for severance once the cuts were made. The downsides, though, were many. For one, it was not a common practice and the union would demand to know why no prospective dues-paying member was good enough for Grean. It would also hint that Trey knew what was going on all along and led a complex deceit. "Led" would be a strong interpretation, but he would be the only visible symbol of the plan once the shit hit the fan. Trey weighed the guilt he felt in planning the expansion with the union against the pain he would feel if it appeared he had been anything more than a low-level functionary, captured by the same circumstance. He quickly discarded the idea of terminating all the new employees after 59 days. He decided not to even mention it as an option to Ike. He hoped Ike would not think of it himself. Above all, he hoped Harlowe would never think of the ploy.

As work concluded Friday afternoon, Trey decided a little liquid refreshment was in order. It was not often he would grab a beer after work, at least infrequent since he had been married, but this Friday he succumbed to the desire. In choosing Warsaw's favored water hole—Karl's Bavarian—Trey broke a sacred rule of Ike's: thou shalt not drink in the neighborhood. About once a year Ike concluded a staff meeting with his advice to all salaried and professional employees not to drink in neighborhood bars. His working theory was neighborhood bars were most likely frequented by plant employees, especially on payday. Ike regaled the team with lectures on his days in the Navy and his observation that alcohol impacts each person differently, but very few positively. Ike noted employees may become more belligerent while under the influence and these same employees did not necessarily have a discerning eye in venting that belligerence. It was also possible all members of management would look generic if that belligerent employee was nursing a grievance from the work week. In conclusion, Ike noted drinking in the neighborhood bars was bad practice. He would not take responsibility for any member of his extended team should they become involved in a barroom brawl. Lastly, if he found out about such a brawl, termination of the staff member would take place no matter the origin or nature of the fight. It was Ike's way of both keeping the peace and sending his staff home to their families instead of the bars.

Driven by fatigue, familiarity and the fact that Karl's had cold draft beer, good bratwurst and was frequented by an older and likely more sedate crowd, Trey entered the bar. Friday night brought a more festive feeling. The locals were supplemented by some legal interns from Newark law firms. The loudspeaker system played German marches and Polish polkas. It was all pretty corny but it was just what Trey needed. After a few minutes, Trey found a table with two of the Industrial Engineers from Grean and sat down with them for light talk and cold beer.

For the first time since Harlowe appeared, Trey felt relaxed and a sense that somehow this would turn out alright. But the good feeling was nudged aside time and again as something seemed amiss. Trey could not identify what was bothering him but the light dread pushed its way forward and receded, time and again. Sometimes Trey just realized this feeling in the pit of his stomach and could not finger the source of the angst immediately, but he always traced it back to this goddamn charade. In the end, Trey chalked it up to the conflict between the tough days ahead as the plan unfolded and guilt over his feeling that things would turn out alright. He tried to wash away this turmoil with another imported draft beer. The beer was winning the battle for his conscience, but barely.

The Industrial Engineers, for their part, were cheered by the activity in the plant and the feeling that good times were ahead. Industrial Engineering was generally the entry rung in the plant engineering department. IEs studied many parts of the production process trying to reduce variability or figure out ways to predict when machines might break down and create methods to forestall or eliminate the breakdowns. After they understood how the product was made they might get an opportunity to do more exotic forms of engineering like design engineering or research and development. After they learned how the parts were manufactured, they were often transferred to product design. Engineers who understood the limitations of the equipment were less likely to design a part with so many design nuances as to make it impossible to manufacture reliably. Most of the Grean engineers were not from top flight schools but had an innate preference for working on the manufacturing floor close to the action. These two particular engineers were authentic to their trade right down to a pocket protector. Trey thought about Ike's rule about frequenting local bars and sized these two up as no real threat.

After 90 minutes and three beers, Trey assessed he was safe for the road and headed home. The extra time at Karl's did allow the Parkway and Turnpike to take on additional traffic that choked the road and made the drive home slower.

As Trey pulled into his driveway later than normal, he thought that perhaps he should have called to say exactly how late he would be. Upon entering the house, that vague sense of dread he had been carrying came quickly into focus. Carole was on the couch, her eyes red from crying. She held a pillow over her lap and a balled up wad of tissues. She vented fury from the second he stepped in the door.

"Did you forget *something*? Where have you been and why weren't you here? How can you not think to call? Am I *never* important enough to make your list?" she said. Her voice was a few decibels below what might qualify as screaming, but not much.

As soon as he saw her on the couch, Trey knew. All that dread snapped into place. They had an appointment with a fertility specialist that afternoon. Not only was he late, he promised to get home early. He'd put off the appointment longer than she wanted so they could get the last appointment of the day to accommodate his schedule. He hoped she went alone to ease the hurt somehow, but he knew that was not the case. Before he could answer she stood and faced him, a red fury filling every blood vessel in her face. On top of the crying, it multiplied the vivid red in her cheeks and ears.

"Where *were* you? I called your office and no one answered. I even called the guard and he said your car was gone so I felt better. Then I thought you were dead in a car accident or something," Carole broke down and sobbed into her pillow. Trey went to say something but Carole wanted none of it and cut him off.

"*Enough* already. Why are *we* last on the list? Your work eats at you and takes you away from us even when you are here. You won't even share with me what you think about. This is why you can't remember the one god...damn...appointment I need you to be here for. I don't get it. I can't get it. You won't let me get it," said Carole, punctuating each word with a jab of a finger toward Trey.

Trey felt awful. This was as colossal a screw up as he had ever committed in their relationship. He went to her and tried to hold her.

"I-I-I don't know what to say, I," he stammered. His idea to get near Carole backfired badly. Very badly.

"BEER!" she screamed. "You smell of goddamn BEER? You went drinking? BEER comes before us and a family? Do you give a shit about us at all?" Carole fell to her knees and buried her face in the pillow, crying in uncontrollable sobs that sucked the breath from her. Trey tried again to hold her, but she turned and pushed him away violently. He fell back on the floor, his back on an easy chair next to the couch where Carole laid, head buried and sobbing. Trey knew silence was best at this moment and wondered exactly how he left this off his mental radar. They did want a family but Trey was never sure when the time was right. After three months of being off the pill to no result, Carole was panicked, more so than Trey. He felt certain they would conceive but Carole wanted the appointment to be sure. She wanted to know if there was a problem so they did not spend months in futility when actions could be taken to get her pregnant. Trey agreed to the appointment but she mistook his confidence and calm for indifference. When Carole announced she made the appointment at the end of the day to accommodate his schedule, Trey knew how serious and kind she was trying to be as he had not asked for such extraordinary measures. He sat on the floor and felt like an utter failure. He questioned if indeed he was subconsciously afraid of all the new responsibilities fatherhood would bring. He knew work only promised to be a misery for the months ahead. He teared up at the unlikelihood that his father Earl would be around to see the birth of a grandchild. Trey placed his palms on his forehead and let Carole's pain wash over him. He was helpless at this moment. He always had the next move, knew the next step. Now he had none. He got onto his knees and stroked Carole's hair, soothing her.

"I do not know how. I do not know when, but I will make this right somehow," he whispered in her ear. "I will not go away unless you want me to but I would rather be here and try to make this better."

Trey just sat with her quietly as her sobs slowly quieted and the room ebbed light as gathering twilight filled the room.

CHAPTER 18

———◆•●•◆———

UNION YES

Saturdays were generally carefree and fun for Trey and Carole, but after his awful screw-up a terrible, uneasy truce fell into place. Carole exhausted herself sobbing and fell asleep on the couch. When Trey realized her breathing was easy and regular, he covered her in a light blanket. After Belvedere hopped up and curled into the curve of Carole's fetal curl, Trey went upstairs and fell asleep in the bedroom. As first daylight snuck into the room's edges, he realized he was still alone in bed. He heard Carole downstairs in the kitchen and recognized the cat's squawks to be fed.

He went down to the kitchen. While she heard him, she did not turn from the kitchen counter where she was preparing Belvedere's dish. Trey touched her on the arm. Carole did not turn but uttered "Good morning" in a flat tone.

"How did you sleep?" he asked.

"Hard. Deep. I am glad I didn't wake at all until just now. Belvedere's purring woke me. It was not a bad way to wake up," she said. She turned to put the cat's food bowl down in a direction to avoid physical and eye contact with Trey. He looked for some way forward.

"I'll go out and grab a couple of bagels," he said. He deliberately phrased it as a statement rather than a question as he could not bear any indifference from Carole. He needed to get out and think about the days ahead. He needed the fresh air and realized the house was stuffy from a night closed up. He opened the sliding glass door to the patio and the air was like a lifeline, gently moving the vertical blind slats.

"Shut that, will you?" said Carole. "I'm cold." Trey slid the door shut.

He realized he and Carole were out of synch in every possible way. He did not want to do anything but help. The biggest help was to get out right now, but not in a huff. He slid on his sneakers, a pair of shorts and a T-shirt and headed out. He knew her favorite bagel and wanted to show some small way he was close to her- that he knew her, even if she felt she no longer knew him.

"I'll be back in a few minutes. I'll get you your poppy seed bagel," he said. There was no answer. He did not deserve any credit but was begging for it. The house was still. He went out the door to the car.

Driving to the bagel shop, Trey realized he wanted to see his father. A few days ago he had a notion to head to his parents' house today. At the time, he knew the extra visit would not get a lot of encouragement from Carole. She would surely not go. She did not like the neighborhood and felt awkward being there outside of holidays and special occasions. She liked his parents but had nothing in common with them. When Trey and his family talked it appeared to her as code with references from a past she did not know or understand. While she would never stop Trey from going, a Saturday visit would seem like a visit better made on a weekday. Trey knew his father was struggling. He was concerned his mother was too close to see the deterioration of her husband's condition. Over 40 years of marriage had made his mother blind to some things. Her love for Earl made her see him through idealized eyes. Trey imagined she saw her Earl frozen in 1944, when they first met. He thought this was a very real possibility. He recalled a time several years ago when he stopped in unexpectedly to see his parents and found his father at the breakfast table, an omelet in front of him untouched.

"Pop, what's up? Have a bad night?" Trey asked.

His mother answered for her husband saying, "Oh he has a little tummy ache so I fixed him something bland to steady him."

Trey looked at his father carefully but could see that this was no garden-variety stomach ache. His father looked up at him and Trey could see yellow, hollow eyes.

"Mom, he's not well. He looks bad. He is the color of a banana. Jaundice is not good."

At Trey's insistence, they took his father to the Emergency Room where they found a failing gall bladder. It was at that moment Trey knew he passed the stop from child to caretaker-in-waiting. His mother's cataracts of love were simultaneously charming and alarming. If she could not see her husband as anything less than perfect, what would she miss today?

Trey wanted very badly to visit them today but knew that it was not the time to be away from Carole.

As troubled as he was at the state of his relationship with Carole, thoughts of his father consumed him. The stories from his father suddenly seemed more than just random tales to pass the time. As he waited in line at the bagel shop, his thoughts drifted to another time, another discussion with his father.

July 1955

When the union lost their organizing bid at Superior Plastics Earl was pragmatic. During the election campaign, management worked from a base of their core supporters and slowly built a coalition outward to a lot of the undecided workers, weaving a subtle quilt of patronage and favors. Once a majority was achieved and the election secured, they had a year to work the other end of the support spectrum and root out any staunch union supporter. Such a practice was illegal, but done skillfully, the actions impossible to prove. Schedules get changed. Scrutiny of the quality of work gets tighter. Raises are denied. Suddenly, the best wages are actually paid elsewhere. The union supporters were slowly drawn by economics away from Superior. One by one, the workplace was cleansed of the strongest union supporters.

Earl was one of the workers lured away. He endured six months on the midnight shift with little overtime until he applied to Global Book Warehouse in Belleville. The three-story building was the northeast distribution point for textbooks and training manuals for most school districts. To qualify, Earl needed to learn to drive a forklift. His neighbor, who worked for the warehouse and tipped Earl to the job opening, snuck Earl in the weekend before and taught him how to operate the forklift and pass the test.

Once hired, Earl found the job quieter and nicer than a lot of factory production jobs. Global employed about 90 employees, about two thirds of them in the warehouse jockeying pallets of books onto delivery trucks. There the remaining third of the employees operated delivery routes to a bevy of customers. The cavernous warehouse was devoid of machinery that heated the air, and that heat created by the armada of forklifts inside dissipated upward into the high-ceiling lofts. The workers were congenial and overtime was plentiful, especially during the summer when school districts stocked up on books.

Business was good and the warehouse was abuzz. A population boom of postwar kids needed to learn to read and write. Global expanded its business steadily but unspectacularly for a couple of years then came upon an opportunity to distribute books to the New York City school system. It was a huge break. One major unexpected stumbling block stood in the way: Global was non-union. The New York City schools were a union stronghold. There were objections to the city using non-union labor as the source for the schoolbooks. Besides, shouldn't the schoolchildren see the union logo on all trucks and goods within the schoolhouse grounds? There was another generation of dues-paying members to be educated here. As Global advanced through the bidding process, officials in the city pointed out Global would be a good partner except for the controversy arising from the non-union status. With a history of good relationships with their employees, Global management evaluated their options. Ultimately, it created an odd marriage of convenience: Global would invite unions in.

When it became clear to the employees it was in their economic interest to be unionized, they began to interview various unions. They lined up like suitors at a singles dance. This was the easiest success a union would ever come across. Minimal organizing costs. A welcoming management. It was almost too good to be true.

The Global employees met and vetted their options. They did a good job of playing the unions off one another to obtain the lowest possible dues structure. By virtue of his involvement at the failed Superior Plastics unionization attempt, Earl was seen as a de facto expert and drafted by the employees as an integral part of the committee to assess the options before them.

The Global employee committee split up the duties and set out to interview each union. A team of three Global employees arranged informational meetings with their prospective representatives. They initially identified eight potential union affiliations and created a book listing pros and cons. Initially, there was great enthusiasm from each of the unions. However, as the weeks went by, much of the initial interest by the unions waned. Some withdrew, citing an incompatibility with their charter. Others felt the 90-man membership unit was too small to be of interest. Another simply stopped answering calls.

While Earl and others found this diminished interest disconcerting, it was not necessarily alarming. In the end, they still had three interested suitors— the Teamsters, the International Warehouse Workers (IWW) and the Brotherhood of Industrial Trades (BIT).

Earl took on the investigation of the International Warehouse Workers and was invited to the next general membership meeting to watch the proceedings. Earl left his forklift job at the urging of Global management to arrive early and get to know the leadership of the IWW. Their offices were a remodeled brick factory in Jersey City. The inside walls were gutted and offices inserted in a crazy quilt of doors and partitions of the various officers and union administrators. Each office looked like it had not been painted in many years, the doors worn at shoulder height where a person might push on the door entering or exiting. Most offices had no ceiling. They looked like cubicles with doors. Cigarette smoke rose from every office, giving it an effect of an odd aluminum bound village with chimneys noting which residents were home stoking the fires. Inside each office it appeared the occupant had built a fort of paperwork around their desk and in boxes behind their chairs. It was not clear who occupied the offices and to what purpose as there were no placards announcing their name or function.

Next to the union offices was a mock-up of a warehouse—the IWW Training Center. Here, out-of-work men (the union felt women's anatomy were not suited to the jarring vibration of the crude forklift on the pitted concrete floors of IWW sites) were trained on the basic operation of a wide variety of material handling equipment starting from the simple pallet jack and extending all the way to monster diesel extended-reach forklifts that rose 25 feet in the air at peak. The training center seemed to be the crown jewel for the IWW. In stark contrast to the business office, the mock warehouse was well-lit and well-marked. Nearly new forklifts were parked in a neat row and in size order. The floor was epoxy sealed and shiny. Warehouse racks in dozens of different configurations extended almost two stories up. The IWW may not have gotten the knack of administration, but their members knew warehousing. The training center was a comforting sight.

Earl arrived early to make informal contact before the larger union meeting. While not yet a card-carrying member, Earl felt an easy comfort with the union personnel and he spoke easily and confidently with them. He was treated as a minor celebrity when he arrived. After a short tour of the facility union President Mike Trach greeted Earl in the spacious lobby. It was decorated with pictures of IWW leadership with various celebrities and politicians, as well as sponsorship plaques for local Little League teams. The teams of 12-year-olds beamed in the best uniforms embroidered with IWW across their hats and T-shirts.

Trach was actually a clipped version of his immigrant parents' name, Trachi. Trach was a large square man with slicked-back, jet black hair exposing a stony jaw. His beefy hand swallowed Earl's in a vice-like handshake that lingered a beat too long. Trach's success was built on self-awareness. He understood every action sent a message and he never missed an opportunity to telegraph toughness.

Trach took Earl back through the jumble of administrative offices to the deepest recesses of the building. Several turns later, Earl was disoriented by the maze and thankful for a host like Trach. Suddenly, the office opened to a much more spacious area. A large waiting room with comfortable couches and easy chairs revealed itself. The area flanked a large reception desk staffed by an attractive young receptionist who wore too much makeup. The rug was a custom-made piece with the symbols of the IWW—a flexed bicep, forklift truck and an eagle. Trach moved quickly past the receptionist. She was on the phone but he pantomimed that they would require something to drink. She nodded as they went by. Her eyelashes looked like bird wings.

Trach's office was a stark contrast to the shabby administrative offices closer to the lobby. His desk was large by any standard, but Earl noticed it was contrasted by slightly smaller guest chairs to accentuate its size. On each side, floor-to-ceiling windows bathed the desk in light. There were two or three large leather easy chairs in the corners of the room and a very large conference table to the side. One wall held a chalkboard and the other a corkboard and some large easels with paper. This was the center of the IWW universe.

Waiting for Earl and Trach were the Treasurer of the International, John Weller, and the Vice President, Gladrey Smith.

Earl was by nature both curious and thorough. At first they went through a ton of mundane details. The International organization chart. The history of the union. Great victories they had gained for their local unions. Upcoming strategies on wages and benefits. Political affiliations and their legislative agenda. Throughout this, Smith spouted off a presentation he seemed to have memorized. Doubtless he had recited this or a similar spiel hundreds of times.

Trach nodded his approval of the performance and Weller sat calmly behind wire-rimmed glasses, glancing at a clipboard of papers that seemed to interest him more than this meeting.

After the basics, Earl went a level deeper in his fact finding. The dwindling number of union suitors for the bargaining unit at Global was a puzzle and he probed a bit. He was still addressing Gladrey when he asked:

"Certainly this situation is unusual—an invitation to unionize—but how do you evaluate our fit with your union? Have you ever looked at a unit and decided it was not worth your time?"

The question immediately grabbed Trach's interest as he cocked his head, not unlike a dog hearing a sound above the range of human reception. Weller looked up from his papers and caught the glance of Trach. Smith was leaning forward to answer when Trach cut him off.

"What would make you ask that question, Mr. Bensen?" said Trach, with a tone of formality creeping into his voice for the very first time.

Earl had struck a nerve and he felt it immediately. He paused to consider his options. His bias was toward the truth as it was easiest to remember, but clearly he was in a sensitive area here. He wanted to choose his words carefully.

"Frankly," Earl began, "we have been surprised that some of the unions have not returned our calls or flat-out withdrawn from the process. We want to understand what we may have done to offend."

"Then why ask us that question?" said Trach, pointing a beefy finger back at himself to punctuate the statement. "We are interested and think you are a worthy group." His signals were unmistakable. By pointing at himself, he made it clear that Mike Trach and the IWW were one and the same. By declaring the Global employees were worthy, he turned the tables on who was making the selection. That finely honed self-awareness was making itself felt. Like a well-rehearsed dance partner, Smith settled back and let Trach take over the room. Earl was surprised at how quickly he felt back on his heels. This would not be a bad trait at the negotiating table but he was trying to feel the brotherhood. At this moment, he did not.

"I try to learn from anyone who seems to have something to offer," said Earl. It was a weak attempt to de-escalate the mood. He realized that his question was not going to receive an answer so he tried to move on to other topics. His prime goal was to understand the IWW dues structure. Initial conversations led to the offer from the IWW to halve the initiation fee and delay any dues collection until the IWW had their first contract in place. Given that Global needed a union contract to penetrate the lucrative New York City market this offer was not as generous as it appeared on the surface. The committee at Global disagreed as to the interpretation of that offer from the IWW and Earl needed to gain some clarity.

"Your offer to suspend dues payment until we have a contract in place is very generous. What our employees want to know is the exact amount of union dues per paycheck, the history of dues increases and how much control the local has of finances," said Earl. While he held a small spiral notepad in his hand, his questions were from memory and he spoke directly to Smith, hoping to rejoin the conversation in a friendlier tone.

This time it was Weller who spoke up. As the Treasurer, he wore a three-piece suit and his tie clasp was an IWW logo. He held a pencil with a large snap-on eraser, presumably because the original pencil eraser had been worn to the metal. As he prepared to speak, Weller placed the pencil behind his ear, the triangular eraser facing Earl. This professional tic somewhat betrayed his polished appearance. He was curt and almost dismissive in his reply.

"Dues vary. It depends on the size of the unit, growth, the issues locally. It'll be hard to say what your dues will be but we will discuss it with you, that is for sure. As for finances, the local has control of their finances, except for what they send to us. Once it gets to the International, your local will have a member on the Board and we will look at larger issues," said Weller. Earl thought it was the tersest non-answer he had ever heard.

Trach was now fidgeting. This meeting had gone on too long to hold his attention any longer. He picked up his tempo.

"Look, I've got to get ready for the general membership meeting. We hold these every month. Your guys are always welcome to come to these. I am sure we are the best fit for your guys. You're a warehouse, no? Do you see anyone else with 'warehouse' in the name of the union? You saw our training facility. Anyone else have that? I am glad you are here. We are made for each other. If you have more questions, feel free to ask them at the meeting. You'll get a better feel there. If your guys talk and you need something else from us, we may be able to do a little something for you. We can send any of our guys down there to talk to you or I can even come myself. Whatever you need," said Trach.

Smith and Weller escorted Earl back through the offices and into the larger meeting hall. A crowd was beginning to gather. They were treated to sandwiches wrapped in white butcher paper and placed in barrels at each end of a long table. Hanging above the table was a large wooden representation of the ubiquitous IWW logo. Underneath the table a keg of beer sat in a vat of ice. A long rubber hose snaked up from under the table and terminated in a tap. Two pyramids of frosted beer mugs flanked the tap. The IWW knew what the local reps wanted.

The pre-meeting was full of genial camaraderie and Earl felt far more at ease among the local reps. Their stories and frustrations were comfortable and familiar. They swapped war stories of recent negotiations and how they won the day. They traded up at this point in life from stories of high school glory on the athletic field to their exploits at the bargaining table. They had a sense of control that bonded them, along with their satin IWW logo jackets.

Before long the meeting began and the free flow of beer made for a loud but orderly session. Earl was introduced as a potential new brother and greeted with warm applause and throaty shouts. He observed the order of business and the kinds of issues being discussed—grievance case status, upcoming negotiations, changes in local leaders.

The meeting ended with an open forum where questions were taken from the floor. Trach sat on a raised stage flanked by Weller and Smith. Beyond them to each side sat senior local leaders on International-level committees. The locals contributed little except to sip their beer. Earl decided to ask a question. There was a dull murmur of side conversations in the room and no microphone so he had to raise his voice to be heard clearly.

"I see the audit committee passed on their report this month. How often do they report and what kinds of things do they look at typically and who sits on the committee?" asked Earl. His questions made no dent in the white noise of beer-fueled conversations.

Weller shot a glance toward Trach to determine if he was to answer the question. Trach raised his palm to Weller to indicate he had the response. The dais had microphones and Trach leaned in saying: "That is a question that is hard to answer completely in a group setting like this." Trach was actually smiling a wide toothy smile now. "So I will ask that we get an opportunity to explain that in a private conversation." Trach then swiveled to find a friendly face in the crowd and asked, "Mikey, can you show Mr. Bensen to the conference room so we can talk? He won't know how to get there."

Mikey was a younger man, pockmarked with scars of an earlier acne *plague. He was tall and slim and had a head of hair that was so carefully coiffed as to hint he doted on his style. Mikey raised his hand high to identify himself and met Earl halfway across the room. It was obvious the meeting was winding down and Earl was anxious to get his answers and get home. The meeting hall was ringed with unmarked doors and Earl had no idea where he might be in relation to where he began his trip. Mikey was expressionless as he led Earl into a dimly lit hallway. He advanced a few steps and then pointed to a lighted conference room.*

"Wait in there, they'll be right with you," said Mikey in a flat monotone. Earl was disturbed by the indefinite time for the meeting and fretted about how late he would get home. He'd wait a few minutes, he thought, but if they were too long in arriving, he would find his way out of this maze and set up a call later in the week.

Earl was not kept waiting long. As he entered the room, he felt an unexpected shove. He lost his balance and stumbled left trying to keep his balance. Simultaneously he tried to process how he lost his balance. Had he stumbled? He used his left hand to touch the floor and try to stand and regain his balance, but he was shoved against a wooden easel in the room. He landed with his back against the easel with a loud crack as the weight of his body slammed the wood frame against the wall. Earl saw two men coming at him and knew he was in trouble.

"Welcome to the fucking Audit Committee, wiseass," said one. He was actually likely the first one who grabbed Earl as he entered the room. He was not very tall but exceptionally strong as he picked up Earl's entire body weight—maybe 170 pounds—and threw him across the room toward the door where he entered. Earl landed on the floor and slid into the corner. He was simultaneously processing all that was going on and looking for an exit. Surely if he got into the halls, they would not pursue him and risk the locals seeing a prospective member getting roughed up. Would they?

"Why insult us if you want to join us?" said the second man, who was taller and heavier but not as fit as the strong man who just deposited him in this corner. Earl knew immediately that this was not a question requiring an answer. He braced for whatever was to come. Fighting against even the weaker of the two would have been an iffy outcome, but Earl quickly calculated terrible odds fighting both. The strong man approached Earl, grabbed his notebook and took it from him, ripping it into pieces.

"The IWW cares about its members. They would never do anything wrong against their brothers. They have never been out of line with the finances. Nobody has ever taken a nickel that did not belong to them. There is your fucking answer. When the audit committee meets, they find it is all in order like it should be. Does that answer your question?" the second, taller man asked. *Oddly, he betrayed no anger. His voice was flat and matter-of-fact.*

Earl was calculating his answer carefully.

"Yes, I understand fully. That is very clear," said Earl. He felt no pain but realized he had a little blood on his pinky. He did not realize he had a small cut on his chin.

The doughier man took his turn to speak. He kicked an aluminum chair out of the way that clanged as it landed. He was pleased that the chair made such an intimidating clatter.

"There is a perfect match here between the IWW and Global. It is a shame that you don't see it and have to ask all these stupid questions. But now I hope you can go back to your committee and understand that we have a lot of strength we can bring to the table. I think you see that now, no?"

"Strength. Yes. Very clear to see. You would bring a lot to the table," said Earl, who was more angry than afraid, but was trying to calculate what would get him out of this situation with the minimal amount of physical damage.

The strong man wanted a more definitive statement.

"So we can put you on record as saying you see us as the fit for your guys?" he said.

Earl thought for a moment, realizing this answer might be critical. He did not want to lie. He considered the fact that right now other members of the Global employee committee were with other unions this very moment. Were they in the same odd spot, professing their preferences? Even as this whirling crisis unfolded and slowed time down, Earl sensed he was taking too long as the strong man took a half step toward him.

"I can make a recommendation, sure," said Earl. He hoped that this half statement would get him through the next few moments but knew his next step was utter capitulation.

"Good," said the strong man. He took another step forward and extended his hand toward Earl, still sprawled on the floor. Earl eyed him to be sure it was not the set up for a sucker punch, but as Earl extended his hand, the man lifted him to his feet with ease with the greeting "Good, Brother, good."

The hallways were narrow. So narrow no two of them could easily walk side by side, so Earl walked a step ahead of the IWW persuaders. Earl's senses tingled as he considered they might try to make one more physical statement to remind him of his pledge, however parsed. But there was no more drama this night. They escorted him through a side door and left him in an abandoned parking lot that abutted the IWW complex on one side. The hot July night sky roiled with heat lightning but threatened no rain.

"You know the way to the bus stop, right?" the dough boy asked. "Be careful going home tonight."

Earl walked three blocks to the bus stop and processed all he had seen and heard. He tried to figure out what to tell the committee and how to serve their interests. As the bus pulled up, there were just two other passengers. Every window on the bus was open and the interior lights were out. Earl paid his fare and the bus driver noted: "The air conditioning is not working so I am leaving the lights out inside so we stay cool. If you want the lights on to read or something, go talk to the rest of them. They want it as cool as they can get it."

Earl nodded and sat in the first open window seat he could find. He had nothing to read. It was a hot, uncomfortable night. He did not particularly want to be seen. The dark suited him fine.

Although he fretted all 17 stops until he got near home, he did not need to. The die was actually already cast. Over the next two weeks, the other unions withdrew their interest in representing the employees at Global. Both of the other unions expressed supreme confidence in the IWW as the best choice and a great example of union ingenuity and pride. They sent glowing letters of recommendation to assuage the employees of Global, who no longer had a choice. The most skeptical members of the employee committee approached Global management with an idea to stay non-union. Global counseled against that tactic. Without the New York school contract, the business would shrink and layoffs would soon follow. Management at Global urged the employees to accept the IWW and assured them nothing would change except for the union symbol on the trucks allowing passage through the Lincoln Tunnel and onto the streets of the city.

Five weeks later, the employees voted to be represented by the IWW. Four months later, the first contract negotiated by the IWW with Global averaged an increase of 17 cents an hour over three years and dues were set at $5 a paycheck. Earl refused nomination as a member of the local leadership. He *began to search the want ads again. His wife was about to have a baby. He needed a better job.*

Trey did not even realize how deeply his mind had drifted. As he plopped into his car, he could not clearly recall the transaction in the bagel shop except that the line was too long and the service too slow. He opened the bag and saw three bagels. None were poppy seed. That awful feeling came back to the pit of his stomach. Where was his mind? He got out of the car, determined to stand in that line again and make the poppy seed bagel himself if necessary.

CHAPTER 19

SETTING THE STAGE

Two weeks passed since Trey failed to keep the appointment at the fertility specialist. Carole had not spoken a word about it. Trey tried gently probing the outskirts of the issue, asking Carole to reschedule the appointment, but she would not engage in the conversation. She would either icily change the subject or just state flatly: "I will, when I'm ready." The relationship settled into an uneasy, tenuous calm.

Trey briefly considered making the appointment himself as an act of initiative and then telling Carole about it but decided that was too risky. The mood had evolved from awful to just tepid. Conversations were pleasant but too stiff to be real. Eventually, Trey would have to bring this to a head, but he wanted to give it some more time. If Carole could bring the issue to a conclusion in her way, he decided that would be best.

In addition to the mess at home, Trey's father was a growing concern. The oxygen treatment seemed to have less impact and Earl's stamina declined in each visit. The days were getting longer, hotter and stickier. The air seemed to suffocate the able-bodied. It was devastating Earl.

Then there was the situation at Grean. The production surge was in full swing. It was as if giant unseen bellows stoked the intensity of the plant in every corner. The pace of the plant leaked out into the neighborhood as well. The plant provided the area with a heartbeat both financially and physically. The physical manifestation of the plant was the low hum and thump. On normal days it was like listening to your own calm heartbeat. Lately, the beat was just a little louder and more insistent. It ran deeper into the night and began earlier in the morning. The sounds were intensified by open windows at the plant and in the neighborhood. It was noticeable to the point the Council of Elders had become aware. One morning, they questioned Trey.

"Hey, Mr. Attorney, what are you guys building over there—secret bombs?" one of the Council members asked.

Trey thought about the secret bombs that were indeed being built but sat unexploded for now. The day Harlowe and Larry would detonate those bombs was fast approaching. Trey smiled wryly at the irony: the build plan was so successful, it hastened the meeting that would cost many their jobs. If the employees were somehow less dedicated, less efficient, those paychecks would keep coming a little longer. It made Trey sick.

Harlowe called earlier in the week to ask for another meeting with Larry Turkel. He wanted to ensure the players knew their lines. Trey arranged the meeting to take place in Harlowe's hotel room later this day. The stakes were high enough to make everyone edgy. It was decided that another jaunt to the country club was too risky. It was unlikely that anyone that mattered would see Larry there but why risk it at this point?

Since Ike was preoccupied with making the plant run at high speed, he reluctantly bowed out of the meeting at the hotel but counseled Trey to be vigilant and supportive. He did not want Harlowe or Larry to leave doubting his resolve.

The Hyatt at Newark airport was a good spot to be anonymous. It was filled with nondescript rental cars and visitors from all over the world. As he pulled into the parking lot, Trey realized that Larry was not one to attempt anonymity. He drove a big, dark blue Cadillac sporting "UNION YES" bumper stickers on both sides of what might qualify as a double-wide car. Equipped to handle the special needs of his size, it even had a pop-down step built in so Larry could descend. In many ways, the huge car only called out in irony, but if Larry understood this at any level, he did not betray it. Larry loved an entrance and the car was just a prop. Trey parked at the far end of the lot away from Larry and gave up any concerns about appearances.

Trey headed to the fifth floor. Harlowe upgraded to a suite, perhaps to impress upon Larry the importance of the meeting. An array of food and drink—enough to feed 10—sat on tables against the wall of the living area of the suite. Larry and Harlowe seemed to be drinking hard liquor when Trey arrived. Larry got in the first salvo and quickly.

"This looked like an important meeting but now Ike sends the 'B' team?" asked Larry. He said this with a mischievous smile to leave latitude to interpret this as a joke or an opinion, but it was clear: Trey's standing in the meeting had been cemented. Larry the alpha dog asserted his spot by pissing on Trey.

After some small talk, Harlowe sat in an easy chair in the corner and Trey on a couch along the wall while Larry pulled the highest chair from a dining set and sat, taking the high ground. Harlowe began the conversation.

"In about a week, Trey will call a meeting through the local union and ask that you join us. He will say that I am requesting the meeting out of Grean HQ in Orlando. He will not know the content of the meeting just but that it is important."

Already Trey understood this would put him in a terrible situation with Mo and Tommy. They would insist that he knew the meeting content. Not knowing he risked becoming irrelevant in their eyes, he pondered whether it was preferable to be a liar or impotent. Heeding Ike's advice, Trey chose not to say a word in this meeting unless asked directly.

"I'll fly in the night before and we will hold the meeting at 9 a.m. I'll lead the management side, which will include Trey and Ike. We will announce that, sadly, a decision has been made to close the plant and move it to several locations. The shutdown will begin within a month and be completed within a year. I will say that we plan to honor all contractual obligations to severance," said Harlowe. Larry felt uncomfortable, even in this setting, to let Harlowe have the floor so long without interruption.

Larry broke in: "I'll remind you of the obligation to bargain about the terms and conditions of the closure. I'll take a caucus and let the guys let off steam. I will come back with a counterproposal that we form a joint committee to look at cost structures and find a way to keep the plant where it is today. I think you'd better take a caucus to think about that." It amused Trey to see such a contrast between the intensity in Larry's eyes and the fact his feet did not touch the floor. The disconnect was absurd, but Trey did not dare allow the tiniest corner of a smile to emerge. He was smack dab in the middle of the shark tank and trying to avoid a feeding frenzy.

Harlowe volleyed, "We can have that meeting, but we can't drag this out. The customer needs us to move this along quickly and once we talk about this with your guys, it could leak and force us to file an intention to close with the state and trigger all kinds of regulatory bullshit."

"Your bullshit is your problem," said Larry. He was establishing that while complicit in this charade, he was not going to be sloppy. "We need to go through the steps and make sure this shows like we have saved a lot of jobs. Remember, that helps you preserve morale."

Harlowe thought about debating who exactly benefited most from this series of events but he wisely demurred. He flashed back to the Grean brothers and their need for speed. He wondered why he had ever agreed to this more complicated scenario, but he needed Larry—heart and soul. He could feel the big payday in his grasp. Harlowe relished his reputation as The Fixer and this might be his crowning achievement if he could pull it off.

"I'll agree to stay in town and talk out of good faith but let's not let more than a day go by," said Harlowe.

The meeting went on for some time as Harlowe and Larry practiced their lines and informed each other of how the session might go. Trey was a very interested, if uninvolved, spectator. He took some general notes on a legal pad in case he was asked to sum up and to be sure he could convey the final format to Ike accurately. Trey could see Larry was eyeing him with some suspicion as he took his notes. If Larry got irritated, Trey accepted he would be the object of his wrath not Harlowe. It had been a good 45 minutes since the last time Larry turned on Trey to assert himself so Trey knew he was overdue.

After some debate, the two arrived at a scenario that Trey marveled at as creative and believable. Larry suggested that when the union returned they would propose a new and lower starting wage scale for future employees only. This second tier would not impact any current employees, so it provided some savings at no risk to anyone employed today. Grean could value this concession however they wanted, and call it a good start, but not totally responsive. This would allow Grean to counter the union offer with a much smaller move of one department of machines plus the second tier of wages for future employees. They could hold additional meetings at any time but this would be essentially for show. Grean would get their move, Larry would appear to save the majority of the plant, and no current employee wages would be impacted. Except for the 50 or so most junior employees who would be laid off and receive severance, there would be no losers. Had the Grean brothers been in the room, they would have flashed $300 million smiles.

Overall, the discussion lasted several hours. Larry eventually left his seat and began pacing the room in a waddling gait, suggesting various scenarios. As Larry paced and mused, he rattled off suggestions to Harlowe how he might change his oratory dependent upon circumstances and who he might have to convince among the union committee .

As the discussions continued, Trey became almost invisible except for an occasional question about the personal situations on various union members. While the answers were factual and neutral, Trey noticed that Harlowe and Larry began to use the information to fit their rosiest world view.

"How old is Tommy Pherrel now?" asked Larry.

"Early fifties," Trey replied.

"Kids?"

"Two daughters."

"College age?"

"Both married now. Never went to college that I know."

Larry chewed on this a bit while contemplating ice swirling in the bottom of his glass.

"Good, just the right age—he'll want to hang on another 10 years so he won't give a shit unless the layoffs reach him, which they won't since he replaced Christ on the job."

Trey knew Larry was wrong. Tommy did not have a ton of seniority despite his age. Tommy had come over mid-career to join Grean. What Tommy had was a rare job title that would not be impacted by the layoffs. Larry was right for the wrong reason and it flashed through Trey's mind to correct Larry but he immediately thought better of it. Why invite the enmity?

Trey realized Larry was likely right in one sense: Tommy was not the kind of guy who deeply contemplated the morality of issues and was more likely to want to understand how existing union rules applied. Still, if this exercise in script writing was also meant to anticipate the day's events, it might be worthwhile to think through a few remote possibilities. But Trey understood his role was to supply facts, not speculate or question.

By the time the session ended, the ice in the buckets on the buffet table was frigid slurry. Harlowe and Larry were satisfied they had accomplished their goals. Harlowe could report back to the Greans all was well. Larry could see his star rise in the International union ranks for having deftly struck a blow for labor everywhere by saving the plant. It all struck Trey as perverse. The whole plan would be set into motion the next morning by Trey and his call for the mysterious meeting.

Since he lost most of the day to this session, Trey decided to go back to the plant briefly and see what was going on. As he arrived shortly after 6 p.m. the parking lot was fuller than it had been in some time. The new employees were more likely to be assigned a night shift so it did not surprise Trey that a lot of the faces he saw on the floor were unfamiliar. The floor shook with the mechanized fury usually reserved for the day shift. The press operators, green and hoping to make good, seemed more attentive than the cool certainty and vague boredom of the experienced operators of the day shift. By virtue of his jacket and tie, Trey was vested with the mantle of great respect by the new employees—uncertain of who might determine their fate of 60-day probationary status. One of the new press operators called Trey over as he walked through. He was covered with a rime of sweat. His hair looked ragged, as if chopped from a much longer style. His left ear bore the hole of a missing earring. He took a deep breath before speaking, hinting he was taking a great risk in what he was about to say.

"How are we all doing? It is great that we are so busy. I can't lie. I need this job. I hope we are doing OK so we can all get in the union. I can't screw around anymore in life. I know everybody here is trying. I hope you guys see that," he said.

Trey looked at him and searched for his badge, which was clipped to his tattered short sleeve and read "KENNY CIESLA."

"Kenny, if you come in every day and know you gave it your best you can sleep at night. Nobody can ask you for more than that," said Trey. He reached out and shook Kenny's hand.

"Have a safe night and keep up the good work," Trey said.

Trey envisioned Kenny living in an apartment with a pregnant girlfriend. Whether that projection was even close to the truth was irrelevant. Trey felt sick, turned away and headed back to his car to go home.

Chapter 20

The Meeting

The day of the big meeting with the union had come. Trey greeted it with a mixture of relief and dread. His past experience led to the conclusion: the more he dreaded events, the less likely they were to result in the worst outcome. Rarely did reality match his blackest pessimism. But this was no ordinary time. Mentally and emotionally, he had been wrapped up in work. Things at home with Carole were improving but at the slowest pace. Trey's decision to let Carole resolve this wound was a convenient excuse on his part for inaction and he knew it. But he dared not begin an active plan to accelerate the healing and then be called into a greater fray at work. The possibility he would be consumed by work in the near term was very real and could not have come at a worse time. No, he knew this indifferent détente with Carole required an undivided attention he could not give at this point, so he waited, uneasily, and counted the days until the meeting and the aftermath.

Arranging the meeting was every bit as painful and emasculating as he had imagined. As he spoke to Mo and Tommy to arrange the logistics, they badgered Trey about the content of the meeting and why they needed the International Representative to be present. Proud of the fact that they could resolve issues without the International, Mo and Tommy vented their anger on Trey, certain he knew the reason for the meeting and livid he would not share it. The damage to the relationship was immediate and deep seated as the union became intransigent on the smallest issues. Trey also knew the union had been searching for more information from various sources throughout management. At least there Trey felt safe. There were

151

no leaks to be had. Only Ike and Trey knew what was about to transpire and Ike was too good a soldier to give a shred of information away.

For the union, the meeting represented a set of contradictions. The plant was surging on all shifts. New employees were hired weekly and the orientation sessions each Monday were crowded with neighborhood locals who were simultaneously eager and desperate. Overtime was abundant. Yet experience told both the newly hired and the seasoned employees that unscheduled meetings called by management did not bode well. The local union leadership was besieged by their membership, many of whom were hooked on overtime the way a junkie gets hooked on heroin. The credit card bills look very reasonable until a 40-hour paycheck shows up when you have been used to the ease 50 and 60 hours pay brings in a relative sense. Just 10 hours—two overtime hours a day—equated to more than a 35% increase figuring in time and a half. The lack of trust spread like a cancer as the rank and file felt their union leadership also knew more than they were letting on. It was getting ugly quickly. Trey needed this over. Now.

About the only person who escaped suspicion was Larry Turkel. When questioned about what he knew, he replied, with some degree of honesty, that it was the local union that contacted *him* about the existence of the meeting and turned the question on its head. He claimed his calls ahead of the meeting to Grean were unanswered. It was a cruel irony that in the days that led up to the meeting Trey and the union locals were tearing into each other and that Harlowe and Larry stood as welcome entrants on the scene, unsullied but splattering mudballs of confusion in every direction.

The 10 a.m. meeting would take place in a makeshift building next to the main plant, creatively named "Building One." Originally built as a storage shed in the 1950s, it was expanded and reinforced several times to the point where it became a meeting and training center. Traditionally, contract negotiations were held there. It was big enough to accommodate large groups and had breakout rooms on the second floor so either side might caucus for a period of time, if necessary. It had a large kitchen that allowed caterers to heat their food and stage it. The building itself had a lot of subtle logistical advantages. It was not connected to the plant so eager eavesdroppers could not get close enough to hear what went on inside. Likewise, the walk to or from Building One allowed a certain staged theatrical messaging. Many times during negotiations, Trey and Ike carefully considered their expression, gestures and even if they might slouch their shoulders or walk with determined purpose as a way to telegraph non-verbal messages to both hourly and management personnel who looked for signals as intently as those who watched for the color of smoke from Vatican electoral enclaves.

Because every action sent messages—intended or not—Trey carefully considered the room setup. He arranged the tables and chairs in the style of negotiations. The union side would have three long tables to seat 10, while management would have two tables for five potential participants, although in this case there would only be three. If this was the OK Corral, the management side looked outgunned in the arrangement.

Harlowe arrived the night before and dined with Trey and Ike at the country club. Ike's always-nervous hands trembled a bit more in contrast to his words of calm assurance to Harlowe that all would turn out alright. For his part, Harlowe took smugness to an art form, his mouth curling into the smallest telltale smirk at the corners as he went over the intended flow of the conversation with the union.

Trey slept unusually well the night before the meeting, exhausted by the anticipation. Although he intended to run early that morning, a soaking rain changed his plans. He knew that without a run, his energy would be higher than normal and hoped for a quick meeting so he would not end up feeling like an unrelieved coiled spring. By 9:50, the meeting was just minutes away and Ike, Harlowe and Trey ducked into a pelting, wind-whipped rain with umbrellas providing scant shelter.

Over near Building One, a lone handicapped spot was created close to the main entrance, primarily to accommodate Larry. Because he did not like the designation of "handicapped," Larry lobbied for a reserved spot, but for Grean, that was a concession too far. Given the choice, Larry reluctantly accepted a handicapped spot. At five minutes to 10, the spot was still empty. The Turk loved to make an entrance.

Inside, the union governing board gathered around a stainless steel coffee urn, adding powdered creamer to weak coffee. The governing board was a carefully constructed group of seven stewards. Their qualifications took two forms: for one, they had to reflect the diversity and face of the membership. They were young and old. Black, Hispanic and white. They came from all departments. Male and female. They ranged in seniority from three years to almost 40. Second—and most important of all—they had to defer to Mo and Tommy, which in large part they did. The stewards liked their title, but preferred the heavy lifting be done by their leaders.

At 10:10 Trey spotted the outsized bright headlights of Larry's car cut through the gloom and rain and reflect on the far wall of the meeting room. Although close to the front door, Larry got quite wet walking from his car and entered the room, mopping his hair into a wet mess on top of his head.

"This better be good," he growled as he came in and immediately called a union caucus. Always looking to control the pace and flow of every meeting, Larry kept the union in their upstairs meeting room for close to an hour. Although smoking was not allowed in the building, almost two-thirds of the union committee smoked and the smell of lit cigarettes wafted down to the first floor. In any circumstance, Ike and Trey would turn a blind eye to this violation of rules, especially today.

Harlowe was getting bored, peering out the window as the rain found every low spot in the pavement to form impromptu lakes. Large drops of rain in the storm sent out overlapping and expanding rings in the vast puddles.

"What the fuck is he doing with them up there, writing the Gettysburg Address?" asked Harlowe.

"If he's pissing you off, he has just achieved his goal," said Trey, who was right but impertinent and the comment earned him an annoyed squint from Harlowe.

The union arrived in the room shortly before noon and arrayed themselves in a pecking order with Larry as the centerpiece, flanked by Mo on the left, Tommy on the right and the rest of the committee on each side. It struck Trey that this was the most bizarre rendering of the Last Supper imaginable.

On the management side, Ike, as the Plant Manager, sat in the middle flanked by Trey and Harlowe, but it was Harlowe who delivered the message, quickly, almost eagerly. Although Trey's official function was note taker, he carefully watched the faces of the union as Harlowe spoke.

"I am afraid I have some bad news. This plant in East Newark has been an important part of the Grean legacy. It is where it all began. But all things come and go. I am sad to announce that Grean Machining has decided to close this facility over the course of the next few months. Operations will be dispersed to various Grean locations around the country, absorbed or eliminated in some cases. As always, we will honor our contractual obligations to the union and the severance provisions contained in the contract."

Mo's eyes got large but just for a second. Even that tell was an amazing concession from such a seasoned negotiator as Mo. He quickly gathered his expression into an impassive, almost-bored stare. Tommy appeared to blow a shallow breath from billowed cheeks. The stewards were less nuanced. Some sat back while a couple edged closer to look down toward the middle of the table for cues from their leadership. Several ran nervous fingers through thinning hair. If they expected a quick and explosive reaction, they were disappointed. Larry answered calmly but firmly.

"We are all touched by how important this place is in history and how you treat its importance. We want a caucus," said Larry, with just the proper drip of sarcasm.

Harlowe looked like he was about to say something but Larry was already out of his chair and leading the charge to the doorway that led to the stairs and the caucus rooms. Some of the stewards at the far end of the table did not hear the statement from Larry and lingered. They appeared unsure if they were even invited to the caucus until Mo turned around and motioned for them all to join this hasty retreat. It had all the grace of the exit of grade school actors tromping off stage. In less than a minute, the union was gone again.

Trey, Ike and Harlowe repaired to their caucus room for the wait. This was always an awkward time. There was nothing to do but wait for the union to return. In normal circumstances, it could be a feverishly busy time as the management side would create an endless set of scenarios and responses and prepare for whatever the union returned to discuss. In negotiations, Trey liked these sessions in which scenarios were created, rebutted, changed, discarded, buffed. But this was not a normal caucus. This had been so carefully choreographed that there was nothing to do but wait and fidget. In the early days of radio broadcasts of sporting events, breathless announcers took the wire reports of games played far away and recreated them as if they were actually there. This day, Harlowe seemed to be in the union caucus room. He set his squinty eyes across the puddled parking lot and recreated what he believed was going on in the union caucus. Trey and Ike sat at the table and listened to Harlowe channel the recreation as he imagined it.

"The Turk is going to let them vent a while. I imagine a lot of those union guys are calling us all sons-of-bitches right now. They are sweating and Turk will feel them out. He will let them whip themselves into a frenzy. Exhaust their emotion. Drain the room. Cycle them through the stages of grief. I imagine he will let it settle down into a despondent quiet. Then he'll bring them back up that hill with ideas to save the day. They need hope and leadership and he will give it to them. He'll turn that tide and then no one is a loser. We just need to be patient. He does not want them back in there coming at us angry. You know, whatever they come back with, we will need to take a caucus ourselves. We cannot jump at this. We know how this movie ends, but we cannot skip the scenes—it'll look goofy," said Harlowe.

Ike sat nodding as if he was at an evangelical revival. Trey half expected Ike to give out a whooping "hallelujah" but he did not. Trey simultaneously admired and detested Harlowe's sure grip of the situation. It was nice to know there was such a degree of certainty, but as Trey imagined the union caucus room, he saw a group of marionettes tethered with strings, being jerked violently and ceaselessly.

Despite his acknowledgment of a process that needed to unfold, Harlowe grew impatient, quickly. A little past noon, the union called and asked that lunch be sent in. This meant the meeting would not reconvene until after 1:30 p.m. and that got Harlowe agitated.

"I guess those fuckers need to soak us for a lunch too. I guess if that is what Turk needs we need to give it to him, but he is dragging this out to a fare-thee-well," said Harlowe as his lips pursed to almost a sneer. Trey was not sure if Harlowe was totally earnest in his emotion or whipping himself into the state of mind required for the meeting. Ike quietly worked on a stack of purchasing documents he had sent over to pass the time. Trey anticipated lunch and signaled a local sandwich shop to deliver enough sandwiches to feed both union and management three times over.

As lunch morphed to early afternoon, Harlowe began to rehearse Ike and Trey on the order of events in the afternoon. The union would return.

Larry would lay out a union position to potentially save the plant. Harlowe would call caucus. This would last exactly 45 minutes. Harlowe wanted Ike to be the spokesperson at the meeting at that point and lay out some attainable financial goals that would save part of the plant. There would be a period of questions. Harlowe anticipated the meeting could turn ugly at that point if some of the union stewards felt the need to vent but he cautioned that at no point should management engage the emotion. There were times to fight and times to absorb the blow. Given the stakes, Harlowe was unusually willing to be the object of the wrath.

But the afternoon dragged on with no sign from the union they were about to return. It was now 2 p.m.. Harlowe was getting increasingly antsy, although he offered confidence the long caucus was a good sign.

"Turk is earning his dues today for a change. He is really working them hard," offered Harlowe, damning Larry with faint praise. Harlowe was whistling past the graveyard and was increasingly uneasy about the caucus duration.

By just before 3 p.m. Harlowe set a deadline of 3:15. Any later than that with no additional communication and he would send Trey over to get a status. Trey wondered if he could get "Cannon Fodder" added to the title on his business card and dreaded the trip. But Trey's fears were allayed when the phone rang, jolting the management troika to attention. The union was ready to meet again. They needed another five minutes.

The management team went immediately to the main negotiations room. They wanted to see the union file in and look for clues as to mood. The littlest things could be a sign—like if the seating order changed. Outside the hard rains gave way to dim sunlight slanting through the windows and cut odd triangular shapes across the union tables. Soon, the union team filed in. They looked disheveled and worn to Trey. They entered the room single file and took their seats, but there was no sign of Mo or Larry. As the room got quieter, it was evident that Larry and Mo were just outside in the hallway having a somewhat animated conversation. Their tone was hushed but emphatic. Suddenly they both entered and sat at the center of the table. Normally, Larry would take the lead in situations like this. The higher the drama the more he craved the center of the stage. So it was a great surprise when Mo proved to be their spokesperson. He spoke in calm, flat tones informed with the rough edges of decades of

Lucky Strikes. Larry's eyes looked a bit wide and his hair, once a wet mop from his walk in the rain, was a tangled mess on his head. The rest of the union fidgeted in their chairs and played with pencils as Mo began.

"As a union, and I speak for all of us," said Mo emphasizing the word "all" just a little more while sneaking a sideways glance, "we are very disappointed to hear that after all of us have given our lifetime of work to make Grean the company it is today, that you would close this plant and turn your backs on us. This is a betrayal but not an unexpected one after we thought about it. I doubt old Mr. Grean would have done this to us. This was his home and we were his family. But we understand those days are over. We talked this over long and hard as you can see. It took us hours to go over this. One thing we are happy with is you stated you will honor the contract and the law. We think the faster all of us can transition to new jobs the better. We are sure you understand the legal requirement to bargain about the terms and conditions of closure and we suggest we begin meeting on that tomorrow or the next day at the latest."

Then silence.

Trey looked at Harlowe who leaned a bit forward. Harlowe's eyes implored Larry to add something, anything. At that precise moment Larry looked away. The silence probably lasted no more than 8 to 10 seconds, but it was getting very uncomfortable. The script was out the window. Ike finally filled the void, his utterance as unexpected as Mo taking the lead for the union.

"M-M-Management would like to take a caucus conference," said Ike, in a half stutter.

Trey and Ike got up to leave but Harlowe stayed a moment longer, trying and failing in his effort to get eye contact. He finally got up and joined Ike and Trey. His entrance in the caucus room was emphatic as he slammed his fist against the table the second the caucus door closed. The violence of the action coupled with the crack of his fist against the table started Trey in particular.

"He FUCKED us!" Harlowe said in a fury. "He fucked us good. What the hell is that? Why the fuck is Mo in the lead? Does Larry think he can just abdicate his leadership and think he is not accountable?" Trey made a mental note that the affectionate "Turk" Harlowe usually assigned to the union leader had morphed to "Larry." It was reminiscent of Trey's childhood when, in trying to get his full attention, Trey's mother would address him as "Earl Aloysius." Harlowe was reeling around and striking out in many directions. His first turn was surprisingly at Ike.

"Why the hell are you taking a caucus? I have no idea what we are doing in here. I wanted to stay in there and find out more of what the fuck they are thinking. The script is gone and there is not a clue what we are doing right now," said Harlowe.

Ike explained himself saying, "You said we're going to take a caucus and when you didn't do anything. I thought I missed a cue and thought I was supposed to take the caucus." In that short sentence Ike developed a different tic and pushed his glasses up his nose three times in one breath. He did not like being on the wrong side of Harlowe, even for a minute.

"We were going to caucus after Larry proposed our solution. Once that went off the rails it doesn't make any sense for us to be in here with our dick in our hands! We need to be in there figuring out what went wrong," said Harlowe, beginning to pace the room.

Trey felt the need to throw Ike a rope. He stood up to make his point as emphatic as possible.

"Maybe this is just what we need. They were in there almost four hours and we obviously missed something big. Fumbling around in there won't do anything. If anything, if we are off script and say the wrong thing, it could make it worse. There is one person and one person only who can help us here and that is Larry. You can't expect him to just blurt it out in there. We need time, so let's think this through."

"We wouldn't need time to figure out shit if Larry could just keep his fucking word and keep his committee under control," said Harlowe in full froth. In talking out loud, Harlowe realized at some level the situation he hoped for was not the one they confronted at this minute. In an action as close as he would ever come to acknowledging Trey was right in his assessment, Harlowe pulled out a chair and slumped into it and said, "Let's figure out what our options are now."

For the next hour, Trey sat between Ike and Harlowe with a yellow legal pad turned horizontally and sketched out at least a dozen possible responses. They certainly could not go back in and say "only kidding, we don't want to close the plant," but they needed to get to that point. No matter how many responses they prepared, Trey's diagrams kept coming back to one indisputable fact: they needed to understand from Larry what went on in that room and why the union did not want to propose a plan to save the plant. In the end, they decided to schedule another meeting to discuss more particulars of the shutdown, but that meeting needed to be as far into the future as possible in order to recalibrate with Larry behind the scenes. The actual caucus might have been 20 minutes shorter but Harlowe was inconsolable and incredulous and repeated his disbelief that Larry (nee The Turk) had fucked this up.

When the management team re-entered the room, it struck Trey that there had been a reversal of roles since the day began. As he looked across the room at the union, they were gathered in groups of twos and threes calmly discussing things over coffee in foam cups. Other than Larry, who was flitting between the clustered groups like a wayward bee on a pollination run, the union team appeared at ease and in control of their emotions. As Trey looked at Harlowe and Ike, he saw their jaws clenched and taut veins exposed in their necks. If the union was looking for a tell, they had it. They had just given management exactly what they asked for and there was consternation and anxiety. Trey wondered what he looked like and quickly tried to create a visage of contented interest, whatever that looked like. In any case, he wondered if he had a telltale vein showing anywhere. He doubted it.

Harlowe ended Ike's brief turn as management spokesperson. He conjured up his best wily smile as he began.

"It has been a long day and unfortunately we did not get to spend much time together. We are thankful that the union took the time they did and came to such a reasoned decision. We obviously think there are a lot of topics to discuss regarding this action." Trey made a mental note that Harlow referred to "this action" and not a full scale closure. He was a man who was very careful about his lies, Trey thought.

Harlowe continued, "We propose an all-day meeting a week from today so we can both create an exhaustive list of the issues that need to be addressed. In addition, given the sensitive and potentially upsetting nature of this event, I would recommend a mutual agreement of non-disclosure until such time that we agree on a communications plan. Nothing said today should leave this room."

Trey wondered if Harlowe really thought news this big could be contained for an hour, let alone a week. The proposition was absurd and it annoyed Trey. Apparently Harlowe struck a nerve with the union, only this time it was Tommy Pherrell.

"A week?" Tommy began, his voice tinged with testiness. "How are we going to keep this from our membership in good faith for a day nevermind a week? How are we going to understand how to figure out the issues that need to be bargained about this closure if we can't talk about it? No, we can't wait a week and we won't keep secrets from our members. You asked for this. Let's meet tomorrow and meet again as often as we need to."

Tommy's defiant tone annoyed Harlowe more than the words, and red crept beyond his white collared shirt and up his neck. Harlowe looked ready to explode but was cut off by Larry who had been sitting in a deep sulk the entire time.

"We need three days. I can't be here tomorrow and besides, we need to think this through. Let's not rush something this important. The members cannot give us all the lists of demands by tomorrow morning. Besides, we all need to sleep on this," said Larry. Normally, Larry tried to make himself as big as possible in his chair but now he was slumped over, his hands flat on the desk in front of him, stretching forward. It looked like he was in position to be pilloried. It was the first symbolic bone he threw Harlowe's way, a clear signal they needed to retreat and regroup. Harlowe jumped at the opening.

"We'll be here 8 a.m. Thursday then. I regret you cannot honor our request for confidentiality. I do not think this serves either of us well at this point."

Tommy was still in a tense mood and glared at Larry from the side, but Larry and Harlowe were in sync again, if just for a moment. Larry quickly slid off his chair, his feet hitting the tiled floor with a slap and a wave of his hand: "Agreed. See you Thursday."

CHAPTER 21

THE CLUB

The shock of the meeting seemed to physically tire Harlowe, his squint now daubed with a heavy-lidded fatigue. The script was out the window and now both sides were in uncharted waters. Harlowe sat slumped in an upholstered chair in Ike's office, staring into space, flexing his fingers against one another and talking out loud.

"Something went very, very wrong here," said Harlowe, stating the obvious as he pondered. Trey thought carefully about where to interject but every sentence he prepared sounded too much like a version of "I told you so." Trey was also certain that beneath the exterior of exhaustion, Harlowe was a coiled spring of frustration, ready to strike at the slightest provocation, so silence seemed to be the best course of action. Ike did not readily take the mood into account; rather, he took Harlowe's musings at face value and tried to offer a hypothesis.

"I am sure Larry will surface soon and tell us what is next. Maybe he had to insert this as an additional step. Maybe he is trying to be a superhero and pull them from the brink," said Ike.

As Trey thought, the spring in Harlowe was wound tight and it indeed was looking for a target.

"Crissakes Ike, how much glory does that little goddamn garden gnome need? We cannot trust him. He cannot control that union. And he better be on that phone or get us some message pronto. Is he that fucking needy that he has to bathe himself in every ounce of glory?" said Harlowe.

It took about an hour for the three of them to hash and rehash possible outcomes but it was obvious that it was all just speculation until Larry surfaced and explained the situation. At Harlowe's request, Trey made several attempts to contact Larry by phone but the calls were unanswered. Ike offered an optimistic view that Larry could not answer because he was out having beers with the union committee, trying to get the situation back on the rails. They all decided that Larry knew the hotel where Harlowe stayed and would likely reach out to him there, so Harlowe decided to go back. As they filed out of the plant toward the parking lot, Trey's pager buzzed.

"Is that him?" said Harlowe, his voice tinged with what could only be called a childlike excitement.

Trey glanced down and spotted the number. It was not Larry. Besides, Trey doubted that Larry would try to contact him before Harlowe and he told Harlowe that.

"Are you sure? Do you know the number?" Harlowe insisted. He was wearing the unfamiliar face of desperation.

"I'm sure. I know the number. It's not him. For sure," Trey said.

If the management team had any hope about their request for confidentiality, the walk through the plant to the parking lot confirmed the word was out. Had Trey been walking alone he might have gotten the opportunity to start a conversation with a few of the employees, but the sight of Ike and Harlowe was too intimidating and the sight of the three of them together posed too inviting a target. While not addressed to anyone in particular, Trey distinctly heard chatter from the aisles where machine operators plopped parts into material handling boxes.

"Greedy motherfuckers."

"Benedict Arnolds."

"Pigs at the trough."

Harlowe was preoccupied in deep thought and unfamiliar with the noise level so Trey was pretty sure the comments went over his head. By the look on Ike's face, he heard them and he in turn studied Harlowe to see if the words registered. They did not.

Harlowe gave a quick wave as he got into his nondescript white rental car and headed to the hotel, hoping to hear from his beloved Turk. Ike had an armful of file folders that looked to keep him occupied for the night. Trey jumped into his car and drove out of the parking lot. As he accelerated, he listened to the rhythm of his tires on pavement. Satisfied that no one had slashed his tires, he made a mental note to check the paint for vandalism. The day's events were upsetting and the newest employees, buoyed by the hope of their new job, could be emotionally whipsawed and lash out irrationally.

Trey headed in his normal direction toward the Turnpike, but just a block before the normal on-ramp he made a sharp left onto a service road that ran alongside the toll road. As the service road degenerated into a bunch of seedy, weed and junk-infested lots and abandoned hulks of cars, the Turnpike rose on concrete ramps high above the service road. The view from the Turnpike focused on the not-too-distant skyline of New York City, and left the squalor of East Newark largely hidden and forgotten.

Trey continued along for over a mile. The road had not been paved in years and he tried to dodge the gargantuan potholes whose DNA mutated over the course of several New Jersey seasons of snow and ice. Despite his best efforts, the potholes were ultimately unavoidable and jarred him down to the fillings in his teeth. Dusk was throwing long shadows down the side road, cast from the giant concrete pillars that rose 30 feet in the air supporting the Turnpike. Finally, on the right, a garish giant billboard rose like a giant steel weed. It was rooted in the trash-strewn lots of the service road peeking up onto the Turnpike to announce the presence of life below. It was pink neon and announced "BOTTOMLESS PIT: Gentleman's Lounge." The "m" in "BOTTOMLESS" suggested a set of ass cheeks and instructed Turnpike riders to exit and turn right.

Trey glanced up at the giant sign and how it dwarfed the square building that was the Bottomless Pit. He turned into the parking lot.

Once at the door, Trey paid the attendant a $5 cover charge and entered the seedy building. Judging by the size of the parking lot and the number of cars, it was hard to fathom the building held that many people. Once inside the entryway, the place assaulted the senses. Overall, it was much darker than outside. Trey found it difficult to see his feet and tried to be sure he was not about to trip over any unseen step. In front of him was a riot of high-decibel, throbbing music and multicolored lights. The contrast of the dark and light was disorienting and he squinted to try to adjust his vision. Three dancers in various states of undress strutted back and forth to the music, sinuously collecting dollar bills offered by a tight row of patrons that ringed the bar. Not a seat was empty although most of the men stood and leaned over the bar and into the dancers, leaving the barstools empty behind where they stood. Trey thought about Ike's warning not to drink in local bars and figured if there was ever a night a drunken employee might want to take a shot at him, this was the night. Trey's awareness ramped up and fought with the contrasting light, darkness and noise.

The sharp contrast between dark and light was not helping Trey orient his vision as he looked around the room. He sidled through the crowd, hugging a back wall trying to see the faces in the bar, but he was struggling. It all looked like a cartoon with the dancers and barmaids in color and a bunch of silhouettes between Trey and the bar. He squinted trying to get clarity but the atmosphere was not a random accident. Strip joints traded on anonymity.

Trey finished one complete revolution around the bar and was near a hallway that led to the restrooms when a beefy hand clamped down on his forearm. Trey immediately thought it was just someone making their way roughly through the crowd to the door when he sensed that not only was that hand not letting go, but a second pair of hands was on him as well. The two men loomed larger than Trey and pushed him forcefully down the hall. Just short of the restroom door was another hallway. The two men pushed Trey up against the wall. He felt his face flattened against rough, cheap, dark brown faux wood grain paneling. His face was so tight against the wall it was hard to speak. Trey's heart raced wildly.

"Welcome," said the man whose hand palmed Trey's head against the wall like it was a small melon. "If you are an Officer of the Law, we apologize and would like to treat you to a couple of drinks and some amenities."

All of this was happening against the near-deafening din of the music so Trey was trying to process the message and determine if he was hearing clearly to decide exactly what might be his best answer. Before he could answer, the message continued in a very rehearsed cadence by the second man who had him pinned. This was not their first time acting this through.

"But if you are *not* an officer, we would like to know what the fuck you are doing just staring at people like some kind of creep, not buying drinks and just standing around? You are making our paying patrons nervous."

It was at this point that Trey was able to pick up a neon patch on the polo shirts of the two men. The neon barked out "BOTTOMLESS PIT

SECURITY." They were bouncers. Apparently the $5 cover charge had not bought Trey much time. Trey pushed his head back a little so he could enunciate.

"I am looking for some friends. They came here earlier. They said they had a room? But I don't see any room…"

Trey was going to explain in more detail but the bouncers heard enough to understand what to do.

"The Library!" said one of them, although the din and confusion made it impossible for Trey to ascertain which one made the statement.

The two bouncers peeled Trey away from the wall. While they loosened their vice grip on him they hemmed him in and moved quickly further down the dark hall, lit by a single dim bulb maybe every 10 feet. Trey expected to be out in the twilight of evening, forcibly ejected onto the pavement in the parking lot in seconds, but they veered in a direction that viscerally seemed to be further into the bowels of the club. The bouncer on Trey's right kicked a black swinging door open with his foot with some violence. Again, bright light stabbed at Trey's eyes with unexpected fluorescent-lit suddenness. Swiftly, they headed through a small kitchen that smelled of fry grease and stale beer. This was like a ride in a boardwalk funhouse but without the certainty of a safe exit. Finally they pushed him through another set of heavy black swinging doors on the opposite side of the kitchen and into a small square room with a few beat-up couches and a square wooden kitchen table in the middle.

"This who you lookin' for?" said one of the bouncers. Trey thought he was the one being asked the question but he was not. While Trey stumbled forward and hit the table thigh high, he looked up. In front of him Mo Morris and Tommy Pherrell sat in two high backed easy chairs, sipping beer and smoking cigarettes. Mo broke up in a high-pitched cackle, clearly amused at the escort and the entry.

"You know, Ghee," said Mo, addressing a very disheveled Trey, "for a college boy, you don't know shit about being cool in a place like this." He then turned to the bouncers and said, "He's ours, thanks for finding him." Tommy produced a $5 bill from a shirt pocket, handed it to one of the bouncers and said, "Split it with your buddy, huh?" The bouncer's glance marked Tommy as a cheap bastard.

Trey could take a deep breath and get his bearings. This was the place the bouncers euphemistically called The Library. It sat along a row of rooms behind the main stage and bar of the club. On one side was the kitchen that cooked up an assortment of indigestible fried foods and microwave pizzas. Further down the hall was the dressing (or undressing) room for the dancers. In just the few moments he was there, Trey saw there was another door on the other side of The Library. He intuited that dancers entered or exited the stage from somewhere near as he saw them skitter past on impossibly high heels toward a brighter light and a sound that ebbed and flowed as the stage door opened and closed nearby.

"You guys are a fucking piece of work," said Trey, "*This* is where you want to meet?"

Mo and Tommy were very pleased with themselves and laughed out loud. They rose and sat at the table in the middle of the room, pulling up a third chair for Trey. Mo picked at his receding hairline before folding his hands calmly in front of him. He peered over his glasses at Trey.

"Am I wrong or did we fuck with their minds today?" said Mo. His face broke from dead seriousness to a broad mischievous grin.

While Trey wanted to join in the glee, he saw the future in darker hues.

"No doubt they are in shock right now—I know Harlowe is," said Trey. "But people in shock do irrational things. Tell me more about Larry and what he said."

Just then a barmaid in a bikini top overflowing with silicone came by and asked if they wanted something to drink. She bent down to receive payment wherever it might be tucked but Trey placed $20 on her cocktail tray and ordered a round of bottled beer and told her to keep the drinks coming until the money ran out. As she wiggled away on impossibly high heels, Tommy ogled her to the point of distraction. Trey smacked his hand on the linoleum tabletop to bring Tommy back to the conversation but concentrated on Mo.

"It was just like you told us it would happen," said Mo. "To this second I cannot believe how right on you were. I thought you might be fucking with our minds. The Turk came in, let us get some shit out of our system and then told us to think a minute. Then, like he was touched by fucking Moses, he told us about an offer to make some concessions and try to salvage as much as we could. Judas couldn't be so cold or bold," said Mo.

By the end of his sentence Mo was staring off at some unseeable point on the floor.

The waitress returned with their beer and cardboard coasters. The bottles were icy cold and inviting. Tommy held up his bottle in a silent toast and the three clinked bottles and took long swigs. Trey felt it was the first time all day his thirst had been slaked. Some beers are good; this one was restorative.

Tommy picked up the story from Mo then, saying, "We listened to him ramble on but then old Mo over there, he goes into his own trance. He actually closed his eyes so long I wondered if he nodded off but I figured not because all the tension in the room made it crazy. Mo says, 'Let them have it.' That's all he says and it hangs there. Larry's eyes get real big and he started to brush his hair in that nervous way—that's how I know he's under pressure—he runs those little meat mitts through his hair without stopping. Larry asks Mo, 'Let them have what?'"

Mo was eager to take the telling of the story back and he slapped his beer bottle on the table with authority and drama.

"I told them to let them have it all. It's been a good run but this is why we have severance provisions. The guys are older. Most can retire. We can fight this thing all we want but you know they have their minds made up. Let's not waste time and money trying to save something that can't be saved. Let's spend our time getting as much as we can out of the closure. The Old Man is dead. He is the only one who wanted us here in East Newark anyway. Let's realize our time has passed," said Mo, just before taking another long draw on his beer.

"From there it was just hours of chaos," said Tommy. "It is a good thing you two let me in on this because I am not sure I could have sided with Mo otherwise. Larry was having a shit hemorrhage saying we had to save the plant, the legacy, the reputation of the union—blah dee fucking blah blah. I stuck with Mo and the committee came around little by little. Good thing those bastards are so old. After a few hours we had them envisioning retirement on the beach with drinks with little paper umbrellas."

The two told the story over three rounds of beer. It had been a pitched battle all day. Larry pleaded with more and more insistence about trying to save the plant. Mo and Tommy—the only union members tipped to the staged drama made their case that begging for their jobs is exactly what management wanted. By painting the picture of a union losing its long-held dignity and making the case to a fairly senior group of employees, Mo and Tommy built momentum throughout the day.

"At one point just before we went in there I think some of the committee were really ready to tell all of you in management to go fuck yourselves. We actually had to dial it back. I think for a while Larry was ready to try to freelance and probe about saving the plant with concessions but it was pretty clear toward the end if he did all hell was about to break lose and they would have thrown him right out of the building. It was ugggggggg-leee," said Tommy with emphasis.

"Little Judas fuck," Mo mumbled in disgust.

Trey immediately realized the bravado of the day, stoked in emotion, had a short shelf life. The wave of newer, younger employees hired in the surge would see the facts differently. They would want to know exactly what the union was doing for them. Trey laid out some tentative plans.

"I don't know what Larry and Harlowe are up to, but it won't be pleasant I am sure. We need to get back to the table and the sooner the better. You guys have to be outrageous in your demands. It has to be sooo off the wall they cannot possibly accept. Then, maybe WE—Grean—have to come back and say the expense is too great. Then you are in a position of strength here. Just don't offer anything that they can accept and walk away. You don't want some shithead in accounting figuring out the cost is worth it. Go big. And, while you're at it, pour some chemical crap in a hole in the back somewhere for good measure." Trey was being facetious when he talked about the chemicals but as he heard his own voice he began to think about whether that was a bad strategy after all. He quickly erased the thought. Things were complicated enough with what they had in front of them.

The combination of the unabated stress of the day combined with the cold beer on an empty stomach left them all in a pleasant, woozy state. The waitress skittered in again and told Trey the money was gone. He waved her over, gave her a $10 bill and ordered cold water and hot coffee for the table. Pleased by her tip and practiced in her trade of maximizing tip flow, she bent over and planted a kiss on Trey's cheek as a thank you. This was unexpected and Trey wore a look of quizzical annoyance.

"She likes good tipper, Ghee," said Mo. "For another $5, I bet you could fuck her."

A deep tiredness washed over Trey as he sized up Larry, Mo and the day's events.

"If you could tell me how much I need to ensure we all *don't* get fucked in this deal, I'd go get the money now," Trey said.

CHAPTER 22

VISITING EARL

Even though it was getting late, Trey decided to stop by his parents' home to see his father in particular. It was a combination of events that led him to this path. For one, he was feeling the beer from the club. Although he did not believe he was drunk, he knew the police cruising the neighborhood watched for cars headed from the club and were eager to make their quota of DUI arrests. He knew the back streets to his parents' house would give him time to process the beer and get well under any DUI test limits. He also knew he had not seen his father in a while. In recent calls, Trey detected a bit more fatigue and breathlessness in his dad's voice. His mother either would not or could not admit to any deterioration so he wanted to see go himself. Visiting in the early evening meant seeing his father possibly at the low point of his energy level—a kind of low tide Trey could calibrate from fixing the bigger picture in his mind. Beyond all the altruism, Trey also needed an anchor. The events, the drama, the betrayals, the delicate balance of secrets all led Trey to crave something firmer and real. In getting Earl Sr. to talk about his days in the factories, Trey could get grounded again. The day had been sent on the rolling seas. Earl Sr. was terra firma. As Trey added all this up, he really craved the visit and set his course there.

Once at the house, Trey took his key and was about to let himself in when he realized the door was unlocked. He knew his parents' trust in the neighborhood was misguided but unshakeable. They always locked the door before going to bed but left the door unlocked almost all day. They operated under the general premise nothing could happen in broad daylight. But now it had been dark for over an hour and the unlocked door was a threat to the elderly couple. He thought about starting the visit with a safety lecture but knew it would just poison the conversation and he wanted no more conflict this day. He made a mental note to have the conversation about locking doors in the very near future, but not now.

As if to reinforce his fears, Trey found his mother and father asleep in adjoining easy chairs, gently snoring as the nightly news blared and flickered on the TV in front of them. He gently kissed his mother on the forehead so as not to startle her. Indeed he did not. She was so secure in her vision of her safe home; she smiled pleasantly as if it could only be Trey there, not some random crackhead entering through the unlocked door. She patted Trey's face affectionately with fingers crooked with arthritis at the joint but with a soothing maternal touch. Her hostess instinct kicked in almost immediately with great clarity and completeness for a person just aroused from a slumber, no matter how shallow.

"What are you doing here? It's late for you. Long day? Can I get you something?" she asked through slit-sleepy eyes.

"How is he doing," asked Trey, ignoring the question at hand with a nod to his father in the chair, still sound asleep, comforted by the hiss and the oxygen content seeping into his lungs from the green tank next to him.

"Oh, he's good as he ever is. Get him up. He'll be mad as anything if he ever thought you were here and he did not see you. EARL! EARL!" his mother urged. She tried to reach out and touch him to wake him but only the very tip of her finger caught his plastic oxygen tube. Earl stirred a little but Trey brought him to attention with a firm grasp and small shake of his forearm. Earl wore a checkered flannel shirt even though it was fairly warm in the house. Trey sensed a frailty beneath the shirt he had not sensed before. A previously muscled chest wasted away. Earl perked up quickly.

"Trey! How long have you been here?" he asked. Earl slid his arm beneath the tubes and grabbed his son's hand in a happy, firm but cold-skinned clasp. "Sit and tell me what you are up to."

After a few comments about the weather and the changing seasons, Trey got to the point.

"Dad, tell me again about how you ended up in management after all those years in the union."

Earl shifted his eyes back and forth searching his mental files. For a moment, Trey feared the memory was lost but then Earl brightened considerably.

"You mean Wavelength?" Earl asked.

"Yeah Dad, that is it. Wavelength."

October 1957

After leaving the warehouse, Earl found work in nearby Kearny. He put in applications at least a dozen manufacturing plants throughout northern New Jersey. He tried to stay close to the bus lines that ran out of East Newark or at least apply only to jobs that would offset the additional cost of a car. After some months he was contacted by Wavelength Assemblers in nearby Kearny for a job assembling televisions. Wavelength was a contract manufacturer, which basically meant they would assemble a TV for any manufacturer, private label. At the time, TV sales were so hot that company factories of the major manufacturers could not keep up so they outsourced some of the work to places like Wavelength. It was a good job for Earl. It paid better than the warehouse and the Wavelength factory was an easy commute by bus. The only risk for Earl was the fact that Wavelength was a union shop. He would have a probationary period of 60 days. During that period he was not covered by the union and he could be released without cause at any time in those first two months. After 60 days, he would be part of the Electrical Workers Assembly Union (EWAU) Local 55. Because the assembly jobs there were so sought after, Wavelength management was quick to terminate employees in the probationary period for the slightest reason. As a safety net, Earl decided to work the job at the warehouse during the day and the night shift at Wavelength for the 60-day probation. It would be tough but for two months he could handle it. Besides, the extra cash would come in handy with new baby Trey less than a year old. Once he joined the union, he would get an automatic raise to offset his initiation fee and the union dues. In four months, he calculated, he would be ahead of the game.

Indeed, Earl turned out to be an outstanding employee and he actually stayed working both jobs for an additional month until Margaret complained about the lack of family time and the exhaustion creeping up on him. She insisted he quit the warehouse, which he did with great relief. With the extra money he bought Trey a pedal-propelled toy fire wagon with a bell. While

Trey was too young to maneuver the toy by foot, he found the bell easier to operate to his great amusement. Earl's countermove was to mute the clapper with cotton. An uneasy quiet settled in the house. The harsh clang was traded for a steady thud of a clapper encased in cotton-quieter but no less incessant in the hands of young Trey.

At work, Earl experienced great success being promoted to two higher-level, better-paying jobs that allowed him to forsake the premium pay afforded to night-shift employees and move to a normal 8-to-4 day job.

The relationship between the management and the union was a good one at Wavelength with very few disputes. That fact itself did not sit well with some of the union members who felt the relationship with management was a bit too cozy for their liking. They felt the union was too ready to capitulate, won few battles and did not show a strong, determined face when pursuing grievances about working conditions. While the critics of the current leadership had varied and broad but thin support, the most vocal critics were from the Philippines. As the support for the criticism congealed around them, the group became known as—in the twisted logic of the factory—the Cryin' Hawaiians, or simply the Hawaiians. The title of Cryin' Hawaiians was originally coined by the incumbent union leadership in an attempt to belittle the group. The idea backfired as the group—Filipinos and non-Filipinos alike—embraced the name and began to wear brightly colored shirts. Their team now had a cause and a symbol. The isolated complaints were gaining momentum.

After about a year, Earl ran for election as a departmental steward. He won based mainly on the fact he was not part of the established union hierarchy. It placed him in an odd position. Overall he had no beef with the current leadership and depended on their cooperation and support to accomplish his goals. On the other hand, he was clearly elected as a contrast to the incumbent leadership style. The Hawaiians claimed Earl as theirs although Earl did not embrace their imprimatur.

Over time, the internal union strife took its toll. Wavelength managers tried their best to remain neutral. There was a harmonious relationship with the current leadership best served by no changes at the top of the union. Yet to betray any preference was to doom the leadership they sought to sustain. Wavelength had no choice but to watch as the internecine warfare escalated.

The issues inside the union bubbled over in late summer. To begin with, the contract negotiated that spring was ratified by only the narrowest of margins. Many in the union felt the wage increase was far too low and that the leadership had not shown a strong hand. Without a viable threat of a strike, the Hawaiians claimed, management could stand pat and wait out the union. In some management theory, the idea holds that the perfectly negotiated contract is ratified by one vote. If true, the last contract was near perfect from management's standpoint. In the very end, although dissatisfied, the majority did not want to strike and lose wages for an indeterminate amount of time, so the contract passed by the thinnest of margins.

Building on this unrest, the Hawaiians pointed to a string of unfavorable arbitration and disciplinary decisions that occurred over the course of the summer. After losing two arbitrations, the union coffers were depleted and the union committee decided two additional cases could be resolved by compromise instead of costly arbitration proceedings. Coming on the heels of two defeats, the Hawaiians argued the current leadership was impotent and in retreat before the company.

Every action between the union and the company turned into a symbol of distrust and dissatisfaction. When the company signed a contract to repair and maintain the company truck fleet with a nearby repair shop, the intent was to keep money invested in the local neighborhood. But it turned out the shop was owned by two brothers of the current union secretary and the Hawaiians held this up as another indication of the all-too-cozy relationship with management.

By fall, the new union elections were scheduled and Earl unwittingly became a key figure in the struggle.

In truth, the vast majority of the employees cared little for who was in charge of the union and thought it made little difference. The active participants in the dispute inside the union likely involved no more than 5% of the 1,400 employees. However, many of the disinterested liked the fact there was a vocal faction prodding the leadership and saw it as creative conflict. It kept their leadership honest and sent a message to management of a line in the sand, however indefinite. The fact the rank and file ratified their mediocre contract over the objections of the Hawaiians also showed the infatuation with a harder line had limits as well. The election would define exactly how sharply the employees liked their line drawn.

The Hawaiians' leader, Pete de la Cruz, understood this dynamic better than most. He wanted to be union president and walked a fine line. If he espoused radical and extreme positions, he would scare the majority of *employees who wanted more in the way of pay and benefits but did not want to risk a confrontation resulting in a strike. If he watered down his approach too much, his position would not look much different from that status quo. As he pondered his options, Pete sought out Earl Bensen as the key to the success of the Hawaiians.*

Earl had a lot going for him in the eyes of the dissidents. For one, he was soft spoken and well liked in his department. While neither an outspoken critic of the current leadership nor an espoused Hawaiian, he defeated an incumbent steward. He had the additional advantage of not being Filipino by birth or heritage. Earl's blond hair was turning a silver gray. His fair Norwegian complexion could never be confused with the swarthy Filipino employees. He was moderate in complexion and demeanor and Pete saw him as a linchpin to his strategy. If he could add Earl as a union vice-president candidate, it would show Pete was no wild-eyed foreign born anarchist. He had the wise, calm Earl to advise him. Earl would represent those who were less likely to strike. If the time came for a stronger message or action, Earl would appeal to a wide audience. Pete just had to have Earl.

In a short time, Pete buttonholed Earl over a few beers after work. He laid out his argument: the union leadership had grown sclerotic and impotent. He discussed the poor contract terms and the lost grievances. Worse yet, Pete enumerated the issues the union had refused to take up. It was one thing to lose a good fight. It was altogether a different issue to refuse the fight in the first place.

Earl listened and pondered. As a local union vice president he would have prestige. More importantly, the opportunity provided him the intellectual challenge his job did not. Assembling televisions was more complex than most jobs but a union leadership post provided the ability to do good and match wits with a management he both respected and was wary of. Earl understood keenly that the objectives of the union and the company were not opposed to one another but where they did not align, it was important to ensure discussion, not outright capitulation. The effect of a late afternoon of beer had the opposite effect on the two men. Pete left feeling confident he had an ally and a running mate to challenge the current leadership. Earl's natural inclination to be thoughtful could be confused with being wary. He knew right away the risk unspoken by Pete was a union divided, which would be worse than the unhappy mood today. The nomination meeting would not be for another two weeks. He promised Pete an answer in one week to leave time for additional planning.

Wavelength management saw the election as pivotal. As an overall philosophy, they were not hostile to the union. That philosophy had been fruitful for some time but now appeared to backfire. Their refusal to criticize the union or engage in confrontation had somehow morphed into this situation and emboldened a harder-line core of employees. While not actively involved, management knew the leaders of the Hawaiians and the scuttlebutt of friction inside the union. To some degree, the feeling inside management was that as long as the union was fighting among themselves, they would not be a viable threat to plant operations. While successful and profitable, the huge demand curve for televisions was clearly flattening and the early signs of the slowdown would be felt in contract manufacturers like Wavelength. Faced with emerging idle factory capacity in their own factories, the first reaction would be to pull back orders from contractors. In addition, some felt the Japanese, emerging from WWII, would offer cheap wages and threaten manufacturers in the U.S. That threat was not seen as viable and the union scoffed at the point in the last negotiation. The Japanese were defeated at war and they certainly were not going to defeat the Americans on the factory floor.

Weighing their options, Wavelength knew they could not interfere directly with union politics. Not only was it illegal, it was highly inadvisable. Still, it felt as if they were watching a train wreck from afar, helpless to stop it. The worst-case scenario was if the Hawaiians won the election. As the new kids on the block, they would have to back up their claims. They would be ultra-tough on all issues. Precious time and money would be consumed by grievance investigations and hearings. Work rules would be tightened. Overall, it would be a less-pleasant environment. All of this was a theoretical exercise of what might be. But once management understood the Hawaiians' appeal reached beyond their ranks and extended to a guy like Earl Bensen, it gave them great pause. This indicated the possibility of dissatisfaction spread beyond the hardcore to the more moderate employees. If a guy like Earl joined their ranks, the threat of tougher days ahead loomed much more real.

The option of allowing circumstances to play themselves out looked less and less appealing. Wavelength might not have been able to control the direction the wind was blowing but they decided to adjust the sails. Five days after Earl and Pete met over beers to discuss his role with the Hawaiians, Earl received an invitation to the office of the Director of Industrial Relations, Tom Glackin.

Glackin was a veteran on the labor wars and had been with Wavelength for 13 years. He began his career with a clipboard and a stopwatch on the factory floor of General Motors, conducting time and motion studies to determine the optimum assembly methods and the expected productivity and cost of various operations. In this role, he had developed a keen eye for when an employee was slowing down deliberately to gain a lower performance expectation. After a stint in the Army during the war, he parlayed his time at GM into the chance to be a bigger fish in a smaller pond at Wavelength. If he had battled the United Auto Workers at GM, he could certainly handle the EWAU at Wavelength.

Glackin was the architect of the non-confrontational policy with the EWAU and the generally positive results gave him great credibility over time. Now the naysayers were beginning to emerge. Glackin saw the rift in the union as an unintended consequence, but one, if played out poorly, that had potential to undermine his position and bend the arc of his rising star within Wavelength.

Earl was not sure why he had been summoned to Glackin's office. He had heard of him but had never seen him in person nor did he know where his office was. Mindful of his place in the union pecking order, Earl inquired as to whether this was official union business. If it was, he did not want to step on the toes of union leaders and unintentionally escalate an already-uncomfortable situation. Earl was assured by Glackin's secretary that this had nothing to do with union business and invited him to come up after lunch. Glackin's office was on the third floor. In contrast to the wide-open factory with high ceilings and a beehive of activity and noise, the third floor offices were a sterile tomb. As Earl left the elevator, the hallways were narrow. The carpet and acoustic ceiling tiles muffled all sound into a hush. The doors on most offices were closed. Each door was frosted glass and shrouded the activity inside except for the activity hinted by lumps of light and shadow projected by unknown movements and unseen employees.

Earl proceeded down the hall as instructed to the fourth door on the right to a door lettered with

T Glackin
Industrial Reltns

Earl wondered if they had saved money with the abbreviation as he proceeded inside. The layout of the floor distorted Earl's sense of space. The narrow hallways belied the fact that the offices beyond the frosted doors were spacious. Earl had a sense of stepping through an optical illusion as just inside the door sat a young receptionist with a coffee table and couch in an anteroom. Beyond her outpost Glackin's office opened up into a spacious but windowless office. Glackin had silver-gray hair and a jowly bulldog face. He wore his suit jacket at his desk. As soon as he saw Earl, he waved him in before the receptionist could greet him. It made Earl wonder how Glackin knew him on sight.

Once in the office, Earl took a seat on the couch at Glackin's invitation. Glackin took off his jacket, draped it on a coat stand in the corner and retrieved a cigarette from the pocket. He pulled up a chair facing Earl and lit up. An ashtray in the shape of a television sat between them.

"Welcome up! I'm glad you came and I've heard so many impressive things about you," said Glackin, cigarette smoke curling around his head like an angelic aura.

The two men exchanged some chitchat about their families, where they grew up and lived before Glackin wanted to make his point.

"Earl, I told you I've heard great things about you. How you get along with everybody. You seem to be admired by your fellow workers. Your work record is spotless. You work hard. You take pride in your job. But have you thought about the long view?"

Earl was not sure exactly what Glackin meant by the question so he asked him to elaborate. Glackin was very willing. His words flowed easily, as if rehearsed.

"The long view. What are you going to do in the next 20 years? Do you want to stay assembling televisions or can you do something more?" Glackin paused a beat for emphasis and took a drag on his cigarette before continuing. He kept eye contact with Earl throughout.

"We have looked at your record, your work history and tried to gauge your potential. We are a company with a bright future and we need more people like you to lead us. We will need to motivate every employee and we think you have the potential for higher management. We'd like to offer you a chance to go into our supervisor training program and become part of management,"

said Glackin. Now the punchline was delivered. He watched Earl even more carefully for reaction.

Earl massaged his jaw in thought a moment and watched Glackin's cigarette ash grow uncomfortably long. He noticed Glackin was on the edge of his seat, hunched forward, smiling at him. Earl was simultaneously pleased and wary. He was not sure if Glackin was seeking an answer right there or not.

"Tell me more. What does this mean?" asked Earl. It was as if Glackin found his cue on his very own stage.

"What does it mean? It means you are moving up in the world. It is not automatic, mind you. We have some tests for aptitude for supervisory work but I have no doubt you will pass. I have not been wrong yet in offering people an opportunity for the program. You will get training. Your benefits get a little better. Your pay gets better—and best of all—you are not punching a clock anymore. Now, that does not matter to a guy like you who shows up every day, but just think, you don't have to worry about every minute. You would be salaried—same paycheck every week you can depend on—and the possibility of a year-end bonus now, too." Glackin chose the word "salaried" carefully instead of "management," very aware of Earl's position in the union.

Earl agreed to think about it and Glackin agreed to put all the particulars of the offer in writing for Earl's consideration. Glackin noted that in order to set up the next management evaluation tests and schedule training classes, he needed an answer in 10 days—or just days ahead of the union nominating meeting. The two men shook hands, Glackin creating a vigorous tempo in the act. It was as if he was hinting at the secret handshake Earl might learn if he decided to accept the offer.

Earl left the office and stepped back out into the sterile hallway. Life was now very complicated. An already-complicated decision had an additional layer. He knew he could make a positive impact in the union and it was a critical juncture in their history. He liked his coworkers and felt he understood the mechanics of how the union worked and interacted with the management to bring about positive results. On the other hand, he had a family now. The certainty of a paycheck and the higher career ceiling presented by accepting the offer was obvious. While Glackin was careful not to mention the word, Earl realized he was on the verge of crossing the Rubicon and becoming part of management. How he might impact the workplace from that vantage point was unfamiliar territory. How his former union brothers would see his choice and impact his new role was just as uncertain. He felt gratified and sick at the same time.

Before Earl had even reached the elevator to return to the factory floor, Tom Glackin stubbed out his cigarette and closed the door to his office. He picked up the phone and called his boss, the Vice-President of Operations.

"I made him the offer. He is hard to read. I can't say for sure he will take it but I see why the union wants him. That is why we need him. He would make the Hawaiians legitimate and the Hawaiians will make our life miserable. We made the right call here. We need him out of the mix. I don't think he would be a bad supervisor, either. If we have to somehow sweeten the deal—guarantee him day shift or find out what else he values—we should do it. I'll let you know how it goes," said Glackin, lighting yet another cigarette as he talked. He was pleased with his analysis and his strategy to influence the dynamics of the workplace. He was sure he was valuable—in fact, undervalued among the Wavelength management team.

For his part, Earl went home and pondered. His sleep was light and interrupted each night. If he stirred even briefly in bed, his mind erupted in mental debate. He arose silently and went out onto his porch to stare into the cool autumn evenings. The leaves from nearby trees scraped softly down the street, propelled by a soft breeze. It soothed him and Margaret found him asleep on the porch several mornings. For her part, she would not push him in any direction except the one he decided to pursue. She listened attentively as he laid out his concerns on every facet of the choices. Her only contribution: "Do what makes you happy."

Earl wanted to make his decision several days before any deadline to be decisive. One of the nights he fell asleep in a chair on the porch he heard Trey stir and cry before the sound disturbed the maternal alarm in Margaret. He went in and settled Trey and wondered what the child would advise if he could offer advice. Earl only knew he never wanted the world to pull on his son as hard as he felt pulled at this moment.

Trey recalled the first time Earl related the story of his choice to become a member of management. He felt his father sold out. He was glad he left the feeling unsaid. Time had a way of illuminating once-simple forms to reveal detailed facets. Trey felt ashamed he ever felt that way at all. He realized how the choice between family and job is really not a choice at all. In his daydreams, Trey always played out the choice not made and imagined his father as a great labor leader. Trey realized he always rued what might have been for his father when all the while he should have appreciated the love that drove Earl down the path taken.

CHAPTER 23

CHAOS

As a boy, Trey loved to hear his father read Huckleberry Finn to him. Even though it was a long and familiar story, Trey found great comfort in hearing it again. There was something in the mixture of the timbre of his father's voice and the cadence of the story that left him in a place of great peace and made time stand still. As he got older, it seemed silly to even think his father would read to him. Somehow, the retelling of the stories of his life had the same effect. It made Trey wish to freeze time and allow the story to go in an endless loop. While Trey understood the desire, he also knew the story of Wavelength Assembly had taken a long time in the telling and Earl had a finite amount of energy, even in talking. Trey sat at an angle to his father, their knees touching so Earl would not have to project his voice and save precious energy. Trey realized he was almost entranced by the story and his father's voice so he was not so much alarmed as utterly confused at what he heard next.

"Plum, plum, plum, plum."

While Trey was looking right at Earl, he tried hard to process what he was hearing. Trey thought he may have even partially dozed off, but the words and sounds caused him to focus even more intently on his father's words.

"Plum, plum, plum."

Trey glanced at the oxygen bottle tucked next to his father's chair and looked to see if there was a malfunction or escape that caused his father's words to be drowned out with this gibberish. But now looking at Earl's mouth, Trey saw the words form from his mouth. They came faster now, though no more intelligible.

"Plumplumplumplumplum."

Like an old phonograph record skipping, Earl seemed stuck on what was not truly a word but a sound.

"Plum, plum, plum, plum."

Now Trey grew alarmed, his eyes widened. They were in an open room, yet his father seemed to be drowning. Trey dropped to his knees between his father's legs.

"POPS—ARE YOU OK? WHAT'S THE MATTER?"

Trey realized he was yelling. He also figured no matter what the problem, it was unlikely his father was deaf. Trey had no time to get an answer when Earl seemed to crumble in his chair in slow motion. His eyes rolled back in his head and he pitched forward in his chair. Had Trey not been there, Earl might have folded up much like a worn beach chair but his son was directly in front of him. Trey caught his father in his arms and pushed him back in the easy chair. Trey moved so forcefully to hold him up; he sensed the frailty in his father's torso and was afraid he'd broken his ribs. Earl's head lolled and rocked uncontrollably. He was semi-conscious.

Hearing the commotion, Trey's mother entered the room. Perhaps refusing to process the scene, she asked almost sternly, "What are you two doing?"

"Call 911—something's wrong with Pops. He just stopped making sense while we were talking," said Trey.

Trey's mother shifted from stern disbelief to panic in a fraction of a second, shrieked and went to the phone to call 911.

Trey steadied his father with one hand, keeping him upright in his chair. He was amazed how little substance there was to his father's torso. Earl's eyes were glassy and staring into a space in the ceiling. With his free hand, Trey pushed the oxygen tube deeper in his nose and reached around and opened the oxygen tank valve wide. Any thought the oxygen had merely run out was dispelled as the apparatus hissed louder with the turn of the valve. Trey placed his ear on his father's chest. He was breathing, choppy breaths. His heartbeat was regular but rapid. Trey slid his head up from the chest area up to his ear as he cradled his father's head.

"Don't you go anywhere," he whispered. "I love you, so be a tough old bird for me!"

Earl growled something unintelligible. It was "love you" in his head but he knew he did not convey it clearly to his son. Earl felt trapped in an energy-less vacuum and could not escape. He wondered if this was what it felt like to die.

The official report would say it took 14 minutes for the ambulance to respond but it felt so much longer to Trey.

The first to arrive was a short, squat, boyish-faced EMT with a perm in loose curls on top of his head like some kind of odd moss. The EMT surveyed the room, looking at the whole scene as to evaluate escape routes and hazards. His light blue ambulance service shirt was blotched darker blue in the armpits with sweat and rolled up at the sleeves to the elbow, exposing two fleshy forearms. The stethoscope seemed to be choking his thick neck. When Trey saw him, a wave of relief washed over him.

"Baggy?"

The question was utterly rhetorical as not only did his badge nameplate on his pocket read "Baggy" but Biaggio "Baggy" Belfiglio was an unforgettable neighborhood character. Baggy was a classmate of Trey's for 16 years. Baggy was still living at home with his mother as far as Trey knew. He could not count Baggy as a close friend, but to see a neighborhood guy in this situation was comforting.

"Aww, no, no no no no, we cannot have this today," said Baggy. He was calm, almost matter of fact. His nonchalance could have been annoying to some, but in this case, he was reassuring. Baggy had the splayed gait of an obese person as he entered the room and approached Earl. While Baggy slipped on some sterile gloves with a thwack, he addressed Trey and his mother as if he had just encountered them at the dry cleaners rather than in an emergency situation.

"We cannot have this today. Trey, how you been? We all love your dad and I promise we will take good care of him. We will fix him up. He is gonna be all right with me. Tell me what started all this while I check his signs."

There were times that Trey wanted to scold the guys who never left the neighborhood. They had no ambition. Their worldview was small. They never grew or understood life outside East Newark and did not care to. But at this moment, Baggy was an angel sent from heaven. He was no emotionless practitioner. He had been in this house before and exuded genuine warmth and caring. Trey realized there were likely a dozen guys like Baggy in the neighborhood. They might not see their old neighborhood pals for years but would still take a bullet for them just for the fact that they were once neighborhood guys.

Baggy assessed the situation quickly and professionally, stabilized Earl as best he could and recommended that they take him to St. Vincent's Hospital where they could take a closer look at him. The living room filled quickly with a gurney, IV bottles and monitoring equipment. Earl's frailty seemed magnified as he almost disappeared in the white sheets of the cot. The various lines and wires were a clue as to where the pale Earl was located in the white sheets. Baggy's initial nonchalance was a façade. He and an assistant worked swiftly and before long wheeled Earl outside to the curb where a boxy ambulance awaited. Even though he was under an oxygen mask, Earl could feel it was cooler and fresher outside than the stale air of the house and felt a lift just from being outside.

Trey's mother initially wanted to go in the ambulance but Trey talked her into driving over with him on the promise they would follow the ambulance. To keep that promise, Trey had to hustle down the street to get his car. As he jogged down the sidewalk, the adrenaline rush faded and the entire weight of the day hit him. It felt like the energy was pouring out of the bottom of his shoes but Trey knew he had to dig deep for another reservoir of strength.

Oddly, at that moment, he wondered what Harlowe was up to.

Harlowe was sitting in his hotel room, alone. Well, he was not exactly alone as he had his favorite friend, Jim Beam, with him in a glass with ice. Harlowe craved getting drunk but resisted the urge. He knew, or at least he hoped, Larry would call and discuss what the hell just happened. To deal with Larry he wanted a clear head so after downing a first drink, he poured a second but nursed it carefully.

Just about the moment Trey wondered about Harlowe's evening, the hotel phone rang in a stuttering tone. The red light on the dial flashed like it was a nuclear hotline at the Pentagon. Ever aware of appearances, Harlowe let it ring twice. He did not want to appear too eager.

"Harlowe, it's me" said Larry. On his best day, Larry's voice was a growl. After hours with the local union, his voice was a hoarse rasp. He seemed to be conserving words sensing his voice was nearing the outer limits. An awkward pause ensued and it irritated Harlowe.

"Well," Harlowe started, "do you want to tell me what the hell just happened today?"

Larry let out a long sigh on the telephone.

"Sometimes, things don't go the way you want them to. The boys on the negotiating committee got a little fired up. It'll be OK. Once the younger guys see that they are kicking their jobs away they will have a full-scale mutiny. Then let's see what happens," said Larry.

Harlowe was aggravated and itching for a way to release the irritation. Larry's broad pronouncement "all was well" was at odds with all that Harlowe sensed. In addition, Harlowe was the fixer for the Greans. He dreaded having to make the call to them and explain what was not fixed. Larry just lit the fuse.

"Let's see what happens?" Harlowe said incredulously. "Am I to believe you will handle them any better than you just did? It is not OK when you lose control of that group and that is what you did. You lost goddamned control. We are off script. As a matter of fact, right now I don't see any script at all. What I see is chaos and no goddamn plan at all." He punctuated his rant with a swig of the Jim Beam he had been denying himself.

Larry was not one to take a punch without at least returning one.

"Pal," Larry said, his voice dripping with sarcasm, "I think you are forgetting exactly who is your ally here. You are up fuck's river without me, so maybe you should just calm the fuck down about who has a plan and what it will be. Do you have any bright goddamned ideas? Because if you do, I better hear a good one in the next 30 seconds. Then I'll decide if I hang up and let you have your little fucked up plan or if maybe you want to listen to the one guy who has never let you down."

Harlowe was not one to run away from a brawl but this time his better angels led him to the conclusion that silence—or something close to it— was the correct course of action. The two had taken their best shot at one another and vented their spleen. Harlowe allowed some dead air to linger and then replied in a dulcet tone.

"Go on," was all he said.

With what little voice he had left, Larry launched into his plan.

"Your problem is you have all these guys who have been there so many years. They see dollars. Now 50 or 60 grand won't buy you retirement; to these guys that severance looks great. They think they have nothing to lose. What we have to do is find the guys with something to lose—the young guys, the old guys who don't want to be stuck in the house with their bitchy old lady. Guys who won't know what to do if they can't take their morning shit in the crapper at Grean. The committee is all the guys who aren't going to get anything more than what they have now. Their severance maxes at 52 weeks. They get two weeks per year of service and automatic 52 weeks if their age and service equals 80. That is everyone there at that table just about."

Then Larry took a breath. His union negotiating style was on auto pilot and he could not resist.

"One thing you can do is uncap their severance, give them something to lose," said Larry. He recognized right away that he could not even sell that as sincere over the phone.

"Fuck that Larry. Nice try. What else you got?" Harlowe asked.

Larry persisted just a while longer.

"You still think about that. You get your layoffs by seniority so the guys at that bottom won't cost you and if you never close down, it is a cost you never incur for the oldest guys," said Larry.

Harlowe considered the odd logic for just a moment. Larry was reaching but he was right. Sometimes when the union needed a win they could give away benefits that actually had no value in practical terms. You could give the oldest workers 10 years of severance in case of closure—as long as you weren't going to close the place entirely. The union would trumpet it as a huge win for the most senior employees while the likelihood of it ever being paid out was zero. The most senior workers could not be laid off. Then Harlowe realized that these were not normal times. If it had just been the Greans, this might work, but the idea did not pan out for one simple reason: any additional severance cost, no matter how unlikely, had to be accounted for as a liability in the sale price. If the potential buyers saw additional liability, it would drive down the sale price and send a bad signal. Larry was talking and Harlowe realized as he had been noodling the implications through, he was not listening to Larry and hoped he had not missed anything important.

"…so the key is to get all the members together and let the losers in all of this—the low-seniority guys—stir the shit a little. Let these old farts of the negotiating committee feel the heat. Somehow we have to make the loudest ones seem like the majority."

As hard as Harlowe tried, Larry's voice sounded like background noise. Harlowe was deeply entranced in his own calculations. He had been the Greans' fixer for many years and had an undefeated record as far as the Greans were concerned. But like the boxer who loses only his last fight, the loss alone stands out. Harlowe knew this was the payday for the Grean brothers. Jack Grean often spoke with envy about other entrepreneurs and business owners he met in the Orlando social circles who had sold their businesses for "fuck you" money. Harlowe loved the phrase. Harlowe dreamed of "fuck you" money.

For Harlowe, no matter how many bodies he had buried to bring the Greans to the precipice of FU money, all of that would be forgotten if he could not pull off this final act. They needed to show TerVeer the union would not be a problem. As of right now, the issue was invisible to the new buyers. Harlowe needed to somehow show that Grean Machining had the union in tow, even when at this minute they clearly did not. Harlowe was sitting at a narrow desk in the hotel talking on the phone. In front of him was a mirror and he noted even the very few strands of hair left in his forlorn comb over were now graying. He knew this was his payday as well. Without the Grean issues, his value to any other organization was near zero. How do you describe the messes he cleaned up, how to operate in the tiniest margins of the law? How do you describe how you operate beyond the law in the hope that most employees will either be too ignorant or timid to challenge you? At some level the Greans understood Harlowe's value was expanding the limits of the game beyond the playing field. They simply did not want to know how Harlowe was rechalking the lines, only the fact they won the game. Harlowe needed a win and he needed Larry to bring the local union to tow. He realized that while he was pondering all this, Larry was still talking. Harlowe had no idea if Larry had been in his soliloquy 30 seconds or 10 minutes.

"Turk, Turk, TURK!" Harlowe interrupted, trying to break the monologue. "You got it. Do your thing. I'm exhausted. You have my faith that you can do this. Call me when you are done talking to them and we can rehash this again. Just have them all fired up and maybe we can bring this to a close this week. You can't afford to let us close down so go do your heroic union thing and let's get on with it."

After the call ended, Harlowe took stock of where his life had led him: he was drinking alone, in a dingy hotel that was a sour mixture of decades-old cigarette smoke and hotel antiseptic wash. His room was a double-paned sarcophagus to muffle the planes at Newark airport. He could see the fresh air (or as close to fresh air as one gets at Newark airport) but he could not sense its freshness, only imagine it. He wanted to be home in Georgia. Harlowe understood he was the only one in the room, but he needed to hear another voice so he said out loud and to no one in particular: "One hell of a way to make a living."

CHAPTER 24

TURNING UP THE HEAT

It was a typically oppressive day in Orlando, even at 10 a.m. The humid air created a clingy irritability sapping the patience and civility from anyone it enveloped. Inside the Grean Machining headquarters the air conditioning created a personal cold front. So much so, most female employees donned sweaters and most of the men left their jackets on. Despite the chill inside, irritability was quite evident in the executive suite where Cal and Jack Grean pondered the $100 million question: what the fuck was Harlowe Mikkelsen doing to secure their deal?

The brothers had identical offices of precisely the same square footage on opposite sides of a large board room. Each had a private access entryway into the boardroom, all the better to impress guests with their importance. But while the square footage of the offices was exactly the same, Cal Jr.'s office looked and felt larger. As the financial mind, his office was decorated with minimal but impressive art. His desk was the paragon of organization and while he ran a $135 million business, his desk was generally bare except for a pen set, a calculator and perhaps one binder that commanded his attention at that moment. The lack of clutter reflected his taste for absolute clarity and the office intimidated visitors with its museum-like order.

Jack's office reflected what one would suspect was undiagnosed Attention Deficit Disorder. It was a jumble of magazines, plaques, cheap art and pictures with the rich and famous. Most conspicuous was a framed photo of Jack and Ronald Reagan. In the picture, Reagan is shaking Jack's hand and focused on Jack while Jack stared right at the camera, hinting that perhaps Reagan should have the picture on *his* desk to commemorate

191

the meeting. This all was arranged through a high-ranking Republican in Orlando who hosted a $5,000-a-plate dinner for Reagan in his home, thus guaranteeing personal access to the former president. Somewhere deep in the expense accounts at Grean, the $5,000 was listed as "client dinner party." If Jack was going to spend $5,000 of his own money, there needed to be a lot better quality of scotch.

For his part, Harlowe sat in his hotel room and fretted. He was used to delivering solutions. Sometimes his report would be as crisp as "mission accomplished" and then let the Grean brothers decide if they wanted to know details. He knew this would not be the case today; in fact, this was the rare time he had a distinct lack of details. On one hand, the plans were not totally scuttled. Harlowe's experience in these matters led him to believe the destination would be the one intended even if the journey might lead to unanticipated places. Harlowe trusted Larry to make the situation come out right more than he trusted Larry himself. Harlowe and Larry shared a certain pride in making sure their schemes were accomplished. Together they shared a pride in their unofficial status as undefeated champions in their arena.

On the other hand, there were a lot of unknowns at this point. The union local committee was not committed to the prospect of saving half a plant but it seemed ludicrous they would not come around to this point of view. Larry had not delivered precisely on the agreed-to script and Harlowe felt there was far too much that could go wrong as they ad-libbed. Overhanging all of this was the reality that this was not your normal set of stakes on the table. If there were $300 million in chips on the table, the palms were just a little bit sweatier.

In his fantasy, Harlowe thought about not making the call at all, adding to the mystery of what he might be up to and his mystique as the Grean fixer. He quickly discarded that and tried to think exactly how to status the Greans and exactly where to peg their expectations. In the end, Harlowe decided there were too many unknowns and potential outcomes to tell the story in a straightforward manner and gauge how the Greans viewed the situation. Perhaps he was a bit too invested and too isolated in this hotel room to see the big picture. Hearing the Greans' reaction might be the best indicator as to whether he needed to press harder or allow events to unfold.

By the time Harlowe thought through his options for the umpteenth time and picked up the phone, the Greans were getting antsy. Harlowe was not one to keep them waiting so when the call slipped just five minutes past the scheduled starting time, Cal considered sending his secretary on a hunt for Harlowe but thought better of it. He quietly drummed his fingers at his desk as Jack sat in front of him, sketching doodles on a yellow legal pad.

When the phone finally rang, Cal grabbed the phone before his secretary could screen it, a sure sign of the blend of impatience and edginess he felt.

"Harlowe here with the morning news report." His attempt to lighten the impact of his report fell horribly short of the mark and he knew it. He decided to plow on and let it all play out.

Harlowe spent the next 10 minutes describing the events of the past few days. The conversations. The rehearsals. The meeting. The long wait. The union going off script. Harlowe was true to his word. He recited this like a news report and he did not editorialize. He wanted in the worst way to tell the Greans that Larry was an impotent little son of a bitch that could not make good on his plan and had no control over the local. Harlowe wanted to say the whole thing was too complicated from the start but he bit his lip. He knew they needed Larry now more than ever and if eventually they had to double down on risk, he did not want the Greans coming away with the idea that Larry could not be trusted.

Harlowe ended with the idea that the union needed a breather and that Larry would surely prop up the large part of the membership who thought a job—even in a smaller plant—was a good thing. The logic was impeccable. The union would return to the bargaining table to discuss the closure and severance benefits, but somehow Larry would throw out a bone about saving the plant and Harlowe would pounce on it. It might serve the little fuck right, thought Harlowe, if he had to crawl a little. True to his form, Harlowe was not even out of the woods in the current circumstance as he sought an advantage at some vague future point in time.

While Jack Grean had the legal pad, he sat in his leather chair like a prizefighter between rounds and used his to fan himself impatiently. Cal took notes in a journal ruled with two columns. On the left he wrote the facts as he heard them. On the right he jotted notes and questions corresponding to the points in the left-hand column. Had there been a handwriting analyst in the room they would have seen the notes were becoming more clipped and emphasis was being added in the form of more and more underlined words.

"Larry <u>uncertain</u> what drove the decision."

"Next move <u>to be determined</u> after additional caucus with membership."

"<u>Trying</u> to meet sooner."

Cal listened patiently and silently to Harlowe's report. Had they been disconnected, Harlowe would have wasted a lot of time because he did not listen for so much as a grunt or an "uh-huh" from Florida. Harlowe was on a roll and whether he knew it or not, he was engaged in this soliloquy in part because he feared what would happen when he stopped.

At the end, Cal asked, "Is that everything?"

"Yes, sir," said Harlowe in his most obsequious tone.

Cal looked across the desk at his brother Jack for a sign of his take. For his part, Jack had left the details to Harlowe for so long, he seemed as bored at the recitation without a punch line. Jack arched his eyebrows at Cal as if to ask, "Did we win?"

Cal pushed his ledger away ever so slightly and let a pause linger. He laid his hands palms down on the desk and pushed them flat while leaning in toward the speaker phone.

"Time kills all deals," he said.

Jack was not quite sure what Cal was driving at or why he said it at this moment. Harlowe wished he could be in the room to see Cal's face to get the exact measure of his mood.

In short order, Cal revealed all regarding his mood.

"Time kills all deals," he repeated. "There are windows of opportunity. Our friends down the block here at NASA understand that precisely. Come in at the right angle at the right moment at the right speed and you have a nice, soft landing, success and a parade. Misjudge that angle and the opportunity and the ship bounces off the atmosphere or burns in a smoldering heap. We have our window here and it is a lucrative window. But we do not have a plan for this landing. We have a lot of ifs and buts and maybes and our fate in other people's hands who don't give a shit whether we land or burn."

Harlowe wanted the read and he was getting it but it did not mean it was a happy read. Cal was just warming up.

"Harlowe, your skill is making things happen, not watching them happen and you have picked one fuck of a time to climb into the gallery," said Cal. Unlike Jack, Cal rarely cursed, so dropping the f-bomb had additional impact on those who heard it. He did not raise his voice one decibel. He did not have to.

Cal continued, saying, "We may have lost sight of the goal here. We have a golden opportunity to maximize the value of the sale. The most interested bidder—TerVeer Enterprises—is the most interested *except* for the fact that they are not sure how much control we have in our union facility. Their interest is proportional to the fact that we can send them some kind of signal we have control. Time will kill this deal. Harlowe, we cannot drag this out. Make this happen quickly so we can send this signal loud and clear—the union status there does not detract from our value."

Harlowe sat on the corner of an unmade hotel bed listening carefully. He was half-dressed in dress pants and an undershirt. He ran his hands through his thinning hair. He attempted to try to choose his next words very carefully.

"This won't get done overnight, but I will put some giddyup in this, count on it. I understand your urgency," he said.

Sitting quietly for so long was killing Jack Grean. He seemed mildly confused as to whether to be happy or concerned by the call. Everything was somewhat more binary in Jack's world.

"Harlowe, this is Jack. Nobody knows those guys like you do. Go bring this home and we can all go out and celebrate."

Cal was puzzled as to why Jack had to cheerlead at this point. Cal sensed the mission was far from accomplished.

"Harlowe, let us know what additional resources you may need. The union sounds stirred up," said Cal.

"I think I have what I need. I just need to use it."

With that, Harlowe hung up the phone and finished dressing. He had some long days and nights ahead.

Chapter 25

Hospital Hours

Trey could somehow see this day coming but the reality was far more chaotic than anything he imagined. He knew his father could not deteriorate and simply disappear into thin air. Earl was wasting away, but at some point a part of his vital system would be compromised and reveal itself in a jarring event. By passing out into Trey's arms, Earl signaled that event was upon them.

As the ambulance gathered Earl and took him to the hospital, Trey found his car and drove two blocks back to the house and loaded his mother into the car for the short drive to the hospital. He dropped her off in the circular driveway at the main entrance and pulled over quickly to a tall parking garage. It all seemed like an eternity and his thoughts fluctuated wildly between scenarios where they arrived to find his father dead and others where he was sitting up, alert and revived by the medical attention received. The thought his father might be dead was very real to Trey and it caused a lump in his throat. The push of tears caused a pressure behind his eyes and foretold a terrific headache. Trey calmed himself and realized his mother was likely to be ranging between emotions as well. He did not need to push her over into panic or despair. Trey got out of his car and walked to the edge of the fourth floor of the parking structure. He took just a moment to clutch the concrete facing and take two deep breaths. He quickly recalled a boyhood memory to lean on. Trey and Earl were watching reruns of Timmy and Lassie when Trey was 5 or 6 years old. In the episode, Timmy was told to be optimistic with the phrase: "When you hope for the best, the best always happens." Somehow Earl latched on

196

to that phrase and used it half-seriously as Trey was growing up to remind Trey to be positive in the face of challenges. At this moment, Trey used the phrase and the memory to gather himself as he took one more long breath. Listening to the clang and groan of the parking garage elevator, Trey realized chances were good the stairs were faster.

Arriving in the lobby, Trey searched for his mother and considered she might have marched right over to the emergency room. After a quick scan, he decided to walk in that direction in the hope of finding her. The path from the lobby to the ER was marked by a bright yellow line on the floor so Trey found it entirely plausible she had set off to find Earl on her own. As Trey paced the yellow line on worn blue linoleum he kept his head up to see if his mother was somewhere ahead. Walking down the hall, Trey realized one more option when he saw a carved wooden sign that distinguished itself from the standard plastic hospital signs. The sign contained one word and a small arrow. CHAPEL.

Trey was rewarded for his attention. When he first entered the chapel he had to adjust his eyes as the glare of the florescent bulbs in the hospital hallway gave way to soft blue bulbs visually warming the area. The chapel might have been soundproofed too as once the door closed behind him, Trey felt an overwhelming sense of quiet and calm. The chapel faced no outside wall, yet somehow stained glass windows on the wall were illuminated as if they were either dawn or dusk—subtle and suggestive of something yet to come. There was one small figure at a short altar rail. By the size of the figure, Trey was almost certain it was his mother but given he was not 100% sure, he decided to approach and confirm. He could not trust his senses or emotions and did not need to unintentionally assault a stranger and add to their upset and his.

The figure in front of him did not kneel in prayer but stood and used the altar for support with one hand, clutching her coat close to her heart. It appeared the motion was not to fend off cold air, but hold her heart in her chest. As he got within about 2 feet, Trey confirmed what he felt. It was indeed Margie Bensen.

Trey felt no matter how quiet he had been, his presence was known and felt. Even his soft-soled shoes on pile carpet in the chapel seemed to roar. He stood back just a few feet. Wordlessly, his mother turned and took his hand to walk out. Her hand seemed oddly warm and small. It almost disappeared in his larger hand. He matched the squeeze of her hand and headed to the ER.

Once there, Trey's immense friend Baggy was the landmark leading them to the area of the ER where Earl was attended to. Baggy was at the foot of the gurney and seemed to be watching the ER nurses with great intent and admiration. Baggy caught Trey and his mother approaching and waved them closer. Baggy threw his chin in the direction of Earl, who was prone as technicians hooked him up to diagnostic tools, each one with their own required wire.

"He's up and has been talking with them," said Baggy, who never took his eyes off the ER nurses as they worked. Baggy's eyes seemed to dart around the action, trying to ascertain information. "He's improved already. He seems to know who he is and where he is. C'mere you two."

Baggy put his arm around Margie and Trey, bringing them in closer to the action than they might have dared venture themselves. Baggy positioned his head between Trey and his mother and whispered, "Stay right here so he can see you. It will make him feel better." Trey thought this was all very comforting and warm from a guy who once sat on kids in the schoolyard until they surrendered their lunch money.

What they saw was Earl with an oxygen mask and a lot of equipment monitoring vital signs. Nurses seemed to be almost yelling at him asking questions about his name, the date, where he lived. They were testing his cognitive abilities. The vital sign monitors seemed to show a weak but steady pulse and heartbeat with a blood pressure to match. Trey soon realized they were not really yelling at Earl as much as they needed to be heard over the din of all the competing sounds. Earl looked wide-eyed and scared. Margie moved her hand up and clutched Trey's entire arm, resting her head on his shoulder.

For over an hour they probed and poked at Earl. The good news was he was coherent and alert. He had not suffered a stroke. The bad news was they could not pinpoint a reason for this episode. Certainly his deteriorating lungs were not supplying robust amounts of oxygen to the brain but it was not clear what caused his sudden collapse.

By 11 p.m. Earl was in a hospital room. Margie sat at his side and held his hand. Earl appeared exhausted and sleepy-eyed. The normal oxygen tube with one small offshoot for each nostril he wore at home had been replaced by a more formidable mask that forced oxygen into his system at more aggressive rates.

Trey tried to get his mother to go home and get some rest but she would not leave Earl's side. As an alternative, Trey worked with the hospital to bring in a small cot so his mother could sleep more comfortably, at least more comfortably than in a visitors chair in the room. Chair or cot, Margie Benson's greatest comfort proceeded from the fact she was by the side of her husband.

It was well past midnight before Trey left the hospital. He, too, was exhausted, his senses on overload. He was on his way through the lobby exit when he passed the chapel. Remembering the quiet and peace, he stepped inside and sat on a pew-like structure in the back. Small candles flickered in the front and mesmerized him. He allowed his mind to go blank for just a moment.

At about 3:30 Trey was jolted from a deep and restful sleep by a shake to his shoulder. It annoyed him by its intensity. When he awoke he was disoriented but realized he was still in the chapel. Trey realized his neck was sore as his head lolled in an odd position as he slept sitting up. The room was still dark and peaceful and his first impulse was to lay down in the pew. But that was merely a brief, wishful thought.

"Sir, I'm sorry. You can't stay here—you will have to find appropriate accommodations and I can help you with that."

Trey realized he was being addressed by a female security guard. He had fallen asleep in the chapel. The guard was a pretty Hispanic woman with longish hair tucked under her security hat. By her tone and practiced cadence, Trey quickly realized these lines were well rehearsed to balance compassion and firmness. It also crossed Trey's mind that he had been identified in her mind as a homeless person who wandered into the chapel. A quick wipe around his chin reminded him he wore a 20-hour growth of beard and rumpled clothes of a day's wear. He could understand being identified as a vagrant.

"I'm sorry. I must have dozed off. I have to go now. I'll go now," he assured the guard.

Once into the garish light of the hall, Trey took stock of the situation. The first thing he did was find a pay phone and try to call Carole. He knew his disappearance would not be appreciated no matter the circumstance.

Just more evidence of his thoughtlessness. He dropped in several quarters to be sure the call would go through and punched in his home phone. It rang 10 times before an automated voice from the phone company pleaded with him to check the number and call again. No answer? That puzzled Trey but did not alarm him. Carole simply did not answer the phone after 10 p.m. That was a chore left to Trey. There were not many jobs assigned by gender by Carole, but this was one of them: dealing with wrong numbers, drunks and crazies who might call late at night. She might just believe Trey was there. It was also possible she simply did not hear the phone at all. For a brief moment he considered calling again to see if she would pick up out of sheer exasperation but he hung up the phone and collected his quarters from the coin return. As he hung up, he took one step toward the main exit and the parking structure. He saw the female security guard disappear down the side hall. In an instant he decided to head back to his father's room. Trey ducked into the men's room and splashed his face and arranged his hair, improving it from disaster to simple mess. He smoothed his shirt and straightened his sports jacket. If he was going to move around a hospital at this hour he wanted to look and act like he belonged there. He went to the elevator, punched up the floor and strode quickly to Room 507 to find his father. Here the hall lights were dimmer to help the patients sleep and a soothing blue glowing light emanated from 507. His father was asleep lying in his bed at a 45-degree angle. Earl had numerous wires monitoring his condition leading to a box flashing green numbers in rhythmic succession. He was OK for now. His mother pushed her cot next to Earl and fell asleep on her side. Evidently she fell asleep holding his hand but in her drift to sleep it merely lay at his side. Trey did not enter the room but stood at the door admiring the scene. "What did Dad do," Trey wondered, "to earn this kind of devotion?" Mentally, he contrasted this scene to Carole, sleeping alone.

Trey sensed a nurse in the hall who sized him up for a moment, evaluating him as doctor or intruder. He did not even let her speak, but filled the void with his assurance.

"I'm going now," Trey said.

Although his parents were asleep and unaware, he kissed his fingers and waved to them silently as he left.

Seeing that it was now closer to 4 a.m., Trey searched the skies for any sign of dawn but could find none as he made his way to the parking garage. He looked around to see if there were any muggers or addicts in the shadows but decided it had now reached the hour that even the bad guys had gone home. Trey stopped at a White Castle drive-through and picked up a coffee to ensure he would be awake on the trip down the Turnpike to home. The drink—even hot—felt good as his throat and mouth were dry from his nap in the chapel.

He arrived home at 4:20 and came in silently, avoiding every creaky floorboard he had come to know. Belvedere, for his part, was delighted. He must have been sleeping with Carole in the bedroom but the muffled thud of his paw pads on the carpet were evidence of his fondest hope he might be the lucky winner of a bonus meal of kibble.

Trey took off his loafers to be in stocking feet and mimic the soft footfalls of Belvedere. He turned him and pointed him upstairs again with a soft pat on the rump. The cat complied with a small harrumph.

As he ascended the stairs, Trey was not sure what to expect. Carole was a jumble of emotions and Trey understood he was the root of the mood. Truthfully, Trey just wanted even another 90 minutes of sleep. Entering the room, Carole barely stirred. Trey went to her side of the bed and kissed her head.

"I'm home and it's been a long, long day. Dad had a fall. I'll tell you in the morning," he said.

"What time is it? I was so tired I fell asleep. Aren't you here?"

Carole was not making sense.

"Go back to sleep. We can talk in the morning."

CHAPTER 26

---•◦●◦•---

THE HUNKY HALL

The Hunky Hall's proper name was "The Hungarian-American Social Club of East Newark." It was a run-down building in a run-down part of East Newark. Local 412 of the Brotherhood of Metalworkers held their general membership meetings there for several reasons. It was close by the plant. It was large enough to hold even the most well-attended meetings. It had a bar. But the primary driver was most obvious. It was free. The Hungarian community had shrunk precipitously in the last 10 years and the club opened its doors to the general public out of sheer financial need. Past the brick façade was a spacious bar, several pool tables and assorted tables and chairs. Beyond the bar was a decrepit set of room dividers about ready to fall apart from sheer age and neglect. The back area was used for all manner of community celebrations—weddings, bachelor parties, funeral repasts, political dinners and the Local 412 membership meetings.

Only two days earlier the union leadership accepted the proposal by Grean to shut down the plant and expressed interest in bargaining over the terms and conditions of the closure. Immediately thereafter, Mo and Tommy stood in the lunchroom at the plant and discussed the situation in broad terms with whoever was around at that moment. This membership meeting was far more formal and would go into the situation in great detail for all who were interested, which was just about everybody.

The older workers knew there was a severance clause in the contract in case of a shutdown of the plant. Still, it was a doomsday clause they hoped never to scrutinize. If they read it carefully, workers were entitled to two weeks' severance for each year of service to a maximum of 26 weeks per person. But many also knew there was an additional clause called the Rule of 80. The Rule of 80 held that if you added the employee's age and years of service and the result was 80 or greater they were entitled to an additional 26 weeks' severance or a total of one year of severance. Considering many of the current employees joined Grean either right out of high school or after a hitch in the service, there were a whole lot of people who were in their early 50s who qualified for a year of pay. At the time the clause was negotiated, it was actually seen as a poison pill, a cost so dear so as to prevent Grean from thinking of closing the plant while protecting the most senior of workers. But now it appeared Grean would pay any price to shutter the plant.

Still, there was a legion of employees who did not qualify for the extended riches of the Rule of 80 and they wanted to come to the meeting to see what was being done to protect them as well.

The Hunky Hall would normally accommodate the union meeting comfortably but this was sure to be the best attended meeting since they took a strike vote in 1983. The hall itself had a small parking lot to fit about 20 cars. The rest was street parking and anyone arriving late might walk 10 to 12 blocks.

Now Tommy Pherrell sat on a folding chair in the alley next to the hall smoking a cigarette. He fumbled with a badge that identified him as UNION PRESIDENT and attached it to his flannel shirt. He quickly pulled a light windbreaker over the badge as if it would allow him some degree of anonymity. Tommy puffed nervously as he rehearsed his lines and tried to anticipate the reaction. Would he be hailed as a hero who did not grovel in front of management, begging for a few crumbs of employment, or be reviled as a sellout who refused to fight for their jobs?

Mo Morris was inside the hall looking for Tommy and puzzled as to his whereabouts. He followed a curl of smoke outside the side door that led him to Tommy in the alley. There were times the scent of a burning cigarette made Mo long for a return to his pack-a-day habit and this was one of them. He wanted to bum a cigarette off Tommy in the worst way but resisted, at least for the moment. The stress level was only going to get higher so if Mo was going to cave into his vices, he wanted to hold out a little while longer.

Mo liked Tommy and worked well with him but if there was one area he thought Tommy lacked in, it was guts. Tommy was elected to his leadership position as a popular, kind figure but if the conversation got tough, Mo knew he might be alone. Tonight he would need Tommy to put up a fight so he sought him out to both gauge and bolster him.

"What the fuck are you doing sittin' out here smoking in the dark? Are you about to leave me here holdin' the fucking bag?"

Mo was scolding Tommy in mock indignation but like many a truth said in jest, he was really expressing a fear that was oh-so-real.

Tommy did not look up or look amused. He exhaled a stream of smoke in the alley and then looked Mo right in the eye.

"Are we doing the right thing here? We are dancing right on the edge. How do we know Trey isn't playing us? Larry says we can keep most of the plant and that is for sure. We are bluffing here about just walking away and taking our severance but nobody in there will know that. There are people with kids in college and a year of pay won't mean shit to them if they never get another job—and they won't—not like this job."

Mo saw real fear in Tommy's eyes. Things were coming at both of them fast and he did not need Tommy jelly-kneed at this point.

"We talked about this, didn't we? Isn't it time we stopped getting fucked here? We have got to be big boys here and play big-time ball. What we know we cannot say. I am as pissed at that midge Turk as I am at Grean. Why does everybody have to play us for fools?"

Mo let his words sink in a bit and started in again. He did not want this to be a debate.

"Do you have any better ideas? We know they don't want this place closed. If we roll and go back begging like we are little pussies THEY win. Tommy, make THEM up the ante. They want us back at that table. Sure these guys will want to kill us tonight. I did not sign up for this but I DID sign up for doing the best for these guys. Let's face it. Half of them don't know their ass from a hole in the ground and all of them only care about their situation. That's OK. I get it. Every man for himself. But I think we have a shot of making it better for every man out for himself."

There was a stirring from inside the hall that let Mo and Tommy know showtime was near. Mo worried for as split second that he spoke a bit too loud. Tommy threw the small butt of the cigarette at the wall.

"You got that right. I certainly did NOT sign up for this shit," said Tommy. "But we are here so let's see this through."

As they came in the side door, Tommy and Mo saw the largest union meeting they could remember and the hall was split into two large groups milling around. To their left was a small stage set up with a table and a dozen chairs for the negotiating committee. Mo saw that the long banquet tables had no skirts. This would mean the fact Larry's legs did not touch the floor would be clearly visible. This would irritate the shit out of Larry but Mo did not care at this point. He wanted Larry to feel some of the pain, all of it if he could somehow arrange it. That portion of the room was occupied by early birds and those who sought seats in the front as they staked their claim. It was 15 minutes before the meeting was to start officially. Calculating Larry's penchant for an entrance, it was at least 30 minutes before the meeting would begin.

On the right, the harder drinking union brothers and sisters gathered two deep at the bar. This would be a banner night for the Hungarian Social Club finances. The room was humming with dozens of conversations conducted simultaneously.

Breaking all protocol, Larry Turkel walked through the door 10 minutes before the meeting. He was pissed off before he even saw the stage and the naked tables.

"Some asshole is parked in the handicap spot," he announced to one in particular. Larry buttonholed the first familiar union member he could find and handed him the keys to his car. He gave detailed instructions to find the miscreant in the handicap spot, remove the car and substitute Larry's oversized Cadillac into the spot. The Turk could not help but make an entrance wherever he went.

While the bargaining committee worked with Larry frequently, the rank and file seemed a bit star struck upon seeing him. It was an incongruous sight—the little person walking through the hall and the crowd parting like the Red Sea before this miniature Moses. What and where he was leading his flock was open to question, but the fact he was impactful was not in dispute. Some of the more senior workers extended a hand to say hello, while few of the newer employees knew more the legend of Larry the Turk and just strained to see him. His stature made him hard to see and that scarcity only built his mystique.

Reaching the back of the hall, Larry gathered the negotiating committee into a small room that housed banquet tables and chairs so he could speak to them. In fact, he was trying to move them away from their position in accepting the plant closure.

"Look," he began, "I hope everybody has taken a step back. Look at those faces out there. I know it was a shock when they said they wanted to close the plant but we owe all these people a good fight. And if we don't put up that fight, I think we are in for a long night here. They may try to kill us."

Larry searched the faces of the committee for some sign that he was making his point. But before he could even complete his reconnaissance, Mo spoke up.

"Turk, we told you what we wanted. We have this contract and this severance so we can go on. We've seen all these guys in different factories crawl for their jobs and that ain't us. Fuck 'em. Let them have it. I know not everyone here will agree but we will hear them out and if necessary put it to a vote. This committee is here to lead, not to follow. Give us our dignity." Mo spoke in low and firm tones. If anyone on the committee was thinking of wavering, the tone of his comments put those thoughts to bed.

Larry caught himself ready to sneer but he quickly suppressed the urge. A fight with his committee would do no good and Mo above all others knew no fear. Not of Larry, anyway.

"Let's be careful here. I can tell you from experience that people losing their jobs are not happy people—and they shouldn't be happy. Let's not have them feel we are indifferent," said Larry.

While not intending to pick a fight, the word "indifferent" struck a nerve with Mo. His eyes widened and nostrils flared.

"Let's set one thing straight. Neither I nor anyone here is *indifferent*. This is fucking sickening that they can just walk away. But play it out, my union brother. If they have their mind made up to leave, exactly how much do we have to give up and crawl? We get a few jobs back today but in two weeks or two months when somebody has a smaller paycheck or they have half their paycheck going to benefits, what have we done? I have sweated over parts until they fucking rusted. I have done CPR on a man who died of a heart attack lifting parts. I am a lot of things but *do not ever call me fucking indifferent ever again* or no matter what size you are—you and me—we are going to go." Mo's eyes were blazing with unblinking intensity as he looked directly at Larry.

Tommy Pherrell realized his heart was beating just a tick faster as Mo railed at Larry. Afraid they might indeed come to blows, Tommy took a half step forward—just getting into a position to get between Mo and Larry. That proved unnecessary as when Mo spat out his final challenge, he dismissed Larry with a wave of his hand and turned away.

Larry realized he was losing the argument, badly.

"Muhammad Morris!" Larry summoned much the way a mother might invoke a child's given name to gain full attention. "We can't fight among ourselves. This is just what they want—divide and conquer."

Larry grabbed Mo's forearm and extended his own hand in solidarity.

"Let's leave this here. No disrespect intended. We have been through too much together. I just don't want this to end, not this way," said Larry. While calculating his every move, Larry was very sincere in his statement. If he somehow lost this local union it would be an indelible stain on his reputation in the union hierarchy.

Mo shook Larry's hand and echoed "no disrespect intended, none received" back loud enough for the committee to hear.

Larry and the committee got down to brass tacks. The meeting had several parts, all important. First, they needed to present the facts as they were. The rumors in the plant had twisted so many areas. It was important all the members present hear the same thing at the same time. Second, there would be questions. Just because the facts were presented did not mean the fictions would not linger until met and dismissed. The committee even discussed the rumors. If no one was brave enough to bring them up, they decided they would air them and meet them head on.

The main event would be opening the floor to bargaining demands. Because Grean had announced the plant closing, they were obligated to bargain the terms and conditions of the closure beyond the bare bones of what was already in the contract. As with any normal negotiations, the union rules allowed any member to place any demand on the table. All it took was a third of the membership to make it to the demand list. This is where it could get tricky. If the demand was to keep the plant open, that would lead to a design and limit of financial concessions. It was like negotiating in reverse gear.

This negotiating committee caucus took place among the folding tables. The area reeked of stale beer and cigarettes and lasted far longer than intended. The membership filled the time drinking the Hunky Hall beer. The meeting started almost 45 minutes late. The pleasant drunks retreated to the corners. The nasty drunks got louder and nastier.

The meeting began nicely enough but quickly broke down along the lines one might expect. There was a large group of senior employees, some in their 60s, who would gain a large severance package of a year or more. They remembered the plant as it was and realized their fond memories were just that: memories. Their youth would never be recreated. They preferred to remember things the way they were and move on.

A second group of employees were somewhat younger. They had not accumulated the time or the wealth accompanying 25 or 30 years of service. Many had children still in college and knew starting a new job meant starting at the bottom again for all benefits, access to overtime, promotions. It was bleak. Perhaps lower wages and fewer benefits at the same job would not be a bad thing. They needed time and were willing to play for the time in any way they could.

At the very bottom of the barrel was the relatively small group of newcomers. They had five years of employment or less. They were likely to be the big losers no matter what. If the plant closed, they did not get the best severance benefits. If the plant stayed open, they would be the first to be laid off. If concessions were traded to keep the plant open, the concessions would likely fall disproportionately on their shoulders. This was a dispirited bunch who sat in the back of the hall. They had neither the sheer numbers nor the clout of seniority to help them. They were at the mercy of the tyranny of the majority.

The meeting dragged on past midnight, punctuated by several angry exchanges. Tommy wisely told the Hunky Hall to close the bars and send the bartenders home and prepare large urns of coffee instead. He was buying time and hoping the alcohol-fueled anger might simply run out of energy, like a huge wave dissipated into gentle lapping at the shore.

In the end, it was not necessarily logic that won the day. It was a matter of simple math. The largest group there was older and likely to get a large severance package. In addition, Mo and Tommy were able to truthfully convey that the only bargaining chip left was the announcement and timing to close the plant. Larry tried hard to push against the tide of hot emotion and cold beer, but in the end he could not move the conversation his way. There were several times he considered breaking ranks with the negotiating committee. He thought about whipping the group into a frenzy and demanding the plant stay put. That vision had two flaws. For one, his guarantees of union strength rang hollow. Grean just announced they were closing. Second, guaranteeing he could pull the plant back from the brink of extinction ran perilously close to exposing his deception. In truth, he might have been able to pull it off. People desperate for their livelihoods are willing to grasp at the straws of hope. Yet, the ploy required an audacity not even The Turk possessed. As the debate raged into the night, Larry thought there would be other opportunities at the bargaining table to bring about the result Harlowe so desperately wanted: the appearance of a union tamed. Larry's stomach boiled with upset as he imagined trying to explain *this* to Harlowe.

By the end of the meeting, the list of demands for the meeting was 41 items long and contained everything from the ridiculous (double severance) to the thoughtful (guaranteed severance to the family of any employee who might die in the closure period). Still, most of the list was something Larry would privately call "mental masturbation." In normal periods of negotiation, the union would routinely bring a list of demands that ran over 100 items. Less than a half dozen had any real appeal or hope of agreement. Normally management might arrive at the table with a half dozen items. It was this imbalance that allowed the union to pull back dozens of items at a time while management clung firmly to their small list. It was always the greatest moment of theater when Larry could announce the union had withdrawn 50 or 60 demands to just one by management and ask in tones of tortured desperation: "I ask you, is this good faith bargaining?" He would then march the negotiating committee out of the session, promising the exit as a preview of a much wider walkout unless the negotiations began in earnest.

Larry drifted off momentarily to imagine such a scene more as a fond memory because he knew what he was facing in the immediate future was not familiar territory. He was not in his customary position of absolute control. He did not like it and he knew Harlowe would like it even less.

CHAPTER 27

GATHERING CLOUDS

After barely two hours sleep, Trey's head pounded as he tried to sort out all the issues. While he surmised if anything bad truly happened overnight he would have gotten a call, he dialed the hospital number for general patient information and confirmed that his father was still alive and listed as "satisfactory," whatever that meant.

He crept around the house and left Carole sleeping. Under normal circumstances and in better times, he might have waked her to just talk over what happened. When he weighed the alternatives he saw greater likelihood the conversation would careen into dangerous territory so he took the coward's way out and left.

Trey looked to soothe his fatigue with large amounts of coffee so despite running late, he stopped at the Page Deli. His fatigue was so acute it actually felt like a hangover, and that feeling was not helped by either the bright sunrise stabbing the horizon nor the ruckus inside the deli. The Council of Elders was in session and stoked by strong coffee. Today's debate centered on winning lottery strategies.

"All I'm saying is that in order to even have a chance at winning the Lotto you got to stay on the same numbers. If you keep changin' your numbers, it gets harder. Eventually they are gonna have all the numbers called so just pick six numbers and stick with 'em," said Sal, who had the good sense to at least wear a polo shirt this particular morning as opposed to his usual minimalist wifebeater undershirt.

Fat Jerry was having none of it.

"Ya gotta mix 'em up. You got a better shot of the whole thing if you keep changin' 'em up. They throw all them balls in every week all new and you gotta change your numbers too. I'll tell you why your so-called method is full of shit. I keep changin' my numbers and I got three of six numbers three times in the last year. What have you got: shit."

Sal was undeterred.

"You keep your crummy $15 winnings. I tell ya, stay on the numbers and when it hits—it hits big."

Sal spied Trey coming in and attempted to drag him into the lunatic debate but Trey was not in the mood.

"Your Honor—do you think…"

Trey held up his hand to stop Sal mid-sentence.

"I will tell you guys one thing for certain. It will be your unluckiest day when Mr. Kim throws all your dead asses out of his store for cussin' up a storm and scaring his customers out of here."

Howard Kim was standing behind the counter while Trey poured large cups of coffee and seemed to appreciate the intervention.

"You guys are so loud and talk such nonsense. I ought to throw you out—might get a better customer, that's for sure," Kim said with a smile but his words were closer to his true feelings.

"Ah, bullcrap to you Kim," said Sal, his choice of words a small concession to Kim. "We are your BEST customers and best advertisement too. We are like the seal of approval for this dump."

Kim turned his attention to Trey.

"Wow, big coffees today. I guess you had a long night with the union?" Kim inquired.

"No Kim, I had a little emer—what do you mean about the union?" asked Trey. It struck Trey it was unusual for Kim to have detailed knowledge of what was going on in the plant.

Kim leaned in to lower his voice just below the diminished hearing range of the Council of Elders.

"I heard they had a big meeting last night. Maybe the plant will close? I hope not—for you and for them," said Kim. Kim's words contained a deep empathy that surprised and touched Trey. Kim searched Trey for any sign or information but Trey's sunglasses foiled any attempt for non-verbal cues.

"There's a lot to sort out. I wouldn't worry. Things always work out for the best, Mr. Kim," said Trey.

Trey pulled into his parking spot about 45 minutes later than normal but saw Harlowe's white rental car already pulled in to a nearby spot. Given the night's events at the hospital, Trey knew it was a near miracle to be at work at all, nevermind 45 minutes late, but he also knew The Squinty-Eyed Fuck had already noted his tardiness. Trey decided he would not give Harlowe the satisfaction of an excuse.

Ducking in through the loading dock, Trey made his way through the back of the plant to the press room. The plant was roaring with various booms and beats. The clank of parts hitting metal shop boxes could be heard at irregular intervals. Trey approached Pauley Firrigno with a coffee but it was clear Pauley was not in the mood. He glared at Trey from under a very sweaty brow that was already streaked with some industrial oil.

"I don't want your fucking pity coffee. Just leave the money instead."

"C'mon Pauly. What you do is up to you. Go throw this in the toilet if you want but I am leaving it here for you." Trey closed the lid on Pauley's toolbox and placed the coffee on top of it. "Do I look like I make the decisions around here?"

Pauly was unappeased.

"You don't make the decisions but you knew. You all knew. I hope you bring me a coffee at the unemployment line or whatever other shithole I end up in."

The last thing Trey needed was a confrontation so he turned in the direction of the offices. He always preferred to walk through the plant to catch the mood and be seen, but he wondered if today that was such a wise strategy.

As he walked into the HR area, BeBe was in his office dropping off the mail.

"They are looking for you already. I was not sure where you were but I turned on the lights in here so it looked like you were here," she said.

"I had a bad night last night—sick—slept in a few minutes and it all got away from me a little at a time. I'm sorry BeBe—I should have called you. I appreciate what you did but you don't have to cover for me," said Trey.

"Well, that fits because you look like crap," BeBe said with a smile, trying to lighten the mood.

"They want you over in Ike's office as soon as you can. Mr. Mikkelsen is there too," said BeBe.

Trey hated that BeBe gave The Squinty-Eyed Fuck the courtesy of addressing him as Mr. Mikkelsen but understood this was her professionalism on display. Before Trey could acknowledge her comment, BeBe continued with some urgency.

"Can we talk? Soon? So many people are saying so many things and I think they expect me to know and I really could use…"

Trey interrupted, saying, "I promise we will talk today and I will fill you in. In some ways it may be good that you don't know. You can be truthful in pleading ignorance but I know that is not easy either. I may not even have all the information right now. Let me go over there and see what is going on. Think of all the questions while I am gone and we will talk about every one of them. Scout's Honor." Trey punctuated his comment with an odd little salute bearing no resemblance to any known scout troop. This broke the tension and made BeBe smile.

When Trey arrived in Ike's office the long conference table was surrounded by the production planners. It looked and sounded more like a trading pit on the mercantile exchange than a production meeting. Reams of paper and charts were surrounded by cross-conversations of planners who advocated for resources and labor they needed to get their jobs completed. The flood of orders from Grean HQ in Florida created this frenzy.

Harlowe sat in a chair against the wall just behind the conference table. He seemed disinterested in the riot before him and welcomed Trey as something more worthy of his attention. It took him about 10 seconds to stick the knife in.

"Working half days now?" Harlowe said with no visible sign that he was kidding.

Taking a minimalist approach, Trey replied, "Bad night," and moved past Harlowe to catch Ike's eye with a wave.

Ike saw Trey and shifted his priorities. He wound down the production meeting quickly, making a succession of decisions to sort out the various disagreements being debated as to which production orders would run on the floor. When everyone else left, only Harlowe, Ike and Trey remained.

"Where are we now?" Ike asked, looking straight at Harlowe.

Harlowe ran his palms across his temples in a practiced move that slicked the wisps of his hair on the sides without somehow disturbing the tenuous strands of his comb over.

"I know the union met last night to get ready for the meeting. I have a call with The Turk to sort that out at 10. The plant looks busy as hell. Whatever they did last night, it looks like everyone is digging in. That's a good sign. Maybe they want to save their jobs after all. I do know this: We need to speed this up. Time is a-wastin' here."

Ike looked like he was hoping for more from Harlowe, creating an awkward pause he felt compelled to fill.

"The plant may look busy but I am not sure if we aren't making just stuff instead of the right stuff," said Ike.

Trey added, "I can't say what happened last night but I can say that despite the activity you see that beehive out there is not happy." The glare of Pauley was seared into Trey's memory.

Harlowe frowned at the prospect that he was reading too much optimism into the situation.

"Let's keep our powder dry here until The Turk comes back to us."

By 10 a.m. Harlowe was back at his hotel. He thought about taking the call at the plant but decided not to take the slightest chance the conversation might be overheard. Harlowe knew the building HVAC had been reconfigured countless times and he had a morbid fear that conversations taking place behind any closed door might ring through the odd twists and turns and end up being broadcast in a bathroom at the other end of the plant. Harlowe's paranoia ran deep. It was a cruel and ironic justice. There were not many people more devious than Harlowe, yet he could take no comfort in that fact. He ascribed the same devious intents and motives to others and spent unknown amounts of energy trying to foil plots that simply did not exist.

When Larry called, Harlowe was already set up at the cheap desk in his room, legal pad flanked by phone on the left and bottle of bourbon on the right.

When Harlowe picked up the call, Larry did not even wait for a greeting by Harlowe.

"This is fucked up."

"Then unfuck it."

"Let's not start this way, huh?"

The call lasted over an hour as Larry recounted the union meeting. Larry noted there were plenty of people who wanted their job back but there were far more who appeared content to accept their severance and quietly leave. Larry had a better-than-expected grasp of the demographics and the politics of the majority but it seemed lost on Harlowe.

"I cannot believe they have no desire to save their own asses. But cut to the chase. What do we give them to prop up the people who want their jobs?"

"Nothing," said Larry.

The curt response surprised Harlowe. However, the more Larry explained the more it made sense. After coming to the realization there was not enough support to provide any concessions to keep the plant open, the less senior employees spent the rest of the evening creating a wish list of all the things they might be able to squeeze out as concessions. Under normal conditions where they truly sought to close the plant, Grean might sweeten the deal half owing to guilt, the other half public relations value. But this was no normal time. If Grean gave in to any sweetener on the terms and conditions of closure, the junior group might be appeased. If the company took a hard line and offered nothing additional, Larry explained, he could argue that the union had to go to bat for all the employees. Larry warned that Grean should not give one inch, not one red cent beyond the contractual obligation. Once the junior employees had legitimate complaint, the idea of "groveling" to retain jobs might finally look appealing.

Harlowe stared hard at the bottle of bourbon and wanted to crack it open but he dared not. He needed his undiminished faculties to think all of this through. He felt like he stepped into some alternate universe where up was down. He was listening to an International union rep telling him *not* to give an inch.

"I need to think about this a bit," said Harlowe.

The Turk was not moved by the request.

"You can think all you want. This is the only way through this. Go ahead. Start giving. Leave the young guys with any shred of hope and you have a closed plant. You don't want this and I *assure* you I sure as hell don't want to lose this local."

Larry knew he was in the odd circumstance as well. If Harlowe went off script and acceded to any union demands, he assuredly could not refuse them and all was lost. He needed a cooperative partner.

"We meet at the table in four days. Be sure you understand this. You put on your fucking red Santa suit and I cannot pull you back off this cliff," said Larry.

Harlowe let the words and the idea sink in. He was now along for the ride and not driving. He hated the feeling.

"I still have to think about this," he said.

Harlowe hung up the phone and opened the bottle. The size of his drink seemed to be the one thing he could control at this point.

CHAPTER 28

ANGELO, THE JANITOR

The day finally arrived for bargaining over the terms and conditions for the ersatz closure. The expectations for all participants seemed to be out of proportion to reality. The rumors spread and mutated via both hushed and loud tones throughout the plant. Many employees expected the meeting to end with finality and decisiveness. Even though it had just been a few days, the majority was impatient with the uncertainty and wanted it over. It was an itch that needed scratching. Some hopefully envisioned the meeting would conclude like an old western where the paymaster in a covered wagon might back up to the gate and settle up with each employee at sundown. Those movies were in stark black and white. The reality here was filled with wide swaths of gray haze.

In Orlando, the Grean brothers looked out their northern-facing windows with hopeful squints at a threatening bank of thunderheads overtaking the morning sun. The brothers counted on Harlowe to squelch this brush fire and send a signal to TerVeer Industries that the relationship with the union was not problematic and worth writing a $300 million check.

Ike McKnight just longed for some normalcy. The strain of trying to increase production so broadly had taken a toll on him. Ike was a good soldier and would never complain but he was foremost a precise man opposed to jarring change. He finely tuned his plant and it turned like a battleship, precisely and powerfully but slowly. The past few weeks hit the good ship Ike like a tidal wave. This was all exacerbated by the fact Ike sensed the orders were out of all proportion to reality. The unrelenting state of emergency left him worn and he sensed another correction to be managed once Harlowe resolved this situation.

As Trey approached the plant, he realized most expectations on all sides were too high. No negotiation was completed in one session. It just was not the way it played out practically. Simple issues required thought and caucus. Something this complex would not resolve in one day. This was not a one-act play no matter how Harlowe and The Turk tried to write it. The unknowns were fraying nerves on all sides but anyone hoping for a quick resolution was in for disappointment, thought Trey.

Trey felt well rested and prepared as he came to the plant. His gut told him the day would conclude in one of two extremes: a short, terse session or an all-nighter. Either way he was prepared.

Trey got in extra early so he could survey Building One and the negotiating room to ensure it was set properly. He came in through the factory as usual and dropped a coffee off with Pauley. Despite Pauley's anger, Trey continued to drop off a coffee now and then. To do otherwise would be to admit to Pauley's accusations of being complicit. This morning, Trey was so early he arrived before Pauley—a rarity. The giant press sat cold and quiet. Pauley's red toolbox sat as a lone sentry, locked and chained down. Trey placed the coffee on the toolbox, a trail of steam rising lazily like a smoke signal.

After dropping off his briefcase in his office, Trey returned to Building One. Once there, he found the door open and the room being cleaned by Angelo Crocco. Angelo was a janitor at Grean for more than 35 years. He knew Old Man Grean and was the only person Grean Sr. allowed to clean his personal office. Angelo wore that trust as a badge of honor. Trey had seen pictures of Angelo 30 years earlier. He was short, maybe 5 foot 5 inches tall in his heartiest days. An Italian immigrant, Angelo arrived in the U.S. a refugee from WWII. Throughout the years, Angelo never lost the thick Italian accent. Somewhat ashamed he did not speak perfect English, Angelo spoke very little and only when he had to. At one time Trey thought Angelo might be mute. Angelo only spoke to those he trusted and it was a few years before Trey fell into this circle of trust. The old picture Trey remembered showed Old Man Grean with his arm around a slim, black-haired Angelo at a Christmas party as Angelo beamed at the attention. Angelo barely came up to the Old Man's armpit. The Angelo

Trey watched this day was silver haired and pear shaped. He moved in slow motion with a dust rag wiping the tables with slow, precise, hypnotic motions. He carried an unmarked plastic bottle with a clear liquid on his belt like a gun in a holster. Two squirts and a caring, thorough wipe. If janitorial work could be elevated to an art, Angelo was an Italian Master.

When Trey came in to ensure the room was clean and ready, the minute he saw Angelo he thought his inspection was almost insulting. He looked at Angelo and knew one concern could be ticked off his list. While Angelo never made a single part that reached a customer, he performed his job for decades with pride and thoroughness. To Angelo, the job was simple and important. Get it clean. Get it right. Make it look nice. In a few hours the room would be a wreck of papers and noise. The people in the room who might impact the life of Angelo Crocco would never even notice his effort, but Angelo made a life's work out of the effort. Dirty is noticed. Clean is expected.

Angelo sensed Trey in the room before he heard him. He placed his water bottle back in the loop on his hip and left his rag in a neat square on the table. He took a few deliberate steps toward Trey but stopped well short, leaving generous personal space between them. He folded his hands with a little bow that made Trey very uncomfortable. What had Trey done to merit any obeisance?

"Mista Tre. Howwa you and good mawna. I no wanna leave yet. I'ma not ready to retire. Nota yet. Pleasah no fight today, si? I know you do-ah yo bess. But pleasah."

Angelo concluded with a little wave that let Trey know he was done with his plea and turned to go back to his work of preparing the room. Trey was flabbergasted and speechless. He thought about how needlessly complicated this all had become. The words "do-ah yo bess" hung in the air. It was a simple plea by an uncomplicated man.

Trey was ready to leave when he realized he had not acknowledged Angelo in any way. This likely would have been acceptable to Angelo—no offense would be taken—but Trey was at a loss for words.

"Bon Giorno, Angelo."

The good morning greeting made Angelo smile broadly.

"We will all try to do our best. That I promise you."

Trey left Building One and headed back to Ike's office for the customary last- minute pep talk from Harlowe, which would include a description of the various roles and statements to be made. Normal contract negotiations were more like professional wrestling: entertaining but the outcome was pre-ordained. The indignation was scripted and the villains identified. This time it was different. Perhaps it was the fact the stakes were so high or maybe it was just this time that the union committee did not clearly understand their role in the match. When the villain laid them low with a dirty blow they were supposed to arise and win the match. This time they were motionless and submitting to the pin. Harlowe and Larry had to figure out how to get them back on their feet so they could at least proclaim a draw.

As Trey arrived at Ike's office, he found his boss already flipping through reams of production data on neatly folded and printed computer paper stock. Ike held a Styrofoam cup of coffee in one hand. Trey noticed a nervous tremor in Ike's hands and worried that Ike was ready to crap out on all of them in a massive nervous breakdown. Trey wondered if Ike sensed the tremor. He decided that was unlikely because if he did, wouldn't he try to hide it a little better?

"You OK today, Ike?" asked Trey.

"Never better. Why do you ask?"

Now Trey knew Ike was unaware of the tremor.

"These are tough times and long days for you, boss, that's all."

"I've seen worse. This too shall pass," said Ike. He never lifted his gaze from the jumble of numbers in front of him to look at Trey directly. He had a yellow highlighter in his teeth and a blue highlighter in his coffee-free hand and juggled the highlighters to tease out the data needed to bring harmony to the production figures.

Trey heard Harlowe coming down the hall. The heavy step on the tile floor leading to Ike's office betrayed his arrival. Harlowe entered the room with high energy, as if he was making his appearance on stage. He looked refreshed and had on his sharpest dark blue suit. It was showtime for The Squinty-Eyed Fuck.

Harlowe shut the door with conspiratorial quietness even though there was not another soul in that wing of the building. Even though Harlowe already discussed the broad strokes of the plan with Trey and Ike, he eyed them both as if he was letting them in on a great secret.

"Remember, we give them nothing today. NOTHING! I know that seems harsh but we need to give their junior union members something to bitch about. And by the end of today they'll have something to sink their teeth into. Ike, you have to live here after I am back home so let me be the bad guy. I'll say we have no desire to change the terms and conditions of the contract. I'll say that until I am sick of saying it."

This annoyed the piss out of Trey, who noted Harlowe was aware Ike needed to preserve HIS relationship with the union while ignoring Trey who HAD the relationship. Trey had no intention of saying a word at this little pep rally but that was the last straw.

"Harlowe, I know it is too late in the game to change anything, but after you run over the dog in the road he is dead. You cannot perform CPR by running him over a second time. Just wondering: What is the back-up plan if they are still lying dead in the road at the end of this?"

Trey was prepared for the back of Harlowe's hand but nothing was about to deter the confidence he portrayed today.

"In Turk we trust," said Harlowe somewhat mysteriously. "He knows his guys, we have our role and he has his. I guaran-damn-tee you he will get that dog standing again."

Trey thought to press the point further by noting Larry's inability to control his committee just a few days ago but decided not to poke at Harlowe twice. They had their marching orders and Trey was to take notes, shut up and watch Harlowe work. Neither Ike nor Trey was to speak unless invited to by Harlowe. Ike seemed so relieved by this, his grip on his coffee relaxed and what had become a taut ellipse of foam returned to a more familiar circle.

Usually the company committee—represented by Harlowe, Ike and Trey—would walk conspicuously through the plant to put on a little show for the employees. This time, however, they knew tensions were real and raw so they ducked out a side fire door and down a narrow alley to get to Building One.

To their great surprise, Larry's Cadillac was already parked in front. His desire to make an entrance was trumped by his need to get a rein on his committee. As they entered, Harlowe and company found an empty room but they heard muffled voices coming from the second-floor union caucus area.

After about 20 minutes, the union appeared and sat at the long table in their customary places: Larry at the center flanked by Mo and Tommy with the rest of the committee to the sides in rapidly descending importance. Usually the committee beyond Tommy and Mo looked disinterested but today Trey thought they looked uncomfortable and fidgety. In preliminary meetings, a local leader like Mo might open the conversation but Larry took the lead immediately.

"We are gravely disappointed that you would even think to put the loyal men and women of Local 412 on the street and out of work after they built the company after many years from this very spot. We hope you have come here to announce you have reconsidered this terrible and illegal decision."

Larry knew there was nothing illegal about an announcement to close the plant but this was not the time for accuracy and truth.

For his part, Harlowe sat quietly and did not understand Larry actually wanted a response. It created an awkward silence and a bit of suspense until Harlowe stammered, "Um, ah, yes, I mean no. I wish it was the case but we have not reconsidered. We are here today to talk about terms and conditions of the closure." This was an inauspicious beginning for Harlowe.

Larry seemed genuinely annoyed by Harlowe but he was such a practiced negotiator it was hard to tell the difference between real and feigned emotion.

While the union had 41 items to read off, Larry started off with his own addition to the list and it brought an immediate scowl from Mo Morris in particular.

"We are about to hand over our list of 41 demands in regards to the terms and conditions of the closure but I am also adding one demand above all others. Call it demand "A," which supersedes even our first demand. Demand A: Reopen this plant—as is."

While Larry knew the committee did not want to beg for their jobs nor open up a dialogue about concessions, he needed the demand formally on the table for some point in the future if things got sticky. He could not put Harlowe and Grean in a spot of granting something that was never demanded.

Mo glared at Larry from the side of his bifocals but hoped his irritation was subtle and unnoticed. Only Trey picked it up. Mo felt betrayed by Larry, who just ignored the wishes of the local committee—or at least the majority.

It took Larry over an hour to recite each demand. Although he was not asked any questions by Harlowe or the management committee, he often elaborated in detail about the genesis and purpose of each demand. The 41st and final demand exemplified the overall recitation.

"Demand No. 41: Final clothing allowance payment of $1,000 per employee. The normal $100 annual clothing allowance has been a disgrace for years and the brothers and sisters have been reaching into their own pocket for years to repair and replace clothing ruined in the service of Grean. The last decent act you can make would be to send them out into the workplace with a new, clean set of workclothes on their back. You are destroying their dignity. This is one small, decent step toward restoring that. They deserve the clothing allowance."

The recitation had drained the energy out of the room and the mood screamed for a break or a caucus of some kind. But as The Turk announced the conclusion of the list, Harlowe barely took a breath.

"If that is all, I am prepared to respond," Harlowe said with his best squinting smirk. Several of the union committee members at the ends of the table raised an eyebrow in surprise.

"Don't you need to think about what we have just presented?" asked Larry.

"No. There are no surprises here," said Harlowe as he peered down at the three-page list through bifocals that sat precariously at the very end of his nose. "There is nothing here we did not anticipate. It is understandable that your membership wants more. That is the problem here. We are about to close this plant to get closer to our customers in every way. We respectfully decline all the requests here. We negotiated a contract and have done so for many years. The contract lays out the provisions in the event of a closure with regard to severance. We see no need to entertain additional expense of any kind. We will notify you of exactly when we will wind down which operations when. We will work with you on identifying employees impacted by various phases of the closure. We will provide letters of recommendation, which we are not required to do by the way, to any employee who discharges their duties to their last shift. We will honor the terms of the contract we have in place today."

Trey knew this had to shock the fringe members of the committee. They seemed lost. After years of long and protracted negotiation on hundreds of issues far less impactful as these, this was a true punch to the gut. Larry allowed the words of Harlowe to sink in with the committee. He refused to make eye contact up and down the table so several members began to hoarsely whisper to get his attention. He ignored them to focus his full, if insincere, wrath on Harlowe and the Grean side.

"In all my years in representing the workers of America, I have never seen such blatant disregard for the lawfully mandated bargaining process. You sat here for over an hour and wasted my time. You never had a single intention of entertaining a single point we raised."

At this point Larry threw his sheets of demands in the air and let them flutter in various directions. He called for a break and told Harlowe he wanted to discuss the matter with the committee.

"Stay close. We are not about to go away quietly," warned Larry, as he called for a two-hour caucus.

Trey, Ike and Harlowe quickly gathered their notes and left. As they headed out the door, Trey took a quick look back to notice Larry headed to the door toward the caucus room while at least half the committee sat in their chairs looking awfully tired.

Chapter 29

Walkout

Harlowe entered Ike's office and flopped on the couch.

"I thought that list would never end," said Harlowe to no one in particular. The union's list of 41 demands covered three pages but Trey took notes of all the various explanations and digressions made by Larry. Trey's notes accounted for 12 handwritten pages on legal paper. While he knew this was primarily theater and his notes would likely go undiscussed, he played his part of note taker with great earnestness—plus it was a good way to pass the time. Generally speaking, Trey took far better notes than anyone assigned by the union. On the union side, the note taking was seen as an act of hazing for the newest member. Trey was proud of the fact that on several occasions the company had won minor points based upon the accuracy of his notes versus the union version. This time, however, he knew his efforts were about as productive as watering Astroturf.

Ike had his assistant order lunch to be delivered to the office. The three of them took a leisurely lunch of sub sandwiches and small talk. All of them were already fatigued about work so they exchanged notes on favorite cities, restaurants, books, movies—anything but the negotiations or the problems of the plant. When it was obvious the caucus would be long and indefinite in duration, Trey decided to excuse himself and head back to his office. He wanted to check on the condition of Earl Sr.

When he arrived in his area, BeBe was already back from lunch and took a quick glance but did not offer a greeting. She knew he could not say anything about what was going on and she never bothered Trey for details.

But it did not stop her from taking a quick glance to see if her boss looked frayed or composed. This time, she could discern nothing.

Trey called the hospital to find his father's condition was unchanged from "satisfactory" and that no phone was yet installed in his room. Trey intuited that his mother's frugality mixed with optimism for a quick recovery and release from the hospital led her to put off a request for the phone. He fought the urge for a quick drive to the hospital. With his luck he would just be gone when the union called them back into session. Trying to fill time, Trey busied himself with an inspection of the mail and whatever short-cycle duties he would be able to clean up but leave unfinished at a moment's notice.

At the hospital, Earl may have been listed as satisfactory but that was only because they were in no hurry to update the status of a deteriorating patient. Early in the morning Earl awoke and spoke to the doctor making rounds. He did not remember exactly what happened and only recalled talking to Trey and waking up in the hospital. With Margie sitting nearby, he labored through every answer. The short exchange with the doctor clearly sapped him even after a night of sleep. As he rested, he wheezed and tried to suck every available molecule of oxygen from the tubes in his nose. He felt the tip of his nose was cold from the forced flow of air but found little relief. The doctor ordered another battery of tests to see what was happening. A tray of powdered eggs, toast and orange juice went untouched.

About 11 a.m. Margie decided she needed to head home for a change of clothes. This could be a long siege, she feared. She arranged a taxi and kissed her sleeping husband on the forehead. On the way out through the lobby she noticed a nun collecting donations and offering religious medals. Margie took $4 and pressed it into the nun's hand and accepted the medal of St. Bernardine of Siena, the patron saint of lung ailments. She returned to the room and pinned the small oval medal to Earl's hospital gown, soothed his brow and left.

St. Bernardine did Earl no good. This in and of itself was not surprising. Earl was not a believer in patron saints. He generally considered them compromises in horse trading by the Catholic Church to co-opt various sects over time. When he first proclaimed the saints a lot of hokum, Margie was aghast. Earl was never less suspicious of the saints; he merely decided not to discuss it in front of his wife and invite unrest. Of such small kindnesses are long marriages made.

About 45 minutes after Margie left, Earl was jolted awake by a loud alarm at his bedside. He was not awakened as much as aroused as he could not catch his breath and was sure the tubes in his nose were smothering him. He ripped at them to no good effect. He was surrounded by a sea of nurses and orderlies. He looked for any familiar face but could find none. Where were his wife and Trey anyway? Why were they letting these people choke him? He felt powerless as strangers held him down and forced a plastic tube down his throat. His hands were tied at his sides as he tried to resist. He could not even scream but felt like gagging. His immense fear was just about to overcome his fatigue in a rush of adrenaline. But just then he felt warmth in his arm that spread over his body in wonderful relief and he was blissfully asleep again.

Trey was unaware of all of this as he sat in his office killing time. He finished half-dozen small tasks and was getting antsy for the next act. Originally Trey had rejected the idea of walking the plant. The rank and file was too tense and his presence would start rumors. He might face questions he could not answer. But now it was 2 p.m. and Trey felt trapped in his own office. It was getting close to the end of the shift and he thought he might sneak out and see Pauley or Lee for a few minutes. If the mood was awful out there he could just make it look like he forgot something in his car. He was desperate to break the monotony.

As he walked out of the office area, Trey noticed the plant was quieter than anticipated. With so much production flowing every machine was scheduled, which normally would produce a cacophony echoing against the concrete walls near the start of the offices. There was noise and thrum, that was for sure, but not the intensity he expected. He checked his watch. It was already past afternoon break time. Trey wandered onto the floor. He approached the first bank of six cutting machines. Only one was staffed by a lonely operator. Trey identified him as a new employee both by how clean his badge was and the slow, careful output of a rookie operator. The rest of the machines were unattended but clearly in operation in the last hour. The shop boxes full of parts partially machined sat on either side of the machines. Cutting fluids pumped through the machine like blood coursing through veins, but the machines sat idle. Control panels that monitored production blinked a benign yellow indicating the operator had not shut down the machine and just left the area.

While Trey's relationship with Pauley was strained, he still wanted to see him. The absence of employees closest to the office doors emboldened Trey to venture further into the plant. If he could see Pauley maybe he could warm the frost on their relationship. Trey turned the corner and headed to the press room. Trey saw the press pumping away and the clang of parts dropping into metal shop boxes and looked for Pauley. It surprised Trey that the figure watching the press was not Pauley but one of the new employees. While not totally unusual, it meant Pauley was not in the area. He would not leave the giant press unattended. The new employee could do very little except haul away shop boxes when they were full and turn the press off if it jammed. Pauley would call over and get a new employee like this to watch the press on a bathroom breaks or if he was machining a spare part.

Even with limited data, Trey thought the union might have called some additional people over to Building One for consultation. The vacant machines and somewhat-muted roar across the buildings drove him to that suspicion. If the plant activity was stoked by giant unseen bellows, they were currently redrawing and seemed to have temporarily sucked the air from the entire facility.

Trey weighed the cost/benefit of walking toward the center of the plant to test his hypothesis further when he heard his name paged over the plant speaker system. The high ceilings and concrete walls bounced the announcement at odd angles, creating echoes vaguely reminiscent of the introduction of a batter at a baseball game in Yankee Stadium. It also meant that the union was likely done with their caucus so Trey ended his foray prematurely and headed back to Ike's office.

When Trey arrived at Ike's office, the door was shut and there was no sound from inside. Ike's secretary waved Trey through with a nod of her head while she spoke on the phone. Trey knocked with a perfunctory rap and let himself in. Harlowe was still on the couch, although this time he was on the edge of his seat and Ike sat at his desk with his hands folded. Seeing this little scene, Trey was concerned they had been waiting on him. Indeed they were waiting, but not for him.

"Larry is coming down here to see us so we called you right away," said Ike.

That was certainly odd. Larry never wanted to be seen consorting with management in the light of day. Trey knew Larry did not wipe his nose without some intended purpose but he could not figure out this angle.

Trey entered, closed the door behind him and grabbed a bottle of water from a small refrigerator in Ike's office. He barely unscrewed the bottle when the door opened. Knocking was not Larry's style.

Trey was surprised when Tommy Pharrell entered first. In expecting Larry the sight of the gaunt local president was disorienting. Is this the same meeting Larry called? Mo Morris followed on the heels of Tommy. The fact that he made no effort to close the door heralded the arrival of Larry. Indeed Larry did enter, his mop of hair looking quite unruly. He looked somewhat pale but composed.

The three of them stood in some kind of impromptu choreography, Larry moving before his local leadership at a position to simultaneously confront both Harlowe and Ike. Trey was at a right angle in the corner of the room, a forgotten spectator.

"Gentlemen," Larry intoned solemnly while avoiding eye contact with either Harlowe or Ike, "Local 412 of the Brotherhood of Metalworkers is officially on strike."

CHAPTER 30

---◆•◆•◆---

WILDCAT

The word "strike" hung in the air like the crack of a gunshot. Ike's mouth dropped open and Harlowe blinked to take it in. This was not in the script. They were way off script. In fact, this was so far off script that Trey wondered if Larry and Harlowe had their own private play and failed to let anyone else in on it. With one more look around the room, Trey dismissed the thought quickly. Larry looked uncomfortable and shifted his weight from foot to foot. He still had failed to look anyone in the eye. Harlowe's neck and head were starting to turn red.

Tommy and Mo seemed the calmest; their hands in their pockets, softly jingling loose change. Perhaps their calm upset Harlowe the most and made them his first target. Harlowe rose to be perfectly clear he was addressing Tommy and Mo as the local officials. He wanted to stand tall in his most intimidating pose.

"A strike? How the fuck do you guys have the gall to go on strike? Did you forget you have a contract? A signed, legal document? Just because you don't like our answers you are going to pick up your marbles and walk away?"

Harlowe's voice was rising and as it did, the red rash of rage rose with it, consuming all but the top of his head. He was not done.

"This is a wildcat strike. Illegal in any state of the union. Get your lawyers, *brothers*, because we will get a court to stop this bullshit in a few hours. We play by the rules, we honor our contract and goddamn it you better believe we expect you to do so too!" Harlowe just about spat out the word "brothers" in a not-so-subtle mockery of the union. Trey

230

thought Harlowe's invective would have been hilarious in almost any other circumstance. He wondered if he really somehow believed there were any rules to play by in his twisted world.

Tommy, while the union local president, never liked confrontation and looked like he hoped a hole would open up and swallow him so he could escape this ugly scene. Mo never liked Harlowe, was never averse to a fight and had taken all the shit he was going to take.

"Court or no court this is pretty clear that our membership is telling you and Grean to go fuck…"

Larry saw where this was leading and turned to physically push Mo back. His hand just about reached Mo's chest.

"Stop! This is not how we do business. I'll address Mr. Mikkelsen," said The Turk.

Harlowe tried to go back on the offensive.

"Did you guys recommend this? You recommended an illegal action?" Harlowe demanded.

Larry took the floor and stood directly in front of Mo. A tense-jawed Mo continued to glare at Harlowe while Larry proceeded with his thought.

"He does not need to answer that but I will. No, they did not recommend this. In fact, the leadership specifically advised against this action. Even if they had I would understand and applaud it. Our membership decided enough was enough. You back people in corners and they come out fighting. We sat there for hours today telling you what they wanted and you rejected them out of hand. Reap what you sow. Unlike you management toadies who have to kiss the ass of everyone, the union is still a democracy. Maybe you can learn a little from how we operate."

With Larry invoking democracy, Trey imagined a large American flag billowing in the breeze of motherhood behind Larry's stunted body. He wished he could sit down but knew this was not the time to hint at weakness of spirit.

Ike, eyeing his production data stacked in piles on his desk, asked, "When does this start?"

Larry looked at Ike as if he was asked.

"They are leaving as we stand here. The International office is calling out to the night shift. We will also be at the gates telling them to go home. Expect picketing tomorrow, unless you want to change your mind?"

Ike's mouth would not close. Seconds before he was looking at precise data on how to fill the orders demanded by the production system. All he saw on his desk now was useless stacks of paper.

"International office?" asked Harlowe. "That means you had this planned?"

"No, we are scrambling to do the will of our local brothers. Maybe we are just more efficient than management of a large company who does not give a shit."

Harlowe was not placated.

"I suggest that you get your guys back here bright and early tomorrow. Call off this wildcat bullshit. We'll let tonight slide but expect to be in court to explain why you can violate your contract. Get them back in here, I tell you."

"The only people who will be back in here are the people of the negotiating committee. We are prepared to talk to you when you are serious about meeting our demands. You want this over, open this plant," said Larry.

Anxious to get the last word in, Mo spat out: "We'll be here—outside."

The union troika then left. The office area just down the hall from Ike housed all production planners. They sat in an open set of cubicles facing inward with a round conference table set up at the center for impromptu meetings. They already knew the plant was emptying out. Seeing the union leadership leave Ike's office, they popped their heads up like prairie dogs trying to locate the direction of the tornado. They were not sure if it was smarter to work harder to create the schedule or stop trying. As the union leaders left the area, the office got very quiet save the lonely hum of a printer disgorging useless information on schedules that would never be met.

"SON OF A BITCH," Harlowe yelled.

Harlowe slammed his hand on the conference table in a fit of rage. The table was covered with a glass layer. It shattered but did not break into pieces. Fissures ran like a lighting strike through the glass and decreased in density as they moved away from the impact of Harlowe's fist smash.

"That traitorous, lying little son of a BITCH."

Trey finally sat down and realized how fatigued his legs were. He was not about to disturb Harlowe as it was clear *someone* was going to feel his wrath but Trey decided he would not play the whipping boy again. Not this time.

Ike, by virtue of his service and position, decided to speak.

"What next?"

"I don't know for sure," said Harlowe. "But get all your managers here by 8 p.m. I'm going back to the hotel and see if that fuckin' munchkin has the balls to call me and explain this. If he calls, I may be late but don't let them go home until I get back here. We may try to run the plant with management. And don't call the Grean boys—not yet—not until we have a story to tell. We can always get the lawyers out of bed. For $750 an hour they'll get the fuck up anytime we tell them to. We need a plan here. I am sure there is more to this but they better get in line and quick."

Trey actually felt sorry for Harlowe. Usually his bullying was powerful and convincing but nobody could ever hear his words at this moment and not see he was merely a lonely dog barking at the moon.

CHAPTER 31

ROUNDING UP THE WAGONS

Harlowe was still reeling when he left the plant. As he walked to his car, the relative silence in the building irritated him to no end. Each night as he left he enjoyed the roar of the plant as it produced parts in record numbers. Tonight, it sounded like an engine badly out of tune. The staccato thumps and whines of machinery both seen and unseen seemed weak and pathetic. Most of the recent hires stayed on their machines. They were not yet union members, in their probationary period and unsure what to do. If they did not walk off, they risked being labeled scabs and ostracized forever. If they left their machines they would surely be fired by Grean. Most only wanted to put food on the table and figure out how to pay the rent. They never considered they would have to make such wrenching, complex choices. In the last few weeks it seemed like the new employees were as numerous as the union members, but just listening to the few machines echoing off the concrete walls gave lie to that impression. With the union members on strike, the place was a shell—literally and figuratively.

As Harlowe walked slowly through the plant, it looked like some kind of Industrial rapture occurred. Machines surrounded by half-completed production with oily footprints were the only sign of an operator. Production orders were half filled. Machines ran and idled in a purgatory as lubrication systems splashed cooling fluids where cutting tools should have been turning out machined parts. Now they sat spewing brown-green liquid in a circulating pond of scummy metal shavings. Shop boxes sat half filled, begging for the next part. The ventilation system roared. Normally the sound of stale air recirculating through the plant was not noticeable but with the machines idling, the air handling equipment hissed out like white noise. None of it soothed Harlowe. He was fuming. With each idle machine he passed he vaguely recalled the face but not the name of the employee who would normally run the equipment. He silently vowed to get their name and figure out a way to make their life hell when the moment was right.

At the last turn toward the parking lot Harlowe came upon three of the new employees. They were side by side, staffing the simplest metal threading machines. This was about all you could trust the new employees to do: load hoppers that fed the machine with parts, unclear jams and catch the parts as they came out finished. Harlowe was well aware he was in the vilest of moods and tried to catch himself as he passed them. If a lemon and a hemorrhoid produced a love child it would likely bear the face Harlowe wore at that moment as he mumbled a half-heartened good night to the three.

Upon opening his car, Harlowe was surprised to find a note on the seat. It was from The Turk. It instructed Harlowe to return to his hotel and wait for a call. Harlowe was a little unnerved by the fact the note was inside. He wondered if breaking into a locked car was a vestigial skill of The Turk or a subtle attempt at intimidation. Things were too fucked up right now for Harlowe to be intimidated. He got in his car and headed to the hotel but not before heading into a neighborhood liquor store. Harlowe considered buying a fifth of bourbon, but settled on a pint as a mechanism to curb his consumption. Given the circumstances, the pint was too little but having easy access to anything more was simply not wise.

Once in his room, Harlowe thought a glass simply too fancy for the occasion so he uncapped his pint and took a draw. He was on his second pull and in deep thoughtful self-pity when the phone rang, jolting him slightly with a sharp chirping sound.

"Hold your door open with the dead bolt. Now," was all The Turk said. Then he hung up.

Harlowe's patience was low to begin with and the two swigs of bourbon eroded any good humor left over. He was pissed to be ordered around by the likes of Larry Turkel but he was out of choices. He opened the door, engaged the deadbolt and let it swing closed but ajar. Harlowe parked the pint in the nightstand drawer next to the Gideon Bible, stood in the middle of the shabby room with his arms crossed and waited for The Turk to arrive. Harlowe wanted to stand at his full 6 foot-plus height when he arrived. Soon the door opened and Larry hurried in. Harlowe's attempt at intimidation failed miserably as Larry never looked up and pointed over his shoulder with an upraised thumb with curt instructions.

"Shut that fucking thing, I can't reach the deadbolt," Larry said.

The dismissive order almost made Harlowe scream, but he also saw the practicality of it so he did as he was told, quietly closing a locking door and taking a quick look to ensure his curtain was fully drawn.

"This is bold of you, coming here," said Harlowe.

"Unusual times, unusual measures. What do you have to drink?"

"Nuthin." Harlowe was not in the mood to entertain The Turk.

"Bullshit. I smell it on you from here. Share it. I need you alert anyway."

"We have warm bourbon and warm bottled water—and we are up Shit's Creek as I see it," said Harlowe as he retrieved his pint from the drawer. He grabbed two glasses and poured most of what was left in the bottle into the glasses and handed one to Larry. Larry held the glass up in a toast. He hopped up on a chair next to the small sitting table in the room.

"Here's to smoother sailing on Shit's Creek," said Larry.

"Save your little comedy show and tell me what the fuck just happened." Harlowe really wanted to vent on Larry but even the bourbon could not overcome the common sense feeling telling him a fight right now was not a productive step.

For his part, Larry was trying to still look the part of a person in control. He scratched his chin in feigned nonchalance.

"I can't lie to you. They surprised me. We really pushed their buttons," said Larry. He then spent the next half hour describing the events inside the union caucus room. Yes, there had been some anger among the negotiating committee but then resignation followed. The real surprise came when a group of about five of the rank and file appeared at the caucus room door led by Pauley Firrigno demanding an update. The union leadership laid out what happened. Words were exchanged. Tempers flared. Two of the men at the door went back to the floor and rounded up about 20 more members. The situation spiraled out of control quickly. The leadership was branded as a bunch of gutless, impotent sellouts.

Rising to the challenge, Mo Morris lit the fuse by saying: "Gutless? GUTLESS? I'll walk out the motherfucking door right now and hit the streets. Then we'll see if you leave me hanging there and we will see who is gutless and who is just running their goddamn mouth." From that point on it was a tide Larry could no longer hold back. Pauley went back to the floor and organized an impromptu union meeting in the parking lot. Everyone was so tense that it did not take much to set off the mob mentality. It was angry, it was ugly and it was quick. They were on strike, contract or no. The union leadership needed a win to satisfy their membership.

Harlowe was not mollified by this tale in the least.

"So, with all your planning and boasting, when it comes right down to it, you have nothing, you control nothing," said Harlowe.

"I don't see it that way. We let them sit out there for a few days. Carry signs. Knock themselves out. You magnanimously call another session. We talk. We concede a few jobs and you keep most of the plant open. It's over," said Larry, really trying to put forth his most confident tone. It was the nonchalance of the statement that really boiled Harlowe's blood.

"You are delusional." Harlowe realized he was raising his voice and intentionally lowered his voice in deference to the thin hotel walls. "THAT is a plan? Let them knock themselves out? How long will THAT take? Do you recall we are on a tight timeline AND the idea is to show there is no labor issue here?"

Harlowe punctuated the last words with gritted teeth and jabbed the table in front of Larry with a meaty forefinger, causing the cheap table to wobble, rocking the contents of Larry's glass. Larry was not pleased with the tone.

"Does it rain gumdrops where you live, Harlowe? Sorry we can't end this like a fucking fairy tale but we are where we are. You need to get over it and get on with it. Right now this is what I've got. If any opportunity or opening presents itself, I'll let you know."

Larry took the small memo pad by the phone, wrote a telephone number on it and slapped it in front of Harlowe.

"Here, take this number. If you need me confidentially, call this number and just say to whoever answers my prescription is ready for pickup. Then I'll call here at this shithole."

As Harlowe looked down at the number, he noted it was followed by the letters LarRx.

"Very clever, Turk, your little code here. You should be in the CIA. I only wish you were as clever in getting us out of this mess."

"We are where we are. The sooner you understand that, the better off we will be."

Larry took a last but significant swig of bourbon from his glass, hopped off the chair and let himself out.

Harlowe watched him leave then finished his glass in one gulp and fell back on the bed. He stared at the ceiling and soon fell asleep.

Chapter 32

Picket Duty

As Trey left the plant, he was fraying at the edges. The plant situation was a mess. The union was on the street. Harlowe was on the loose and angry, not a good combination. His father was in the hospital in an unknown condition. His wife was barely speaking to him. He was not certain where his mother was but odds were good she was at the hospital. He decided to start at the hospital and see where the evening's events might take him.

Just backing his car out of his parking spot Trey was surprised to see a picket line forming. At one level he knew the pickets were inevitable, but given this was a wildcat action, the speed of the action took him off guard. At the exit gate five or six employees from various parts of the plant carried ragged-looking oaktag placards hastily lettered with broad black markers with "ON STRIKE," "UNFAIR MANAGEMENT" and "TREAT WORKERS FAIRLY" scrawled across them. The paradox struck Trey immediately. The formation of the picket line was unbelievably swift given the events of the day, yet the acceleration left the union organization of the strike and the picket line far behind. The whole thing looked generic, ill-formed and amateurish. The quality of the signs was just a half step above signs held by homeless people at the Turnpike exits. The few picketers left huge gaps across the wide gate. Still, the cars and activity just across the street promised the effort was still in a formative stage as more union members gathered around a panel van containing materials for additional signs. The resources had yet to catch up to events. The reality of it all hit Trey hard. Rather than shift into forward gear and leave the lot,

239

he set his car to park in the middle of the lot and just took in the situation, sighing with a deep breath. It filled him with a great sadness to see the events spinning so wildly out of the illusion of control concocted by Larry and Harlowe. Trey knew these people preparing the picket line. For years they were his coworkers. But the rules of engagement were clear—they were now adversaries, literally on opposite sides of the fence. Trey sat and took it all in with a stooping fatigue. He wanted so badly to drive to the hospital and leave this behind. Despite all the planning and rehearsal, no one had factored in a strike to the calculus of events and no one made plans for additional security. With great resignation, Trey put his car into drive, but only to re-enter his parking spot. He had to call the security company to secure the building in light of the forming picket line. The threat of violence was low in his estimation, but so was the possibility of a strike just days ago. Trey's mind shifted into an analytical mode as he slammed the car door shut and trudged back into the plant.

Three hours later any semblance of daylight had been squeegeed from the sky. Trey doubled all security watches on all shifts. Guards would be outfitted with camcorders as fast as the cameras could be located and tapes procured. Every security guard would be trained in strike surveillance and procedure within the next 12 hours and after that no guard could be assigned to the Grean account without eight hours of strike-duty training. All of this would be expensive but Trey never thought twice about authorizing the expense. If something went bad, the search for the guilty would be relentless. The additional cost to train the guards for this kind of flashpoint duty was a pittance compared to other costs—like Harlowe's bar bill, Trey thought. The security company operatives were happy to bill for additional training. It was an easy call for Trey.

In great part, the security company was staffed by retired police and ex-military lifers supplementing their pension. Trey feared they had itchy fingers, eager to return to action. The strike provided some unknown window of opportunity for the guards to show they were not just a bunch of donut-eating camera watchers. Sensing this, Trey took great pains to set strict ground rules. No guards were to be armed with anything more than a pencil and a flashlight. No guard was to physically engage any striker. They could use the flashlight to illuminate a notepad and the pencil to record the events. If there was vandalism, the police were to be called. The last thing Trey needed was a full-scale riot. Even as the chances of violence were slim, Trey preferred to be emphatic in preventing the spark to ignite the situation. The morning would be dicey. Non-union office workers and management would arrive and many might not even know the union was on strike. Would the union aggressively block the driveway? Would they allow non-union workers to pass? Would any of the probationary employees try to cross the line and then what would happen? Trey knew he needed to talk to Tommy and Mo before daylight. The one thing Trey could control he did: Security was instructed to observe and take notes but under no circumstances were they to physically interfere.

Trey also ordered additional lights to be placed at the gates. On the one hand, the bright lights could be construed as intimidation of the picketers, but on the other Trey wanted no dark spots where actions could be misinterpreted by either the guards or the picketers. Practically speaking, the city gave up maintaining the streets in the area. Nobody cast votes from an industrial area. Lights were better maintained in residential neighborhoods. If the picketing went on all night, Trey did not want someone breaking an ankle in some darkened area where the sidewalk had crumbled and disintegrated. Concern for the safety of picketers on wildcat strike would not be a well-understood motive, so Trey decided to keep that factor to himself.

Just before leaving the building, Trey recorded a message on the company answering machine in case any non-union employee called in asking for status. It noted that the union was on strike but the company was open for business as usual and that all non-union employees were expected to report to work. This recording was another casualty of the truth. Nobody expected anyone other than the highest levels of management to cross the picket line, at least not tomorrow. This was merely what had to be said. False bravado.

With Harlowe and Ike already gone, Trey was making command decisions. He knew he was leaving himself open to criticism and second guessing but voids were appearing out of the chaos and they needed to be filled, if only temporarily. Harlowe's usually dismissive second-guessing had the effect of emboldening Trey. What could Harlowe do that was any worse than in the past? Besides, Harlowe had bigger fish to fry.

As Trey exited the plant the second time, the picket line was still undermanned but somewhat better organized. There were about 15 picketers and it looked like they had at least found someone with handwriting evolved beyond serial killer quality to create their signs. As he pulled near the driveway exit, Trey realized he might be the first to test the line. He anticipated no trouble and got none but he proceeded with great care, inching past the line slowly with a smile and a wave. Trey understood one of the many ironies of such a situation: usually those closest to the bargaining table were afforded the widest berth on the picket lines. It was an understood professional courtesy. But Trey also understood this was uncharted water in an alternate universe where none of the expected rules applied. Nobody was there to train these novices on strike courtesy and those on the line were frustrated. Trey inched carefully past the line and headed toward the hospital.

Once at the hospital, Trey bypassed the elevator and took the stairs just to get some exercise and hopefully increase his energy level. His father was moved to a room on the fourth floor and the stairs emptied Trey out mid-floor. As he approached the door Trey could see his mother asleep, sitting up in an easy chair next to his father's bed. She looked tired but blissful. Earl, however, was a mess of plastic tubes. They wrapped around him like so many snakes. His hands were tied at his sides to prevent him from pulling at the tubes. He, too, was asleep but his calm appeared to be morphine-induced via a slow drip from a bag and canister above his bed. He appeared closer to lifeless than resting, his body sagging in a heap. The mere sight of his father in this condition somehow shocked Trey. He physically recoiled as if hit by an invisible rogue wave. Trey felt his weight shift back to his heels. He went to the hospital to be with his father but now he found it all too much. He could not enter the room. He had no emotional reserve left. Trey leaned against the wall just outside the room and processed the scene mentally. If he went in, he knew he would fall apart. That would be no help to his mother. He took a few large gulps of air, massaged his temples and then his eyes trying to gather himself. He sensed a nurse or hospital employee coming down the hall and he did not want to interact with anyone. He took one last deep breath and headed back to the stairs and down to the hospital lobby.

A few moments later, his mother stirred and looked out the window into the dark night. She wondered where Trey was and what he was doing that was so important—more important than being with her and her beloved Earl at this moment. She nudged her chair toward Earl's bed and wedged her hand into his. With her other hand she dug into the shallow pocket of her sweater and fished out a Rosary. She grasped the beads between her fingers and prayed in silence.

Trey left the hospital. It was almost midnight. He was amazed and annoyed at the traffic. It did not take much for the narrow urban streets to become choked and the hospital had no circadian clock. Cars picking up and dropping off workers, the injured, the near crazy and visitors created a maze of congestion. It seemed that at no hour would there be free flow of traffic. After several minutes at crawl, Trey burrowed into the more residential section of town. The houses were largely dark except for a stray flicker of the television murmuring behind thin, cheap window shades. He was moving faster now as the makeup of the streets turned ever-so-gradually industrial and more foreboding. Large warehouses cast long shadows across the streets. Eventually, Trey found the service road beneath the Turnpike. Pockets of homeless men hunkered down for the night. They did not seem to be disturbed by the cast of his headlights. Soon Trey was back at the Bottomless Pit. Like the hospital, the streets adjacent to the strip club appeared to be a beehive of activity. Trey guessed correctly that parking would be available closer as some of the patrons began to stumble home. After only one visit, Trey moved confidently inside the club. He took out a $5 bill and quickly identified one of the bouncers and jammed the bill into the pocket of his polo shirt.

"I have friends in The Library who are waiting for me," he said.

He spoke with a false confidence but he knew it was working. The bouncer seemed assuaged by Trey's knowledge of even the existence of The Library. In contrasted to his last visit, the trip through the bar and into the bowels of the club appeared straightforward. Within seconds he was in The Library. This time Mo and Tommy were in a foul mood.

"I hope you are coming here with some answers, Ghee, otherwise you might as well go the fuck home," said Mo. Trey guessed he was at least mildly buzzed as three beer bottles sat in front of him. Two were empty and the third looked about done.

Tommy looked no happier, his eyes irritated by the day and the endless string of cigarettes now sitting in a heap in front of him in a dented faux gold alloy ashtray. He merely glared at Trey with one eye in a squint.

"Did you two think this was a half-hour sitcom that gets wrapped up in one episode? I think you are better off knowing we are far closer to the beginning than the end of this," said Trey.

"That better not be true," said Mo, taking the last swig of his beer. "Because they are about to kill us down there."

"I just came from the plant. Your guys looked closer to disorganized than an angry lynch mob."

"That's the thing. Right now they may be more pissed at us than you," said Tommy.

Mo and Tommy noted the support for the strike was far from unanimous. The union meeting had been stormy and acrimonious. As expected, the younger members were livid the union was not prepared to negotiate some package of concessions. The older members gave Mo and Tommy the benefit of the doubt. They were tired. They wanted to go home, not picket or negotiate. They just wanted a conclusion, any conclusion. Mo and Tommy were in an odd spot—every faction had a different outcome in mind—but everyone wanted a swift conclusion. Now Trey had relayed the bad news: The last thing on the horizon was a definite conclusion. As Mo explained the situation, he became more frustrated than angry, but the end result was pretty much the same.

"You're the one who got us into this—feeding us all this information, telling us we can jam them up, but you aren't the one taking the heat in those union meetings. Now you tell us to be cool? Ain't gonna happen, Ghee. You didn't say we needed time, because if we do, the game is lost. We ain't got time. You better not leave this room until you tell me the way through this—but do not—and I repeat DO NOT tell me we need time." Mo punctuated his last statement by emphatically jabbing the table with a crooked forefinger.

Trey knew the emotion was not contrived so he let the words settle into the curl of smoke from Tommy's freshly lit cigarette. The smell of sulfur from the match assaulted Trey's nose like smelling salts in front of a groggy fighter. He spoke in a firm, determined tone.

"I got nothing for you two. We are where we are. I am telling you the only truth I know and sometimes the truth is I don't know where we have to go right now. I know where we have to end up but I have no idea what Harlowe is up to. Ike is going to do anything that covers his ass. The one thing I need is for you to be sure your guys on the line don't do something stupid or crazy. That is why I came down here, really. The pickets are setting up. Do they have any guidance as to how to act out there?"

"We tried to pair up some of the older guys who are a little settled down and who have been there before with the younger hotheads. We just don't know who will show up at any hour. But they know enough not to burn down the place where they have to get a paycheck," said Tommy, adding a belated and unsure, "I think."

Trey described the security measures in great detail plus the stand-down instructions given to the security guards. He wanted Tommy and Mo to understand there would be additional security visible but the purpose was not to inflame but deter emotion. Given what he heard about a fractured sentiment on the part of the strikers, it was critical that the union leadership be able to speak with informed confidence. They could express it as a guess to their membership but the more often they turned out right, it gave them a more secure foothold on opinion.

Trey had a beer with them more as a gesture of goodwill than any desire to drink. He was bone tired. If Tommy and Mo wanted to fight, they, too, seemed stooped with fatigue and agreed to assess the landscape in the morning.

By the time Trey plopped into bed, it was 2:30 a.m. Carole stirred just a bit as he got in bed.

"You smell like shit," she said before rolling over and drifting back to sleep.

CHAPTER 33

TICK TOCK

I f you travel on business long enough there comes a disconcerting moment when you wake up and truly do not know where you are. There is a mild panic as your mind reboots and recounts recent events to mentally find your location. This was the panic Harlowe felt when he was jolted out of a sound sleep. This sleep was fueled by bourbon and supplemented by a deep mental funk. Oddly, Harlowe slept best in a crisis. Sleeping people do not have to face the issues and Harlowe fell into the deepest stage of unconsciousness.

The jolt of an electronic bell was supplemented by a red light flickering. It lit the pebbled ceiling of the drab hotel room like distant lightning. Harlowe immediately identified this was not his alarm clock, the tone was too shrill. He knew he was not home but he could not immediately recall where he was. Was this a fire alarm with a red flasher? Where were his shoes? Was it raining outside? What time was it? Must be the middle of the night; it is so dark and quiet.

Slowly Harlowe found his bearings. Maybe it was only 15 seconds but it seemed much longer. He pieced it all together. He was in the hotel room in New Jersey. That sound was the phone. The red light was the phone flasher to assist hearing-impaired guests. It was indeed dark but that was mostly the black-out curtains provided by the hotel. The daylight edging around the curtains created an almost perfect rectangle; it almost appeared neon in intensity. He ever-so-briefly considered he had died in his sleep and the rectangle was heaven's door. And his head hurt.

"Yeah," Harlowe answered. It was the best he could do while still triangulating all the data in his aching head. He was at least relieved to discard the idea he was dead.

"We were beginning to think something happened to you."

The tone was flat and calm. It was Cal Grean Jr. The slight echo on the line hinted he was on a speaker phone. Harlowe knew immediately Jack Grean was somewhere nearby. It took about another second to confirm that as another louder voice chimed in.

"Sheee-it Harlowe. That is a nice way to say we thought you might be dead. It is so quiet from your part of the world. I know no news/good news and all that crap but we are dying down here. What the hell is going on?"

Harlowe was dreading this call and being caught by surprise out of a sleep was not the least bit helpful. The dry air of the hotel room left him unable to speak. Harlowe excused himself to cough and clear his throat. He quickly opened a bottle of water on the nightstand and took a swig to regain his voice. Normally a booming baritone, he struggled to a hoarse squeak.

Jack could not help but run Harlowe's actions through his own filter of experience.

"Are you hungover, Harlowe? Are you up there partying on our dime?"

Cal Grean had no time for such nonsense. He shot Jack a sour look of displeasure and tried to wrest the conversation back to some useful state of decorum.

"Tick-tock, Harlowe. Time kills all deals and I feel like our deal is getting sick. Tell me it's not. What is going on there?" Cal Jr. asked.

When the boys were much younger, Harlowe mentored and entertained them with parables drawn from his career and upbringing. The boys particularly loved when Harlowe taught them the phrase "so quiet you can hear a rat pissing on cotton." These glib exchanges reminded them of happy, simpler times. This was why Harlowe searched for a story to soften the harsh facts. He struggled to remind them of his status as family friend.

"Boys, I know the clock is ticking and I'm up here doing my level best. But if your Bible group arrives and the cake is supposed to cook at 350 for 30 minutes, you can't crank it up to 700 for 15 minutes. You go find another Scripture to read."

Cal Jr. washed his hand over his face with noticeable irritation. Somehow, even over the phone, Harlowe sensed the annoyance and immediately filled in the details. He walked them through the session to the breakdown of the talks and the walkout. He quickly noted that Larry still felt the situation was in hand and that the walkout—while not ideal—was just another step in the process.

The word of the walkout stunned the Greans. The whole point of sending Harlowe to the East Newark plant was to show TerVeer Enterprises how benign the union was. This was not the signal to send. Jack Grean saw his payday slipping away and needed comfort.

"But you have the thing ready to be fixed, right Harlowe?" He was almost pleading.

Harlowe so wanted to guarantee a happy ending but he knew it simply was not true. It was time to lower expectations.

"I can't say this is how I wanted it to go but these things have a way of sorting themselves out. They have a lot at stake, too, so once we get them back to the table cooler heads will prevail."

Cal Jr. was not comforted.

"Harlowe, we have a lot riding on this. One thing for sure is we cannot have this getting back to TerVeer. Keep a lid on it. Make it go away. Get them back to the table and work with your little friend to resolve this."

The condescending tone as Cal Jr. called Larry his "little friend" struck a dark chord with Harlowe. At that moment he wanted to remind the brothers of how he and his "little friend" were doing a lot of dirty work so they could walk off into the sunset with bags and bags of cash. He really wanted to call Cal Jr. a little shit but thought better of it.

"Yes sir, I understand," said Harlowe.

"I'll call the labor attorneys and see about the legality of the strike. The problem with the courts is they are slow and very public. Not to mention expensive," said Cal. In his heart he knew getting an injunction was the last way to demonstrate to TerVeer the free and easy relationship with the union.

Cal continued scribbling geometric patterns in the margins of his legal pad.

"Harlowe, I'm not sure I really understand how you are going to make this happen. Let's touch base again tomorrow morning. These gaps in communication are not good at this point. If TerVeer calls, I really don't know what the hell to say unless you keep me up to date."

"Tell them we are thorough and this is a complex but achievable goal," said Harlowe.

"They don't want complex. They want complete," said Cal Jr. The minute he said it he realized that his words were too harsh. Perhaps not a bad thing, but too harsh. He changed his tone to encourage Harlowe.

"You and I know it is complex but they don't give a shit. I know you are doing your best. You always do. You have our confidence," said Cal. Across the room from Cal, Jack rolled his eyes and made a gagging motion indicating Cal's insincere encouragement was sickening. But he would not leave his brother hanging.

"You have never failed us, old man," Jack chimed in.

Harlowe knew he was being manipulated, but he did not care. He needed the encouragement. He felt his left eyelid twitch involuntarily. Not a good sign.

"I'm doing everything I can," Harlowe said then hung up after agreeing to a call the next morning.

He rolled back and rested his back against the headboard and assessed the situation. Usually he controlled the game and knew the next move. This feeling of being out of control and without a clear picture of the end game was driving him nuts. He was staring into space in an unproductive haze of thought. It might have been a minute, it may have been 15, but the phone jolted him again. He dreaded to think it was the Greans calling back. It wasn't. He was actually relieved to hear The Turk's growl on the phone.

"Get your dead ass ready in 30 minutes. Order some breakfast up to your room and then we are going to meet someone who is going to solve our problems."

"And who are we going to see?" asked Harlowe.

"Nevermind for now. I'll explain it to you when I see you. Just be ready when I get there. I can't have eggs. Too much of that cholesterol shit. Just get me something with bacon and a lot of coffee. Then we are going for a ride."

CHAPTER 34

MEET THE MAYOR

Newton's First Law of Motion states a body at rest stays at rest. There probably should be some corollary of political inertia in New Jersey at the municipal level. If promulgated properly it would state: once elected, a mayor remains in office until either indicted or embalmed. It often seems mayors in particular inhabit their seat for life. Upon closer inspection the truth is a mayor appears vested for life once reelected. The key to the first four years is to co-opt the machinery of patronage, keep the electorate happy with a series of high-profile/low-impact projects and wring hope out of any challenger to the throne. Then consolidate popularity and the patronage machinery to ride through a seemingly endless series or reelection bids unchallenged or with token resistance from poorly financed cranks and crackpots.

So it was in East Newark. There were but three mayors in the last 65 years and the third and most recent mayor was Thomas Glynn Thomson. Thomson followed two dynasties; the first lasting 20 years, the next 44. Thomson was born at the right moment in history as the previous mayor was debilitated by age and Alzheimer's disease. At 35 and two terms as ward councilman, Thomson mounted a shrewd campaign defying the evolving demographic landscape. Thomson split off just enough of the votes in the black and Cuban neighborhoods while dominating the older, whiter sections of town to win narrow election. While barely two years in office, he had the air and savviness of a veteran of several terms. He was a natural dynast. He was at every grade school graduation, cut every ribbon on the smallest new business in town and generally made sure his picture was in every edition of the local weekly newspaper. He clearly understood the papers were starved for content and while the editors were sick of seeing Mayor Thomson's blotchy face, they knew the new business owner would run out to buy 25 copies of the newspaper and run a Grand Opening advertisement. The mayor understood with great clarity one reelection likely foretold employment for life.

Thomson himself was not an imposing physical figure. In fact, he was short. No more than 5-feet 6-inches tall in stocking feet but nearly 200 pounds. His thick midsection was deftly camouflaged by $1,200 tailored suits designed to draw attention to his broad shoulders. The pasty complexion was topped by fine reddish hair often combed over only by a brush of his sausage fingers. He knew he was no Adonis and he maniacally controlled how and when he was seen. He had zero trust in the photographers sent to cover his public appearances so he retained a photographer on staff at the city who was a former campaign staffer. The photographer knew the sublime angles to flatter the boss and the mayor spent hours each week poring over dozens of photos of his appearances before approving one to send to the local papers. For their part, the newspaper quietly cut back their photo staff. The mayor was good to their bottom line.

The mayor was attentive to every detail. Once elected, he renovated the Office of the Mayor for the first time in half a century. While the rugs were ripped out he added a 4-inch platform beneath his desk and chair. It had the effect of raising his stature subtly and creating an almost imperceptible air of authority and power in the minds of anyone who entered the room.

Mayor Thomson's keen self-awareness made him uncomfortable this morning. Thomson was elected in part by union campaign contributions and the strong endorsement of the union establishment. It was all part of the fragile coalition vaulting him to his 4-inch pedestal. So when the mayor's chief of staff cleared an hour from the daily calendar to meet with Larry Turkel of Local 412 and an unknown guest from out of town, the mayor was simultaneously disturbed by the host of unknowns surrounding the visit and pleased to make time for anyone connected with the good working people in his constituency. Mayor Thomson straightened his tie and looked at his watch. He wondered if there might be a photo opportunity in this meeting somewhere.

When it was obvious Larry would be late to the hotel, Harlowe jogged across the highway in front of the hotel to a diner and picked up two breakfast sandwiches and two coffees to go. As Larry pulled up in the hotel cul-de-sac, Harlowe stood with a white paper bag betraying a widening grease stain. Heeding Larry's disdain for eggs, Harlowe ordered an egg sandwich for himself and a Taylor Ham and Cheese on a hard roll for Larry. Harlowe was more annoyed than surprised when Larry, upon arrival, rummaged through the bag and commandeered the egg sandwich for himself.

"I know what I told you but that egg sandwich just smelled too good," said Larry, taking a bite from the middle of the sandwich, scattering egg and hard roll pieces throughout the car.

Getting into the car, Harlowe was mesmerized for the moment by the apparatus in the driver's seat permitting a dwarf to drive the vehicle. He felt like he was backstage at a magic show as he tried to make sense of the various extensions, pulleys and knobs enveloping Larry, allowing him to drive so effortlessly. To Harlowe, Larry resembled a one-man band on stage. He half expected to see cymbals strapped to Larry's knees. As Larry drove pieces of egg dropped in his lap, bouncing randomly through the apparatus like some kind of odd pachinko machine. It briefly occurred to Harlowe that the egg might foul the apparatus somehow and send them careening off into the median. He quickly brushed the bizarre thought out of his mind to get to the point.

"Mind telling me NOW where we are going and why this is such a stroke of genius?" demanded Harlowe.

Larry was driving like a madman, cutting back and forth between lanes. He put his sandwich in the empty side of the cupholder on the console, picked up the coffee and took a swig to wash the sandwich down. When he put the coffee down it sloshed onto the sandwich. "Pig" was the word flashing through Harlowe's mind.

"The first thing we have to do," said Larry, "is get there on time, which is why you see me driving like a fucking maniac. We don't have a lot of time for me to explain a lot so just follow my lead. I trust you on that. You are good at it."

"Follow your lead on WHAT with WHO? Give me SOMETHING to work with here," pleaded Harlowe.

"Follow me and hang on. The guys in the local don't know what they want and they are not listening to me like they should. You need to keep a lid on this or you are up shit creek, right? The good thing is that your plant is down there in industrial no-man's land. But the one person who needs to understand what we are doing is the mayor of East Newark. If he finds out too late there is a mess down there he cannot help us. We are going to see the mayor."

Harlowe, always the poker player, tried to hide his every emotion. He felt his eyes widening in disbelief so he was glad Larry was preoccupied with driving this contraption of a car and did not see the tell. Larry nearly missed the exit leading to city hall and careened across a lane of traffic and swerved recklessly down the exit ramp. Harlowe was not flustered by the maneuver. He was still too puzzled.

"The mayor? How does he help us in this? And what am I telling him?"

Larry made two quick turns and pulled quickly into a handicapped spot close to the side door of the large old building. He put the car in park and turned to Harlowe.

"Tell him all the tax dollars you and Grean have poured into this town and how committed you are to keep this place here if the local union will let you. I tell you I had to mortgage my left nut to get this meeting so quick so just trust me when I tell you follow my lead and that I trust you enough to know you won't say anything stupid."

It was odd but Harlowe felt a pride in kinship in such faint praise from Larry. He could be trusted not to be a fuck up.

Larry led Harlowe through the side door. City Hall was a grand old building in many respects. Built during the Depression by the Works Progress Administration and courtesy of Franklin Delano Roosevelt, it had wide hallways and high ceilings. The walls were made of a goldish polished stone that marked so many WPA constructions. The stones and linoleum floors amplified every footfall announcing even unseen people around corners. Because the WPA did not foresee things like air conditioning and computers, the beautiful architectural lines inside were marred by a patchwork of grafted-on ductwork everywhere. It was like seeing your grandmother with breast implants.

None of this caught Harlowe's attention. Despite being a good 2 feet taller than Larry, he lagged behind him in the halls. Larry knew where he had to go and did not want to dawdle. Who knew who might see him and be related to one of the local union members? He ducked down a side hall and into the men's room, waving Harlowe in behind him.

"The mayor's office is straight down this hall. Give me a 30-second head start and I'll be waiting there. Probably no one here knows us but let's create a little distance."

Larry then lit out before Harlowe could even react. To give him a lead, Harlowe washed his face with warm water in the sink. He looked at himself in the mirror and saw a very weary version of himself.

As Harlowe walked into the mayor's office a dowdy female civil servant sat at the front reception desk. Larry was nowhere to be seen. Harlowe briefly considered he was in the wrong place but the receptionist noted with no small amount of irritation: "Go right in that first door, they are waiting for you." It was as if she blamed Harlowe for wasting the precious time of the mayor. Harlowe wanted to strangle Larry at that moment.

Harlowe opened a wood panel door and had an Alice-in-Wonderland moment. The Office of the Mayor was grand. Stepping through the door, everything was larger and more imposing. The ceilings were even higher. Floor-to-ceiling windows looked out on a shopworn East Newark neighborhood. At the far end of the room sat an enormous mahogany desk. Larry stood there, the top of his head barely reaching the desktop. Mayor Thomson stood behind his desk and another man—presumably a mayoral staffer in a three-piece suit—stood at an angle to the mayor facing Larry and Harlowe. Larry beckoned Harlowe into the office.

Larry introduced Harlowe to Mayor Thomson and his aide, Bergen Krupp. The mayor extended his hand only so far so as to make Harlowe reach further and more awkwardly across the desk. The aide had a lifeless handshake that repulsed Harlowe.

Larry got right down to business.

"Mr. Mayor, Grean Machining has been part of the community for most of this century, providing jobs and tax dollars. Because I know you are concerned with all the businesses in town, I thought you should know about a little problem we have right now. After years of mutual respect where we have worked out many differences, we find ourselves today on strike."

The mayor already was not pleased and wondered how Krupp did not know this little fact. He tried to calm himself knowing his pale face would betray any agitation. He wanted to seem cool and in charge.

Larry continued.

"The mere fact we appear here together should be a sign we believe we can work out our differences and come to a logical and agreeable conclusion. As we examined the situation, we realized all of us—the union, the company and the city—all have an overriding and common need," said Larry.

To this point Harlowe sat, listening intently, looking for a cue to contribute. This dramatic prelude left him uncomfortable. He had no idea what word would come out of Larry's mouth next and it bothered him.

"Privacy."

It might have been the last word Harlowe would have offered at this point. A terror gripped when he considered he would have to comment or embellish this gem. It would be like polishing a turd. Luckily, Larry was nowhere near done.

Over the next several minutes Larry laid it all out. The union and the company needed some space to conclude their business. It did the city no good to have a lot of publicity about the strike. The union itself was not pleased about some miscommunication between the local here in town and the International union organization. Normally, it would be the union that might notify the press to drum up public support for the position of the working man. In this case, Larry assured the mayor the union had no intention of drawing attention to this unfortunate situation. Likewise, it would be normal for the company to call the police department and notify them of a picket line and request a larger police presence. In this case, no such request was forthcoming. Such a request would draw attention of the press. Coverage might cause negotiations to be conducted in public. The plant sat in a remote industrial neighborhood. While this would not be a secret forever, it was important to let the two sides work this out quietly and without a lot of attention. Passions would not be inflamed. Positions would not harden.

Just a few days.

Mayor Thomson shot a glance at Krupp who refused to acknowledge it, preferring to keep his eyes on Larry and Harlowe. Further, Krupp had no idea what to make of this request. The mayor certainly did not want to think about a visible or messy labor issue. He was glad to know it was happening although annoyed he was behind the curve. But nobody just showed up without asking for something. He waited for the punchline. The ask.

Larry was not yet ready to lay out the request. He was still arming the mayor. He noted that while the plant sat in East Newark, the wages enjoyed by the employees via their union representation allowed them to purchase homes in more affluent and status-rich suburbs. Fewer than 25 employees actually lived in East Newark, although business taxes and the ripple of lunches, gasoline and other purchases made by the employees in their commute contributed to the economic welfare of the town. The point was driven home: not a lot of votes down there to be had.

Larry was in absolutely high gear at this point. He spouted off statistics that mesmerized the mayor. The only problem was it was absolute bullshit. Larry had no idea how many employees lived in East Newark nor where they purchased their gas. He never let the facts ruin a good speech. He was merely giving the mayor something he could quote with great confidence at a later date.

Likewise, Larry assured the mayor that if indeed the word got out about the strike, it would look like breaking news not something withheld from the public and Grean and the union would take full responsibility for the news gap.

Harlowe sat and said a silent prayer he would not be called upon by the mayor.

As Larry paused, Mayor Thomson was doing complex political calculus in his head. He heard nothing of great alarm. Strikes were not pleasant but neither were they unknown. It did not appear there were a lot of votes at stake. Perhaps Larry sensed the ambiguity from the mayor, so he decided to draw a clear picture.

"A lot of people get flustered and anxious when they hear the word 'strike.' It doesn't bother us," said Larry, extending his hand to draw Harlowe into his frame of reference. Harlowe never hated Larry more than at this moment. Larry continued.

"A strike does not bother us. It is part of the process. It can be a productive contrast. The people who are panicked by the word may call the town and ask for the police to intervene or do something. We think that would only make things worse. Let's keep a lid on this. Let's not blow this up into something bigger. Give us a few days to work this out. But through it all you know we are down there resolving this."

As slimy and mean-spirited as he could be, The Turk excelled at just this kind of soliloquy.

Mayor Thomson got the signal now. Keep the police out of the area. What was not clear was why? Did Larry and Harlowe just want a news blackout? The reporters combed the police reports daily so this kind of made sense. But was there another possibility? A question to be avoided? The mayor's sixth sense was confirmed almost immediately. Larry changed the tone without necessarily leaving the topic.

"Mr. Mayor, you have always been a friend to labor and you proved it today taking this meeting on such short notice. Is your campaign office still open and taking donations? I feel we are overdue," said Larry, not an ounce of shame in his voice.

The mayor understood what Larry needed: He wanted the police to avoid the area at all costs. It was time to end the conversation.

"Gentlemen, I know that negotiations are best conducted in private and not in the public eye. The less posturing the better. It ensures nobody gets into a position where they can't back down. I am very glad to see you both in here and working together to find a solution. I will do what I can to honor your request." The mayor waited a beat, hoping to separate topics to the best of his ability.

"As for any campaign donation, it is an honor to receive your support. The election is a way off but it is good to get a running start. Mr. Krupp knows all the details of how that is supposed to happen and he will work with you."

The mayor stood to indicate the meeting was over. Harlowe was trying to figure out what he just heard and thankful he had not been called upon. Chief of Staff Krupp walked Harlowe and Larry to the door of the large office. When he heard the click of the door indicating the mayor had left the chamber he leaned over Larry and positioned himself to make eye contact. His voice was quiet but firm.

"You understand the method to make such a contribution? It has not changed, bless your Sacred Heart."

"No, I remember," said Larry, "and I cross my Sacred Heart it will be there tomorrow." The tone of the comment was significantly less polished and more sarcastic than his address to the mayor.

The walk back to the car was less hurried as Larry seemed spent by his performance. Harlowe tried to strike up a conversation on the walk but Larry cut him off with the wave of a hand. When they finally reached the car and got inside, Harlowe wanted answers.

"Follow your lead? What the fuck was all that in there?"

"First, you are going to church in the morning to pray. Then we are going to get this local to repent their sins for not listening to their International."

CHAPTER 35

———◆•◆•◆———

RECKONING AT HOME

The alarm clock went off at 5 a.m. as usual. Carole never fiddled with Trey's alarm as he often pushed through almost any fatigue to conduct his morning run. But after only two and a half hours sleep, Trey could not quite identify the source of the noise in his deepest sleep trough. He wondered exactly the origin of the noise. The clock radio played on for what seemed like an eternity. "Where is that music coming from?" he wondered. Slowly, he came to the realization of where he was and the source of the noise. Arising from a rested sleep he would deftly locate the alarm and silence it before Carole stirred from her deepest sleep. This morning his eyes burned as he opened them even to a slit. He waved fruitlessly at the alarm clock snooze button but connected just enough to send it sailing to the floor with a crack indicating the device may have sustained significant damage. The combination of noises sent Belvedere in a panicked run through the house. Trey craved just a little more sleep and surveyed the damage with one groggy eye.

"Thanks," said Carole. "You are batting a thousand aren't you?"

At this point Trey thought even if he went to sleep and had a nightmare it might be an improvement over his current situation. He found himself falling into a light sleep when he heard Carole in the bathroom. His klutzy movements awakened her and now she was making zero effort to muffle any noise. Even in his fatigue, the noise was just enough to keep him from falling asleep. Despite being awake, his body would not rise but seemed to sink and formfit into the mattress. The sound of the shower in the next room was soothing and put him back into a light but restful sleep, but somehow when the water stopped it woke him to a full but weary consciousness.

He struggled out of bed to find Belvedere sniffing the clock on the floor. The outer casing showed a crack but it seemed to be keeping time with a low, grinding gurgle he had not heard before.

Trey staggered to the bathroom and washed his eyes with warm water. Carole was behind him, toweling off, and he leered at her in the mirror. Her body was clean and beautiful. He felt like if she wanted a baby he could make one now, but he knew his advances would not be welcome.

That point was driven home quickly as Carole looked up and caught his semi-lecherous look.

"How many times have I asked you to just call me when you are going to be that late?"

She was clearly annoyed.

"Then you come in smelling like a garbage dump and the real cherry on top is banging around at this hour. Have some consideration. Turn the alarm off if you don't intend to get up."

Trey thought back to the night before and the daisy chain of events. She was right. He did have time and opportunity to call. But it was a blur.

"We are on strike," he said. It was a statement of fact, but Trey had some glimmer of hope that it would be some kind of excuse for not calling. A non-excuse excuse of sorts. He wanted so badly for Carole to carry the conversation a little further so he could clear his head. She made no such move so he charged ahead.

"They are on strike. On the street. It was a mess. It is a mess. I am not sure what we are looking at today."

Trey realized he still had not apologized for not calling.

"I'm sorry. I could have called. I don't know where the time went. It got late. It all got out of hand."

Carole looked at him as she wrapped a towel around herself.

"OK. You were working. But why do you stink like a lit cigarette put out in a beer can?"

Trey smelled it now more than last night as he wiped his face with his undershirt. As he fell into bed last night he never changed. He realized the cigarette smoke from the strip club clung to him like pond scum.

"We were working out the details of all the fallout from the strike.

We went for a few beers. I stopped by the hospital. Dad is no better. My mom was there but she was asleep. He looks horrible. I went back for a few more beers."

Trey knew he was telling approximate and hazy truths and trolling for sympathy. He miscalculated badly.

Carole was angry but somewhat indifferent.

"So you have a crisis. Load yourself up with beers. See your Dad. Get yourself upset. Drink beer and drive around in the dark and decide not to call me so I worry. Does that about sum it up?"

"That would not be entirely wrong."

Trey was not trying to be glib and evasive. He was hoping to endure the conversation. He could not think of a good answer at this point. He tried to fill the void.

"I'm sorry. I cannot seem to do the right thing. If there is a wrong outcome, I'm picking it right now."

Carole was not mollified by this at all.

"I don't know what you are doing right now. You are drowning and you are not letting anyone help you. I can't get in your head. You have a sick father, a crisis at work. Maybe I need to be second fiddle right now. Third fiddle even. But I don't have to like it. I could even bear taking a backseat if I knew what was in your head."

Trey could tell Carole was near tears. On top of all this he could not bear the tears. She turned her back and tried to hide her face as she composed herself. The whole dressing room was lined with mirrors. At one angle Trey could see her wipe at the corner of her eyes. She did not want to share her emotions with her distant husband.

As the silence lay heavy between them, Trey thought their relationship was at a crossroads. Maybe not a crossroads. More like a traffic circle. They were stuck going around and around. Even the image in his head made him slightly dizzy. The room seemed to move just a little, not so much a spin but nervous little jerky jumps before his eyes.

Carole tried again.

"We can get through this. But you cannot shut me out and expect me to watch while you implode. Don't mess me up. Don't mess us up. Do what you need to but tell me what the hell is going on."

Trey thought about her words but he was almost sick. He had no energy for the fight and no time to explain. They could be there for hours and he needed to pull himself together and get back to the plant—or was it the hospital?

"I need to lay down," he said. "Maybe just 20 or 30 minutes, but I need to close my eyes. We can talk tonight, I promise."

Trey approached Carole and touched her arm, but she just looked at him and walked back in the bathroom. Trey went and plopped in the bed. It felt like heaven. He must have drifted off immediately. If Carole was still banging around the house in anger and frustration, he never heard it. He drifted off to a dreamless, deep sleep. When he awoke he wondered if Carole might still be in the house. Once he saw Belvedere snoozing at the foot of the bed he knew Carole had to be gone or the cat would be following her in search of food or affection. No, she was gone. He never heard her leave or start her car. It was lighter outside than he expected but he could not focus on the clock. Finally, he saw the time. It was 8:20. A lot later than he thought. He jumped out of bed. They would be looking for him at the plant and who knows what the hell was happening. He was showered and gone in 20 minutes.

Chapter 36

Hospital Rounds

As Trey headed up the New Jersey Turnpike he wished he had taken an additional 10 minutes to look at the weather on TV. The sky to the north was black and threatening. He left his umbrella resting just inside the garage. It looked ugly ahead.

Just before he left the house he told BeBe he would be late but had his beeper on. He noted he wanted to stop at the hospital again. It was not truly his plan but the string of events made it a fortuitous excuse to be late. He really did want to stop and see his father and his little nap made him late to work. Oversleeping was not a welcome excuse. Attending to a sick father was noble. The fact he was using his father as an excuse made Trey ill. He wondered if he could sink any lower.

By the time Trey reached the hospital the skies opened up, creating large, shallow puddles in the visitor parking lot. It would be several hours before official visiting hours so the lot was pretty empty. He found a spot not too far from the stairwell leading to the entrance. Even so, without his umbrella, Trey was uncomfortably wet by the time he reached the lobby. In jacket and tie, he looked enough like a doctor that he could stride past security if he was confident enough. For good measure, he clipped his ID badge from Grean on his shirt pocket. Even the wrong badge was still a badge to the rent-a-guard. He made it past the lobby and onto the Critical Care floor without a single challenge.

This time as he entered the room his mother was up looking at the sheets of rain pouring down. Earl looked no better. A scatter of tubes and wires. One good sign was he was breathing on his own now. The dreaded

263

respirator was gone. His vitals looked steady if weak to an amateur observer like Trey. He made a little noise so as not to scare his mother, who seemed pensive. When she saw him, she hugged him a little longer than usual.

"Where have you been? I just wanted to see you, be with somebody," she said.

"I was here last night. You were asleep and I did not want to wake you. How is Pop?"

"I don't know. He slept through the night but I am not sure what all these numbers mean," she said with a nod to the blinking panel readouts above his bed. Trey thought this might be the best time to catch the doctor on rounds so he went to the nurse's station to see when the doctor might be by. They told him the doctor was on rounds and the best bet was to return to the room. When Trey returned to the room there was a tray of hospital breakfast food on the stand at his father's bedside. Trey wondered exactly how they calculated the nutritional needs of a man in a semi-comatose state. As bad as it probably was, the aroma of scrambled eggs activated a great hunger pang in his side. He swiped the orange juice off the cart and took a sip. It was weak but sweet.

"I'm sorry I can't stay long right now. We have big problems at the factory. The boys are on strike." Trey saw his mother's eyes widen at the mention of the word "strike."

"Nothing to worry about. We can handle it but it is crazy. You know my pager number. I can be here a while longer but I need to get them settled there. I'm a 10-minute drive away," said Trey. He wanted to get his mother some breakfast but he knew if he did he was certain to miss the doctor. There was no patient in the other bed so he grabbed a visitor's chair and pushed it on his father's side. There he sat next to his mother. He laid his hand on top of hers. It was warm and soft but frail. It reminded him of the times she would touch his forehead and cheek when he was sick with a fever. They were comforting hands and he wished he could stay there forever. The rain slackened but still beat against the ledge just outside the hospital room window. The hypnotic quality of the rain's rhythm was broken by the arrival of the doctor, who entered the room in a burst of energy. Trey tried to get a glimpse of his badge or nameplate to address him personally but the lapel of his coat hid any identifications. The doctor was a tall, thin man with a gaunt face. He had long wavy, thick black hair that receded in the front and was long in the back. It had the effect of making him look like he was sitting in a strong gale, even indoors. It accentuated his eyes and nose. He appeared to be Indian.

"I'm Trey, his son," he said with a nod to the bed and the man entangled in the web of wires and tubes, "and this is my mother."

"I am Dr. Daniels."

Trey thought he did not hear the name clearly as he was expecting a far more exotic foreign-sounding name. He shot a quick glance again for the badge or nametag but still could not locate it. Trey hoped he got the name right. No sense pissing off the doctor treating your father. Trey settled on a safer, but less formal greeting.

"Dr. D, how is he doing?"

After entering the room at a frantic pace the doctor downshifted his cadence and leaned against the wall, indicating he would take time for the family. He was clearly kind and perceptive in gauging the surroundings.

Dr. Daniels sat with Trey and his mother for almost 20 minutes. He explained that the lung condition was chronic and deteriorating. The lack of lung function was slowly sapping Earl's energy. The lack of oxygen ate away at the function of every critical organ. This episode was a capitulation. The progression of the disease was personal and depended on many unique factors. The age of the patient. The general health before the onset of the disease. Their mental state and sense of optimism. He asked Trey and his mother to perform that calculus on their own to determine probability of recovery.

"I have seen patients who rally and actually emerge from one of these episodes in improved condition for a time. Others do not. I wish I could tell you I knew who rallies and who does not. But I would be lying and I do not like to mislead patients or their families. I will say this; the next day or two will likely be very telling. Seeing you here tells me he has a lot to live for. Many patients have no one."

Trey's mother began to weep and buried her face in Trey's chest. He wanted to break down in tears as well, but he fought them back. He wanted to be the rock now. The tears, forced back, felt like they balled up behind his eyes, forming a massive pressure and headache. Dr. Daniels placed his hand on his mother's shoulder in comfort.

Dr. Daniels went on to explain the measures he would take to

minimize discomfort while treating the underlying lung condition. Trey
was thankful for the patience and explanation but he was absorbing little
of it. He was just happy Dr. Daniels was there.

Just then, a noise startled all three of them. It was a low, guttural rasp.
"I am so thirsty. Is there water?"

It was Earl. Awake—at least for the moment.

While Trey and his mother tried to process the sounds, Dr. Daniels
moved forward and poured water from a plastic jug into a small foam cup.
He pushed Earl into a more upright position so he could drink without
threat of choking. In the space of seconds, color reappeared in Earl's face.
He looked unkempt but far more alert. The rally Dr. Daniels hinted at,
right before their eyes.

There was not room for all of them in the space beside the bed so Trey
let his mother approach his father first. She took the cup from Dr. Daniels
and trickled the water into Earl's mouth. In between sips she moved wispy
white strands of hair on his head. Trey knew her hands were magic. A few
strokes across his head seemed to create a semblance of his normal look.

Dr. Daniels stood back to let Trey approach. Trey kissed his father on
the forehead. Being that close he drank in the smell of his father. It was
familiar and comforting.

"Where ya been, Pop? We've been waiting for you."

"Dunno. May have missed the bus."

CHAPTER 37

A CHURCH-GOING MAN

Harlowe Mikkelsen traveled light but came prepared for almost any occasion. On this morning he found his white shirt and dark blue suit. He rummaged through the bottom of his bag and found a blue striped tie. It was polyester but a pretty good fake. Good enough for today, anyway. He took an extra few moments to comb his thinning hair. It was like a fat woman in a bikini: Thankful for whatever is covered but what is covered is never enough. It had to do.

Satisfied that he looked solemn and professional, Harlowe donned his raincoat as the rain poured down outside the hotel room window. He patted his pocket of his vest jacket compulsively. His envelope was there. He looked at his watch. 7:40 a.m. No time for coffee.

He retrieved his white rental car from underground parking. As soon as the elevator opened at the parking level he smelled the rain as it washed the air, pushing small bursts of air through the garage. Harlowe followed the directions he was given precisely, pushing through the rush-hour traffic down city streets. He avoided or yielded to any Yellow Cab. Their pace was unaltered by the rain or the traffic signals and appeared to Harlowe to take insane risks. Any other day he might jockey with them but not today. He did not need an accident today. Too many things had already gone wrong on this trip. Wrecking a rental car and missing this meeting would be just another unbelievable screw up. He let every cab have the best part of the road. Harlowe's careful driving was rewarded as he finally found Ridge Road and proceeded through several well-kept, yet worn neighborhoods. Before long, Harlowe tossed aside the directions. He did

267

not need them. The 232-foot spires of his destination appeared in the gray sky like something out of a gothic novel. He could just drive toward them like the North Star.

Sacred Heart Cathedral sprawled and dominated this piece of urban neighborhood. Harlowe drove around the church once looking for parking and found a large empty lot surrounded by a 12-foot fence and barbed wire set aside as parking for the parishioners. It was large enough for parishioners at a Thursday morning mass. Harlowe could not conceive how this lot accommodated a Sunday service for such a mammoth building. The barbed wire on the lot amused Harlowe.

"Oh ye of little faith in your fellow man that he shall not steal your car," he muttered under his breath, as he pulled into the lot.

The rain let up just enough that Harlowe was able to navigate the stone steps without hurrying and risking a fall.

The cornerstone of the church read 1899 but the massive construction project was halted several times over several decades. While still unfinished, it opened for worship in 1928 but had not been dedicated until 1950. It seated well over a thousand, although a Thursday morning service might only attract 20 or 30 of the most fervent worshippers. The actual interior covered about as much territory as a football field—365 feet from entrance to altar and 50 feet across. The ceilings were 35 feet high in places, decorated by lamps that looked like they could only be lit by angels.

Harlowe, as a Southern Baptist, felt uncomfortable with the size and scope of the building. He felt it was built to intimidate, not welcome. He thought back to his childhood and how 60 or so locals jammed the small Baptist church on hot Sunday afternoons. His little church was a tenth of the size of this leviathan. He could not imagine where Sacred Heart would put the spread of food and jugs of lemonade and sweet tea. He was getting annoyed. But he had a mission. This whole thing felt like a pebble in his shoe.

While the crowd may have numbered about the same as his hometown service, the 60 or so worshippers here were swallowed by the facility. Entering from the back, Harlowe walked by at least 35 pews before he saw one occupant. He continued to move forward toward the front and the altar. He hoped nobody would come by and try to be friendly. He did not think friendly was what he had to worry about. The cathedral was cold and gray. It depended upon sunlight through stained glass to warm its vast interior but on such a gray day, the muted lights above were swallowed by the interior. The rain beating on the cathedral windows and roof created a white noise.

Harlowe went to the seventh row and sat down. He had one prayer. Let this service be brief. He need not worry. Midweek masses in the Catholic Church are notorious for their brevity. Worship lite.

The acoustics of the large church mixed with the rain outside made everything hard to hear and understand. It looked and sounded enough like his worship service to be familiar and odd at the same time. Kind of like listening to the news on the BBC. He pieced the words he could clearly understand with the images before him to get the most general idea of what was going on. He took his cues for standing, sitting and kneeling from observation but he felt wildly out of place.

Halfway through the mass they passed the collection baskets. Six ushers held the baskets on long wicker poles, waving them in front of the worshippers who placed their offerings inside. Harlowe sat on the aisle. He took a small mustard-colored envelope from his vest pocket. Inside there were 35 $100 bills fattening the envelope in the middle. He put the envelope in the collection basket, staring straight ahead at the altar, now a welter of activity as altar boys and the priests prepared the communion wafers and wine. The six ushers were overkill given the crowd but they did their job solemnly and piously. Once they completed the collection, they marched the collection baskets to the rear of the church near the vestibule and emptied them into a larger wicker basket. There, the head usher remained behind and took all the offerings to a small office stenciled with the words "PRIVATE: CHURCH USE" on a frosted privacy window. Once inside, he dumped all the envelopes and cash on a broad copper-topped table. The few coins in the collection clinked around the table, with several quarters rolling off. The rest was a sea of green. Some of the green was cash, ones and fives mostly, the rest were mint green offering envelopes imprinted with SACRED HEART CATHEDRAL and an image of the massive church on the sunniest of days. One mustard yellow envelope stood out by its color and odd shape so thick in the middle and tapered at the ends. The head usher picked up Harlowe's offering envelope and placed it in his vest pocket. He gathered up the remainder and counted it out. One hundred thirty-two dollars and seventy-five cents in cash. Seven dollars in checks. One coupon for a free bag of dog food. One New York City Subway token.

The usher put a rubber band around the collection with the checks on top. He left the subway token on the desk. Someone would grab it. He put the dog food coupon in a mail slot for Monsignor O'Connor. No doubt it was intended for him and his scraggly little terrier, Smitty.

The head usher left before mass concluded. He walked under cover of an umbrella and directly down the steps to the curb. There his car sat in a special zone reserved for church officials. He drove out of Newark and into East Newark. He parked a block from city hall and picked up a newspaper. He placed the fat envelope inside the newspaper and bound it with a rubber band. Still under cover of his umbrella, he went inside East Newark City Hall and proceeded to the office of Bergen Krupp, Chief of Staff for the Mayor.

"Your newspaper, Mr. Krupp."

Krupp took the newspaper and placed it inside his leather briefcase without so much as removing the rubber band. He had an urgent meeting with the mayor pending.

Chapter 38

—————◆•◆•◆—————

Pauley's Puzzle

Pauley Firrigno leaned on the railing of his front porch. The porch itself was in dire need of a coat of paint. Grey curls of weathered semi-gloss stood up under his feet like so many snails. He gently kicked at the paint chips and saw them flutter away, powered by the breeze of the rainstorm. He was angry. Maybe more irritated than angry. He should be working right now, up to his elbows in his huge press, stamping out parts two a second. He was scheduled for overtime today and this weekend. He liked the overtime and the larger-than-normal paychecks of the last few months. Instead he was standing on his porch, looking at the rain and on strike. In the normal rhythms of the contract he knew when the negotiations would start. Subtly, he would hold back on a few purchases in case of a strike. Put away a few dollars in case of a short stoppage. But this was ominous and uncertain. It looked like no matter what, the certainty of a paycheck was in long-term doubt. They could go back in and negotiate their own doom or stay out now and…do what? Lose this week's paycheck? The frustration just rose in him. It was all out of his control. Pauley realized he was gripping the railing of the porch so tight he did not immediately feel his hands getting wet by the billowing rain. He stepped back and wiped his hands on his work pants. The idea of carrying a picket sign in the rain was absolutely disgusting to him. He knew he had to go soon but decided he could wait a few more minutes to see if the rain would let up. He plopped down in an aluminum frame beach chair on the porch that listed badly to one side.

The house itself dated back to World War I. It was sturdy but frayed at the edges. And as much magic as Pauley could perform in getting a 50-ton press to beat like a giant heart, he had neither the skills nor the desire to maintain the house. There was the practical matter: The house was not worth the investment of time and money. Housing values were actually declining in the neighborhood and had been for the last five years. The nicest house in a bad neighborhood was not a bargain. For Pauley, it was warm and dry and represented the most stability he ever had in his life. After years of living as ward of the juvenile system and living in a boarding house in one little room, this dilapidated house was his castle. It was where he could count on Pilar making sopa de zanahoria, a hearty carrot soup perfect for a rainy day. But most of all, the house reminded him of Tomas. Tomas, almost 8 now, was Pilar's grandson. While attached by neither blood nor legality, Pauley had a deep and emotional bond to the boy. Exactly what drew Pauley to Tomas is hard to say but ever since he laid eyes on him, Pauley found it his mission to create a safe and joyous place for the boy. Tomas returned the affection and adored Pauley's attention. The two played on the wooden floor of the living room for hours with plastic toy soldiers or building blocks. They orbited each other in a warm and loving relationship delighting Pilar. While her love for Pauley was not amorous, she loved him for loving Tomas. If Pauley and Pilar fought over money or chores he would often retreat to his safe place and play with Tomas. This retreat was pure and visceral, an almost primal need on his part to return to the person who most loved him. It was not calculated. But when he did retreat, Pilar would simply melt and forget she ever was mad at Pauley.

Tomas was never far from Pauley's thoughts. When the boy appeared on the porch with a bang of the aluminum storm door it startled Pauley, momentarily mesmerized by the thrum of the rain.

Tomas was a slight boy with close-cropped hair that lay flat on his head—a youthful Caesar. He put a pile of textbooks and notebooks down on a small plastic table next to Pauley and climbed into his lap, further straining the lawn chair that creaked out a warning of imminent collapse.

"Aren't you going to work? You're late, aren't you?" the boy asked.

"I'm not late. We are starting late today. We have special work today."

"Are you staying home? Can I stay home and do stuff with you?"

"No, I'm not staying home. Wish I was, though. I'll be leaving in just a few minutes. You need to be in school and learning things and getting smart enough so you don't have to work in a factory."

"But you have fun at your job. It sounds like fun—maybe something I can do. You say you have fun all the time."

Pauley closed one eye to size the boy up. Every day after school Pauley would quiz Tomas about school and what he liked about school and his day. When it was Pauley's turn to discuss the day he always told the boy work was fun. He thought it was good for Tomas to see work as a happy spot, but now he was not sure about the tactic.

"There are a lot of places you can have more fun than a factory. It's OK for me but you'll be smarter than me so your fun will be different. Now go to school and make your brain bigger than mine." Pauley said this as he gave Tomas some light noogies on top of his head. Tomas picked up his stack of books with a light air of dejection, but quickly regained his smile. Before he left the porch he put on a rain poncho and wrapped his books and notebooks in plastic grocery bags. He cinched the hood of the poncho around his head tightly and headed down the porch and onto the puddled sidewalk.

"Have fun at work," Tomas shouted with an excited, exaggerated wave.

Pauley sighed deeply and looked at the sky. It was not promising anything but more rain. The picket line promised to be anything but fun.

As Trey left the hospital the day was bleeding toward mid-morning. He knew Harlowe and Ike would not look kindly on his absence at this moment of crisis—no matter how manufactured it was. Still, nothing could blunt his soaring mood having seen his father rally as he did. As late as he was, Trey took one look at the hospital vending machines and knew he would invest another five minutes at the Page Deli to get a decent cup of coffee. Caffeine was sustaining him at this point.

As Trey moved through the side streets near the plant he hoped the late hour might free up a valuable parking spot right in front of the deli. Luck was not with him and he had to park almost a half block away and jog back up the street through the fierce rain. This was how much coffee meant to him at this point. As he got closer to the door, he had another hope: perhaps the rain had deterred the Council of Elders from their unofficial lodge inside the deli. It was not a lucky day. The rain had the reverse effect. While normally they might be bored and actually leave the

273

deli to go home by mid-morning, they in fact were now dug in like ticks. They were slightly bored watching the puddles form in the potholes in the street so when Trey appeared, they pounced in delight.

"Mr. Attorney, what is going on out there? Did you throw those guys out?"

"You locked them out, right?"

"What the hell is going on over there?"

Trey was not about to be drawn in by the Council but he knew ignoring them would be futile. They were interested to a degree but harmless.

"I simply do not know," Trey said. "I come in late one day and they are on the street. I would guess they are protesting the fact that I am not there."

As Trey made his coffee in the largest foam cup he could put his hands on, Howard Kim, proprietor, appeared at the cash register.

"Rain, rain, go away—and maybe they go away too," Kim said as he rolled his eyes in the direction of the Council of Elders in mock disgust. But then he leaned in to Trey with great seriousness, adding: "You OK over there? Everything going to be OK?"

"These things have a way of working themselves out," said Trey, dropping change on the counter to cover the coffee. "This just needs time." The words sounded sage to Trey as he heard his own voice. He immediately wondered if he was trying to convince himself. Trey realized he had only one cup of coffee and thought about Pauley. A wave of sadness washed over him.

Once in his car, Trey pulled slowly around to the plant parking lot entrance and saw pickets bobbing slowly in time with the picketers' gaits. The oaktag signs were a soggy, illegible mess bent in the rain. It was hard to distinguish one person from the next as they were all clad in some kind of rain gear. It looked like some kind of zombie line, one slowly following the other in a disorganized circle. As Trey pulled up, the picket line spacing opened to let him through. He proceeded with great care and caution. He did not want to throw up a splash of filthy water and add to the indignity of the moment. In a second he flashed to an imagined image of a fearful Harlowe accelerating through the line with a torrent of sewage-grade water going everywhere. Trey was snapped out of his daze by a rap on his driver-side window. It was Mo Morris. Mo squinted at Trey as rainwater ran down off his hood and off his face.

"Get the fuck in there and get Tommy and me called in for a meeting, damn it. Set the next bargaining session so we can tell them something or they will have my ass out here."

"I'm just getting here so don't expect any miracles. I don't even know who is in there right now."

"The Squinty-Eyed Fuck is in there, I can tell you that," said Mo, referring to Harlowe.

"Where is The Turk? Water too high for him?" asked Trey. The minute he said it he regretted it. This was simply not the moment to crack wise. Mo waved Trey into the parking lot in disgust.

When Trey got into the plant he stopped a moment just to listen. He always felt he could hear the plant and know if it was running efficiently. Each machine had a cadence and easy rhythm when running at high speed. Added layer upon layer, it was less a cacophony than some kind of symphony. Today he expected silence and arrhythmia. So he was surprised when he heard something more like a murmur. A beast wounded or at rest but definitely alive. Presses thumped slowly but defiantly. Lathes whirred a great high-pitched whine. Parts clanked into metal shop boxes. Trey was simultaneously comforted and disturbed. Who was running the machines? Did some of the union cross the picket line?

Taking a few steps inside it all became clear to Trey. With the union out on strike, management was running the plant as best they could. Since most of the engineers and management came up through the machine shop, it was a pretty easy transition. In some ways it was like a strange holiday. The engineers, schedulers and office personnel were out on the floor running whatever machines they knew how to run. Freed from the union rules, they ran several machines simultaneously. They set the speeds slower but moved from place to place to feed the machines parts or clear minor jams. Trey nodded as he went through the shop floor.

Trey went to his office. The light was on in BeBe's office but she was not there. He assumed she was somewhere on the floor making parts. He threw his rain-damp sports jacket over the back of his chair and headed over to Ike's office.

When he arrived, Ike's office looked like a trailer after the tornado passed through. Piles of paper sat in every corner of the office. The walls were covered with large sheets of computer paper with various arrows and calculations. Obviously this had been the center of activity at some time earlier but now it sat still and eerie. Trey stepped into the office carefully and began to examine the paper on the walls to see if he could make sense of it. He was starting to understand the rough ideas expressed on the first sheet when he was startled by Ike's voice behind him.

"Where've you been? You missed all the fun this morning," said Ike. He was almost chirpy in his tone and he wore a broad grin.

"It's amazing what you can do without the union rules," said Ike. "We have about two thirds of the place running already and we have only scratched the surface of the capability here."

Trey knew the place was running on adrenaline right now. This was great fun—like bring-your-child-to-work day. When all the office workers returned to their desks to see their regular work piled up it would not be fun for very long. Trey knew to keep his mouth shut though—even to Ike.

"Where's Harlowe? What is our next step with the boys out on the picket line?" asked Trey.

"Out on the floor, I guess, bucking up the troops. He should be here any minute."

The concept of Harlowe as morale officer annoyed Trey but he let it pass. Trey explained his absence to Ike and described his father's hospitalization. Trey knew family was an important part of Ike's makeup and he wanted Ike to blunt any grief Harlowe might give him about his late arrival.

Trey took a seat on the sofa in Ike's office. It was not long before Harlowe arrived. Trey took one look at him in his dark blue suit and thought it was odd attire. It was obvious Harlowe had no intention of dirtying his hands making parts. Not today anyway.

Harlowe started in on Trey almost immediately.

"Well, nice of you to show up today! We thought you were out on the illegal picket line!" said Harlowe, voice dripping with sarcasm.

Trey shot Ike a glance to see if he might intervene, but Ike was busying himself by making neater piles in the stacks of paper on his desk. With no help on the way, Trey decided to just push forward with business at hand.

"What's our move now? They will want to know when we are meeting. Are the lawyers filing an injunction?"

"We do nothing," said Harlowe. The statement caught Ike's attention as he stopped shuffling papers and looked up at Harlowe.

Trey echoed the word with incredulity: "Nothing."

Harlowe strode across the room to the small windows in Ike's office and raised his hand to point out the sheets of rain coming down. "We have beautiful weather here today. They went on strike—an illegal strike as we all know. But we don't need the lawyers yet. Let them soak up some of this. It isn't supposed to stop for a few days. Let them see how they like their decision. We are in no rush right now. The plant is humming. Let's see how today plays out anyway."

Trey noticed Harlowe had a swagger that was conspicuously missing yesterday. Trey had to test Harlowe a little to figure this out.

"What good do we do by pissing them off? For argument's sake, they know the weather forecast as much as we do. If we bring them in now one could argue we have a little more leverage. Let's face it, the bargaining committee will feel the heat to do something and not let the rest of those poor bastards drown in the rain."

Harlowe hated when Trey spoke in hypotheticals and hid behind imaginary persons arguing other points of view. He thought Trey was too weak to speak his own mind.

"They stay out there. We do nothing. Let them fucking drown for all I care. And if you want to disagree, there are a couple of Greans sitting by the phone down in Florida who would love to hear from you."

Harlowe was in full bully mode at this point. Ike rededicated himself to the busy work on his desk. Trey understood that Harlowe was in charge and not to be questioned. Trey also knew the confidence to bully his way through the argument did not come without consultation with The Turk.

Miraculously, Trey's pager went off, allowing him a semi-graceful way out. He looked down at it in wonder and begged out of the room.

"Let me see what crisis is brewing—it could be anything today." Trey did not look at Harlowe as he escaped the room. He got into the foyer and looked at his pager again. "7006 3615." In the dyslexic world of pagers, it read "side door" when held upside down. Trey went into the plant and ducked down several rarely used passageways to isolated parts of the building. If anyone really asked what he was doing, it was just a routine security check. In reality, he wanted to be sure that Harlowe was not following him. Trey's knowledge of the nooks and crannies of the plant made it possible for him to disappear and reappear in various spots.

He moved quickly down a row of pallets stacked three high full of semi-finished work. He then walked down a seam where two buildings had been joined decades ago, but left an odd, unusable space between them. The building smelled of damp walls and the rain dripped in above him at random intervals. In years gone by, the plant had received coal for the boiler and stored it in bins that were below street grade. The trucks would just pull up and dump the coal into the bins. The bins had fallen into disuse but the doors next to the chutes remained. It was a place where employees could go out for a smoke on a hot day and escape the heat of the plant as the door was below grade, shaded and cool. Today, the only people who knew about this little cubby were out on the picket line. Trey tried the door once to no avail but then he pushed into it with greater force and it groaned open. It did not open far before it jolted to a stop, hitting something. Actually someone. Actually two people, Mo Morris and Tommy Pherrel. Both clad in rain ponchos but still soaked to the bone, ran inside quickly as Trey pulled the door shut with a bang.

"You think you're funny leaving us out there in the rain after we page you like that?" Mo Morris was not a happy man. He punctuated his comment with "Motherfucker" directed at no one in particular.

Tommy was happy to be out of the rain for no other reason than he could now light up a cigarette. There were all kinds of motions beneath his oversized poncho and suddenly his two hands appeared—one with a cigarette, the other with a lighter. He lit his cigarette and showed relief as the nicotine brought him some calm. Trey wondered if the cigarette smoke might betray this tryst. Mo got right to the point.

"When are we meeting?"

It was the question Trey did not want to hear.

"We're not."

"What the fuck do you mean we are not meeting? Let's start dancing—give me some times," said Mo, a small puddle forming around him at the edges of his poncho.

"You are going to have to get Larry and push this thing. Harlowe wants to leave you out there to soak up some rain," said Trey.

"You make me laugh. You know if Harlowe says leave us out here, he did that with Larry's blessing. Harlowe don't shit without Larry's say-so."

Mo glared at Tommy, who seemed content to watch in silence and have his smoke for the moment. Mo knew he was in this alone.

"I don't care what you think Harlowe and Larry have agreed to. You need to go kick Larry's ass and get him to pressure for a meeting. Harlowe is not doing shit. I'm sorry. It's your move," said Trey.

"You ain't doin' shit for us either, you know," said Mo ruefully.

Trey knew he was at the precipice of a very loud and angry argument that would have no effect except to perhaps echo through this empty part of the building and bring attention to their position.

"Stay here as long as you like and dry out. I gotta get back before they miss me," said Trey.

CHAPTER 39

UNION MEETING

Heavy downpours pelted the picket line all morning but subsided around noon. Although another band of heavy rain was predicted, the break was so pronounced it allowed peek-a-boo sun from streaks of blue sky. Local roach coaches quickly learned of the picket line and sensed a business opportunity. Several of the stainless steel clad trucks showed up and offered the strikers discount lunches, hoping to stir goodwill for better days.

As the sun persisted the street congealed into mottled variations of gray macadam, the water seeking the lowest levels and potholes in the street. A few straggling pickets continued their walk by the entrance to the Grean plant while the majority grabbed cheesesteaks, burgers and veal patty sandwiches and ate on the curb facing the plant. There were three different food coaches now lined up, engaging in a price war and expressing support and sympathy for the strikers.

Mo Morris was simply not hungry so he paced somewhat aimlessly and ran his fingers through thinning hair, surveying the situation and thinking through next moves. There was virtually no traffic on these back streets in an industrial area and he was lost in his thoughts in the middle of the street when he realized a sedan was headed slowly toward him. It took Mo a moment to realize it was a East Newark police cruiser moving slowly but deliberately down the street. Mo motioned for them to stop. As they did, Mo ducked his head in on the driver side.

"What's up, officers? Care to join in and support your union brothers in the cause?"

"Nah. Good luck but we just wanted to see how things were here. It all looks pretty peaceful. Looks like no trouble or nothin'." There were two young officers in the squad car. Both seemed fairly indifferent and grateful there was no reason to get out of the car.

"As long as being wet is not a crime, I imagine we will be OK out here," said Mo.

"We don't plan to take any special trips out here. You don't need us looking over your shoulder. I am sure you know the drill." The officer tapped on a PBA union button on his pocket in a small sign of respect for Mo and the union. "We will leave you be as long as we don't get called out here."

The officer looked at the ragged crew of picketers eating sandwiches on the curb. It looked a little more like a homeless camp than an angry mob at this point. Mo shook his hand and the cruiser pulled away. As he did it struck Mo a little odd. Although there was not a long history of strikes, Mo had been on the picket line before and the police were a constant and visible presence. It was a different time. The Grean family was on site back then so they may have demanded the attention of the police. There was a new mayor so maybe this relaxed attitude was part of a different outlook. Maybe Trey called off the police as an olive branch of trust and to cool things down a bit. As the squad car disappeared around the corner, Mo had bigger things to worry about and was just glad the police would not be one of them.

As the picketers ate their fill, the food trucks packed up and moved on to the high schools for the 3 p.m. dismissal. The blue breaks in the skies now filled in with darker, more ominous clouds. It was likely Grean could only run one shift with management on the machines so the plan was to discontinue picketing around 6 p.m. If any real zealots wanted to picket overnight the union would let them but strictly on a volunteer basis. The plan was to resume and continue at 6 a.m. the next morning, before the management people would arrive for a 7 a.m. start. The idea was to scare away any weak of heart types and make the rest feel guilty as hell.

Any fleeting pleasantness created by the dabs of sun was completely gone. It was not raining, but a new cold wind blew insistently ahead of yet another front. The daylight took on a dusk-like tine as the sun disappeared permanently behind thickening clouds. The picket signs bent in the wind and were difficult to carry. As impossible as it was, the swirling winds seemed to create headwinds for the picketers walking in either direction. This was just wretched luck for the union.

Shortly after 2 p.m. two large, white, unmarked vans came down the street. Mo and Tommy were walking the picket line and both thought it might be a local news crew. Tommy froze immediately, even anticipating the possibility of being called on to speak into the cameras as the union president. He was searching for any way he might defer to Mo.

The two vans stopped about 50 yards short of where the picket lines began and the side doors slid open in the first van. Four men got out. They were young – maybe late 20s. Each was dressed somewhat alike. Their black short sleeve T-shirts were a size too small and showed off preening muscles. They all wore blue jeans and sneakers. Their hair showed no signs of gray at all but was a tad longer than mainstream. Maybe they were lost and wanted directions but were just wary seeing the pickets. They walked purposefully toward the strikers. The leader of the four was also slightly bigger than the others—a little over 6 feet tall.

"Who is in charge here?" he asked.

Mo was simultaneously piqued and irritated by their arrival and the tone of the question. He quickly got out in front.

"How may I help you?" Mo asked. There was a tinge of edged determination in his voice.

"We understand that you are out here on strike even though the majority of your union brothers want to be in there working. We understand you are trying to give their jobs away when you have a chance to save them."

Mo felt the anger rising in him already. A few enormous drops of rain fell in large blobs, their moisture simply too heavy to be suspended any longer in the gathering clouds. Mo hardly noticed them as his eyes narrowed into tight slits. Mo was probably 25 years older and 25 pounds lighter than any of the three men in front of him but he gave no ground.

"Who the fuck are you? Who the fuck sent you? And have I told you yet I think you are lost? So let me tell you where you are: You are standing on the corner of Who Gives a Fuck What You Think and Get The Fuck Outta Here."

As Mo spat the words out, he leaned forward. This flash point alarmed Tommy immediately and he stepped in between Mo and the guys approaching. Tommy's back was to the three men. It was risky but he wanted to show he had no fight to pick with them. Besides, he wanted to make eye contact with Mo and calm him down. Tommy was staring directly into Mo's eyes, imploring him to step this down a notch but Mo was staring directly over Tommy's shoulder. He locked on the three men with laser-like focus. Mo's jaw was tightly clenched. The blobs of rain came splattering around like miniscule water balloons, rewetting the recently dried pavement. Tommy knew he should not lay hands on Mo at this exact moment so he threw his hands in the air and moved ever so slightly forward. He hoped he could shepherd Mo gently backward but Mo gave no ground. The rest of the picketers were taken aback at the sudden turn of events. Most of them stood back a bit to take stock of the situation. The only one who stood forward and close to Mo and Tommy was Pauley Firrigno. The morning rain rendered his hearing aid useless so he was getting closer to the conversation. He could hear almost nothing but he did not like what he was seeing. Tommy needed a Plan B.

"Let's talk this over a bit and see what is going on, huh?" said Tommy. His hands were still in the air to signal his role as peacemaker. Tommy heard a noise behind him to indicate the three visitors may have taken a step back so Tommy turned to face them and assess the situation. He saw that the men relaxed their posture a bit, but he also saw more men getting out of the one van and the door to the second van was sliding open as well. It was also raining—now with smaller drops but with increasing intensity.

The front man identified himself.

"Let's take it easy here. I meant no offense. My name is Jackson. We are your union brothers, too. Some of your local guys came to the International building and said they had not been heard so we were concerned. We wanted to hear your side too, of course. But when we heard the frustration, we wanted to do some—should we call it quality control?"

Mo was unappeased. Tommy now locked eyes with Jackson but took in the wider view of the men gathering from out of the vans. It was almost unreal. Like one of those cars at the circus where clowns kept getting out—except these were mighty big clowns. Tommy had a firm but inconspicuous grip on the forearm of Mo and he gave it a little squeeze. Mo was coiled like a spring.

"What business is this of yours, *Brother Jackson?* I ain't never seen you anywhere. And I surely would not be so bold as to tell you what to do in your local. We don't need no Quality Control and certainly not from you. Who the hell sent you and what do you want from us?" demanded Mo.

The group from the two white vans now emptied onto the street. They numbered about 12 and seemed oddly disinterested in the conversation Brother Jackson was having with the picketers. They looked young, large and oblivious to the fact it was raining at all. They talked quietly among themselves.

"We all need help now and then. It is our understanding that the International advised you not to walk out. We understand there is work available right now and maybe a way to save some jobs. I don't know why we at the locals pay dues if we aren't going to listen to the International? They know the big picture. They have never steered us wrong. So now you older guys milked it, get your severance and want to cut and run. How is that right for guys like us—at our age? We have a long way to go. After I've heard all this I'd say get out of the rain and go back in there. Listen to the International. They know how to run this."

Mo sized up Brother Jackson. Indeed Mo was not paying close attention to all the new employees hired as probationary employees. They were not dues paying. He could not represent them. Some of them would now be around the 90-day probation period. Now Mo wished he paid closer attention to the new employees. Was Brother Jackson part of the new group? He could not recall ever seeing him either at Grean or at the International building or meetings. It was bad enough battling with Grean and Harlowe The Squinty-Eyed Fuck but now he had to deal with some part of his own union?

"Where is Larry Turkel? Did he send you here? If he did go tell him he better get his little ass down here and deliver this message himself," said Mo.

Brother Jackson was quick with his reply.

"I know Larry but he did not send us. Your own members asked us to come down here and talk some sense to you because they feel they were not heard. If there is one thing worse than management fucking us it's when we fuck our own and believe me, they feel they are getting fucked here."

The rain now fell in an intense waver and slicked down the long hair of Brother Jackson as well as the other two men standing behind him. It made their hair look even longer. Just the sight of them triggered Mo's temper as he stepped around Tommy and pointed a finger.

"We got NOTHING to say to you whoever the hell you think you are. Just get back in that van and get the fuck out of here."

"The International has jurisdiction here and you should listen to them. Why won't you talk to us or even listen to your own members?"

Mo and Tommy were the only two on the picket line close enough to hear Brother Jackson clearly but the whole conversation was confusing. Who exactly was this guy and where was Larry Turkel? The International had no standing to override the local in this case. What exactly did these guys and their friends in the van want? The guys on the picket line got a little closer to see what the commotion was all about. It rained a little harder.

Pauley Firrigno was just behind Tommy and Mo—the next closest person from the picket line to the conversation. Still, Pauley's understanding was muddled. Under the best circumstances Pauley's hearing was compromised but Mo was speaking directly at the men from the van and away from Pauley. The sound of the rain created a static in the hearing aid, making it hard for Pauley to understand clearly. About the only thing clear to Pauley was Mo was upset. He and Mo worked together for years. Pauley respected Mo and what he stood for. He wanted to help Mo but could not understand so Pauley took two steps past Mo and Tommy and turned his head to cock his left ear—the one without the hearing aid- toward Brother Jackson. It was a terrible mistake.

With his head turned at such an odd angle, Pauley never saw it coming. One of the two men behind Brother Jackson took two steps forward and clubbed Pauley with a forearm blow that drove him to the ground in a heap. Mo saw it coming but too late. Mo drove a shoulder into Pauley's attacker's midsection. As he looked up, he saw the dozen or so men who had been lingering at the vans rush forward. It was chaos.

What followed was a street riot. It was such a mismatch; the term street fight did not apply. The picketers outnumbered the men in the vans by about 2-to-1 but the local union could not have foreseen the ferocity of the attack. The local members were an older, sedate, peaceful bunch by and large. They were soaked, cold and leg weary from a day of marching in the rain. The men in the van had fresh legs and were on a mission. The attackers waded into the picketers, knocking them to the ground, kicking them and hitting them with small burlap sacks filled with something heavy. Some of the picketers fled immediately. Some of the old men on the picket line had not been in a brawl in 25 years—or ever. They were overcome by the speed and ferocity of the attack. A few tried to swing their picket signs like weapons in self-defense but the signs attached to the wood acted like a fan, causing wind resistance, reducing the defensive blows to ineffective taps. The attackers from the van ripped the picket signs from their hands and drove the short wooden handles between the picketers' ribs. Mo might have been one of the spryest and physically fit, but he was quickly overcome. He knew his was a losing cause so he balled up into a fetal crouch on the ground. He felt the hot sensation of blood coming from inside his mouth and saw the rain dilute it on the pavement, turning from bright red to a light pinkish color as it washed away in arcs.

The whole thing lasted less than five minutes but it seemed a lot longer to those who endured the attack. The men from the vans watched but did not pursue the picketers who fled. A couple of the attackers broke the picket handles over their knees. One of them barked out quick orders: "Let's go. Let's go. NOW." The men piled back in the vans quickly. Once inside, both vans threw into reverse gear and fled back out the way they appeared. Either they did not want to risk running over someone in the street or they did not want to risk someone clearly seeing a license plate. In any case they left, tires screeching. The scene on the street looked like a battlefield. Minutes before, it was an organized marching circle. Almost all who stayed and fought were on the ground, assessing their injuries. None of the picketers who fled in fear were even close enough to help. The injured flexed their arms and felt at the cuts and bruises inflicted by their attackers. It was pouring down as hard as it had at any point in the day.

Inside the plant Trey was at his desk preparing labor cost analysis in case it was needed in negotiations. He was deep in thought, looking for novel ways to portray cost savings when the door to the HR area slammed open. It was Jeffrey Scotto—one of the lathe operators on strike. He was terribly wet and wild eyed.

"CALL THE POLICE. CALL THE FUCKING POLICE. NOW!!"

Trey was taken aback and could not process it fast enough for Scotto, who came in and grabbed the phone and tried to dial 911 but failed in his hysteria. Trey's first thought was one of the old guys on the picket line had a heart attack.

"Give me the phone back and slow down," Trey said. "What do I tell them? What just happened? Is everything alright?"

Scotto was near hyperventilating but described the attack in some detail. He was one of the many picketers too far away to hear what was happening, but he was getting angry.

"It was you guys who hired these strike breakers, right? It wasn't enough that you take our jobs, you had to kick our ass, too?"

Trey realized this could get out of hand right here in his office. It was bad outside—that much was certain. Trey was also secure in the knowledge the people outside were not management-hired goons. Then he thought about Harlowe and doubt gripped him. He just hoped that doubt had not leaked out in his expression to Scotto. Trey dialed 911 and shouted there was a medical emergency at Grean and hung up. He hoped the lack of detail might bring any available resources from the city quickly. Scotto's wild eyes and fear unnerved Trey. He grabbed a bright yellow windbreaker normally used in safety fire drills from a coat tree in the corner of the office. Trey grabbed Scotto by his wet arm.

"Let's go. Show me what's going on," said Trey.

Scotto seemed to hesitate for just a second. His fear froze Trey as well. What were they going out to see? As they moved through the hall and into the plant he saw a half dozen more of the picketers. Some sat on the floor looking shocked and exhausted. A few were waving their arms in wild pantomime. Trey had seen enough. He immediately worried his 911 call would be seen as a crank call. This was serious. Just before Trey went out the back door he saw a fire alarm and pulled at it. It did not budge. It had likely never been used. Trey grabbed a bin of machined parts, lifted it over his head and threw it at the wall in the direction of the fire alarm. The bin hit the red fire box and the metal handle seemed to explode off the wall, sounding a shrill two-tone alarm through the building. More police and fire seemed a better plan than less. Scotto, amazed by what he just saw, dismissed any idea he had about the attackers being management agents.

As Trey sprinted out the back door he was buffeted by a driving rain obscuring his vision. He struggled to make sense of what he saw. Based upon what Scotto said, Trey expected to see a full-on brawl. Instead, it appeared a lot of the picketers were resting, sitting with their backs on the chain-link fence. They were scattered in clumps of two and three and four over a space of maybe 50 yards. He did not see the attackers. It seemed preternaturally calm. He could not figure out why anyone would be sitting in the huge puddles on the ground. As he got closer, he understood. In the first group of three, one of the picketers had a large gash above his right eye. It was bleeding profusely. Still, he was in much better shape than others. Just to the right, another man on the ground looked like he had been hit with a tomato in the face. It was not a tomato but pieces of his nose splattered over his face. The man with the bloody eye tried to gingerly dab at the blood splatter on the face of the man on the ground to see where the actual wound began.

The rent-a-guards inside were comfortable in the warm, dry building but one just now ventured out. Trey grabbed him, directing him to go back inside and locate every first aid kit possible. He also directed every guard to gather at the fence line. It occurred to Trey that whoever did this had the potential to return in an effort to finish the job. Even if they were only rent-a-guards they might look like police until the real ones arrived. He evaluated whether it was better to stay here or bring the injured inside for safety. He listened for sirens but heard only the hiss of the rain and the groans of the injured. Where the fuck were the police and medics?

Trey searched the street and saw Mo. He was on one knee like a boxer trying to get up from a knockdown. Mo's lower lip was split and the blood gushed down his chin. Tommy leaned on the chain-link fence holding his left side with both hands.

Then he saw it.

At first he thought it might be a pile of coats in the street but then he saw the arm, thickly covered with hair.

It was Pauley Firrigno. Faced down and not moving. That arm was exposed from under a rain slicker pulled up over the elbow. His arm was at an odd, uncomfortable angle from his body. Blood was puddled around his head. Trey ran over and as he did, Mo along with several others realized Pauley was badly hurt—maybe even dead. Trey put a finger to Pauley's neck and detected a pulse. He was not dead but he was gravely injured. Finally, the whine of sirens rose from a distance. Abruptly, the rain stopped as if someone shut off a faucet.

"Do something for him!" yelled someone in the gathering crowd. One of the guards showed up with a first aid kit in a blue plastic box. The Band-Aids and Mercurochrome packets looked pitifully inadequate to help Pauley. A police car came roaring around the corner, lights on but no siren.

"Don't touch him," said Trey. "It looks like he has a head or neck injury and the pros are here now."

A couple of baby-faced patrol cops ran up to assess the situation. They seemed to be looking around for a car collision or a bus tipped over. They could not calculate how all these people on the ground got hurt. Trey was resting on the balls of his feet in a squatting position. He merely rocked back and sat in a big wet puddle as the first EMTs hovered over Pauley.

Trey looked at the scene all around him. The blood. The pain. The street awash in the detritus of the city washing down the gutters, congealing in small black pools.

"What the hell have we done," he muttered.

CHAPTER 40

TOASTING EXCESS

Several hours later, the police, the fire department and the EMTs finally left. Pauley was surrounded by a host of medical personnel, gingerly encased in a neck brace and hooked up to several IVs before being loaded into an ambulance. He was unconscious. Most of the others were treated for cuts and bruises although there was one person with several dislocated fingers. Tommy Pherrel took his own car down to the ER to get his ribs x-rayed. He suspected they were broken. Every breath was agony. Medics thought Mo needed stitches in his head and lip but he refused for the moment out of sheer stubbornness. He did not want to admit he absorbed more than a superficial wound from those goons.

Trey was one of the dozens of witnesses who gave statements to various officers investigating the incident. The fire department seemed particularly interested in how the false alarm was set off inside the building and away from the picketing. Not wanting to get into messy explanations, Trey expressed surprise and shock that anyone could do such a thing and posed a theory that a stack of finished goods toppled over amid the hubbub and general panic, knocking the fire alarm off its moorings. The fire inspector dutifully recorded the theory and did not question exactly how the parts not only toppled but jumped about 6 feet across an aisle. He was rewarded in his job for closed files not probing questions.

Walking back into the plant Trey found it silent except for the hissing of compressed air lines. He was not sure if the violence scared the management team out of the plant or whether they just shut down for the day via order from Ike. Trey straggled in to Ike's office and was mildly surprised Ike and Harlowe were still there. Trey looked a mess. His pants were still damp and stained from sitting on the ground. His knuckles scraped raw and bleeding, were wrapped in gauze and bandages.

"Next time they cast the lead for Mother Teresa in a movie, you ought to try out. You looked a natural treating the sick and wounded out there," said Harlowe with a sneer.

Trey ignored Harlowe for the moment. He wanted to sit down somewhere but knew he was filthy. Rather than sit on any of the couches or chairs, he plopped on the floor. He recalled somewhere in the afternoon looking up and seeing Harlowe and Ike observing the scene from the loading dock, about 75 yards from the street and behind a barbed-wire fence. Ike was a bit more empathetic.

"Any idea what happened out there? And who was that they carted away? That looked pretty serious."

"Pauley Firrigno. It is bad. I don't know how bad and neither do they but he was not conscious, I'll tell you that."

"And I'll tell you what happened," said Harlowe, eager to interject. "They have themselves a little civil war going on amongst themselves. The young ones want to be working, not standing in the rain."

Trey finally had it with Harlowe.

"Didn't we tell them the place was closing? Hard to want to see how all that desire to work leads to a riot."

"Union brothers. Union brotherhood. Cain and Abel were better brothers." Harlowe just about spat out the words in derision.

"Our guys say they never saw the guys who started this before. Are you saying our young guys—who can't make the rent—paid leg breakers?"

"You call them 'our guys'? What part of these guys being on strike makes them 'our guys'? Take a look at whose name is on your check on Friday, boy." Harlowe was willing to move the topic in any way to get a foothold and humiliate Trey.

Trey struggled to his feet awkwardly.

"The guys who have been getting a Grean check just got the shit kicked out of them by some guys who never did a thing to help Grean survive all these years. I'm going over to the hospital to see MY guy Pauley."

Trey walked out to try to have the last word but Harlowe shouted out the door and down the hallway.

"Don't forget to get him flowers."

When Trey arrived at the hospital it was just about peak visiting time. The block before the hospital was clogged with cars backing up the street trying to get into the visitors lot. Impatient, he swung into the emergency room parking lot and parked in a spot marked "PICK UP AND DROP OFF ONLY." He would take his chances that the guards here were as vigilant as at the plant. He breezed past the ER intake desk with the air of authority that made the desk clerk assume he was a doctor. As he got back into the ER Trey scanned the environment looking for some sign of Pauley. The walls of white curtains created a milky maze, shrouding each patient. At the far end of the ER, an open area emerged where a patient was just removed. The floor was cluttered with a wide range of medical debris. Trey recognized one of the EMTs from the street and approached him.

"Was this the guy you took from the picket line?" asked Trey, with a nod to the empty gurney behind the pushed-back curtain.

The EMT recognized Trey from the scene on the street.

"Yeah—he was really in sad shape. Did they run over him?"

Trey had not considered that possibility but no one on the street mentioned anything about a hit and run.

"I wasn't there until after it happened but I don't think so."

"Jeez then, I've seen people hit by cars that looked better."

Trey hesitated to even ask the next question. It stuck in his throat for a minute but he got it out.

"Is he going to make it?"

"I can't say one way or the other. They took him away to OR. I was not close enough in there to see much and really tell." The EMT suddenly realized he was saying too much and added hopefully, "You're a relative, right?"

"Half-brother," Trey answered.

Across town Harlowe left the plant right on the heels of Trey's departure. As he left, he sized up the idling machines and knew he had to figure out a way to get them running again and soon. Harlowe left directly for his hotel room. When he got there he was startled to find Larry Turkel in his room along with several trays of room service food.

"Jesus, Larry, help yourself. Remind me not to stay in this hotel again. The security sucks."

Larry licked his fingers and peered over his reading glasses at Harlowe.

"Maids belong to the Service Workers Union. We got them a great contract last time. Chefs, too. You won't even see this on your bill. Best part is the booze," said Larry, pointing to a bottle of champagne in the ice bucket.

"What are we celebrating? That those old tired farts got the shit kicked out of them? Connect some dots for me, here, will you Turk?"

"Sit down, relax. You've won and you don't even know it."

Harlowe grabbed a piece of a club sandwich and flopped in a sitting chair in the corner.

"Enlighten me, Turk."

"Those boys were from the union—kind of. Maybe off-the-books types. The locals cannot stray from what we tell them. Not too far or they will think they don't need us. Our boys at Grean ignored me so we had to get them back in line. I've never steered them wrong. Now the young guys who want the jobs will be in charge. You can call a meeting anytime you want. I think they will listen now."

"And the police—they were all over there taking pictures. The vans had license plates. How does this not come back to the union somehow?"

"For me to worry about. I never asked them to do anything but talk to those guys. I think the guys on the picket line went after these guys first. I bet the license plates were not good and I bet the vans are on a train to auction somewhere in Florida. Just guessin' is all I'm doing of course," said Larry as he popped a chicken tender into his mouth.

"And as long as we are all guessing, I suppose the police may be stumped by this whole case?"

"Crappy cops in East Newark. Well-known fact."

While Harlowe slugged back a beer Larry soothed Harlowe with a timeline. The Turk thought they could wrap things up in less than a week. Harlowe did the math in his head. The ability to get an agreement with a smaller union would please the Grean family. Harlowe envisioned his retirement in a place considerably nicer than this dump in New Jersey. Somewhere warm. Maybe Phoenix, he thought.

Back at the hospital Trey was at loose ends. Pauley's condition might not be known for some time. He was assessing his next move when his pager went off. It was an unfamiliar but local number. Trey was still moving boldly inside the hospital. Rather than go to a pay phone he grabbed an unattended phone in the corner of the ER. He guessed "9" would get him an outside line and guessed right. He dialed the number nagging at him from the pager. A soothing female voice answered as Trey identified himself.

"Mr. Bensen, I am Nurse Smallwood. I am at St. Vincent's Hospital assisting your mother. She asked me to get a hold of you through your pager and she was not sure how to do that so I am helping her. It's about your father. Your mother thinks it would be a good idea if you came here to see him. Can you get here soon?"

Although her tone was not grave the words made the hair stand up on the back of his neck. It felt like the weight of his body was redistributed to his shoes. Trey told Nurse Smallwood he was in the hospital and would be there momentarily. Trey weighed whether he indeed wanted to ask the next question, but he did anyway.

"Is he OK? I mean, is he alive?"

There was some muffled rustling on the other end of the phone that made Trey wonder if Nurse Smallwood heard his question. It turned out she did.

"Yes, he is still with us. But your mother would like you to come see him as soon as you can."

Trey got off the phone to hear his pulse ring in his ears. He took a few deep breaths to compose himself and headed up the stairwell.

When he got to his father's room it was dark and he hesitated thinking he had been moved elsewhere. The room was dark, still and tidy. Then he realized there was somebody in the bed. It looked like his father but something was not as he remembered it. A lot of the tubes and wires were gone. It looked like the bed linens were changed. They were clean and unrumpled. His father was in the bed, the sheets covering him precisely at mid-chest with a neat uniform fold. His hands, once restrained to keep him from pulling at the tubes, were unrestrained and relaxed aside each hip. The bed was tilted ever so gently upward behind his upper torso. He looked so peaceful and restful. But so much of the apparatus was now gone. Was this a miracle recovery?

"He took a turn for the worse. He's dying."

The voice came from behind Trey. It was his mother. Her peace and calm was astounding.

"I asked them to call you." she continued. "You should be here. He wants you here I am sure."

Trey's mother recounted the hours since morning. Indeed Earl had a remarkable rally just as Trey left. He was up and alert and in full grasp of the situation. But it was as if the rally drained the last ounces of energy. A few hours later the difficult breathing left him gasping and incoherent. He lapsed into a comatose state. His vital signs deteriorated. For a few moments it looked like he had died but his breathing began again, slow and shallow. Frantic consultations began. Earl's organs were in a death spiral of shutdown. Machines and tubes and wires were attached and inserted.

"I hated that. I asked them what would happen if we stopped all that nonsense. He will never have the quality of life again he would enjoy. They told me he would die either way. I had them remove all this stuff. He is in no pain. The only thing he has is morphine now. We tried to call you earlier."

Trey instinctively felt for his beeper. He then thought back to the chaos in the streets. There was no way to explain. No sense to her understanding why he could not respond.

Trey's mother anticipated the next question. She read it in Trey's eyes.

"It could be an hour. It could be a day. It could be two. I just could not torture him. I hope you think I've done the right thing."

Trey's mother was looking past Trey to where Earl lay in great peace and cool white sheets.

"You did, Mom. I'm sorry that I..."

"Shhh," she said, moving forward and placing her hand gently on Trey's arm. "Don't say it. He loves you and you provide as he provided. There is nothing to regret."

She walked past Trey and pulled him gently to Earl's bedside.

"I like watching him now. Watching him breathe. When it is quiet you can hear him breathe—even now. It's like him talking to us somehow."

Together they sat in silence, time slowing all around them. The room was dark except for a soft light above the bed. It gave Earl an other-earthly glow. Together they watched and listened to him breathe. The noise of the hospital business in the halls was muted and faraway. A nurse came in occasionally and looked at the monitor above the bed, scrolling like a declining stock market ticker.

For over an hour, they sat in silence. From an almost Zen-like stage of calm and reflection, Trey allowed the creep of the reality outside the room to enter his consciousness. It ate at his calm from the edges a nibble at a time. How was Pauley? Where was Mo? Were Tommy's ribs really broken? Would the police catch the people who incited the riot? And Carole; he needed to call Carole above all.

Soon Trey was consumed by the deterioration of his calm. He realized he was tapping his foot. He got up and kissed his mother on the head and left the room. From her cocoon of serenity, she seemed hardly to notice.

Trey slipped out of the room and back down to the lobby. Less brash now, he decided to use the pay phone in the lobby. He tried to call home to Carole to explain the events of the day. He was simultaneously pleased and perplexed when it went to the answering machine. It was past 7 p.m. and Carole should have been home already. He listened to his own voice inviting him to leave a message after the beep. Trey called out to Carole to answer in case she was busy or just screening the calls. If she was home she did not pick up but he let her know he would be late.

CHAPTER 41

LONG GONE

There were so many fires burning in Trey's mind he struggled with which one to address. The calm he felt in his father's hospital room was long gone, replaced by a deep restlessness.

He decided he needed to find Mo and Tommy to see what they knew about the melee and what might happen next.

He knew if they were anywhere, they were at the club, so he hopped in his car and headed back under the Turnpike, guided by the glow of the garish neon sign outside The Bottomless Pit.

Trey knew the drill now. Pay the cover charge. Find a bouncer. Ask for Mo in The Library. He was moving at high speed. Except for one thing: Mo and Tommy weren't there. As a matter of fact, the bouncers eyed Trey suspiciously. They thought he might be running a con to get behind the stage. Maybe he was a stalker or a pervert. Now Trey had no idea how to reach Tommy or Mo. Assessing his options, he decided to stay put a while and see if they did show up.

Trey went to the bar and ordered a beer. The topless dancers wandered by, trolling for dollars. The light and the music overwhelmed his senses. He wanted to disappear into the corner so he did, sitting at a pub table behind the main bar. There were not too many because these were the cheap seats. The dancers called them cheap seats because these were the seats where the cheapest customers sat. Sitting at the bar it was almost impossible not to tuck a dollar into some string of lingerie. Back here the oglers sat nursing beers. Occasionally one of the dancers coming on stage or going off stage would wend her way through these tables hoping for a few bucks. It was almost an act of shaming the back corners. Being midweek though, some of the tables were open and Trey retreated there.

By heading for the dark corners, Trey lost sight of the TVs suspended directly above the bar. Normally the TVs would show a hockey or baseball game. Tonight, the game had just ended and the station switched to local news. With most of the attention on the girls shaking in their g-strings, no one noticed sports had melted into news. The loud music drowned out any sound but the picture was a live shot of the street behind Grean Machining. The reporter was lit with klieg lights and it looked like she appeared from a dark abyss. She pointed to a torn and tattered union hat, drenched in the fetid wash of the gutter water and storm runoff. Another shot showed a pile of bandages and medical supplies piled up on the street. The last shot showed what appeared to be blood on the whitish concrete of the curb. The reporter waved her arms at the black panorama behind her with some degree on wonderment. No one in the bar even noticed. When someone finally did see the news was on he alerted the bartender, who promptly changed the channel. It was the third inning in Seattle. The Mariners were tied 2-2 with the Tigers.

Trey nursed his beer and waited. While the dancers ignored him as a cheap weirdo, the barmaids eyed his beer bottle carefully and fed him a fresh cold one even when he had a third of his warm beer left. The beers went down easily and tasted good. Their effect was even more pleasant, taking the edge off this rotten day. Trey gave the waitress a $20 bill and told her to let him know when his tab ran out.

Somewhere in the course of events he peeled off another $20 and watched for Mo and Tommy less carefully. The padded swivel barstool got very comfortable. The beer was the right temperature. The music and lights less grating. Trey was slipping into an easy place of odd comfort and shutting out the world. The Bottomless Pit embraced him in loving arms.

Around midnight it became obvious that Mo and Tommy were not coming. To soothe the disappointment Trey had one more drink. He was feeling the effects of who-knows-how-many beers. He sat and nursed one last bottle in some booze-soaked theory his body needed time to metabolize the alcohol. If he drank this last one slowly he would burn off more than he consumed. A dancer named Amber came and sat with him. She was working here for tuition money. It paid better than bagging groceries and it was more exciting anyway. She wanted to be a pharmacist.

Trey looked at his watch. It was 12:40 a.m. There was nowhere he wanted to go but he knew he had to leave. The bar emptied out to a few of the most hard-core patrons. However sad, this group appealed to Trey more than anything waiting for him outside the door. He stood to leave and felt his body sway under its own weight like an overfilled tureen of soup. He made his way carefully to the parking lot. He got into his car and sat there, trying to sober up. He knew he could not stay there overnight and he also knew the police may be lying in wait; a DUI trap here was easy pickings for them. He took several deep breaths and then made his way slowly down the service road. He looked carefully for police tucked behind the giant concrete pillars rising to support the New Jersey Turnpike above. He was not exactly sure what he would do if he saw them but he was vigilant scanning the landscape on either side of the road.

As Trey crept down the side roads and up onto the Turnpike the studios at the local TV affiliate were busy with their overnight activities. They were already piecing together what might be shown on the morning news, trying to fit a 22-minute jigsaw puzzle 90 seconds at a time. They took another look at the report about the street fight at Grean. Given nobody knew much about the brawl, there was some question as to whether it would make the morning news for one more airing. In the end, they deferred a decision and hoped an overnight fire might have enough footage to displace the Grean story. Still, the visuals and the mystery surrounding the brawl were tantalizing. Who had the fight? Where were they now? Would there be more violence? How had everyone disappeared into the wind? An overnight film editor at the station blinked at the screen through a veneer of cigarette smoke emanating from the unfiltered butt burning perilously close to his fingers. He felt the increasing heat burning his finger and absentmindedly stubbed it out in a gold gilt ashtray in front of him. He could not decide if the piece was good enough to run on the morning news but something about the visuals arrested him. The blood on the curb. The storm runoff washing around bandages. The people gone—unseen. Almost like the Rapture touched down in East Newark. He knew someone in the network might see something there.

"Numbnuts!" he barked at an eager intern. "Pull this piece on the fight at Grean and put it up on the satellite. Somebody with time to fill might want it—but damned if I'm sure how."

Within seconds the carnage on the street shot electronically into the air, bouncing off a satellite 200 miles above earth.

Meanwhile, Trey felt better once he made it to the Turnpike and back down toward his home in Seawell. As he gripped the steering wheel in tension and fear near the club, he felt more in control somehow on the well-lit eight-lane highway. He relaxed a bit as he exited the Turnpike. The toll taker seemed totally disinterested in his condition or well-being. But just as he began to relax heading home, he felt his anxiety rise again. It was 1:30 a.m. He was getting home late and he was sure he smelled and looked awful. This was a recipe for another fight, another wedge between him and Carole. Any excuse he considered seemed lame and trite. He felt his heart pound as he pulled into the driveway of his townhome. He killed his headlights a half block early so they would not shoot through the house on approach. In the moonless night he could not see much beyond the front of his car. Even in his haze of alcohol and grief it occurred to him that he was living his life the same way—limited visibility—outdriving his ability to see what was not immediately in front of him. Barely averting one collision before reacting to the next crisis. Walking in the door could be his next crisis. He wanted to lie down and sleep. He only hoped to slip in unnoticed.

Trey took a deep breath and steadied himself as he prepared to put the key in the lock and walk in. He knew he could not stumble in and make a big commotion if he hoped to pull this off. Perhaps he could even lie on the couch and fall asleep. If there was a fight it could wait until the morning. No, that was cowardly, he thought. He would go up and lie in his own bed.

He entered almost silently, checking carefully for obstacles near the door he might kick. He used the porch light so he would not have to turn on interior lights. He was careful not to let a curious Belvedere out but the cat was nowhere to be found. In fact, it was too dark. Carole was a stickler about leaving on a couple of small night lights near the door and stairs, but it was pitch black once Trey closed the door quietly behind him. He crept carefully back to the kitchen and turned on a set of small lights over the counter to focus his eyes and fix the situation. He felt grimy from the day and quietly washed his face in the kitchen sink. He used the dish detergent as his face soap hoping the lemony aroma might wash away the stink of the day. Even with his entrance—no Belvedere. This was odd. The chubby little cat was a great opportunist and eternal optimist. If there was anyone in the kitchen it was a chance to be fed. It was just as well. A mewling cat might provide as much noise as a stumbling drunk husband.

Trey went up the stairs longing for bed. He removed his clothes down to his boxers in silence. A few more steps and he could feel the relief of sleeping in his bed. As he got to the bedside he listened for Belvedere as much as he looked for him in the dark, but still he could not feel him near. As he reached for the sheet, he began to realize something was not right. Instead of feeling the sheet and comforter, he felt the bedspread. His eyes strained in the darkness to make sense of what he was feeling. Something was not right. The tiniest bits of light around the edges of the window could not make a dent in the bottomless blackness. Trey ran his hand down the bed to feel only bedspread. He switched on a small light next to the bed. Carole was not there. Trey's heart raced and his head was swimming. Did he just pass her on the couch downstairs? His eyes lit upon her dresser. Always meticulously organized, it was now Spartan-bare except for two small atomizers. Trey ran to the walk-in closet where only a few hangers sat, clearing a large space until his clothes packed the far end of the closet.

She was gone.

Chapter 42

Sending Signals

Dear Trey,

I'm sorry. I just can't take it anymore. I want to be there for you. I want there to be us. But right now this cannot be and I am not entirely sure why. I feel shut out and alone. I don't know where you are or what you are thinking. You are trying to go it alone for some reason I cannot understand. Your father is sick and your work is a mess. You are not here with me. Since I met you I felt we could face anything and accomplish anything if we did it together. Right now you do not want us to be together and I cannot stand it. Right now we need to be apart and figure these things out. I'll call and let you know where I am. I thought about talking about this but I knew you would not be part of such a conversation. I almost hate to ask: Is this a shock to you? If it is then maybe you need to start there.

There is no one else. I could not stand anyone else. I just need to be alone. When you are ready to be the Trey I know and love, maybe we can work it out. In the meantime, we need to be apart because if I stay you might hurt me—hurt us—in ways that cannot be repaired.

Maybe my leaving is the worst thing for you, but maybe it is the only way. I do not want to hurt you. I just want to stop hurting.

Love Always,
Carole
PS—I have Belvedere.

Trey found the note in the middle of the kitchen table. It was handwritten in her beautiful teacher's handwriting on a yellow legal pad. It was tattered at the top where she tore it from the husk of the pad, folded it in half and left it in the middle of the table. He missed seeing it as he crept through the darkened kitchen just a few minutes earlier. Trey felt foolish. He tiptoed in darkness through an empty house, clueless that his own wife just left him. The house was now ablaze as he turned on every conceivable light trying to see exactly what Carole left with and hoping for some hint this was not real. He sat on the edge of the chair at the kitchen table and re-read the note several times. Every time he read it, he read it more slowly. He pored over it like a detective looking for tiny clues. Any blotches to indicate she may have been crying? Did she underline any words? Was the fact she said "Dear Trey" a hopeful sign? He liked "Love Always." Definitely good. Could he find her now? Was she sleeping? When did she leave? If he called earlier could he have stopped her? What could he say now? He had no answers for her questions. Who was he kidding? His head throbbed and his face was a grimy film of beer and strip club smoke. He felt like a total failure.

He felt like he could fall asleep right there in the kitchen but knew he would regret it, so he dragged into the living room and collapsed on the couch. He fell asleep with the letter on his chest minutes after his head hit the couch throw pillow.

In Chicago, NCN—National Cable News—was working through what viewers on the East Coast would see on their dawn update at 5 a.m. The overnight producer, Jeanne DeSmedt, looked up at a dozen screens as she pulled all the content she could off the satellite. The first update at dawn is important but tough to program. People are half asleep. She was always looking for a grabber. As she scanned the screens she always envisioned people bleary eyed, turning on the TV as much for background noise as anything. Beyond the latest crisis in the Middle East, what would make them put down their wet towels as they stepped out of the shower and turn up the TV?

She searched the screens, hoping something would grab her eye. It was 3 a.m. in Chicago and deadlines loomed. She was already on her fifth cup of coffee. She had a rough lineup of stories, but they needed a story to tease coming out of the national news to lead off the show. What would make all those sleepy people come back and want to see the first story after the first commercial of the day?

She scanned house fires, jackknifed semis spilling chickens across a highway and a cat with wheels for back legs.

"Hold 3. Bring 3 up. What the hell is that about?" she said to the technician filling the screens before her.

In an instant, the silent image on screen 3 was shifted to a larger central screen that allowed her to add audio. She almost did not care about what the story was given the images. What she saw was a very low shot of bloody bandages. It was almost shot from below and the small wad of gauze looked 6 feet tall. Behind it the empty street looked like a battle zone, but barren of all life. If this was another massacre in some third-world country, she was about to toss the whole thing. Nobody wanted that in the morning. Then she listened to the entire feed. This was not some war-torn god-forsaken outpost. This was East Newark, New Jersey. Some factory and strikers. Good and evil. Hardworking stiffs getting cut up. She had her hook for the break. She took a big gulp of coffee and then talked into her headset with great urgency.

"I need a writer and an editor up here. We've got 54 minutes to recut this piece so it makes sense somewhere else than fucking Jersey."

Trey had only been asleep for a little over two hours but he was in a deep, dreamless sleep. The phone rang and it jarred him awake. For a split second he was disoriented before remembering he was on the couch. He had to listen for the phone again to think through where to answer it. Even in his stupor, he hoped it was Carole. As he sat up her letter fluttered off his chest but he grabbed it in midair, refusing to let it out of his sight. He shuffled into the kitchen in his stockinged feet and grabbed at the phone, trying to prepare something positive to say to Carole. Except the voice on the other end was not Carole. It was his mother.

"He's gone, Trey."

Her voice was calm and matter-of-fact.

Trey was not processing the information.

"What? Who's gone? Where?"

"Your father, Trey. He's dead. Just a few minutes ago."

"What happ—"

"He was such a good man. A good provider. So good to you. So good to us."

The words broke her stoicism as she began to weep into the phone.

"Trey, darling. Can you come now? I'm at the hospital and I don't know what to do now. I'm sorry to wake you but I could use you here." She was in a full breathless sob.

Her weeping stabbed at Trey's heart.

"Of course, Momma. I'll be there as soon as I can."

As Trey took a quick shower, hoping to wash the stink of the last day off of his body, National Cable News started the morning broadcast with a story from Washington DC about a controversy in Congress over balancing the budget and closing tax loopholes. That was followed by protests in the Middle East over terrorism. Hoping to hold the audience through the commercial, a well-coiffed anchor dutifully read his teleprompter with a voice steeped in gravitas. The picture showed an empty street streaked in rain and what appeared to be blood.

"A picket line brawl in New Jersey leaves dozens injured but no clear picture of who was involved or why the violence erupted. What police are saying there and your overnight lottery numbers when we return."

CHAPTER 43

THE NEWS

The NCN Morning News roundup returned from the first commercial break of the morning with a shot of the street just outside Grean Machining from the day before. It was a long shot of the street showing several emergency vehicles, lights flashing, EMTs tending to battered and bleeding people. The street was littered with medical debris. The voice-over from the anchor almost seemed flippant.

"Police in New Jersey are trying to figure out what triggered a brawl on a picket line outside a factory in East Newark. Authorities there say several people were injured-one seriously—when a fight erupted on the picket line. Union officials deny that the fight was among union members and say they want a full investigation to see if the management there had anything to do with the violence. Police are still investigating and say at least some of those involved in the fight fled the scene before authorities arrived. The workers are on strike protesting job cuts there."

The video ended with a shot of storm water washing what appeared to be blood down the street.

The television carrying the news program was suspended from the ceiling by sturdy cables above a row of treadmills, stationary bicycles and rowing machines. The TV abruptly shut down and condensed the picture to one vertical line before the screen went entirely black.

Duncan Rucks, Vice President of Mergers and Acquisitions for TerVeer Enterprises, pumped ever more furiously on his bike, head down and ignoring the news he just saw. He hoped it was some kind of mirage but he knew it was not. He looked up at the black screen with disgust.

He was already up at this early hour, multitasking. He was combing the Asian markets for bargains while riding a stationary bike at the company gym and catching up on the news when he saw the flash. Even without a mention of Grean, he knew immediately where this riot took place. Duncan calculated all the implications in this 45-second clip and was already anticipating the arc of the ripples.

The brawl meant the union in New Jersey was out of control.

The deal for Grean Machining was dead.

His reputation for selecting the right deal was tarnished.

TerVeer still had no way to reduce costs for their machined parts.

He could be dubbed a failure.

None of these were good and he had to cut his ties to this debacle quickly.

Still sweating profusely, he mopped his head with a towel and walked from the gym annex into the main part of the office, which was dark and quiet. He opened his office and called his assistant, leaving her a message on voicemail to get out a certified letter, signature receipt required. The whole time he sat on the edge of his desk chair, not out of anxiety but to be sure he did not soak his office furniture in sweat. He quickly scribbled a few thoughts on a pad. These were loose ends that had to be sewn. Some were formal and others were social. Some calls he had to make to contain the damage. Repositioning his recommendation of the Grean acquisition as a long shot and perhaps not as strategically important as once thought. The current suppliers of machined parts could be beaten down in price a bit more and provide even better value than all the headaches associated with Grean. Then he went back to the gym. He needed to find another acquisition, something to make people at TerVeer forget about Grean.

By 9 a.m. the message was conveyed to a courier service in Orlando to be delivered before noon.

About this same time Trey emerged from his shower. While he had the TV morning news on as almost background noise, he missed the broadcast on NCN regarding violence at the plant by just a minute or so. The story was replaced on the screen in the bedroom TV by a weather map with a big, smiling sunshine face. Even the low volume of the news grated on Trey and he shut off the TV almost peevishly. He felt oddly relieved, even in his grief. He plopped back on his bed, "our bed," he thought. His momentary relief receded and was replaced immediately by a deep uncertainty regarding his marriage. How was he going to contact Carole? Where was she? When would she reach out—if at all? Any serenity was extremely short lived in his mind as his attention flitted from crisis to crisis. His marriage. His father. His mother. The plant. Harlowe. As hard as Trey tried to compartmentalize the issues and prioritize his day, they seemed to spill over one another. They tangled together in his mind in a giant knot. Perhaps the same knot he felt at the base of his skull where the neck muscles throbbed.

As he landed on the bed, Trey felt like the most comfortable place in the universe at this given moment and the house was filled with a vacuum-like quiet. He knew he needed to get to the hospital quickly but he gave in to the peace and shut his eyes for just a moment to soak in the stillness. He succumbed to this cocoon. It was just another mistake as he fell off to sleep in just seconds.

CHAPTER 44

SCHOOLYARD NIGHTMARE

*T*rey *could not remember exactly how he got there but he was standing in front of his old grammar school. The school was built on a bluff and stood high above the street level, bound by two steep driveways on each side and a wide set of stairs down the middle. The stairs recognized the steep ascent with not one but two landings that allowed the person ascending to rest with a couple of steps forward before continuing the climb. The school itself stood almost fortress-like, defending some point unknown behind it facing the Essex River in the distance. It was as if it had been built by the Department of Defense to defend East Newark from privateers from New York City when in fact it had been built by the city shortly after WWI.*

On this day, Trey stood looking up at the school. The sky was a translucent steel gray/blue. The kind of sky you get in July just ahead of a thunderous rainstorm ready to wash the skies and the streets in one convulsive five-minute event. There was a flagpole that stood at the top of the stairs and extended 25 feet in the air. The flag whipped almost straight east in a gale, appearing much stronger 50 feet up (allowing for both the rise to the bluff and the flagpole that sat atop it) than where Trey stood at street level. It was quiet. Preternaturally quiet except for the snap of the flag and the occasional clang of the flagpole hardware against the steel pole itself. The strong wind blew cold from behind Trey and he felt a strong need to walk up the driveway toward the school. He was not afraid of the possibility it might storm but sensed almost an innate homing signal calling him toward the school.

As Trey ascended the steep macadam driveway the wind blew freshness into the air around him. He walked deliberately but effortlessly until he was at the corner of the schoolhouse. He felt almost weightless. The gates to the side yard of the school were unlocked and opened, inviting him in. Trey remembered the old school doors were heavy and uneven, layered with season after season of paint. The lumps of paint combined with age and wear and made it impossible for the doors to close flush with the door jamb. In winter Trey recalled how snow might pile up just inside the misshapen door if the storm was strong enough. The snow could seep in every warped spot. But the old doors were now replaced with shiny new aluminum hardware, made flush and tight with the building. It was like grafting a prosthetic arm or leg onto an old body. It was functional, but it looked odd and out of place with the weathered building. The aluminum door was shiny and silver, the building a pile of pitted red brick.

As Trey approached the door he saw that the upper third of the door was glass reinforced with fine wire to discourage brick-throwing vandals. As he looked in he saw the familiar sight of a floor landing painted with a glossy institutional gray paint with stairs that led either down to the basement gymnasium or up a floor to classrooms. He was looking down toward the basement when a movement on the floor above caught his attention. The movement startled him. The building seemed vacant and dark except for the glare of the pre-storm sky illuminating the interior, leaking in at odd angles from any side a window was available. By the time Trey looked up he could only catch the glimpse of a right leg from the knee down, attired in gray workpants, and a black shoe and a white sock. Even though he did not see the person as he passed, Trey recognized him immediately as his father, Earl. It was not a literal recognition, but a sense. A sure sense. Trey processed the image like a subliminal message flashed for a millisecond on a screen. Yet he was 100% certain the fleeting image of the pant leg disappearing past the upper landing belonged to his father. Immediately he knew he had to see him. Trey tugged on the aluminum door but it did not move, frustrating him terribly. He pulled on the door harder and harder, shaking the doorframe until on the last tug, the door popped open, throwing him momentarily off balance. Trey was afraid the door might close again before he could gain entry, but he slipped in just ahead of the aluminum click of the door behind him now. Immediately a high, tinny alarm sounded. Trey stepped in, still obeying this homing beacon he felt. He knew the alarm bell would bring security—maybe even police— so he moved quickly up the stairs. He did not run. Inside the air changed immediately. Outside the breeze blew fresh and clean. Now, the air was warm *and comfortable but stale, filled by the chalk dust and aging paper of 75 school years. There was a clean antiseptic smell of glazed interior brick walls washed down God-knows-how-many times, mixed with decades of layers of gray floor paint. The smells were comfortable, but he had no time to linger—his father was just ahead of him. As Trey reached the top of the landing to the first floor, he turned smoothly and silently on the shiny floor. This time he looked down a long hallway of classrooms on the right. Each had its doors closed. The hallway was dark except for the light filtering through the windows on the classroom doors. Each door threw a triangular light slice into the hall. Dust seemed to be suspended in the light and settling softly. That infernal alarm continued to scream and quickened Trey's heart rate. At the far end of the hall Trey saw the gray pant cuff again, this time turning left. This time it was the left leg disappearing in a fleeting image. It confirmed again to Trey it was his father.*

Trey moved down the hall quickly, flickering through the mottled light until he reached the end of the hall. As he turned left at the end he expected to see his father but the hallway was empty. The dust swirls suspended in the soft filtered light betrayed a movement down another corridor to the right. The alarm told Trey he was running out of time and he moved down the hallway, turning right. The hallway opened to a vestibule and a double-wide set of exit stairs and down one flight again, past more newly installed aluminum security doors and back outside to the glowering light and winds, which now swirled cold ahead of a storm promising to be brutish.

Once outside, Trey instinctively knew to turn left around the large school building again. He could still sense his father's presence. The gray pant leg was burned into his consciousness. The alarm continued to ring but fade in the distance. Trey was relieved to be outside. He moved left into a corner where the school walls were all brick with no windows. They sheltered him from the wind but cast a long shadow. His father was nowhere to be seen. There was a narrow alleyway where the building came close to but did not touch a retaining wall, creating a boundary to the school property. Trey knew it was the only path his father could have taken, but his signal was lost. The strong beacon of certainty was gone. He knew he could pursue, but the effort would be futile. He lost him. He wanted to keep that picture of that gray pant leg frozen in his memory forever. How could he make that memory permanent? More desperately, how could he find the homing beacon? He became aware again of the alarm ringing faintly inside the school. He felt it was shrill. He wanted to get out of the shadow and back into the light but feared even the light was filled with cold air now. The cold air rushed down on him from the sky.

Trey gasped for air and sat straight up in bed. He was sure he had just experienced a nightmare but recalling the dream, he could not figure out why it was scary. He was sweating and panting and he gulped the air. When he fell asleep on the bed he was naked and warm from the shower. Now his sweat was cold and chilled him to the bone. He wondered what a nervous breakdown felt like. If it was being frightened by things you could not even understand, this might be what it felt like. He grabbed at a T-shirt hanging on a doorknob and wiped his face to dry it and then got to his feet with great effort. His head hurt like a sonofabitch. He looked at the clock in a panic. He had only been asleep about 20 minutes but the day already seemed to be slipping away from him. He got dressed quickly and left for the hospital.

CHAPTER 45

ICU

As Trey pulled into the hospital parking lot he realized he had no idea how to find his mother. He headed to his father's room but certainly he was removed to either the morgue or the funeral home by now. Instead of heading up a side stairwell to the patient rooms, Trey entered through the lobby. He did not get very far. He immediately saw Mo and Tommy asleep on couches near the security desk. He thought for a moment to ignore them and sneak by, but he could not stand to walk by, indifferent. Trey sat down roughly on the couch to rouse them but it did not work. He had to physically shake them to bring them to attention. They both looked and smelled awful. A day's growth of beard and dirty clothes on both of them betrayed the fact they were in the lobby all night. Both wore bandages with peek-a-boo blood stains on their hands and faces. Trey was surprised they had not been removed by security. Trey pushed on Mo at the shoulder. He awoke but fell over onto Tommy, who protested with a grunt.

"What are you guys doing here?" asked Trey.

Mo washed his face with his hand and focused on Trey.

"We should ask you the same fucking question. Come to see what's left of us?"

"Not now, Mo. I'm here because my father died last night and I have to go see where he is and get my Mom, too."

Mo softened immediately and rubbed Trey's knee.

"I'm sorry for your loss," he said in a growl.

"Who's still here? Is Pauley out? Is he OK? How is everyone else?"

Tommy tried to sit up from where he was slumped over the couch but he could not bring himself to a sitting position without rolling onto this shoulder and pushing up with great effort.

"My fucking ribs," he groaned before rising to the edge of the couch and continuing.

"That is why we are still here. Everybody else is out and beat up but OK I guess. They won't let us see Pauley. We know he had surgery. We think he has a cracked skull. No one will tell us anything but we ain't leaving until we find something out. We will wait these bastards out."

"Where's Larry? You mean with all his connections the little swindler can't check on his union brother?" Trey asked. Mo gave Trey a withering look to convey all that needed to be said. Tommy made it explicit.

"We haven't seen that little fuck. He's been talking to the press about a management conspiracy but he has not come down here—unless he snuck by when we fell asleep."

"So what the hell happened out there? Who started it all?" asked Trey.

Mo scratched the stubble of afro remaining in his receding hairline to reflect before he answered.

"They said they were union. Talked like they were union. But when they started swingin' they were not any union brothers I've ever seen. Your guess is as good as mine. The Greans coulda sent them for all we know. They were as young as our guys who are pissed but not our guys for sure. We sure as shit are going to find out."

Trey knew he could not linger much longer but decided he needed to see where Pauley was.

"They'll let me by to find my mother. Let me see if I can roam and see how Pauley is. Go home if you want to. I can hit your beeper when I find something."

"We are here this long," said Mo. "We ain't going nowhere until we get some info so do what you can. We'll be right here."

Trey knew already moving around the hospital had less to do with security and more to do with the air of confidence he could muster. He fished his Grean ID badge out of his pocket and attached it to his pocket. He loosened his tie to add a sense of informal urgency and carried a notepad against his chest. He breezed past security with a knowing nod and into the elevators to the patient floors. Once on the second floor, he called back down to security and asked where to deliver flowers to Mr.

Paolo Firrigno and found out he was in ICU—Intensive Care Unit. Trey reboarded the elevator and stopped at Floor 5-ICU. Still moving with authority, he hustled past the nurse's station but took a quick peek at the large white board serving as a messaging center for the staff. He saw P. Firrigno in a dry erase marker in the box denoting area 15-1. The ICU was divided not into rooms but areas separated by floor-to-ceiling curtains. This allowed the space to shrink or expand per each patient's needs for care and equipment. As Trey approached area 15 he noticed there were no other patients nearby and it looked like Pauley had a lot of space to himself. Trey immediately felt good that Pauley had a little room and privacy with no one crammed next to him. Still brimming with faux authority, Trey charged past the curtain in space 15. But the bravado and good feeling were quickly replaced by horror.

If there was a human being in the bed, he was obscured by a tangle of tubes and pumps. A life support system pumped life-sustaining air in and out of this crumpled body. For a split second, Trey thought perhaps it was a training device of some kind as the place where the person's head would normally be appeared to be a comically overinflated purple balloon. Then Trey realized it was not a balloon. It was Pauley's head. It was grotesquely swollen and covered in a light gauze veneer. Trey could not figure out exactly how human flesh could stretch that far without splitting. It looked like Pauley might explode and send shards of his face everywhere. His left eye was a slit, swollen shut. His right eye seemed to be shifted out of place, pushed by the swelling on the left into some dislocation. It was worse than any horror movie he had ever seen.

As Trey entered two nurses were tugging on the knot of tubes, trying to optimize their location. At once, they turned and sensed Trey in their space. They seemed like they might be awaiting expertise and relief from their predicament. Trey's eyes caught sight of a Hispanic woman seated at the foot of the bed. He assumed it was Pilar, Pauley's wife. She looked bedraggled and clutched a string of rosary beads. Her eyes never left Pauley. The eyes of the nurses in their struggle alarmed Trey. He had really overstepped his bounds this time. He excused himself with a mumble of excuses about being in the wrong area and ducked into the first bathroom he could find. It was one of those oversized hospital restrooms built to accommodate wheelchairs and walkers. He locked the door and wept over the sink in a wrenching sob.

Slowly Trey gathered himself and doused his face in cold water. He needed to be calm and controlled for his mother. He could not be a blubbering mess no matter how much he wanted to be at this moment.

How could he find his mother? He decided to go back to the lobby and see if there was a message at the reception desk to direct him. On the way back he passed the doors to the chapel and stopped in his tracks a few steps down the hall. He poked his head in the door. It seemed to be the perfect temperature and softly lit. He adjusted his eyes to the light and saw no one in the chapel until he scanned to the very back row. That is when he saw his mother, her gray hair in a tight perm, head bowed in prayer. Trey slid silently down the pew toward her, not wishing to interrupt her prayers and thoughts. As he neared, she grabbed Trey by the back of his neck and brought him down to her shoulder like a child. They hugged in silence for what seemed an eternity. Trey was glad he was all cried out. He just wanted to be a rock right now—whatever that meant.

CHAPTER 46

DAWN IN TONY ORLANDO

The sunrise over Orlando promised a sizzling day. Cal Grean Jr. already had the air conditioning cranked up in the car as he approached his office and was thankful the cool night air still hung in the parking garage as he made his way to the office.

It was a few minutes before 8 a.m. and the most eager of his subordinates made it an obvious habit to be at their desks as he arrived. His secretary always started at 7:30 to ensure the coffee was hot and the day was organized—or perhaps, re-organized. When Cal arrived his schedule was already printed and sat in the middle of his desk. Folders containing documents pertinent to topics of each meeting were in a pile for his review.

Cal was perplexed by the silence from New Jersey and Harlowe. He wanted an update but decided to wait for his brother Jack to arrive to track down Harlowe.

Jack arrived shortly after 9 as was his habit. He, too, wanted to find Harlowe. Jack still liked Harlowe a lot but he sensed Cal's growing irritation with being left in the dark. Jack considered a side call to Harlowe to encourage him to call in and smooth things over a bit with Cal but he discarded the idea as too complicated. Harlowe was a big boy and could handle himself.

Cal was indeed occupied by the pile of folders on his desk that morning and the topics crammed inside them. Cal and Jack discussed lunch plans and a good time to call Harlowe when the courier arrived. The letter was received by Cal's secretary and she brought it to him as soon as she digested the contents.

Cal knew the note was impactful by the urgency of his assistant. He scanned it once, took a deep breath and read it aloud to Jack.

We regret to inform you that TerVeer Enterprises hereby withdraws interest in pursuing acquisition discussions with the Grean organization. We thank you for your active participation in all phases of this process and wish you luck in pursuit of your objectives.

Please be reminded that all documents, discussions and exchange of information regarding financial and technical issues remain bound by the terms of non-disclosure and confidentiality provisions executed in the course of this due diligence.

Sincerely,

Duncan Rucks

Executive Vice President

Mergers and Acquisitions

TerVeer Enterprises

Jack saw his island life fading away. Cal felt emptiness in the pit of his stomach. He rarely experienced failure and he remembered why. It tasted like a shit sandwich. He had no appetite for lunch now. He needed to find Harlowe.

Harlowe operated so long in the shadows the Greans never suspected he would be in plain sight. The fact was Harlowe was back at the plant camped out again in Ike's office. With Larry's encouragement he was planning a victory lap as he addressed Ike.

"Keep it together out there another day or two, Ike. After that ass-kicking yesterday the guys who want to work and get back in here are firmly in control. We'll have this place up and humming again within the next week."

He took a quick look at the clock and grumbled about Trey's whereabouts.

"Where the hell is Bensen anyway? Is he still out there holding their hands on the picket line? Goddamn Molly Pitcher is what he is cut out to be."

Ike knew Harlowe's sneer was unfair. Trey's relationship with the union was positive and trusting—a bridge that allowed things to function.

Still, Ike was not about to mount any defense. He knew better than to challenge Harlowe—especially now.

The phone rang in Ike's office. Upon first answer, Ike's face lit in a half-smile but then sobered quickly.

"Harlowe? It's for you. Sounds important. Orlando calling."

Harlowe took the phone but never got to say a word. Ike heard a dim, relentless chatter bouncing off the receiver. Harlowe was turning pale. His eyes narrowed to his famous squint.

Trey was not anywhere near the picket line or giving the union any comfort as Harlowe suspected. Trey was at the Runge Funeral Home, making arrangements for his father's funeral, which would take place in three days. Trey and his mother were in the middle of the casket showroom. Each casket was lit from the ceiling with a beam of heavenly light. The room was warm and soundproof to buff any harsh noise to a comforting hum. Price tags gently offered a "suggested" price. It was all surreal. As hard as Trey tried to compartmentalize all the pieces of his life it was in the middle of the casket tour when he realized he had not yet alerted Ike and Harlowe about the death of his father. Then he realized he had no idea how to reach Carole. Then he wondered about Pauley. Somehow Trey envisioned Pauley's wife and wondered if she, too, would be in this room before long to pick out something for Pauley. Then he realized the funeral director had been extolling the features of each casket as they went through the showroom.

"Trey, honey. Which one should we choose? I can't do this. I know you will do the right thing," said Trey's mother. She seemed vacant and nearly in shock. After all the tough decisions she made about her Earl, she was played out. Trey came back to the present but was not prepared.

"I'm sorry, Mr. Runge. I'm going to have to ask you to repeat yourself," said Trey. He blocked out all the distractions to try and focus on this awful task at hand. The complex compartments of his life were coming apart at the seams.

Back at the local TV station, they were getting calls about their NCN piece, which had been picked up nationally. Originally, they had no plans on a follow-up story but the national attention revived interest. They dispatched two crews to see what was new. One went to the hospital for a live shot about those treated in the brawl. The second returned to the original site of the melee to find a diminished picket line of just four strikers carrying signs. The search was on for Larry Turkel to make a statement but he was unavailable due to "ongoing negotiations."

After Trey finished the arrangements at the funeral home he brought his mother back home. It was the first time she had been there in nearly two days. His father was everywhere and nowhere at the same time. An argyle sweater sat waiting on his easy chair. A half bottle of water sat on his side of the nightstand. His favorite hat—a plaid cap—hung on a peg near the door ready for his next walk. These things all seemed hurtful and mocking. While Trey's mother got out of her clothes and into a duster for comfort, Trey picked up his father's sweater and put it over his nose, inhaling deeply. It was his father's scent, so vivid and strong in the absence of his person. Trey felt like an animal picking up on a trail. Even if he suspected his mother was doing something similar, he did not want her to see him smelling the sweater so he placed it back on the chair carefully so it looked undisturbed. He gave his mother two aspirins with a mild sleeping aid and put her in her bed for at least a nap. He told her he would be back in a couple of hours but he needed to go home for a little bit.

"Give Carole my love," she said. It made Trey feel awful but this was not the time to talk about his marital problems. The fact was he had no idea what to say anyway. He needed that compartment air tight for the moment.

"I will. She sends her love, too. Rest. I'll be back soon. Call my pager if you need me sooner. I won't be far."

Trey drew the shades to darken the room. Hopefully the neighborhood would be quiet for a while and allow his mother rest. He took an extra moment before leaving and sat in his father's easy chair. He looked around the room. He wanted to see the world as his father last saw it. He somehow hoped Earl Sr. left some wisdom by the seat of his pants and Trey tried to soak it up. Soon he felt foolish, got up and quietly left, locking the door behind him.

CHAPTER 47

A CRACK IN THE CASE

As Trey got to the curb in front of his mother's house he assessed which compartment of his complicated life he needed to address next. He thought about going to the plant and informing Ike he'd be gone a few days. But then he thought about Tommy and Mo sitting in the hospital lobby. If there was some additional news on Pauley's condition it would be a good piece of information to leave with Ike. Even though he knew Harlowe might be at the plant, Trey could only imagine talking to Ike. The thought of seeing Harlowe made him slightly sick to his stomach. It was now getting on to midafternoon. Trey fussed at his watch. If he hurried to the hospital he could complete his task and be back before his mother awoke to an empty house.

As he neared the hospital Trey thought his recently acquired familiarity with the facility might allow him to move around and perhaps get access to Pauley's area again. This time he had to be prepared. He wanted an opportunity to talk to Pilar, comfort her and get better information on Pauley's condition. He needed composure.

He was deep in thought as he moved through the streets of East Newark. When he pulled into the parking garage he strained to remember exactly how he got there. It was still before visiting hours so the parking was plentiful. He grabbed the first spot he found, even though it made for a longer walk to either the service stairs or the lobby of the hospital. He grabbed his jacket to look somewhat official and headed across the lot. Bright sunshine now shrunk pools of stagnant rainwater from the day before and he hopped around them to avoid getting his shoes wet.

Because of the puddles and concrete parking lot stops, Trey trained his eyes downward to be sure he did not trip. It was then he realized the presence of a stabbing headache. The sudden onset of the pain was alarming and confusing. His senses were further confused as the ground seemed to rush up to meet him. A white parking line on the ground seemed to expand five times its width. He was disoriented and realized, despite his most careful efforts, he was falling. He struggled to put his hands out and break his fall but it was as if his hands were in sand at his sides. He felt sure his face would hit the pavement before he could even move his hands. He saw the pavement approaching—almost in slow motion. He could not process why his hands did not move. He hit the pavement face first. His headache intensified as his nose hit the garage floor. It felt like the bridge of his nose exploded into his head. His temples ached. It all went black. For how long? A second? A minute?

As Trey processed what was happening he realized his head ached from the base of his neck forward. He was still face down, carefully rolling to one side fearing he would leave parts of his nose on the ground. He felt the back of his head swelling immediately even though he fell face first. None of it made any sense. As he rolled to one side, sunlight stabbed his eyes. He saw someone hovering over him. Trey was embarrassed to think someone saw him fall so awkwardly. But then he recognized the person standing over him.

It was Harlowe Mikkelsen.

Harlowe's large, balding head was finally of some use as it partially blocked the sunlight. He stood over Trey, jaw tightly clenched. In one hand he held a length of pipe—the kind the machinists used at Grean to push parts down conveyors. Suddenly clarity came to Trey. This was no headache or stumble. Harlowe just clocked him in the back of the head with the pipe.

"You turncoat son of a bitch," Harlowe said, lips barely moving. His voice was even and low and menacing. "I don't know exactly what you did, but I know it wasn't good. You queered this whole deal for us somehow. You and your little union buddies. I heard you talking with them at the side door, you sneaky bitch. You think you are smart. You threw a wrench in this and I am about to throw a wrench into you."

Trey was in agony from the first blow and felt like the top of his head might explode. His vision was blurry from the impact of the blow and the fall. Somehow, he was not afraid of Harlowe but it was clear The Squinty-Eyed Fuck intended to inflict more harm. Trey saw Harlowe raise his hand with the pipe again. He calculated how he might move to deflect or avoid the brunt of the blow. Remembering how his hands refused to obey his impulses, Trey wondered if his body would respond and move quickly enough. He prepared for more pain as he began to calculate the impact from the pipe hitting his already-aching head.

Once again, Trey was betrayed by his senses. He saw Harlowe lean in to strike him but this time Harlowe seemed to get bigger and bigger. It looked like Harlowe was going to leap on top of him. Trey tried to figure out how to fend off Harlowe. What the hell was he doing?

A split second later Harlowe landed on Trey with a thud. More excruciating pain as the weight of Harlowe knocked the air from Trey's gasping lungs. Trey monitored his body to feel for a knife wound and looked to see what Harlowe might do next. But he did nothing. Harlowe was physically bigger and heavier than Trey. He landed mostly on Trey's right side, pinning him to the floor of the parking garage. Trey struggled for breath and leverage and found neither. Harlowe suddenly and awkwardly lifted off Trey. It was then Trey saw another face. It was Howard Kim from the coffee shop. His round face and dark, doll-like hair was now in the exact same spot in the blue sky above Trey. Trey saw Howard was drenched in coffee. Harlowe was nearby but not moving, just kind of groaning.

"You OK Trey? Jesus what happened here? This guy was trying to kill you. Lucky I was coming by to teach nurses self-defense. Next time give him your wallet—not worth a life. You can get new wallet," said Kim, holding a hand out to Trey.

Trey accepted Howard's assistance at first but then a pain shot from his head and through his eyeballs. At that point he knew trying to get up would be excruciating and futile. He was sure that the pain could not get worse but somehow it did. The last thing he remembered was rolling his head to the side, looking for some position to relieve his pain. He saw a dead rat drowned in a puddle of water in the corner of the parking lot. Then everything went black again.

CHAPTER 48

THE FUNERAL

Three days later Trey opened his eyes in his own bed in a largely empty home. At least it no longer hurt to move his eyelids.

He was still groggy from the lingering effects of the painkillers to help him sleep. He actually slept half upright since he got out of the hospital. It was the only way he could comfortably sleep in the neck brace. It was a contraption designed to keep him from rolling his head in the night—an action triggering searing pain. He was diagnosed with a severe concussion but no skull or vertebral fractures. He had two black eyes and bruising around his face, an outcome of the broken nose suffered smashing face first into the floor of the parking garage.

Staring at the ceiling of his bedroom, Trey was torn. On one hand he was thankful for the utter quiet in the house. Even a neighbor's screen door slamming two doors down was jarring the first day home. Today he felt a little better. The passing hum of a car on the back street did not set his head thumping in rhythm with his pulse. But the quiet now was a reminder that Carole was not there. The house was more than empty. It was barren without her.

Struggling to one side, then up on an elbow, he propelled himself to a sitting position. That hurt. It felt like the fluids surrounding his brain sloshed inside his skull. He waited quietly at the side of the bed for the throbbing to stop. He would need a lot of coffee to break the fogs of the painkillers, that was for sure.

As he steadied himself, Trey stared at the answering machine. It blinked full and refused to record any additional messages. He cleared it once when he first arrived home. It contained a hodge-podge of well-wishers, calls from the attorneys from Grean in Orlando, Ike wondering how he was and several florists who could not figure out how to deliver flowers. Trey was unsure the flowers were get-well wishes or condolences but it did not matter. The two calls on there that did matter were from Carole. She called to talk, but left no number, merely saying she would call again. The fact she did not want Trey to know her number or call was troubling to him. He hoped it meant she did not know about his concussion. All of this he needed to sort out, but he was weak and shepherding his strength.

Trey needed to be the best version of himself today. It was the day of his father's funeral. He begged the doctors to let him go to the wake but they sternly ruled it as out of the question. Even as he sat up to argue his case the pain and double vision made him realize they were right. After a short discussion with his mother, they decided to proceed with the wake. Other than custom, Trey had no desire to sit and stare at his father's lifeless body in an open casket. The tears that welled up in private mourning created a pressure behind his eyeballs hinting they might burst. He did not want his mother to extend her period of grief and the few living relatives had already been notified about the arrangements. No. Once people heard about his injuries they would understand. But Trey also knew he could not live with himself if he did not attend the funeral.

Trey crawled downstairs in his boxers and a robe. The thought of a fall was terrifying so he took his time, taking each stair as a separate event. As much as he missed Belvedere, he was happy he was not underfoot.

As Trey waited for his coffee to drain into the glass pot he seated himself gingerly at the kitchen table, stared blankly out the back sliding glass door and watched the squirrels bounce past. He recounted his last 72 hours. He woke up three days ago in the emergency room. He briefly thought he might be paralyzed but realized he had been immobilized as they checked his injuries. He figured out the metallic taste in his mouth was the iron content of his own blood as it seeped back from his broken nose and into his mouth.

He spent one night in the hospital, heavily and mercifully sedated. They wanted to keep him another day but the doctors reluctantly released him after he threatened to sign himself out. He wanted to be home, even if that home was empty. He also knew going home provided his mother great solace and a signal he was on the mend.

Harlowe was taken to jail after the statement from Howard Kim. The detectives assigned to the case came to talk to Trey but he feigned incoherence and they went away. They, too, could wait for another day. Trey hoped that this lack of cooperation somehow extended Harlowe's stay in jail. Trey then recalled at least one of the calls on the answering machine came from the detective investigating his assault at the hospital. It could wait another day.

One thing he could not remember was how Pauley was doing. The fact gnawed at him because he remembered asking and being told. He simply could not recall the answer.

Trey consumed the entire pot of coffee in silence. It tasted great and seemed to clear his head of grogginess and pain. He caught sight of his face in the shine of the toaster and realized he was a grotesque mess. He had not shaved in three days. His eyes were still swollen and the blackness around his eyes curled around the side of his head. He had six stitches in the back of his head and a knot at the base of his skull where Harlowe landed with the pipe blow. The swelling prevented him from lifting his head backward and upward. The feeling there was no permanent damage but recovery might be slow and tenuous for a while. The whole incident rattled his brain around inside his skull pretty thoroughly.

For the next two hours Trey gingerly groomed and readied himself. Shaving carefully around the scratches on his face rubbed raw on the pavement. Picking out a shirt that had always been a size too big so he could leave his collar loose and avoid an invitation to a headache. Dark glasses would be expected in such a state of mourning but he needed the largest pair he could find to hide his blackened eyes and bruised face. He donned his black suit, wincing at bruises and strains that revealed themselves only now. He felt like he had been dropped off a building. He briefly considered a painkiller but settled for six Advil. He did not need to fall asleep during the funeral Mass.

Because he was not yet cleared to drive, Trey opted for a limo from the funeral cortege. He felt at odds with such a fancy car. He was mourning a man of simple tastes and ducking into a luxury car behind dark glasses like a Hollywood celebrity. He hoped none of the neighbors saw him, but he noted a few blind slats raised by the curious.

Trey settled comfortably in the limo. The seats felt like pillows. He said silent thanks for the extra cushy suspension absorbing the potholes that would otherwise jar his head. He was taking in the sights, darkened into soft green shadows by the tint of his sunglasses. It was well past rush hour and he saw people in their cars, oblivious to him and the limo. He envied their routine and reflected how just a few weeks earlier, he was one of them. Now everything had changed. He thought about how he had to be strong for his mother and decided he would hold these images of all the people on the Turnpike oblivious to his grief and think of them whenever emotion gripped him, threatening his stoic serenity. Just another day.

But as much as he tried to think about the task at hand other urgent issues began to emerge from the shadows and push into his consciousness. Like ping pong balls submerged in a vast pool, the thoughts eluded his best efforts to keep them submerged. The detectives and their questions. Pauley Firrigno. And Carole. Especially Carole.

It suddenly occurred to Trey: Carole and her absence at the funeral was an urgent issue to be faced immediately. What would he say to his mother? Her absence at the wake was understandable. He briefly considered that in all the activity he might not have to explain it at all. But he knew he was just avoiding the issue and childishly hoping to bury it. It had to be faced. But why now? He submerged that ping pong ball for now, preferring to settle into the comfort of the ride—at least for the moment.

The limo arrived at the church in good time and well before the ceremony and the arrival of his father's casket from the funeral home. It was Sacred Heart, the same gothic behemoth where Harlowe offered his donation to the first church of the mayor's office—although Trey did not know this. The church had a huge but largely aging parish population. Thus, it was all too common that funeral masses were tightly scheduled and executed with machine-like precision. The Bensen funeral was listed on a small message board at the curb as scheduled for 11 a.m. Since it was only 10:30, Trey was not surprised to see another hearse and a cortege of cars lined up directly in front of the church main entrance. The cold business of grief.

Rather than wait in the car, Trey opted to go into the church. The mass in progress wound down as Trey sat in the back row. He was thankful for the relative quiet and darkness. It washed him in a soothing reflection as he examined the stained glass windows and how they picked up the light. He thought about how as a little boy he sat so much shorter than his father as he looked up at the windows and his father. It seemed to him at the time his father was part of the stained glass vignette, transposed into the particular saint depicted in some heroic or healing act.

The memories caused the emotions to rise and the tears to flow. This led to a stabbing pain in his head and sinuses. He pushed the emotional ping pong ball down again below the surface. He thought about all those people on the Turnpike who could not give a damn. It worked. He was in control again.

With a sudden need to do something, Trey got up and went to the prayer sanctuary in the corner. Hundreds of devotional prayer candles rose in tiers like so many fans in a stadium, curved 180 degrees around a series of prayer benches. The smell of sulfur from the slowly burning wicks rose pleasantly. He took a $5 bill out of his pocket and placed it in the offering slot. There were precious few candles not lit but he spied one unlit votive in the perfect spot. It was on the top row but way off in the right-hand corner. It somehow seemed to be appropriate in remembrance of his father—not front and center, but present. Intense and illuminating, yet still softly muted somehow. Most effective as part of a greater set of objects with a common purpose. He took a long wooden taper and lit that lone candle. The pain returned to his head again. He forced his thoughts back to the Turnpike. How many ping pong balls can one person keep submerged in such a vast pool and for how long? He gauged he needed to endure about two hours.

As Trey turned his attention back to the church he realized the funeral mass in progress had ended. The pallbearers bore the casket down the center of the church, past Trey and out the door. There were about 50 mourners, a decent number, but the enormous church dwarfed them.

Trey followed at the very tail end of the procession to see the pallbearers struggle to get the casket into the hearse. It was then he saw his father's hearse and cars lined up the block clogging traffic in the narrow city streets. It occurred to Trey that Sacred Heart needed a hearse traffic controller. At least there was not another funeral mass until 2:30 p.m. Nobody would be hurrying Earl Bensen through his rites.

As the concluded funeral pulled away, the Bensen procession waited respectfully for a minute or so before slowly pulling up to take their place. Trey waited on the steps. Already he was feeling weary and he knew he needed to tap into some reservoir of energy. He wavered a little but caught his balance. The thought of navigating the set of stairs up and down scared the hell out of him. He thought about the grief he would add to the day if he went tumbling and had to be carted away by an ambulance so he stood still and gripped the brass bannister on the stairs. As the casket wheeled closer up the approach path, clouds cleared and the sun intensified. Trey ducked inside to get relief. His intention was to join his mother as he entered just behind the casket. His entire attention was focused on the casket as it gleamed in polished mahogany in the sun.

Looking back at the line of approaching mourners, Trey was surprised but pleased to see both Mo and Tommy. They looked extremely uncomfortable in dark blue suits, narrow ties and shirts so baggy the collars looked like SkeeBall target holes.

Trey scanned the mourners, rifling through his mental notes for names of uncles and cousins only seen at weddings and funerals.

It was then he was startled out of his intense focus by a touch on his arm. His jump was a reaction out of proportion with the gentleness of the contact, probably a product of being jolted out of his focus and a lingering reaction from the assault. The touch progressed from his forearm and slipped gently into his hand. It was a touch of a person trying to calm a skittish bird and communicate help and tenderness. It was Carole. She looked stunning in a black dress and clutch bag. Even behind the dark glasses she sensed his surprise at seeing her.

"Did you REALLY think I would not be here for you?" she asked, her voice stern but soothing.

She nodded and directed Trey to escort his mother as she neared. Then Carole lowered her voice to a level she was sure only Trey could hear.

"You actually look more handsome with all those lumps on your head."

She squeezed his hand and placed her cheek on his arm.

CHAPTER 49

---•◦◆◦•---

FIVE YEARS AFTER

Ames, Iowa

"Let's go girls! The Daddy Bus is leaving!"

It was only 7 a.m., an hour before school began, but there were several stops to make before school and preschool drop-offs. Bryn, age 5, stepped carefully down the stairs from her upstairs bedroom, deliberately planting her foot and watching its placement before proceeding with extreme caution. Faith, age 3, hopped down with a small jump and thud on each stair step with a shriek of pure joy—each footfall and adventure.

Trey smiled, noting the contrast between the stern demeanor of his older daughter and his daredevil imp. They were perfect in his eyes. He marveled as they changed before his eyes each day in how they expressed their personality in each smile, accomplishment and challenge. Faith carried her bright yellow rain slicker even though there was not even a hint of foul weather. But she was using it as a pretend parachute, jumping from stair to stair as if skydiving.

Trey waited for them to pass him at the foot of the stairs and scooted behind them playfully to their waiting breakfast. As they clambered up on chairs around the kitchen nook he opened the curtains and let the early morning sunshine warm the eating area. Carole was already dressed for work but busily putting the finishing touches on breakfast as well as lunch bags.

"I see you did the girls' hair—I guess you forgot your own. You are a mess," she said, playfully mussing at his uncombed hair as it spiked in every odd direction.

The house was warm and settled. It was now five years since they moved from New Jersey to Iowa. They arrived about four weeks before Bryn was born as the construction of the house lingered several months behind schedule. By the time they moved in, Carole could do little but point at where the boxes should go. They painted Bryn's room a muted pink the day after she was born. Slowly, the chaos gave way to an emerging routine that just seemed to fit.

The move to Iowa was unexpected to some degree. The violence on the picket line and the collapse of the deal to sell the business created panic at Grean Machining. The Greans tasked Trey with figuring out what a fair agreement with the union might look like. Because the existing contract had more than a year to run, just the promise not to close the factory was enough to bring the union back in from the picket line. In the following contract, Grean pledged investments in new machinery and training; the union sought and gained rich severance benefits in the event of closure. This all but guaranteed the plant would exist for another generation. It also forestalled any environmental cleanup Grean would face for what lurked in the ground beneath the plant. Few government agencies want to burden an existing employer with the high costs of such a cleanup. They could kick that can of reckoning down the road a bit.

After completing the deal, Trey knew he did not want to stay on any longer. He applied for an academic job at Iowa State University teaching Industrial Relations. He was surprised when they hired him after only two rounds of interviews. The only thing that kept Trey even longer was the settlement of the civil suit against Harlowe for his injuries and trauma. Trey was sure he could have won a larger judgement but he rode a fine line. It was large enough to ensure Harlowe would be eating dog food in retirement but not so large he would declare bankruptcy.

In another delicate dance, Grean offered Trey a generous severance package. In no case did Grean offer severance to an employee quitting but deep within the document there was a codicil where Trey surrendered his right to sue Grean for any reason. It was the kiss goodbye and closure for Trey and Grean. Harlowe served 60 days for battery, reduced to 25 for good behavior and an inexplicably clean record. Ever the good soldier, Harlowe never ratted anyone out. It was never clear to Trey exactly who paid the damages in the civil suit, but in the end he did not care. Seeing Harlowe in an orange jumpsuit was priceless. The Squinty-Eyed Con.

As his girls finished bowls of cereal topped with strawberries and bananas, Trey's mother appeared in the kitchen. She walked with a slow but certain gait and the assistance of a cane. Her late and grudging agreement to join them in Iowa significantly altered the house architecture. The last plans added a granny flat connected to the main house near the family room on the main floor. She stubbornly resisted moving out of New Jersey until Carole's pregnancy became obvious and the thought of grandchildren so far away loosened her allegiance to East Newark and the Garden State.

Gram Meg, as she was called, caressed the cereal-soaked faces of her grandchildren with a gentle hand and cuddled in near them at the table. The house would be quiet as soon as they left for school, so she drank in their chatter and fidgets.

Carole worked in the Student Affairs office at the college. The hours were a bit shorter and allowed her to be home midafternoon each day when the girls came home. She helped Trey escort the girls to the large van in the driveway and buckle them in the back seats. They were off by 7:30 a.m., overcoming another morning of jammed zippers, leaky juice boxes and sloppy kisses for Gram Meg.

Traffic was light. It always seemed light compared to the northeast. Trey moved the van carefully through the intersections, always cognizant of his precious cargo. They had one stop before school and they pulled into the circular driveway. Trey got out of the van and slid open the side door, exposing a wide steel ramp.

"Let's go!" Trey demanded. "Time's a-wastin. I have young minds to bend!"

As soon as the little girls saw the man rolling down the concrete ramp, they shrieked with an intensity that belied the fact they had just seen him yesterday at this same time.

"Good morning Uncle Pauley!"

Pauley Firrigno rolled out of his wide front door in his wheelchair. Pilar initially tried to assist him but he gently slapped her hand away in mock annoyance. Tomas, now a blasé teenager, trudged out wearily to the van with his backpack crammed with books. Tomas got in first and took a seat in the back bench of the van as far away from Bryn and Faith as he could manage. It was definitely not cool to be seen with little girls.

After Tomas got in the van, Pauley propelled himself up the ramp with strong, sure forearms. He could stand and walk a few steps if he had to, but they had a schedule to keep and this was faster. He got in the wide open area just behind Trey's shoulder, pivoted around and secured his wheelchair with seatbelts for the ride.

Overall, Pauley spent five months in the hospital and another four in physical rehabilitation after the riot on the picket line. His beating left him with permanent motor instability. While not paralyzed, he would never be able to return to work. Trey visited him every day in the hospital and at the rehabilitation facility—always bringing him the strong coffee he craved. The union and Larry Turkel announced a series of fundraisers to ensure all of Pauley's medical bills were paid. Although they never found his attackers, Pauley became a minor celebrity in the union at the International level as a martyr in the labor movement.

In addition to the union's campaign, Pauley collected an undisclosed sum from the city of East Newark for failure to provide reasonable police protection and coverage. Mayor Thomas Glynn Thomson staged an elaborate press conference at the plant several months later to bemoan the lawlessness in his city and pledged additional resources to make the citizenry feel safe again. It was beside the point that there was not a residential address within six blocks of the crime. His redirection of the issue to underline his love of law and order was a masterstroke only Tommy Glynn could carry off.

For his part, Mayor Thomson did gain reelection with at least some use of the money Harlowe deposited in the collection basket at Sacred Heart Cathedral. However, the reelection did not guarantee another multi-generational dynasty at city hall. The shifting currents of demographics ran too strong, accelerated by the flight of people like Trey's mother to places outside of the city. A rising star on the city council who made his way through the Cuban refugee experience campaigned hard against Mayor Thomson and unseated him partially on the support of term limits. The former mayor now made his living via his law degree by suing the municipalities for damage done by the countless potholes to the cars of unsuspecting taxpayers.

As Trey contemplated leaving the area and moving to Iowa, his bond with Pauley, Pilar and Tomas grew strong. He convinced Pauley to make a joint move and a fresh start. It actually surprised Trey when Pauley agreed to the move even before Gram Meg conceded. It wasn't that hard for Pauley. All he had to do was consider the quality of life for Tomas and then realize how a run-down property in New Jersey translated to a virtual palace in Iowa and he was sold.

Picking up Pauley, Trey was in the home stretch of his morning commute. First he dropped off little Faith at preschool. Trey tried to take her by the hand and escort her to the front door but the tug of the adventures pulled her out of his grasp and into the door with an excited wave goodbye.

Tomas and Bryn were next as they were dropped off at the grammar and middle school complex just outside the university. Tomas dropped his skateboard with a noisy crack on the pavement and rode off quickly to minimize the time he might be seen with a kindergarten girl and two parents. Bryn carefully counted her books and rechecked folders containing pictures proving her grasp of colors before departing somewhat solemnly.

That left Trey and Pauley for the last leg of the trip. They talked easily and freely as best friends do about topics of great and minor importance. Once at the university Trey pulled into a handicapped spot. Pauley let himself out of the van with a deftness borne of many days of practice. He let Trey push him up a gentle rise to the coffee kiosk he managed at the school.

Trey looked at his watch and saw that he had just 20 minutes before his class was scheduled to begin. He breathed in the clean, fresh air. He knew he would make it on time. He always knew he would make it.

ABOUT THE AUTHOR

With 40 years in and around manufacturing plants in a host of roles including labor negotiator, John F. Schierer has first-hand knowledge of the complex and layered motivations of both labor and management and how these motivations twist the traditional objectives of each group.

He began his career as a reporter and editor of a weekly newspaper in New Jersey (The Hillside Times) and later entered the field of human resources negotiating labor contracts and integrating acquisitions into large corporations. He has been published in various human resources publications including HR Magazine and Forefront Magazine.